Out the Summerhill Road

A novel

by

Jane Roberts Wood

Number 5 in the Evelyn Oppenheimer Series

University of North Texas Press
Denton, Texas

10 9 8 7 6 5 4 3 2 1

Permissions:
University of North Texas Press
1155 Union Circle #311336
Denton, TX 76203-5017

The paper used in this book meets the minimum requirements of the American
National Standard for Permanence of Paper for Printed Library Materials,
z39.48.1984. Binding materials have been chosen for durability.

Library of Congress Cataloging-in-Publication Data

Wood, Jane Roberts, 1929–
    Out the Summerhill Road : a novel / by Jane Roberts Wood. — 1st ed.
        p. cm.
    ISBN 978-1-57441-299-4 (cloth : alk. paper)
    1. Murder—Fiction. 2. Teenage girls, White—Fiction. 3. Texas, East—Fiction.
I. Title.
    PS3573.O5945O95 2010
    813'.54—dc22

                                                                        2010020914

Out the Summerhill Road is Number 5 in the Evelyn Oppenheimer Series

Interior design by Joseph Parenteau / Pronto

DEDICATION

For Dub

Again and always

Acknowledgments

I should like to thank the remarkable staff at the University of North Texas Press, especially Karen DeVinney, whose editing has been thoughtful and liberating.

And my publishers/editors: Ellen Temple, Carole Baron and Fran Vick, whose readings enriched my novels and whose friendships enriched my life.

And Victor Sidy, Dean of Talisman West, who designed this house where I write and who playfully and generously designed the perfect house for Jackson, a character in this novel.

And Jeannie Davis and sadly, posthumously, Dr. Nancy Castilla who listened to my readings for twenty years with affection and intelligence.

PART 1

Girls in White Dresses

Girls in White Dresses

It was horrible! Just horrible! Rosemary Winslow murdered! Her body found in the Park the night, the very night, of Sarah's slumber party! Rosemary Winslow. A nice girl. Who could believe it? Not her best friends who waited until three in the morning before they woke up Sarah's parents to tell them they didn't know where she was or why she hadn't come. When the girls saw the grim look on Mrs. Claiborne's face and watched as Mr. Claiborne threw on his robe and rushed down the stairs to the telephone, they began to realize that something was horribly, dreadfully wrong.

But even as the police were called and a search was begun, nobody dreamed it would end in a nightmare. Who could believe that? Not Rosemary's father, who, after the call came from Sarah's dad, hugged his wife and said, "Stay here. By the phone. In case she calls." And Jacob Winslow threw a coat on over his pajamas, jumped into his car and drove slowly, *forced* himself to drive slowly, so that he could look down every drive between his house and the Claibornes' for his baby girl's blue convertible. But when he saw the two police cars blocking the entrance to the Park, saw a policeman holding his cap in his hand and with his face turned to stone, Jacob knew it was bad. He stepped out of his car and threw up before the policeman could say they had found a young man's body in the Park beside a blue Chevrolet convertible and that a search for his daughter had already begun.

One hour later Rosemary's body was found. When that news came, Rosemary's best friends—young, innocent, heartbroken—tearfully told the police they did not know a thing that might have triggered the slightest alarm about Rosemary's safety while they waited for her to show up. And then, after a few questions, the girls were shielded by their parents from insensitive questions asked by the police, questions that bore no fruit and that might cause psychological distress to their sensitive daughters.

By good daylight telephones were ringing all over Cold Springs; parents were tiptoeing into their teenage children's bedrooms to be sure they were safe, and later that morning, the terrible news came from church pulpits, news sad beyond the telling of it.

At Bryce's cafeteria, the Gleeboff twins swore they would find the man who murdered Rosemary. They called their buddies in Troop 18, called all the guys who could finagle a car, to meet at the high school and form a search party. Bane and Hollingsworth, with red-rimmed eyes, said they would be there with their gas tanks full. Aston, red-faced and sweating, brought up the rear in his dad's old Chevrolet, but when the dozen or so cars arrived at the Summerhill exit that led into the Park, the boys found that road had also been closed.

❄

On the night of Sarah's slumber party, a kind of madness had come over the girls. After all, they were seniors! Seniors in Cold Springs High School and about to go off to college where their lives could begin. Seriously begin. The night Rosemary was murdered not a one of Sarah's guests had arrived at Sarah's house before ten o'clock, and Sarah herself had shown up only a few minutes before ten.

For weeks rumors had been flying all over town about the Park. Tramps taking a short cut through the Park had worn a trail between the Summerhill Road and 29th Street. And by 1946, a year after the War, soldiers had begun to hang out at the Park. With its great old native oaks and loblolly pines, its spring-fed lake and narrow dirt paths winding through the woods, the Park brought these men the sense of camaraderie they had known all through the War. During the day, they looked for work; at night they hung out together and looked for women. "Bless them all," the people of Cold Springs said about their heroes and meant it. Cold Springs was grateful, but . . . still, the soldiers were too old, too experienced for their young daughters. And there was this: at times it was hard to tell the difference between a tramp and a soldier.

Just last Saturday Isabel was driving through the Park when a veteran (she was pretty sure about this), leaning against a tree, raised his bottle of beer in a toast and hollered, "You wanna screw, Sweetie?"

She slowed down. "Not with you, Buster," she said and sped away.

When Isabel told her friends about it, they stared at her. "Isabel, you didn't! You didn't say that to him!" exclaimed Sarah. "What did he say?"

"Who knows? I was out of there before he could think what to say." Then Isabel raised her eyebrows. "But I'll bet it wilted his pecker," she said, setting the girls off into spasms of giggling.

And there was this other delicious, scintillating rumor: somebody—high school boy, tramp, veteran, who knows!— *was* sneaking up on couples parked out there. When the girls talked about it, they invariably broke into nervous giggling. But there *was* a Peeping Tom at the Park. There really was, although nobody took him seriously.

A couple from New Boston had seen him—a shapeless, hooded form, caught in the headlights of their car as he sprinted into the woods. When the young man from New Boston caught the bastard in his headlights, he had jumped out of his car and chased him all the way to the Spring House where he vanished. The Cold Springs boys agreed on one thing. Although the coward could run, he would be caught sooner or later. Armed with tire tools and hammers, every boy in high school was halfway hoping the S.O.B. would creep up on his car when he was parked out there with his best girl and if that happened, he swore he'd beat him to a bloody pulp.

However, on this balmy, star-filled night in May, the girls had promised their parents they would not go near the Park. "If you want to park somewhere, you can park right here in your own living room," Sarah's dad had told her. She took that with a grain of salt. A quick goodnight kiss from a boy was as much as her dad would tolerate. A long kiss brought on a malfunctioning porch light.

But afraid of the Park! Their parents' belief that the Park was dangerous sounded silly to the girls. It was, after all, their Park. Their very own Park that they loved better than any place in the world! Knew better! As far back as Junior High, the four would ride their bicycles out there, let them fall to the grass and then step into the coolness of the Spring House, kneel, cup their hands, and drink the cold, sweet spring water. Afterwards, more times than not, they would ride around the lake to a grove of pine trees, throw themselves down on the sun-dappled grass, lie back on folded arms and tell secrets. At other times, they would squeeze through a torn-away screen to enter the abandoned dance pavilion where their mothers and fathers had danced all through the War to "Sentimental Journey" and "I'll Never Smile Again" and "In the Mood" and "Don't Sit Under the Apple Tree." Humming, singing words they all knew, the girls would dance alone or with each other, keeping the beat, their saddle shoes stirring up the dust motes lit by shafts of sunlight coming into the pavilion.

But now the War was over, thank God! And they were grown. Their parents said it. Their teachers said it. They said it to each other. They would soon be on their own, meeting heroes coming home from the War who were going back to college and these ex-soldiers, hundreds! no, thousands! would be waiting for them on campuses across the country.

Still, just days before graduation, their parents, despite what they said about adulthood, treated them like children. However, on this night, this Saturday night, the moon was full, the War was over, and to the girls danger seemed as distant, as removed as the stars, and they were determined to have fun. But not at the Park. Of course not! Unless . . . and unless. . . .

✻

Rosemary was delirious with happiness. Her senior year was almost over and she was sixteen and practically on her way down to the University of Texas at Austin where she could begin a new life. And she had a late date! It was a secret. Not even her best friends knew about Mark. And after her late date, she was going to Sarah's slumber party. Then she would tell them about Mark. They would be excited and asking questions: "Can he dance?" And, "You went to the Park?" And, "You didn't kiss him on a first date! You didn't!"

She could hear the giggling now. They would have to bury their heads in their pillows so as not to wake up Sarah's parents.

When her mother had died in October of her freshman year, Rosemary began to feel as if she were drowning in sorrow. Smothered by it. Diminished. Disguised by weak smiles and silly remarks from friends and strangers alike, sorrow followed her around like a lost and hungry dog. She gave the imagined dog a name. She called it Sorrow.

By Christmas of that year she had become nothing more than *the girl whose mother had died.* Everybody seemed to have forgotten the Rosemary who made them laugh, who even made old stone face Lawson smile when he saw her coming down the hall; everybody had forgotten the Rosemary who could diagram whole paragraphs in Latin. They had forgotten the cheerleader who was tossed higher and higher to the beat of the drums and the roar of the crowd at football games.

The end of the week. The end of a semester. The end of cheerleading practice. The beginning of the Christmas holidays. Sorrow was at her heels. She had never realized life was so full of sad beginnings and endings.

"What are you going to do this summer?" Mary Martha had asked Rosemary at the end of their freshman year as the girls were sitting on the steps of Cold Springs Junior High School, waiting to be picked up by Isabel's mother. Waiting for her answer, Rosemary's friends, her three best friends, looked at her and smiled gently, smiled sadly.

"I don't know what I'm going to do!" Rosemary snapped, glaring at her friends. "But I'm not going to hang around with the three of you and whine. I know I won't be doing that!" she said. Turning away to hide her tears, "And I'm going to walk home by myself. I *want* to walk home!" she declared. Then *the girl whose mother had died* had straightened her shoulders and stalked away.

It had been sudden. She had had no time to get ready for it. They were shopping together, Rosemary and her mother, when her mother stumbled over a curb and fell, hitting her head on the bumper of a parked car. Rubbing the side of her head, laughing as Rosemary helped her up, "I'm fine," she said. "I'm perfectly all right." But she wasn't. She died the next day. "From a hematoma," the doctor said.

In the months that followed, "Don't feel sorry for me," Rosemary would say to Sarah. "It doesn't help." Or to Isabel, "Stop crying. Your mother's doing just fine." And then she would flash that brilliant smile she wore as a shield against pity all through her high school years.

But today she had a white dress for the prom and, maybe, a date for it, too. Although not superstitious, she was feeling lucky again, and maybe, just maybe, she had just about seen the last of Sorrow.

She looked at her watch and now she was hurrying, hurrying. She slipped on her white linen pleated skirt and white cotton sweater with the orange tiger on the front. She bent from the waist and brushed her hair forward. When she straightened and looked in the mirror, she saw that her hair was a thick, luxurious cloud round her face. She loved her hair, loved the way it moved when she jitterbugged. Leaning close to the mirror, she brushed on green eye shadow over her green eyes. When she was all grown up, she might be pretty. She knew she was smart. And she was still *the cheerleader who flew!*

Grabbing her overnight bag, she hurried down the stairs.

"I'm leaving," she called into the living room.

Her father came into the hall. His face was round and friendly. He put an arm around her shoulders. "Have a good time at Coach's party."

"Oh, I will, and don't forget, Dad. I won't be home tonight. I'm going straight to Sarah's after the party."

"Be careful, Baby. Stay away from the Park."

She turned to blow him a kiss. "Don't worry. I'll be fine," she said and was gone.

The party had been exactly like all Coach Edwards' parties with Mrs. Edwards handing out cokes and Dr Peppers and popcorn, and everybody being polite and trying to think of something to say to kids they had seen yesterday and the day before and the day before that. Finally, she could take French leave and slip away early for her late date, and she did just that so that hours later the only thing anyone was sure of was that Rosemary had left the party early and alone.

※

Unfortunately, Isabel Jessup had seen Rosemary after she left the coach's party, *unfortunately* because if she told anybody about seeing her it would ruin her reputation. The sound of Rosemary's convertible had brought her from her bed, where she had been reading, to the window. Unlatching the window screen, she leaned out into the darkness. Muffled laughter floated up through the leaves of the magnolia tree outside her room. Rosemary's laugh. It was Rosemary's laugh. Rosemary's convertible. She leaned farther out. How could Rosemary do this to her? And never mind that Jackson was a party to it. Rosemary was her best friend. Rosemary would be at Sarah's slumber party tonight. Isabel leaned farther out the window to accuse, to confront, to question Rosemary. Then it dawned on her. Jackson needed a ride! That's all it was. That was the reason Rosemary's car was underneath her window. Jackson could never get the family car. His father was too stingy to let his son have the car!

More laughter floated upward, whispery laughter, followed by Jackson's voice. Then Jackson slapped the hood of the convertible, once, twice, Rosemary's lights flashed on, and Isabel followed the curving path of her headlights as she drove off the Jessup property.

Now Isabel made out the white blur of Jackson's shirt as he emerged from the shadows, moved into the center of the drive and trotted toward the house. When he reached the tree outside her window, he whistled his whippoorwill's call and then segued into the song. "When whippoorwills call, and evening is nigh," he sang.

Giggling, she leaned out her window. "They're not here," she said. "I'll come down and let you in."

But he was already climbing the tree.

Although Isabel had always had an iron allegiance to virtue, she was tired of virginity. She was, after all, almost seventeen years old. She would be going off to Ward-Belmont in the fall.

Before this happened, she yearned to be initiated into a new world, the adult world. However, she was of two minds about welcoming Jackson into her bedroom and, just possibly, her bed. He was undeniably handsome and funny and no other boy in high school could set her heart to beating so fast that she had to put a hand over her breast to calm it down. Why his heart-stopping grace when he was shooting hoops or the look of wonder on his face when he answered a question about Shakespeare or about a poem by Robert Frost made her forget where she was or what she was doing. But, and this was a serious *but,* Jackson lived in a trailer. However, a bottle of her father's whiskey waited on her dresser just in case.

When Jackson came laughing through the window, he took her into his arms. "Izzy. Izzy. Let down your hair," he whispered, kissing her hair, her neck. "Way up here in your tower let down your hair." His voice was husky; his hand cupped her breast.

"Wait! Wait!" she said, pushing his hand away. "Let's have a drink. Don't you want a drink? Whiskey and coke?"

"This is all the drink I want," he said, kissing her lips. "Come," he said, pressing her down on the bed. Then "Oops!" And moving the book from underneath his elbow, he saw what it was. He sat up on the side of the bed. "You're reading *Gone with the Wind*! How did you sneak it out of the library?"

"I haven't read much," she said, proclaiming innocence. "I probably won't even finish it."

"Isabel, grow up. Let's grow up together," he whispered, and took her in his arms again. "Izzy, you're beautiful. Did you know that?"

Isabel did know that. She took it for granted since she'd been twice voted the most beautiful girl in high school.

"Wait," she said now, hurrying to the bathroom. "Wait!"

In the bathroom, she mixed coke and whiskey. She looked at herself in the mirror and, pleased with what she saw, she smiled and, watching that self glamorously leaning against the counter, she drank. Counting the swallows, coughing, she emptied the glass, feeling pleasantly dizzy. And oh, how she would love a cigarette now! Smoking in front of her mirror, gesturing with sharp, emphatic gestures like Bette Davis—this was one of her pleasures.

She picked up Jackson's drink and finished it. Then, feeling different, very different, as if she had left her body and was watching herself, watching Isabel, she swayed back to her bedroom and slipped into Jackson's arms. Minutes later, her slacks lay on the floor, her panties too, then his, hers, a jumble of clothes, all tossed to the floor, and he was thrusting, thrusting himself inside her.

Gasping, groaning with pleasure, he rolled off her when it was over. "Wow!" he said, sighing. He sighed again, running his hands down his chest and over his hip bones. He turned toward her, his head propped on his elbow. "Izzy, that was wonderful!"

"No. It wasn't."

Isabel's voice was calm. Detached. For she had already begun to worry. Could she be pregnant? This soon? Was her egg and his sperm matched up together somewhere inside her? Doing this little wriggling dance? She shuddered. If she were already pregnant, it would be with twins. A terrible thought, but twins ran in her family. There had been twins in the family for six generations. Would her father shoot Jackson if he found out? Or shoot the twins? No. But she was absolutely certain, and this was the most dreadful of all possibilities, that she had handed Jackson a weapon to use against her for the rest of her life.

Quickly, they rinsed the tell-tale spots from the sheets and remade the bed, while Jackson protested by alternately chuckling, "This is pretty funny, Isabel," and growling, "This is pretty crazy. Willie B. could have washed your sheets."

"Are you crazy?" she said. "Willie B. would go straight to Mother with the evidence. Jackson, you've got to swear by all that's Holy you'll never tell anybody we went all the way. Swear! Swear it!"

"Isabel, I love you. As soon as graduation is over, we can go to Oklahoma and get married." A frown appeared on Jackson's forehead. "Do you think your dad would let you have the car?" he asked.

Feeling years older than this boy who stood before her, "No!" she said. "I'll never marry you, Jackson Morris! I'm going off to school in the fall!'"

That was when she pushed Jackson, volubly protesting, out the window and dropped his clothes down over his head.

Then, standing before the mirror she examined her body. She lifted her breasts and squeezed them together. Still, no cleavage. Nothing had changed. Nothing! Despairing, she turned away from the mirror. She had thought that after sex, she would look different. Voluptuous, maybe. But only one thing had changed. Jackson could ruin her reputation! If he said a word to anybody about tonight, her reputation was gone! Down the drain. Sighing, she took a bath and dried off all traces of her affair. Consoled by the idea that Katharine Hepburn was as flat-chested as she was, she dressed carefully and waited for her parents to come home and take her to the slumber party.

※

Mary Martha had seen Jackson jump into Rosemary's convertible. And a few hours later Rosemary was murdered. This was a thing she would never forget. What was she supposed to think? What would anybody think? She would tell the police that Jackson was the murderer. The only thing she would never tell was that she had gone to the Park to meet him.

She had asked for the family car at the supper table.

"Of course you may have the car," her mother said. "A slumber party at Sarah's. Daddy, is the car full of gas? Are the tires all right?"

"Now, Mother. You know the answer to those questions."

Mary Martha hated it when her parents called each other *Mother* and *Daddy* rather than Maybelle and Thomas. It spoke of something less than . . . , well, less than *something*. She was sure Isabel's parents never called each other "Daddy" and "Mother."

She looked down at her plate, separated one English pea from the others and chewed it carefully. Then, "I want to get there before dark," she said stiffly.

Her parents smiled at her, smiled at each other. "You've got your head on your shoulders," her father said. "You girls have a good time tonight and Mary Martha, do not, do not! take a shortcut through the Park. There's enough gas in the car to circle around it."

She groaned inwardly. "Thank you, Father," she said formally, and then, "I'll be just fine."

How easy it had been to lie when she was meeting Jackson in the Park. She hurried out to the '39 Ford, a car way too modest for her taste, backed down the driveway, turned the corner, and only then did she pick up speed. The speedometer showed fifty. She slowed to forty. She didn't want to arrive too early. Better to keep Jackson waiting. She drove out Pine, crossed over to Broadway on 29th Street and turned off onto the curving dirt road that ran through the Park. When the paved road ended, she drove alongside a dirt road past the Spring House and as far into the woods as the trees would allow. Then she rolled down her window and leaned back against the seat.

The wind lifted, bringing with it the aromatic scent of pines and the bracing smell of the silt-laden, spring-fed lake. The silence was nice. And even nicer, just as the sun was setting, she heard the songs of tree frogs followed by the raspy song of a bird. Jackson would know what kind of bird it was and when he came he would tell her.

Sighing with pleasure, she reached into her bra and pulled out Jackson's note and unfolded it. Although it was full of ink blots, she could read it. He had written:

> *. . . little minx. You have bewitched me. Pretending to be shy so that I, only I, know how . . . you really are. Prove it by meeting me at the . . . House in the park tomorrow night about sundown. If you don't show up, I'm coming straight to . . . you. Who cares what people say! You are my . . . love!*

At first she had not believed it! This note dropped onto her desk during the fire drill. But when she was hurrying down the stairs to P.E., Jackson had put his hand on her shoulder. "Be careful, honey. We can't have anything happening to you. Not now."

Then she had believed it, and reading Jackson's note again, she was suffused with happiness. She had not told a soul about Jackson. Her parents would never let her step foot outside the house with a boy who drank too much and lived in a trailer.

At one time, Isabel had had a crush on Jackson, but nothing had come of it. Isabel's mother liked Jackson, even though she knew he had a terrible temper and drank too much at dances.

"Girls, be kind." Isabel's mother said this all the time, especially when they gossiped, and she told everybody she was a Democrat. That explained a lot. Mary Martha's parents never talked about politics. For all she knew, they were Communists.

Suddenly restless, Mary Martha realized the falling darkness was turning the trees into dark shadows and the sky black. Growing impatient (Where in the world was Jackson?) she jumped out of the car and ran to the Spring House. Here she felt completely safe. She had always felt safe in the Spring

House, but after a while the stone floor where she sat grew hard and cold, and, still, Jackson had not come.

Now, she heard the sounds of a car's engine and voices: "I need . . ." It was Jackson's voice, and then, "She said she . . ." What did Jackson need? And who was he talking about? Now it was Rosemary's voice, ringing out over Jackson's deep laughter. "Jackson, get out! Get out of my car!"

"Wait!" she tried to call! "I'm here for our date. Over here. In the Spring House!" But her throat was paralyzed. And now, the convertible's engine was racing, its tires screeching, and they were gone, leaving behind the smell of gas fumes and burning rubber and the sound of Jackson's laughter.

She was alone again, in the darkness, the only sound that of the spring bubbling up and splashing down upon the rock floor. She began to cry. The note had not been meant for her. She had been stupid to think it was. And she'd never be as pretty as Isabel and, even though Sarah was a little over-weight, who would notice that when they saw her Elizabeth Taylor eyes—like jewels. Now she realized that she, Mary Martha, would never have a date. She knew it. She hated her-self. She hated her friends. They would laugh at her. No, they would be too embarrassed to laugh. They would fall silent, dumbfounded, if she told them she had thought the note on her desk was meant for her. She could never tell them that!

Little girl, you have a good head on your shoulders. Her daddy's voice. She stopped crying. Her daddy was right. She would think this through. Jackson *was* common. He was vile. She hated Jackson.

Suddenly, she heard the snap of a branch, a footfall on pine needles. Her heart stopped. A tramp? A soldier? That Peeping Tom everybody was talking about? What *was* she doing out here in the woods by herself? She shivered. Her daddy would die if he knew it. She would never get the car again. Sobbing, she ran to the car and locked herself in. Her hand trembled so she couldn't get the key into the ignition. Hurry! Hurry! It was in! Thank God! The car was moving. She was out of danger, but Jackson had almost gotten her killed. She had heard his footsteps. He was out there in the Park somewhere. Waiting.

She drove as fast as she could to Sarah's slumber party, drove with this terrible secret on her shoulders. She had always been proud. She lifted her chin. At least she still had her pride. That must remain intact.

❋

Sarah had just come home when Mary Martha arrived, and sometime later, thirty minutes later? An hour? Isabel had been delivered.

"Oh, I'm glad you're here," Sarah told them. "I've got great news. I'm not going off to Sweet Briar. Eddie and I decided that tonight. I met him inside the movie. It was scary. Ingrid Bergman's husband almost killed her. Let me take your things upstairs. My folks will be home soon. But the downstairs is ours tonight."

Clattering back down the stairs, Sarah began again. "We drove through town looking for you," she said. "We wanted to tell you the news." Frowning, she looked at her watch. "Wonder where Rosemary is. Well, never mind. She'll be here in a minute. My folks don't like Eddie. But they don't really know him. He is really, really sweet. I love him. I really do. Tonight Eddie and I decided we'll go to the Junior College right here in Cold Springs. When William and Lois Evelyn (Thinking about possible confrontations with her parents, Sarah used her parents' given names.), get to know him, they'll love him as much as I do." Satisfied with her plans, she smiled that wonderfully beguiling smile of hers. "When Rosemary comes we can plan our futures." Her Elizabeth Taylor eyes sparkled. Suddenly aware that her soliloquy had been met with stony silence, "What in the world's the matter with you two," she asked. "Have you been struck dumb?"

Mary Martha blinked, shrugged her shoulders. "We were just listening."

"I've got the curse," Isabel said, praying it was so. "I need an aspirin and a coke."

"Sure," Sarah said, leaving them with the silence and returning with a bottle of aspirin and a tray of cokes. Dropping a couple of aspirins into Isabel's hand, she narrowed her eyes. "Something's up with you two," she said. A cozy, pretty girl, she stood, frowning down at them. "No? Yes! Cat got your tongue? Well, never mind. Let's get into our pajamas. When Rosemary comes, we'll get it out of you two."

The three girls dozed, popped popcorn, played records and dozed. Not until three that morning did Sarah wake her parents to say, "Rosemary's not here yet."

Her mother opened her eyes, blinking. "What? What time is it?"

"What? Girl, what did you say?" her father, already out of bed and pulling his robe on over his pajamas, demanded.

Following him downstairs to the telephone in the hall, her voice a whisper, she said, "She's not here, Dad. We don't know where she is. We kept looking out the windows, waiting for her but . . ."

Before she could finish her father was speaking into the telephone. "Jake, your girl didn't show up here last night. We thought maybe. . . . Oh, God, tell me that she's there, asleep in her own. . . . Okay. Okay. Jake, we'll find her. I'll call the sheriff. We'll organize a search party."

By five that morning, the sheriff had found a young man's body near Rosemary's convertible, its radio playing, "I'll Never Smile Again." Not knowing much about irony, the sheriff shook his head in wonder over that. An hour later, Rosemary's body was found a mile away from her convertible.

And wasn't he the boy from Mount Pleasant? the town wondered. And who could have committed such unspeakable murders? The murderer still out there. Somewhere. Not knowing made it harder to bear.

✳

Those who had seen Rosemary at that last Thanksgiving game remembered as if it were yesterday. Petite, so *perfectly* petite, she had always been the one tossed higher and higher so that her orange and white uniform, streaking through the air, flying up toward the stadium lights, became a flash of bright color against the dark sky. At that moment it seemed to the roaring crowd that she had transformed herself into an exotic bird, perhaps a rare, brightly colored rain forest bird. *Boom! Boom! Boom!* The drums would sound, silence would fill the stands and Rosemary, standing on the steady hands of the strongest of the cheerleaders, would catch her breath and then she would fly up through the air, fly endlessly through the air. Up and up and up she would soar, and when she came laughing down to earth, "Again!" she would cry. "Please! One more time!" And up she would go, up and away from her reserved stepmother, away from her sympathetic friends, away from Sorrow.

And now she was dead. One day her friends, her best friends since kindergarten, had been excited about a slumber party and suddenly, unbelievably, astonishingly, Rosemary was dead. Their vibrant, saucy, brave friend—dead! And even more horrible, murdered! Who could believe that! Rosemary hadn't an enemy in the world.

At first the girls, stunned and shocked into grief, thought the murderer would be caught right away. During the following days, the F.B.I. and the Texas Rangers and the Cold Springs police swarmed over the town. Tramps were arrested. Even soldiers, the town's recent heroes, were picked up and questioned. High school boys were invited to the police station to answer "a few questions." Some came alone, and some came with representation. Others came with their parents *and* representation. Even the high school bandleader, who wouldn't have hurt a flea, was questioned. A Texas Ranger came out to Mary Martha's house one afternoon and asked a question or two before her father ushered him out of the room.

In the middle of the rumors and speculation and paranoia, Jackson Morris was questioned. After visiting with the sheriff on Friday, Jackson was asked to come down the following Monday for another "little visit."

"I asked that boy a question," the sheriff told Officer Gates, only two years out of high school himself. "He said he couldn't say where he was the night the girl was murdered. We'll see what he says when he shows up down here."

On Monday, the police chief waited until noon and then sent Officer Gates with a warrant for his arrest to the school. There the officer found that Jackson had been marked absent in all his classes. Then Gates drove out to the Morris house trailer, but by the time he knocked on the door of the trailer house, Jackson had disappeared from Cold Springs. He never came home again.

In just those few weeks, a kind of innocence was lost. Belief in the certainty of life fell away. Rosemary's three best friends were frightened into silence by the fears of their parents and by the men in uniform asking questions that might suddenly draw their heart's blood toward the truth and change their lives forever. The silence became a wall around them, a barrier not to be breached. Besides, what good would the truth do? To them? To Jackson? Jackson had disappeared. And year-by-year, the three girls outgrew the past. They outgrew the truth.

The murders were never solved. The Phantom Killer, as newspapers across the country called him, had gotten away.

PART 2: 1980

The Women of Cold Springs

The Bridge Club

Like the swampy estuaries of Red River, rumors encircle the town and then the very word—*Jackson Jackson Jackson*—rises above the willows and swamp magnolias and bois d' arc trees along Red River, to threaten the peace-loving citizens of the town of Cold Springs. When the body of a woman who had been shot and dumped into Red River was found miles downstream last year, "You suppose that Morris boy . . . ," Mr. Olson said to the men unloading A-grade pine at his lumberyard. Leaving the thought unfinished he lit a cigar, blew out the match and put it in his pocket. "I knew Jackson Morris. Knew him too well! When he was in high school, that kid almost burned up my lumberyard."

And when a widow living on a farm fourteen miles outside town was found shot to death in the living room of her farmhouse two years ago, "You reckon that Jackson Morris had something to do with it?" Miss Oates, the Cold Springs librarian, asked.

"Well, he could have," her assistant, a high school senior, replied and added, "My mother said that if Jackson wasn't guilty, he wouldn't have run away four days before he was supposed to graduate."

This latest rumor is that one of the Lawrences saw Jackson Morris, or a man looking like an older Jackson would most likely look, step out of a real estate office on the Richmond Road. "Something about the way he carried his shoulders," Trey Lawrence said. "Sure looked like Jackson. Course, it's been almost thirty-five years, but I'm pretty sure it was Jackson."

But this was only a rumor. *Jackson would never come back,* the town said. *He wouldn't dare. Even if he's still alive, he'd never come back home,* they said. But when the four women in the Tuesday bridge club heard the news and considered it, their responses ranged from mild excitement to a shaky uneasiness, for who knew what this day would bring, what one of them might say, inadvertently or not, over the course of an afternoon colored by small glasses of sherry. While they did their hair, slipped into their clothes, found their car keys and hurried to their bridge game, they brushed all thoughts of Jackson away. Still, the *idea* of Jackson hung in the air like fog, blending with the smells of sawmill and pine and the fetid sloughs of the river.

Since the '60s, there have been these four for bridge on Tuesday, three of them friends since Miss Patty's kindergarten. Gaynor, the youngest of the four, is a newcomer, having arrived in Cold Springs in the early '60s.

Isabel Jessup Arnold is from an old Cold Springs family. Tall, her black, curly hair threaded with gray and, with a little weight on her, she now has a full-blown beauty she lacked in high school. There is an evocative languor in the way she moves, and she is irrepressibly open-armed about life, despite moods that send her spirits soaring and, then, inexplicably, spiraling downward. Her moodiness, it is thought, had been caused by the death of her college sweetheart, killed in Korea, and the untimely death of her husband some years later. Paradoxically, the town maintains the belief that Isabel has enjoyed a charmed life, living as she does in her perfect house and having reared two perfect children.

The second of the four, Sarah Carter was born with the proverbial silver spoon, but her money has been lost through a series of risky ventures by an entrepreneurial husband who, then, promptly abandoned her and their two children. The town believes that *her* children, unlike Isabel's, are irresponsible and strange. Still, despite her, some would say, failed life, she has a buoyant breezy manner which exudes an air of centered serenity. An early blooming rose, the earthy smell of a gathering rainstorm, an endearing gesture of one of her children—any of these are enough to send hope bubbling up. A pretty blowsy woman with straight blond hair and a smattering of freckles across her nose and cheekbones, she is short, full breasted and overweight. When Sarah smiles, her face comes alive and her eyes sparkle like sapphires. Upon hearing the sound of her deep, warm chuckle, a room filled with strangers will often break into smiles.

The third Cold Springs native is Mary Martha Mercer who is as different from the others as a sparrow from a flock of parrots. She is wispy. There is that lisp in her voice together with the thin tendrils of brown hair that frame her face and the chiffons she wears through the summer and into September. She has a pretty heart-shaped face that is transformed into sharp points when she becomes upset—a rare occurrence. Mary Martha has lived a life of missed possibilities and knows it. In choosing a life of reticence and caution—a life withheld—she has become as mysterious as a nun to her friends. And it is a fact that she has the wide-eyed innocence and candor often associated with those who have taken the veil. Her voice is gentle. Her movements are imbued with a postulant's air. And because she is a devout Janeite and an excellent bridge player, the assumption is that she thinks deeply. But if the roots of friendship that bind her to her friends are invisible, they are deep and strong.

The newest and youngest member of the Tuesday bridge club is Gaynor Trevor-Rogers. Seven months after Gaynor's husband was killed in a plane crash, his twenty-five-year-old Irish bride noisily and outrageously arrived in Cold Springs. With her diamonds flashing and her spiked hair a flaming red, she had stepped out of a taxi in front of her dead husband's home, lifted her chin and breathed deeply. "My God," she said. "It smells like County Kerry." Because she was bare-legged and wearing scuffed shoes and wrinkled cotton housedresses all over town, *Tacky*, the town said, and, "Imagine Betsy's son marrying a woman like that!" they said, "And married to her just days before he died! It shouldn't count," they said. But Gaynor had a way of capturing one's attention even before she spoke, and when she did speak it was with lyrical cadences and a voice like a bell. Gaynor now has become very much a part of the small town, although earlier there had been talk about her, talk that still might send her running back to Ireland.

Just a week after Gaynor arrived (and this in the early sixties), Sarah called her. "Do you play bridge?" Sarah asked.

"I can learn," she said. And so Gaynor had stayed on in Cold Springs.

They play the second and fourth Tuesdays of each month, and if a divorce, a wedding or a funeral interrupts the life of one of the four, the others wait until it is seemly to cut the cards and deal again. They waited three weeks after Isabel's husband was carried out of his house on a stretcher, carried out dead. And nude.

The remaining three became her handmaidens; *seeing her through*, they called it. After hearing Gaynor's clipped, abrupt, "No, not this morning. She's not available. You may ring back tomorrow, if you like," Sarah and Mary Martha looked at each other with raised eyebrows, nodded in agreement, and hurried to preempt Gaynor's telephone duties. These two, Cold Springs bred and born, knew which of the callers Isabel would want to speak with, which to put off. "Oh, yes, Isabel would want to speak with you," they said, or, occasionally, "I'm sorry. This just isn't a good time right now. You do understand, don't you?" they would ask, their voices gentle, their words like honey. Gaynor dutifully kept lists of who brought what, who came, who called. The three set the table, washed dishes, answered the door and took out the trash. They were at Isabel's side, every step of the way, were there when her mother said firmly, "Isabel, if anything like this ever happens to you again, get his clothes on him!"

Hearing this, Sarah had exploded with warm, rollicking laughter. Isabel's mother, frowning, finger to her lips, whispered, "Oh, Sarah, shush. Shush now, Sarah," even as she looked toward Mary Martha for a reasonable response, but Mary Martha's response was a staccato burst of giggles. Then she looked toward Gaynor for support, but Gaynor, bent double with laughter, was already stumbling out the back door. The others followed Gaynor down the steps and out into the backyard where they huddled together, laughing, holding their sides, gasping for breath, but when Isabel's giggles dissolved into deep, heart-wrenching sobs, her friends, seeing her in such a state, also began to cry. Holding on mightily to each other, they wept as if they would never stop while Isabel's mother looked on anxiously. "You have no control over your emotions," she pronounced from the top of the steps, setting off another round of laughter. "When will you ever grow up! Not a one of you has any sense at all," she said, before whirling and going back inside the house.

Their Tuesday schedule seldom varies: two or three rubbers of bridge, then lunch, followed by another rubber or two, and, finally, the homemade cookies and sherry. Along with the sherry and the tallying of scores, the testy, *sometimes* testy, replaying of hands and snappy conversations finish the evening. By then the sun will be falling and evening shadows gathering and remonstrance begun: "Mary Martha, you've got a long drive. Now keep your eyes open when you drive into that dark garage! Why *don't* you put a light out there?" And, "Gaynor, keep your car doors locked until you get home! Wearing those diamond earrings and living way out there from nowhere, I declare a robber's going to come in on you some dark night and slit your throat."

Standing, gathering up their things, smiling at these old warnings, they airily kiss each other's cheeks and say their goodbyes. For, although they do live alone, at least publicly alone, however in the world could they be threatened by such talk? They have survived floods (an awful one in '62 when the Red River overran its banks and rose as high as the Tanyard bridge), and the Korean War when Isabel lost her young fiancé ("How will she ever get over losing that boy?" they chorused, as they waited for her to get over it), and after that there was the fatal heart attack of Isabel's husband. "George never was the right man for Isabel," said some. "Too old and too serious, but," this last said grudgingly, "pretty tall when he stood on his billfold."

For Sarah, there was all that trouble with both her children going off to the University and four years later coming home changed, utterly changed. And then, Sarah's great old house had burned. To-the-ground! And her children had to move out. "Thank God for that!" Cold Springs said. "And for the insurance!" But not in thirty-four years have they told each other the whole truth about Rosemary's murder. The burden of guilt that each girl carried was heightened by fear and by over-protective parents. Silence was kept, at first by the girls, hardly more than children, and now as women grown. For where does the truth lie? Who knows the complete and inviolate truth?

Still, a certain smile on the face of a stranger will remind them of the brilliance of Rosemary's smile after her mother's death. "Don't feel sorry for me," she would tell them sternly. "It makes me cry. It doesn't help," and then that wonderful smile she wore as a shield would spread across her face. Or seeing a couple on the dance floor would remind them of Rosemary, dancing. For who in the world could jitterbug the way she could, that left arm flung back, her right hand placed saucily on her hip when her partner swung her out. After all these years, memories of Rosemary swirl, lift, drift away. *Rosemary. Murdered. Her murderer still out there. Somewhere.*

Because they live alone, usually, their offspring worry, but what can grown children do with women like these? At times, the whole town worries, especially when something terrible happens to some woman living by herself, even as far away as Ohio or New York, for awful things happen, have happened, in Cold Springs.

Mary Martha

On Tuesday morning Mary Martha is awakened earlier than usual by the noisy coupling of alley cats. When she looks out her window, the cats are nowhere in sight, but she notices the unseasonable fog drifting through her azaleas and down into the dry creek bed that runs alongside her bedroom windows. This kind of thinking is what she has managed to avoid most of her life. Her imagination knows no bounds when she thinks of it: at first the easy sweetness, then the barely noticeable drift leading to the blood rush, and, after that, there is no turning back from the maelstrom of sex. She has seen it happen to her friends, seen them forever swept into the endless whirlpool of demanding husbands and faithless lovers and careless children.

As if the cats and the fog are not enough, yesterday she had seen a gray-headed man standing beside a smoking car on I-30. Unable to believe it was Jackson Morris, she stopped and then she had seen the smile, the blue eyes, the sauntered walk as he came towards her. "I'd rather pick up a snake," she told herself before speeding off. Glancing in the mirror, she saw a man with his hands on his hips, standing as if lost in the middle of the highway. Was the man Jackson? In the bright light of morning she is not at all sure.

What with the cats and the fog and the man, Mary Martha's world is off balance this morning. She picks up Jane Austen's *Letters* and tries to read, but the words before her eyes make no sense. She turns her face into the pillow and closes her eyes. There is no escape from the past. If she could change the past, do it over, she might tell the truth, the whole truth.

❈

She had been fifteen, and Jackson Morris had asked her for a date! She had gone to the Park to meet him. She had seen him jump into Rosemary's convertible. She had heard him say, "How do you know I'm not the Peeping Tom?" And then Rosemary and her friend had been murdered.

A week after Rosemary's murder, a Texas Ranger had come to her house. He came, hat in hand, apologizing to her parents. "I need to ask your daughter, Mary Martha, isn't it, a question or two."

"She doesn't know a thing about it. Terrible isn't it? Some outsider. A tramp riding the rails, maybe. A soldier, even."

"Mr. Mercer, that may be. But we need to talk to her, and I just thought, considering how young she is that. . . ."

"She's just a child."

"Yes sir. I thought it would be better here in her own house than down at the station."

Nodding, her father had stepped out of the room and called up the stairs: "Mary Martha, baby, come on down here. Ranger Gonzales wants to ask you some questions."

When she had entered the room, she had seen the Texas Ranger towering over her father. She had seen the gun in the holster at his waist and the white cowboy hat in his hand. She sat on the sofa between her mother and her father to answer the Ranger's questions.

"Mary Martha. I understand you saw Jackson Morris leaving the Park the next morning?" Ranger Gonzales said.

"Yes!" she said, eager to say it. "I was coming home from Sarah's slumber party, and I saw him stepping out of the woods. When he saw daddy's car, he ran back into the woods behind the springs."

"Now, you know this boy pretty well, do you? You sure it was Jackson?"

She had seen the Ranger was ready to doubt her. It was in his eyes. "I've known him all my life," she had answered truthfully.

"Mary Martha, do you like Jackson?"

"Not anymore," she had said, bursting into tears. "I'm afraid of him now." And this, too, was the truth.

Then Mary Martha had seen her daddy's face, frozen into impenetrable stiffness, as he ushered the man toward the front door. "This is an ugly business," her daddy said. "My daughter is not involved. Not involved in any way. She has told you all she knows."

Then her daddy took the man's arm, and they stepped out on the porch and closed the door behind them while she sat on the sofa and cried.

※

None of that matters now. She had skirted the truth, had not told the whole truth. Sins of commission and omission. But when Jackson disappeared, the truth hadn't mattered. Running away was proof enough of his guilt. And one undeniable fact remained. Jackson had jumped into Rosemary's convertible that night, and a few hours later Rosemary was murdered. Jackson had murdered Rosemary and her friend from Mount Pleasant. Mary Martha is sure of it. But who would believe her after all these years?

And now if Jackson has come home, the rumors, the gossip, the paranoia will flare up all over again. If the sheriff asks her, she will tell the whole truth. "I saw Jackson get into Rosemary's convertible shortly before she was murdered," she will say. But for now, she will simply wait.

She glances out her bedroom windows. The fog has lifted and the only sound she hears is the song of a mockingbird. It has been good to reach a decision. Turning from the window, she plumps up her pillow and reaches for the *Letters* on her bedside table. Repose is needed now. She opens Miss Austen's letters and reads:

*I am not surprised My Dear Cassandra, that you did not
find my last letter full of matter. I wish that this may not
have the same deficiency.*

This one paragraph is enough to bring a smile to her lips.
The charm of Jane Austen's letters is that they are seldom "full
of matter." She settles more snugly into her pillow, savoring
each word:

*But we are doing nothing ourselves to write about, and I
am therefore quite dependent upon the communications
of our friends or my own wits.*

How satisfying! How reassuring Jane's thoughts are! And
how much alike the two of them are—their personal lives
tranquil, circumscribed, yet filled with observations. But how
different are the lives of their friends! The lives of Mary Martha's friends are quite chaotic, at times even dangerous, when
compared to the lives of Miss Austen's friends. Satisfied that
if she, Mary Martha, wrote letters, which she has no intention
of doing, her letters would easily be filled with matter, she
closes the book.

Padding barefooted into the bathroom, she turns the faucet on full force and, stepping into the tub, she unwraps a bar
of hotel soap and bathes. When she travels, confiscating the
small bars of hotel soaps and bottles of shampoo and conditioner is one of her favorite ways to save. However, unlike
Miss Austen who often mentions money, Mary Martha never
discusses her economic situation with her friends. She takes
enormous pride in keeping her financial condition from the
world, although she enjoys hearing Albert Aston, her banker,
tell her she needs to spend her money. Looking at her with
his round black eyes, "Mary Martha, better spend some of
that money! You can't take it with you!" Albert always advises
from behind his carved mahogany desk.

She glances at her watch. She has plenty of time. Sitting at
her mother's dressing table, she luxuriously cleans her face

with lavender-scented witch hazel. She sometimes wishes the whole world smelled as clean. When he was young, Albert smelled a little like witch hazel. He was fat even then, but not bad looking. She had considered going out with him, but he had never asked her until after her parents died. By then he had, of necessity, taken over the management of her money.

She had stopped in one morning to see him on business. After a long desultory talk about Mary Martha's investing some money in a Certificate of Deposit, "Not too much. Have to keep a balanced portfolio," he had advised, and then, with no warning at all, he had pushed himself out of his chair, walked around his desk and stood so close to her his stomach brushed hers. His face was covered with a fine sheen of perspiration. He smelled nothing in the world like witch hazel.

"Mary Martha," he said, "let's cut to the chase." His breathing was harsh, whether from passion or nervousness, she could not tell. When she took a step backwards, he reached out, put his hand behind her neck, and pulled her face close to his, so close that all she saw were the straight, black hairs jutting from his nose. When he tried to kiss her, she had turned her face away.

He had drawn back, taken out a white handkerchief and wiped his face. "Something came over me, Mary Martha. I'm rushing things." He took a deep breath and whistled it out through his teeth. Then he said, "Mary Martha, there's a movie at the Paramount with Gregory Peck. How about a movie Saturday night? Think you would enjoy a night on the town with me?" he said.

"No," she said softly.

"Well, I heard you lost someone in Korea," he said, handing over an excuse for her refusal.

"I didn't," she said.

He had exhaled slowly. He turned and walked over to his office window and stood with his back to her. Then he turned around and looked into her calm gray eyes. "Mary Martha," he had said angrily, "you are too goddamned honest."

Now, remembering Albert's response, Mary Martha feels a tinge of sympathy for him. However, when she imagines his privates hanging down there, somewhere below his belly button, it is enough to make her want to close her eyes and never open them again.

Oh, dear! she tells herself. Thinking of Albert could ruin a perfectly lovely day. She drops Albert back behind the desk where he belongs and, picking up her eyecup, she rinses her eyes, one at a time, blinking until each eye is perfectly clear. She lightly applies pink lipstick, blots it and adds a smidgen of rouge to her cheeks. She buttons the ruffled, rose-printed, chiffon blouse and zips up the linen skirt. Slipping her feet into Italian pumps, her single extravagance, she holds one foot up, turning it this way and that. She has always been inordinately proud of her slender feet.

Today, they will be playing at Isabel's. Thinking of Isabel's flower garden, Mary Martha steps outside and, turning her face away from the raw odor of the sawmill, she hurries to her car. She turns on the air conditioner and breathes deeply, prepared to enjoy the smells of baking bread and newly pressed linens and lemon oil at Isabel's; the breezes wafting through French doors that would be open to the terraces sloping down to the rose garden, just to the left of the fish pond. As soon as she rings the doorbell, Willie B., Isabel's sassy old maid, will be hurrying to take her wrap and bring coffee, flavored to her taste (a heavy dollop of cream and two teaspoons of sugar), and for lunch, sandwiches made of freshly baked bread and Isabel's own apricot chutney and liver pate; and, after the last rubber, Willie B. will slide a tray of homemade cookies and sherry-filled glasses into the middle of their gossip.

Mary Martha knows that Willie B. could take a seat in the gossiping section. Isabel herself says that if Cold Springs knew how much Willie B. knew, not all from Isabel's bridge friends, they would lie sleepless in their beds at night. Word gets around.

The drive from Genoa to Cold Springs is 20 miles, a long drive just for bridge, but nice this time of year. Mary Martha's little red Buick hums along satisfactorily, and now that the interior of the car has cooled off, she can turn off the air-conditioner. Coming up to I-30, Mary Martha slows to look at the pines caught in the gauze of fog and the glint of sunlight.

When she sees a young man standing at the end of the Arkansas River Bridge, his right hand out, thumb up, she slows. He is wearing a hat and holding a book close to his chest. Is it Sarah's son? Is it John Carter? It is! Easing to the side of the highway, she tells herself Sarah needs to take a firmer hand with her children. Picking up a guitar case, the man hurries toward the car. The old felt hat he wears masks his eyes, but when he reaches the car she sees they are a watery blue, the irises rimmed with black. He does not look a thing like John Carter. He is years older than Sarah's son.

"I thought you were John Carter."

"No ma'am. I'm Jake Ramsey." He takes off his hat and steps back.

"You know John?"

"No, ma'am."

Polite. Clean-looking, except for the shaggy hair and the earring, she thinks. "Where are you going?"

"Dallas."

"I can take you as far as Cold Springs," she says, wondering why in the world she's said it as soon as she says it. "As far as the Summerhill Road. You won't have to wait long for a ride there."

He moves to open the front door of her car. "No, I've got all this stuff up here. Hop in back."

She watches as he carefully places his guitar case on the seat. His clothes are damp. Drops of water roll down his face.

"You look like you might have swum across the river," she says, pulling out onto the highway.

"I spent the night in the Bottoms."

His voice is scratchy. At the sound of snaps, she glances in the rearview mirror and sees that he is removing the guitar from its case.

"It was wet down there, water dripping all over everything. I couldn't find a way to keep dry. My book got wet."

"You were out in all this weather in the Bottoms! For goodness sakes! Why?"

It isn't any of her business, but the Bottoms is full of mosquitoes and snakes and tramps. And now she has invited one into her car.

"Why would anybody go down there to spend the night?"

Another question. And now her head is swimming and her vision is blurred. Since the cats woke her up, she's had too much excitement. She blinks. Nonsense. She can see perfectly well. She presses her lips together. It was that ridiculous story about Jackson. She is being silly. But she will be glad to get Jake Ramsey, if that is his name, out of her car. What possessed her to pick him up in the first place?

"Why the Bottoms?" she asks again.

"An old man took me down there."

"Who was it?"

"I don't know who it was. Some old fool. He said I could spend the night at his deer lease."

Some old fool. When he gets to Dallas, will he describe her that way? "An old fool picked me up," he will say to his friends. Feeling years older, she repositions her hands on the steering wheel and draws her elbows close. She steps on the accelerator.

"Whoa-a-a," he says.

She steals a look into the rearview mirror. His eyes meet hers. Before she can look away, he leans forward.

"The old man had a deer blind on the river. Said I could stay there. He had an old dog down there, chained up. Whining. Nothing but skin and bones. Lordgodalmighty," and now his grimy hand is draped over the front passenger's seat, "that was a pitiful looking hound. In the middle of the night I turned it loose, and we took off together. The dog stayed with me until daylight. Then he turned around and went back home. Guess he knew I couldn't feed him."

He leans back and strums his guitar. "She don't like being out in the weather. She needs a fine-tuning." Then, "Like a woman," he adds.

A totally inappropriate remark. Insulting, really. She glances at the speedometer. The needle's on 85. She hadn't known her car could go that fast. She glances into the mirror again. His eyes are there, filling the mirror. His nose is sharp; his face narrow. The right side of his mouth turns downward. How could she have thought he was Sarah's son?

"Hey, didn't you go to Cold Springs High? You did, didn't you?"

She tightens her grip on the steering wheel. His mirrored eyes hold hers. "Yes."

"You were in my algebra class, a Miss Smarty. . . ."

"Definitely not! No!"

He gives her shoulder a dismissive pat. "Whatever you say," he says, sitting back. His eyes disappear from her mirror. "You're a pretty cool driver," he says. He strums a C chord, then a D, then C again. Satisfied, he strums the C chord again. "This here's an old Gibson. My folks gave it to me."

Folks. The word speaks of normalcy. "Do your parents live in Arkansas?"

"As far as I know, they're still dead," he says lightly.

After a second his answer registers. *Oh, Jesus*. She takes a deep breath. How far has she driven? Are they inside the city limits? Where exactly are they? Just ahead, there's the Cold Springs water tower. It couldn't be more than five miles to the Summerhill Road. She *is* inside the city limits. Suppose a policeman stopped her. Would she say, "I'm scared of this boy I picked up." She slows to thirty. A few more minutes, and he will be out of her car.

"Play something," she says, afraid of the tremor in her voice. "I like guitar music."

"Here's an old song you might know."

Old. That word again. She steals another look. He bends over his guitar, his thin face intent. She begins to remember him in school. Vaguely.

He strums a chord and begins to play "I'll Be Seeing You," the song she was humming this morning. Her right eye begins to twitch. As she furiously rubs it, the car veers off the pavement. She quickly corrects it, both hands on the wheel again.

"Sing it," he says. "It's an old song. Don't you know it?"

Mocking her. Her hands are sweating against the steering wheel. She wipes her hands on her skirt. She is a fool. Why did she pick up a tramp? This has gone far enough. Too far. Abruptly, she steps on the brakes and swerves to the side of the road. A long, angry blast sounds from a passing truck. She puts her hands over her ears.

"Get out!" she says. "Please." Her voice is trembling.

"What in the hell's . . ."

"Get out. Please. Just get out. I've made a mistake."

He opens the door. "Look, lady, I'm sorry. I use slang. I'm sorry. Hell, I'm sorry."

Her foot taps the accelerator.

"Wait!" he shouts. "My guitar!"

She brakes. Grabbing the guitar, he curses, slams the car door. "Hell, lady, you are a trip. You're crazy."

She presses hard on the accelerator and, tires screeching, pulls out onto the highway.

"Fuck you, lady!" he screams. "Fuck you!"

In her side mirror, she sees the guitar waving in the air, a fist gesticulating.

Minutes later she turns onto the Summerhill Road and from there onto a small graveled road. She stops beneath the shade of a tree and puts her head on the steering wheel and weeps.

❄

Their chairs pulled around a library table, the three women have finished their coffee and watched Willie B. whisk away the cups and saucers. Now they simply wait.

The large, rectangular room where they wait is painted a soft yellow that sets off the carved moldings. Shabby Persian rugs are scattered over the mahogany floor. Two long sofas, their faded slipcovers, one a flowered design, the other an animal print, carelessly, artfully matching, are placed on either side of the marble fireplace. Between the sofas is a gracefully carved round table. A whimsical chandelier hangs over the bridge table that is placed at the opposite end of the room. The chandelier is a metal, gold-colored, beribboned balloon, under which six golden candlesticks, each holding a tapered electric bulb, are tethered. Of all the things in her house, the chandelier is Isabel's favorite.

"Mary Martha is never late," Isabel says now.

And from Sarah, "She's always early."

"It may be all that talk about Jackson. If Mary Martha heard it, maybe she couldn't get out of bed this morning," Isabel says. Standing, she walks over to the windows and looks down her winding drive. "She would have called us. Something's happened."

"If she's heard that Jackson's come home, she's probably scared," Sarah says.

"Why would that frighten her?" Gaynor asks.

Her question is met by silence. Finally, Sarah responds. "It all happened so long ago. We were children. It would take days to tell you. But there are some who think. . . ." She looks guardedly at Isabel before continuing.

"Go on. Finish," Isabel says coolly.

"Some who believe Jackson murdered a young girl whom we knew." Sarah shrugs. "It's true, Isabel," she says lightly.

"It is true," Isabel says. Then briskly, "I'm going to pour more coffee." But, instead, she lifts her long, slender hand to her throat, stroking it. "I think about Jackson, Sarah. I'd like to see him again. I would!"

"Why?"

Frowning, Isabel shakes her head. "I don't know why," she says.

"Oh," Sarah says, "you can't mean that. Let's forget about Jackson. Mary Martha will be here any minute, unless she's had a flat or something."

"She has new tires," says Gaynor.

"She'll be here," Isabel says firmly. Smiling, she moves toward the bridge table. Her teeth are white against her dark skin. "Let's shuffle the cards. Gaynor? More tea?"

Isabel is wearing a white linen pants suit and, under the jacket, an apricot cashmere sweater. Summer cashmere. On this early day of spring, her appearance evokes a kind of tropical lushness due to the contrast between her dark hair and skin and the bright apricot and white pants suit.

Sarah has turned her chair toward the terrace, sat down and stretched her legs out in front of her. Never mind that Sarah, all in beige—skirt, jacket, shoes, her straight hair, beige too, and her only jewelry a single strand of pearls—is a little on the heavy side. When Sarah smiles, as she is smiling now, her freckles scatter, her eyes brighten, her face is alive. The warmth of Sarah's smile diffuses Isabel's defiance. They pull their chairs close together as Isabel pours more coffee and, for Gaynor, tea.

Gaynor, by Cold Springs' standards, plainly dressed, except for her diamond earrings and red hair, has also relaxed into a chair at the bridge table. Looking out onto the terrace, "Isn't it grand, that bower of white roses!" she says. "Cheerful in April. What is it then?"

"It's a Lady Banks rose," Isabel says. "And it's about to take over."

"Ay, the same as in Ireland," says Gaynor. "But I do love the flower."

Sarah sits up straight. "Let's cut for deal," she says. "Ah. The jack of spades, and I'm Mary Martha's partner. I'll deal for her."

But here she is, Mary Martha, hurrying in. Taking note of her reddened eyes and flushed cheeks, their welcoming smiles encourage her to the table.

"We're glad you're here," says Sarah. And, "We've cut the cards. You're my partner."

Watching as Mary Martha shrugs off her summer shawl and deposits it with her handbag on the settle bench, they lean slightly towards her.

But they have been talking about her. Mary Martha knows it. She always knows. It is one of the senses one develops when one lives alone. Of course, they all live alone. But their lives, entangled with the lives of children and dead and living husbands and lovers, at times, border on the scandalous. And they live alone only intermittently. Well, *she* Mary Martha, has something to talk about today. She decides that if the cards come her way, she will tell them she picked up a hitch-hiker. Over sherry.

As Mary Martha settles into her chair, Sarah puts the cards she has just shuffled to her left instead of her right. Isabel picks up her hand and stares at a three of spades for a full minute before arranging her cards.

Smiling faintly, head canted, Gaynor studies Mary Martha. Texas women remain a quaint and curious puzzle to Gaynor. She has lived all this time in Cold Springs and, still, there is a part of their lives that remains closed to her.

Now Mary Martha adjusts her chair, hastily arranges her hand and smiles. "Sorry," she says.

Hopefully, they smile back at her. Although Mary Martha seems mysterious to them, her daily schedule is an open book. But, why was she late? Politely, they wait for her to continue.

She looks around the table. "One spade," she says firmly.

Imagining the flurry of excitement her news about the hitchhiker would have caused, she gazes at the hand she has deliberately underbid. She had thought she would tell them about her adventure right away. "I picked up a hitchhiker," she might have said casually. But the thought of Clovis flying in to see about her aunt had sealed her lips. Clovis. When she had broken her arm last year, Clovis had been called. When she had had an episode with her heart, Clovis had been called. And considering the long, worrisome telephone calls that followed was enough to render her mute on subjects such as picking up hitchhikers.

It is this last idea, almost a threat, that causes her to over-take her partner's high spade. Hearing Sarah's heavy sigh, she presses her lips together. "Sorry, partner."

It was silly to be upset. He was just a young man, down on his luck, trying to get to Dallas. A middle-aged hippie, probably. She supposes there are a few hippies, still around. Somewhere. And those earrings! Gypsyish. If it hadn't ended the way it had, it would have been something to talk about. A little excitement. She could have taken him as far as the Summerhill Road. Her friends would have been shocked if she had told them. The truth is she had been scared. There had been his thin, dirty hand on the seat, his eyes filling her mirror. And she has not been as excited in a long time, not since she had gone to the Park to meet Jackson. Thinking about Jackson, her scalp tingles. All at once, as if from the edge of the world, she knows . . . *something*. Something is going to happen. It is not too late. It could happen tomorrow. Or the next day. To her.

Buoyed by this feeling, she finesses a nine of spades to make her bid. "That's the rubber!" she announces, almost giddily.

Later that night, she listens to the news before going to bed. Students in Iran have taken over the embassy and are holding Americans hostage. President Carter has threatened military action. Jean Harris, the headmistress of a fancy girl's school, is being tried for the murder of her former lover. Later, she lies on her back, idly wondering if it was the rumor about Jackson or the caterwauling cats or the fog that had caused the day to take such a curious turn, a turn as amazing as the idea that Jackson might still be alive and buying property in Bowie County. At this thought, rather more stimulating than is needed at bedtime, she opens *The Letters* and reads:

> *My Dear Cassandra—You cannot imagine—it is not in human nature to imagine—what a nice walk we have round the orchard. The row of beech look very well indeed and so does the young quickset hedge in the garden. I hear today that an apricot has been detected on one of the trees.*

A walk would be just the thing for her, too. Tomorrow she will walk. Early. She might even walk along the creek. When she has gone no more than a hundred yards, she will be deep in the piney woods. An early dogwood might be in bloom or

the swamp iris flowering early. One year the Monarch but-
terflies had migrated through the woods and along the creek.
Had Miss Austen been there, how thrilled she would have
been to see the wonder of that! Imagining this—a walk with
Jane Austen—she closes the book and sleeps.

❄

Two weeks later Isabel gets up in the middle of the night.
She sits on her terrace under the full moon remembering the
night Jackson had climbed into her bedroom holding a white
flower as bright as day in the moonlight. Her memory of that
night is searingly vivid. *Jackson.* What if Jackson has come
home? She has always believed he would. Someday. *Stop it!*
she tells herself. Think about tomorrow. Think about tomorrow and bridge at Mary Martha's. Think about Mary Martha,
more and more mysterious. Think about her wide-eyed innocence. As pure as a nun. She might as well be a nun. Clois-
tered. Revealing nothing. Think about Mary Martha's house.
Strangely comforting. In that house, not a vase moved, nor
a stick of furniture, not a room painted—nothing changed
since her mother had died. Untouched by Mary Martha, the
house remains inhabited by memories of her mother. It is her
mother who comes in from the kitchen, who sits at the organ,
who rattles the pots and pans, who calls out a greeting as, all
the while, Mary Martha drifts, drifts through the house. Like
smoke.

A breeze from the garden, bringing the intoxicating scent
of gardenias, ruffles her hair. In April there is always this
heady pleasure. She imagines forsythia, a bee coming to the
yellow blossom, feels the word on her tongue. She remembers
rumpled beds and ice-cold champagne. Their honeymoon.
An early morning view of the Eiffel Tower from the George V
Hotel and from below the scent of chestnut blossoms. George
always smelled like a pipe, although he never smoked one.

Damn! She needs her sleep, but how can she sleep thinking of George? Of Jackson. Think only of Mary Martha's house, she reminds herself. She knows the house room-by-room. The square living room with its faded silvery wallpaper. The pictures of Mary Martha's grandparents and great-grandparents, in sepia, marching up and down the sides of the huge walnut framed mirror; the old organ, its moth-eaten, felt keys, standing dismally against the wall in the library. A house in stasis.

But Mary Martha is not in stasis. She has changed. Something is going on with Mary Martha. Coming late for bridge two weeks ago. At Isabel's house. Briskly arriving after the three of them had had more coffee and cut the cards. Mary Martha has always been early! Never late!

Late.... Isabel sees her late husband carried out on a stretcher. Nude. His nudity caused by nothing other than a hot Texas night. Let them think what they would, the men in the ambulance, frowning their sympathy, forcing their embarrassed smiles into tight-lipped soberness. Even in shock, she had noticed the hospital attendants forcing themselves to look away from her braless, skimpy T-shirt, her short denim skirt. Get a life! she had wanted to tell them. She misses George. George cared about the world. She misses George's mind. George, sometimes rudely, refused to suffer the banalities of life. He would have been concerned about the Soviets invading Afghanistan? He would have voted for Carter, but what would he have thought about Carter's canceling the Olympics to show he was mad? *Absurd,* he would have said. And George would have made Afghanistan seem as close as Arkansas or Oklahoma. Sighing, she thinks of the day ahead. She hopes the cards come her way. If she gets the choice, she and her partner can sit the way the bathtub runs. Isabel is superstitious about bridge. She needs all the luck she can get when she plays against Mary Martha. Mary Martha is a Janeite, the only one in town as far as she knows. "What in the world is a Janeite?" Gaynor had once asked Mary Martha, unable to resist the urge to tease her. "Is it a secret society of some kind? Are they feminists? Do they burn their bras? "

Mary Martha does not like to be teased. She had taken three tricks before responding. "I think Rudyard Kipling coined the word," she had said carefully. "A Janeite is a person who reads and contemplates the writings of Jane Austen. Just now, we're reading *Emma*."

"What's it about?" Gaynor asked.

"It's about a woman, a very young woman who doesn't know herself. Not at all," Mary Martha had answered. They were leaning forward listening, so interested that she had added. "Emma is totally self-delusional."

Isabel had been intrigued. Since then she has thought about reading about a self-delusional girl named Emma. She, Isabel, is certainly not self-delusional. She knows herself very well.

After a minute Mary Martha tilts her head and says, "Gaynor, it is your lead."

Gaynor can never resist the urge to tease. Gaynor. Irish through and through, with her red hair and her hearty laugh, but just below the surface, the keening, still, for her dead bridegroom.

On bridge days, they sometimes parade Texas, warts and all, before Gaynor, parade it like some mismatched, misbegotten parade of wit and witlessness. Over sherry at Isabel's house, Gaynor had once said, "I like Carter. But what's all this about religion? Like Ireland, is it?"

"We don't fight about stuff like that in Texas," Sarah had chuckled. "It's football here, pure and simple."

Now, yawning, Isabel stands, stretches, and goes back to bed. On her way, she notices the chandelier. Plumping up her pillow, she makes a mental note: *new bulb for the chandelier.* Thinking this she turns over and falls asleep.

Surprised by sunlight pouring through her bedroom windows, Isabel lies in bed the next morning. Fully awake, she wills herself not to think about Jackson. She will think about her taxes or the mole on her shoulder. Still in her robe, she poaches an egg, puts it on dry toast and takes a bite. She puts down her fork, and studies the egg, watches it slowly congeal on her plate. She should take a shower and dress. She sits on. She looks through the windows onto the kitchen terrace. She sees a blue bird after a grasshopper. Her mind swirls away from the grasshopper's murder. And ... *Jackson is before her eyes.*

She sees herself, a girl, rail-thin, looking down, blushing, turning, turning away from his ardor. Remembering, she is filled with wonder. At seventeen, Jackson knew all about ardor. It is all there, like a dream, this sixteen-year-old girl, pushing Jackson away, and turning, turning, running away from his outstretched arms.

❀

Isabel had always loved men and said so often. She looked forward to marriage and sex, "and in that order" she laughingly told her friends. Flirting indiscriminately, she had dated just about every boy in high school. "Yes!" she said to Billy Joe Webster, whose father was a plumber. And, wide-eyed, demurely, "Yes" she said to Otis Strickland, a fumbling, mumbling boy of whom nobody had ever heard, when he asked her to the Boy Scout Troop 18 picnic. And to Stephen Smith, whose mother worked at the *Five and Dime*, "I was hoping you'd ask me," she said confidingly, even though Stephen had not the slightest idea what to do with his feet on the dance floor.

Yet, there had always been Jackson. Isabel was acutely aware of Jackson. Without a cent in his pocket and always on foot, she had always said "yes" to Jackson. "Yes" to his asking if he could walk her home, "yes" to helping him with Latin, "yes" when he asked her for a dance. Yet, Jackson was no more than a friend until her senior year.

With her wide smile and gleaming teeth, her bronzed skin that even in the middle of winter gave her the look of having just come from the beach, she was usually thought of as beautiful. She was not. Her nose was mildly crooked; her chin mildly stern and, occasionally, her expression took on a steely look. However, with her nimble mind (she was very funny), and generous spirit, neither her friends nor their parents, and certainly not the teachers nor the school's custodians nor the help at the Country Club, almost nobody in fact, noticed her flaws. From the first grade, she gave valentines to every classmate and, at Christmas, presents, too. By the time she was in high school, she led the tin foil drive and volunteered once a month to roll bandages for the wounded soldiers. Everybody loved Isabel.

But in September of her senior year, she, unfortunately, had fallen madly in love with Jackson Morris, *unfortunately* because Isabel was a closet snob. Old family, old money, the right schools meant everything to Isabel. How could she then love Jackson? Although Jackson was funny and smart and so handsome the sight of him coming down the hall made her heart jump, she was unable to separate him from his family or from their serious lack of family money. Jackson was poor! He lived in a trailer. Her house. His trailer. A chasm separated them. Although the money in Isabel's family had shrunk considerably, she was well connected. She had Harvard and Yale uncles and dozens of Ivy League cousins. She had ticked off the pluses and the minuses, as carefully as the figures in her checkbook. Still, who knows what might have happened, what might have changed her whole life and, thus, made her deliriously happy, had Jackson not disappeared from high school and from Cold Springs five days before his graduation.

By the time she finished Ward-Belmont, George had proposed to her at least three times. Ten years older, he had finished Harvard and Harvard law school and had joined his father's law firm as a junior partner by the time she came home with a degree in Fine Arts. She accepted a ring on Christmas Day, and they had been married on New Year's Day. Together, they had lived, contented, *mostly* contented, lives. They were pleasantly reasonable with each other. Their lovemaking was satisfactory. They had two perfect children, well educated, who now lived independent lives in far-off cities.

Luckily, she had not been forced to choose between Jackson and George, choose between two lives she might have had. Still, she wonders. Living her staid widowhood in her perfect house and seeing her precious children from time-to-time, she has always wondered. And now? Jackson in town? She is consumed with memories of Jackson.

❧

That very night of Rosemary's murder, Isabel had seen Jackson emerge from the shadows into the moonlight and jog toward her window. Whistling his whippoorwill's call, he had climbed the tree outside her window, and swept her up into his arms. Smilingly Isabel remembered that although his hands were all over her body, their kisses remained chaste because she had strongly believed in the danger of tongue kissing. But when he took her nipple into his mouth she was unbuttoning her blouse, unfastening her bra, and his mouth was moving down, down, and then there was no resisting Jackson's hoarse whispering: "Izzy, Izzy, Izzy." Afterwards, she was crying softly and, sounding like the Shakespeare play they were reading, she was whispering over and over, "My reputation. My reputation."

The next morning the police had found Rosemary and Mark Hollins dead, and Isabel's world was forever changed.

Mark had been changing a tire on Rosemary's convertible when he had been viciously murdered by blows to the head, and Rosemary had been brutally strangled and . . . *molested.* The word, too terrible to say aloud, never appeared in the *Cold Springs Gazette.*

Three days after they "had slept together," and how quaint the phrase sounds now, Isabel had met Jackson in the parking lot and opened the Bible she held in her hands. *"Swear,"* she said. "Swear you'll never tell a soul we slept together. That would just about kill my parents."

Lifting her chin with his hand, he smiled. "Isabel," he had said gently, "look at me. I love you. I'll always love you."

Brushing his hand and his love away, "Swear!" she commanded.

His expression suddenly serious, he put his hand on the Bible and swore.

"It's over between us," she had told him then. "I'm going off to school after graduation is over, and I'll probably never see you again."

He had run away right after she had said those things to him. One morning he sat in his Senior English class, his arms folded, looking indifferently at Isabel, at the teacher, at everybody. The next day he was absent. He never came back. She never saw Jackson Morris again. She had lived with an indefinable regret for awhile, but after all these years even that is gone. But now she has heard that Jackson has come home. She will not allow herself to believe it, although some part of her has always known she would see him again.

❊

"Where is the white lady of the house?" Willie B. calls now, her laughter bouncing into the kitchen. Hands on her hips, Willie B. stands, frowning down at her. "What you doing in here? Sitting over breakfast. The sun way up in the sky. You knows what day it is. You better get on out of here. I got my work to do." Willie B. turns on the water in the sink and, raising a great clatter, she scrapes and stacks the dishes. "You playing at Miss Mary Martha's? Don't blame you for not hurrying over there. I wouldn't want to spend all day over there myself," she mutters through lips as still as those of a ventriloquist.

Willie B. is tall. Her shoulders are broad; her chin strong. Her lips are rarely still. Portraying every thought, revealing every emotion they twitch, widen into a smile and narrow, as if pulled by a drawstring. Isabel knows that when Willie B. speaks without moving her lips, she is trying to stay out of Isabel's business.

"Now, Willie B.," Isabel says mildly.

"You're thinking about that noise all over town," Willie B. says, her lips narrowing. "I'm hoping to the good Lord ain't nothing to it. Too much water gone under the bridge. No use in dragging it all up now. Too late to make it right if'n there's somebody knows what the right is."

"Willie B., it's true. He's here in town."

"You seen him?"

"No, but I got a feeling."

"Baby, you white. You ain't supposed to have feelings."

"What are you talking that black talk for, Willie B.? You mad or something?"

"I don't know. I guess I'm worried."

"Well, is it true? Has Jackson come back?"

"Maybe he has. But now you can't go messing in all that now. You get yourself up and dressed. You don't need to be thinking about what's nothing but pain and trouble."

The clock chimes. Isabel counts the chimes. Nine. Think about dressing, she tells herself. She sits on.

"If you're gonna mope all morning, that's up to you. But you need to find someplace else to do it. Look at this kitchen. Look at this mess. I got to clean this up."

"All right. I'm going. I'm going," Isabel says, standing up, patting her flat stomach, patting Willie B.'s shoulder as she leaves the room.

In the shower she lets the soapy water run over her shoulders, her breasts. She rubs the sudsy water over her pubic hair, wishing the hair on her head were as black and as curly. She'd like to be black, just for one day, black and tall and skinny and wearing four-inch heels and walking into "The Blue Parrot" like she owned it. She'd be wearing a black dress with black sequins, and she would float by tables with men leaning toward her. "You're looking good, baby," and "Light my fire, baby," they'd croon to her swaying hips.

Willie B. has told her all about the Blue Parrot, said she'd take her except for her reputation.

"I'm not worried about my reputation," Isabel had answered.

Willie B. laughed. "It ain't your reputation I'm thinking of," she had said.

Isabel dries off, sprays on perfume and rubs lotion on her elbows and legs. Hurrying now, her spirits rising, she slips into panties and fastens her bra. She grabs blue linen pants and a blue and white silk sweater from her closet and slips into them. Sitting on the bed, she fastens her high heel sandals and tosses a French-blue, silk scarf around her neck.

Going through the kitchen, she sees that Willie B. is at the table, drinking coffee and eating doughnut holes. Covering her mouth, Willie B. grins at her.

"Willie B., you're looking mighty comfortable. Sho is now," Isabel teases.

"Well, I am. And you've come to yourself. I knew it when I heard you coming down the hall. Clickety-clack, clickety-clack."

"Nothing cheers a woman up like looking good and knowing it."

"Ha! That's for others to say." Frowning in mock seriousness, she looks at Isabel's sandals, her blue slacks, her sweater. "If I say you're looking good, you're looking good." She frowns. "I say you're looking good," she laughs. "Now get on out of here. This is gonna be another fine day." Hearing the garage door open, she frowns again. "I hope to the good Lord it's gonna be," she adds.

In the darkness of the garage, Isabel's blue Chrysler shines. She slides onto the seat and backs quickly out of the garage. Halfway around the circle drive, she smells flavoring, then the yeasty smell of a cake baking. Instantly, her mother is before her, gray hair in a French twist, pearls around her neck, a Christmas apron around her waist, anxiously (always that, always anxious), stooping to take a cake from the oven. Tears fill Isabel's eyes. All her life, her mother baked fresh cocoanut cakes for Christmas dinner. Now, she's had two Christmases without them. Without her mother. "Damnit, Mother," she says, "I thought you'd always be here."

Driving slowly down the winding, gravel road, she sees that the highest branches of the redbud trees are in bloom. And the little dogwood at the end of her drive is about ready to blossom out. She turns onto the Summerhill Road. She will be at Mary Martha's in half an hour.

She flips on the radio. "You walked into the party like you were walking onto a yacht," Carly Simon sings. When she gets to the chorus, Isabel sings along with Carly: "You're so vain, you probably think this song is about you." By the second time the chorus comes around, she and Carly are belting it out, and what with their duet and the trees in flower, and her scarf flying round her shoulders, she imagines flying over to Paris. The chestnut trees would be in bloom, and she would be wearing her French-blue scarf, this very scarf she is wearing now that has made the day so glorious. Isadora Duncan was strangled by her own scarf caught up in her convertible's wheel. *Strangled, like Rosemary.* She will not let herself think about Rosemary. *The horror of it! The cruelty of it!* Turning up the volume, she pushes away all thoughts of Rosemary.

Coming up onto I-30 she sees the hitchhiker. He sits perched on a bridge railing. He is wearing an old-fashioned hat, and he is reading a book. A guitar case and a backpack lie at his feet. Charming, really. When she slows to turn onto the highway, she finds herself looking directly into his eyes. He nods and lifts his hand in a quiet salute, as if he has known her distantly or has some knowledge of her. His gesture touches her. On this impossibly beautiful spring day, everything pierces her heart. She turns the radio down and loosens her scarf from around her neck. By the time she has driven a mile, she has forgotten about the hitchhiker. She believes she will always remember budding trees against the blue of the sky, the puffy Gulf clouds, the touch of silk around her neck. She has no idea that the hitchhiker's image is what she will remember the rest of her life.

When she pulls into Mary Martha's driveway, she sees the garage open and empty. As she gets out of her car, Sarah and Gaynor, in Sarah's Buick, drive in behind her.

"Well, for goodness sakes," Isabel says, "She's not here."

They troop up the walk to the front door and ring the doorbell. When Mary Martha does not answer, Gaynor tries the door. "It's locked," she says.

Sarah turns and, shielding her eyes from the sun, looks toward the highway. "This is weird," she says.

"Here she is!" Isabel says.

They watch Mary Martha turn into her driveway and speed toward the garage. Sarah throws back her head and laughs.

"Sarah, what are you laughing about?" Gaynor says, grinning.

"Mary Martha speeding into her own driveway."

"I don't think I've ever seen her speed."

And now the three smile as they watch their friend pull only halfway into her garage. And this, too, is odd.

Seeing her get out of her car, pop open the trunk and turn toward them, her arms full of groceries, they rush to help her. When Isabel takes the sacks from her arms, she sees tiny beads of perspiration on Mary Martha's forehead.

"Are you all right?"

"Oh, yes. And here I am, late. And I hate being late. Especially when we're playing at my house. Come on inside. Let me get these things in the refrigerator. You won't believe what we're having today with lunch. No. Let's have a glass now. We'll have champagne right now."

Disbelieving, Isabel watches Mary Martha un-sack the groceries—green beans, black-eyed peas, corn, still in silk and tassel, and strawberries—all this on the white counter next to the refrigerator; two loaves of bread, a blackberry cobbler and a roasted chicken on the wooden island in the middle; pots of flowers just inside the door; and, finally, two bottles of champagne in the sink. Such largesse! Such bounty! And how unlike Mary Martha's usually stringent fare.

Mary Martha has always been predictable. Keeping a lace handkerchief in her handbag, but always using a tissue instead. Holding her breath until she has arranged her cards and, afterwards, releasing it with a long shuddering sigh. But who can read anything from Mary Martha's sighs. She should have been a poker player. Not by a flick of the wrist or movement of a facial muscle or shuddering sigh does Mary Martha ever reveal what kind of hand she holds. But today Mary Martha is a flustered woman with flushed cheeks and disheveled clothes.

"Mary Martha, all this looks wonderful! Such a feast!" Hands on her hips, Sarah beams at the counters filled with food.

"I found an open-air market this morning. It is like a small grocery store with the produce and flowers out in front and ovens for roasting and baking in back. It was nice."

"An open air market? In April?" says Sarah.

"That's where I bought the champagne," Mary Martha says.

Sarah raises an eyebrow and puts her hands on her hips. "You bought champagne from an open-air market?"

"A woman sold it to me from her refrigerator. Her private store. She lives in a small yellow house right next to the market."

Now they are looking at Mary Martha like she's opened the bidding with six hearts and not a heart in her hand.

"It's called *Green Mama's*," she says through narrowed lips. "And her yellow house is next to it, set way back in the trees."

"Mary Martha, you're full of surprises today," Isabel says. Sliding off the bar stool, she looks down at the strawberries. "Aren't these gorgeous? Now. I'll help you get this put away," she says, giving Mary Martha a hug. When she feels Mary Martha's shoulders stiffen, she drops her arm, picks up a strawberry and eats it.

"It is early," Mary Martha agrees. "I was surprised to see the market myself." Although mollified, she is not quite ready to let go of her frustration. "All that stuff doesn't come from around here," she adds. "They fly it in from all over. New Zealand. Colombia. No telling where it's from. It was so nice that I looked at everything. The time got away from me." Leaning against the counter, she holds her glass high. "To luck!" she says.

Another puzzle: There are smudges of dirt on one pant leg and a small tear on the other. How unlike her this is. And she looks smaller than usual and more vulnerable. It may be that her niece, Clovis. . . .

But before Isabel can finish her thought, Mary Martha begins to drink her champagne in great, audible gulps. Seeing her do this, Isabel decides that they have to talk to Mary Martha. Whether Jackson has come home or not, the three of them need to put it all together, everything they saw and heard the night Rosemary was murdered. Mary Martha is convinced that Jackson murdered Rosemary. She would gladly testify. She has said as much. But Isabel has a voice, and she would tell everybody in Cold Springs that Jackson was with her that night. What time *did* he leave? She wishes to God she knew.

Now Mary Martha fixes her wide, gray eyes on Sarah. "Sarah, you're the gardener," she says, her lisp becoming more pronounced with each word. "I found a cluster of wood violets in the creek bed. Would you go down there, and tell me if I can transplant them. Else they're going to be washed away the next hard rain we have. Will you?" Leaning forward, Mary Martha sways slightly, places a hand on the counter to steady herself.

"Sure," Sarah says doubtfully. "Where are they?"

"Under that old oak. The biggest. The creek bed's nice this time of year. You all go with her. I'll get our lunch ready."

"Mary Martha, are you sure you're O.K.?"

"Yes. It's just what I said. The time got away."

Walking around a boulder as high as their heads and climbing over smaller ones, they dutifully make their way down to the creek bed. The two of them watch as Sarah, holding on first to the trunk of a tree, then to a wild grape vine, and finally, grasping the side of a tall, jagged rock, makes her way down to the creek bottom.

Sarah strolls, hands clasped behind her back, head bent, minutely examining the rills and rocks and small plants she sees. She stops to pick up a smooth, dark blue stone, tosses it toward them, and points toward a frog hopping out of her path. "Here they are! And they are beautiful," she exclaims. Pushing the small heart-shaped leaves aside, she examines the delicate lavender flowers. "They are well-established here," she says.

"Can they be transplanted?"

"They'd be better off left."

Gaynor leans over and holds her hand out to Sarah. "Come on up," she says. "You'll be telling Mary Martha about the violets. Let's go back now. I'm hungry."

After an unusually good lunch, they desultorily play two rubbers of bridge, and it is Mary Martha who suggests they stop a little early. They replace decks of cards, take glasses to the kitchen, return chairs to their usual places.

Willie B. is right, Isabel tells herself. An entire day at Mary Martha's is too long.

It is at that moment, when they are caught up in gathering their handbags and car keys, that Gaynor remembers the gossip she has heard. "Oh, by the way, the neighbor, Teddy, was by way of telling me that some rich toff has bought the prettiest place in the county. It's just off the Richmond Road. He's fenced it and he's got some cattle out there. Teddy says he'll be building a house out there. The old Tanner farm, it's called."

"Well!" Isabel takes a deep breath. "Did he say who bought it? Did he say who it was?"

"He said the name you spoke about last month. Jackson, was it? But his wife said the name wasn't Jackson. She said it was an Arkansas horse trader who bought it."

"It couldn't be Jackson. He wouldn't dare come back here," Mary Martha says.

"Not after all these years," Sarah says. "Jackson's probably dead by now."

"No," Isabel says. "Jackson's not dead. I'd know it if he were."

"If he has come back, he will be arrested," says Mary Martha.

Isabel, her hand on the doorknob, looks sharply at Mary Martha and sees her cheeks a blistered red, as if she's been in the sun too long. Her face is taut. At this moment Mary Martha looks vibrantly alive! she tells herself. Angry, but alive.

"We have to talk about it," Isabel says firmly. "It's been thirty-four years. Let's sort it out."

Swinging her handbag, Sarah moves toward the open doorway where Isabel stands. "If Jackson has come home, we need to talk. I'll make some calls about this place on the river," Sarah says. She touches Mary Martha's shoulder, puts her hand on Isabel's arm.

"If he has come back, I want to see him," Isabel says. Turning the doorknob, she steps outside.

Raising her voice, Mary Martha says, "I want to see him in jail!"

"Now, now," says Sarah, "We don't have a real sheriff. I'll never know how a man named Rock Dallas got elected."

At that Isabel breaks into laughter, and then smiling, "You're right, Sarah. We don't have a sheriff."

Mary Martha, somewhat placated, smiles thinly. As they turn to leave, "Wait!" Mary Martha calls. "I forgot to tell you! My Aunt Bossie is real, real sick. She can't live long."

They stop, turn toward Mary Martha, their faces filled with sympathy, their hands outstretched. "Oh, I'm so sorry," Sarah murmurs.

"No wonder you were late. We could have cancelled the bridge," Gaynor tells her.

"No. Oh, no. Aunt Bossie wouldn't want that. She would want me to go on with my life. I'll keep you posted. I'll call you tomorrow. "

"Oh, do! Call us tomorrow," they chorus, leaving hesitantly, walking slowly, heads down, to their cars.

Isabel turns and walks toward her. "Let us know what we can do," she says.

※

After they leave, Mary Martha makes a cup of decaffeinated coffee and wanders into the living room where she stands, gazing at the pictures of her ancestors. *You've looked at me long enough,* she tells them and, taking them down one-by-one, she stacks them on the lamp table. She sits on the sofa studying the blank wall filled with white rectangles. Thinking of the look on Albert's face when she told him she would be spending more of her money, she is filled with satisfaction. She hears a whistle. Jackson used to whistle. Looking out the window, she sees a little boy looking like Huck Finn headed toward the creek. Her imagination is driving her crazy. On her way to the bank last week, she had almost stopped when she saw a smoking pickup with its hood raised. The driver thought she was stopping to help and began to walk toward her car. When she thought it might be Jackson, she had sped away. But looking at him in her rearview mirror, she realized it couldn't be Jackson. And now, this morning she had put her life in danger again by picking up another hitchhiker, this one at the open air market.

At first the man had seemed gentle and polite, far more polite than the young hitchhiker she had picked up a couple of weeks ago. As she had walked along tables filled with fresh produce and flowers, she had become aware of a man sitting on a wooden bench just outside the shed. He wore a faded army shirt and boots. When she glanced toward him, he smiled. When she turned back to the strawberries, a girl with long, black hair and round hoops of golden earrings was hurrying toward her.

"My friends are coming for lunch," Mary Martha said.

"I will help you," the girl said. "Ees easy. You buy this chicken," she said, holding up a nicely browned, roasted chicken. "You slice it, the white meat. No! I slice it for you. You put the slices on the baby spinach. With the olive oil, the lemon juice, the caper." Her voice trilled like birdsong. "Everything. It is here. The strawberries, also."

"And sherry. Do you have sherry?"

"I have not the license. But I sell you champagne. From my own refrigerator. There is my house," she says, gesturing toward a small yellow house, just to the side of the market. "That is where I go for the champagne."

Dazed by the unexpectedness of the market, the woman's melodic voice, the smell of sun-warmed produce, Mary Martha shopped unhurriedly. With her arms full of produce, she stepped into the sunlight and saw the man she had noticed earlier. He came towards her.

"Ma'am, let me help you with these sacks," he said, and, even as he spoke he was easing them from her arms. He gently placed the sacks in the trunk of the car and closed it.

"Thank you."

"Which way you headed?"

"That way," she says, waving her hand toward the east.

"You're not by any chance going as far as Bois d'Arc?"

Oh, dear, another one. "I'm not going quite that far," she answered.

When the man turned away, it occurred to her that giving him a ride would atone for the shabby way she had treated Jake Ramsey. She took a deep breath. "Wait!" she called. "I can drive you to Bois d'Arc. It's only a couple of miles farther."

He turned back, opened the car door and eased into the front seat. "I take this as a favor," he said, closing the car door. "I've been sitting on that bench an hour or more, waiting for the energy to put my thumb up, but you never know who's gonna stop. Could be dangerous."

She glanced at him. He was looking straight ahead, his profile grim, all signs of kindliness gone. A small *frisson* went down her spine. She took a deep breath.

"How long have you lived in Bois d' Arc?"

"If I live anywhere it's Bois d'Arc," he said. "I came on back home after the war. I wanted to go back to farming."

"The Korean War?"

"Oh, God, no. I'm not that old. I was in Vietnam for three years."

She glanced at him again. He was looking at her as if waiting for an answer. Her mind was blank. She could think of nothing to say. They rode in silence.

Then, he said, "Times haven't been so good since then. I tried to farm for a while, but a man came through offering big money so I sold out," he said. "I guess I sold out in just about every way a man could." He coughed lightly and turned his face away. "God help me! I'm no good to anybody. I end up hurting everybody I come in contact with."

Hurting everybody. She was mute. *He doesn't mean me,* she thought.

Crossing his arms over his chest, he said, "I saw too much. We all did. We saw too much."

"I can't know . . . I cannot even imagine," she began.

"Lady, don't even try," he interrupted. He coughed again, cleared his throat.

He broke the silence. "All of it was bad," he said hoarsely. "There was this little girl. I can't get over her." He stopped and gazed out the window. "Don't seem real, does it."

"What?"

"That tractor out there. Those hay fields. Not to me. But that little girl stays with me day and night. When I dream, it's always same dream. In the daytime I still see her. And at night, too. Can't never get away from her." He shifted his body so that he was turned halfway toward her. "I don't believe in spirits, but it's like I didn't do what I could. You can't do the past over."

When she glanced toward him, she saw his eyes brimming with tears. "The little girl. What happened to her?"

"She lost her arm. We had stopped in a village. Nobody there but old women and children. We were giving them candy. The old women, too. That's all we had. Hard candy wrapped in shiny gold and red papers. One second this little girl was reaching for a piece of candy. The next, her arm was gone. Gone. 'Where *is* it?' she cried. Like she was mad. 'Where *is* it?' She said it twice. That little girl wanted her arm back. That's all in the world she wanted. We tried to find it. Her grandma wanted to bury it with her."

"Oh, my," she said. "Oh, Lord! Nobody should have to suffer . . . , no little girl should have to see . . . "

"Lady, let me out. I've got to . . . Stop. I'm sick."

She pulled over. His head lay back against the seat. He swallowed and swallowed again. "I shouldn't have gotten started on it. It don't help. It's mine to bear."

He opened the car door and stood braced, legs apart, arms hanging limply by his side. His face was white, his shirt darkened with perspiration. "I'm not crazy, lady. Well, maybe in a way, I am." When he tried to smile, a shudder ran through his body. His lips were trembling, his chin quivered. "I do thank you for the ride," he said. He looked down at the wild grasses under his feet. He lifted his head so that his eyes met hers. "You better get out of here," he said quietly.

He reached into his pocket and pulled out his handkerchief again. Carefully wiping his face, he gazed at the trees behind her. Then he walked to the edge of the highway and half-walked, half-slid into the roadside ditch. He climbed up the other side and, stopping now and then to disentangle himself from the thickly hanging vines, he disappeared into the woods. Shaken, she had driven home.

❈

After her friends have left, finally, Mary Martha straightens her kitchen and then she walks along the creek. When darkness falls, she takes a bath and slides gratefully into bed. Feeling as if she has come to herself, she wonders if she has had a mental breakdown of some kind. Her friends, especially Gaynor, had been puzzled. And no wonder. She could imagine what they would think if they found out she had been picking up hitchhikers. They would put in an emergency call to Clovis. Plumping up her pillows, *Balance,* she told herself, *balance is what's needed.* Isabel and Sarah had thought she was upset about Aunt Bossie. She is sad about her aunt. But it was the hitchhiker's story that upset her. She will never be able to sleep unless she can regain her composure. Counting to ten, she breathes deeply and exhales slowly. And, then, she begins to read:

> *My Dear Cassandra—Here is a day for you! Did Bath or Ibthorp ever see a finer 8th of April? It is March and April together, with the glare of one and the warmth of the other. We do nothing but walk about. As far as your means will admit, I hope you profit by such weather too. I dare say you are already better for a change of place.*

What she needs is her old life back, a life as careful and as circumscribed as Jane Austen's. She closes the book and settles herself comfortably in her bed. While Jane Austen's letters are seldom full of matter, they are filled with observation and serenity. And how alike the two of them are; one having already lived a careful life, and she, Mary Martha, *resuming* a life of careful observation. After hearing the hitchhiker's story, she is more determined than ever to return to a life of quiet contemplation. And she does need a change of place. If something happens to Aunt Bossie, she will take a trip afterwards. A trip is exactly what she needs. Satisfied, she picks up Jane Austen's *Letters* again.

Aunt Bossie's Funeral

Rumors like wildfires! When one dies down, another more outlandish than the one before, flares up. Jackson Morris has returned and bought a farm. Jackson has not returned, but is planning to return. Jackson came back, stayed at the farm a few days and flew off in a little red prop plane, just took off from a country road. This last is an image so outlandish and titillating it sends a shiver down Sarah's spine although she doesn't believe a word of it. Jackson would never come back to Cold Springs. Whatever else one might say about Jackson, he was nobody's fool.

Today, she is going to the funeral for Mary Martha's old aunt, dead at ninety-three. The funeral will be sad. Only a few of Aunt Bossie's old friends are still alive. Those who are able will come on walkers or in wheelchairs or, cane in hand, they will walk unsteadily down the church aisles.

Later on she will have dinner with Hite Bennett, an old friend and sometimes lover. Come Tuesday, they will be playing bridge at Betsy's house because, as Betsy says, it is far more comfortable than Gaynor's. Sarah had thought Mary Martha would not want to play so soon after her Aunt Bossie's funeral, but "No," Mary Martha had said. "The last thing Aunt Bossie would want is for me to change my plans." Well, that's fine with me, Sarah tells herself. But it has always amazed her that everybody seems to know exactly what the dead would want. To her mind, Aunt Bossie might just as well have said, were she still alive, "Mary Martha, for this one time it won't hurt you to miss your bridge game."

Isabel had called to say she wanted to sit with Sarah. "Please stay out of the garden! Get to the funeral on time!" she pleaded.

"I will. Gaynor's coming with Betsy. Let's all get there a few minutes early and meet outside."

"That way we can sit on the aisle so Mary Martha will be sure to see us."

"Perfect!" Sarah had said.

After breakfast, Sarah glances at her watch. She still has plenty of time. And minutes later, here she is, in her garden, snipping white roses off the Lady Banks rose bushes. After arranging them in a silver goblet on the sofa table, she steps back to admire their beauty. Then, she showers and dresses. And now (Where has the time gone? she asks herself), she has to hurry or she'll miss the funeral!

Arriving after the service has started, she finds herself tiptoeing down the center aisle, looking for a seat, while Miss Cugee Case sings, "Just As I Am." She tiptoes past Gaynor and Isabel, crowded in with latecomers, late no doubt because of her. Darn! She will have to sit with Aunt Bossie's family, but then, thank goodness! she spies a seat right behind Mary Martha and whispering, "Excuse me. Excuse me," to the people who are already seated, she settles into a seat just as Miss Case finishes her solo.

Before she has time to read the program, Brother Tinsley is coming forward to give the eulogy. "Let us pray," he says and bows his head. There is not a whit of uncertainty in Brother Tinsley's prayer. His prayer sounds like a neighborly conversation with a fishing buddy as he prays that all the fish will be netted just as Aunt Bossie has already been netted in her Master's net. After another hymn, he begins his eulogy. "All of us, oh Lord, every one of us, believers and sinners alike, can rest assured that Aunt Bossie is with her Maker. Let us not doubt it for a minute," he says. "Aunt Bossie, a saint on this earth if there ever was one, is looking down on all of us from heaven." Then Brother Tinsley looks toward the ceiling and in a reasonable voice, says, "Aunt Bossie is at last in heaven with the Lord God and happy to be there with all the saints who came before her."

Sarah has no idea where Aunt Bossie might be right now. She didn't know her all that well, but she hopes she *is* happy. To Sarah, Brother Tinsley's eulogy is beginning to sound questionable with his claims to know both Aunt Bossie's location and her state of mind.

Sarah could preach a better eulogy. She would find just the right words from the poems she had loved in high school. In her younger days, Aunt Bossie's face was so freckled you couldn't count the freckles. For her, Sarah might begin with Hopkins: "Glory be to God for dappled things," she might say. And she does love the psalms, the beauty and solace of the poetry. And she likes the word *bless-ed,* the way it's pronounced in the beatitudes. By the time Sarah has planned a better eulogy, the funeral is over.

She is making her way out of the church when she feels a heavy hand on her arm. The hand belongs to Mary Martha's neighbor, the ancient and tottering Miss Willoughby. Over Miss Willoughby's head, "Sorry," she whispers to Isabel just in front of her.

Turning, "Gardening!" Isabel hisses.

Then, "Why, Miss Willoughby," Sarah says. "What a sad time for all of us. But it's nice to see you, even under these circumstances."

But Miss Willoughby is too overcome by grief to respond. Her hand and her grief grow heavier as they slowly make their way out of the church, Miss Willoughby dabbing at her eyes with her lace-trimmed handkerchief and holding on to Sarah's arm with an iron grip as Sarah's friends sail on out of the church. Then, as she and Miss Willoughby carefully make their way down the three church steps, Miss Willoughby, clinging and weeping, collects herself enough to ask: "Sarah, how is your dear mother? You know we've been friends all our lives."

This was so. Sarah knew it was so. And looking into Miss Willoughby's faded blue eyes, brightened by a frail spark of hope, how could she bring herself to say, "Miss Willoughby, my mother's been dead almost two years now." Miss Willoughby *had* truly loved her mother, and Sarah's first thought is that she might collapse into Sarah's arms, right here on the church steps, if she said these words to her.

Reassuringly, she covers Miss Willoughby's hand with her own. "Miss Willoughby," she finds herself saying, "Mother's not doing too well right now."

"Oh, child, I'm sorry to hear it," Miss Willoughby says and smiling hopefully, steps off, rather more sprightly than Sarah expected, to her waiting car.

By the time Miss Willoughby has disappeared Sarah is so tickled at the absurdity of what she has said to her, she has to tighten her tush in order not to wet her pants. Over dinner that night when she tells Hite Bennet about her ridiculous answer to Miss Willoughby's concern about her mother, she gets tickled all over again. When Hite seems puzzled by her humor, she suggests a martini. She drinks hers too quickly, and then she orders wine.

Sarah has always had a weird sense of humor. She laughs when somebody falls, or when an umbrella turns itself wrong side out in a rainstorm. She laughs when someone says the wrong thing. She laughs at pretense. She laughs at her own clumsiness.

Two days after Aunt Bossie's funeral, Sarah is properly sympathetic when the women arrive (Mary Martha is the last), at Sarah's house for lunch in order to return the dishes brought to Mary Martha's house when her aunt died. In fact, Gaynor and Sarah are strolling around her garden (Sarah does have the sweetest smelling, the greenest, the most abundant garden, no matter the season!), and that alone is enough to put Mary Martha out of sorts because the doorbell goes unanswered, and she has to walk around the house to find her hostess. During lunch, however, she recovers from her friends' thoughtlessness, and she even feels mildly excited as she daintily nibbles small chicken salad and pimiento cheese sandwiches. When the dessert is served, she takes a bite of the lemon meringue pie and, "delicious!" she pronounces enthusiastically. Then she carefully places her fork on her plate and turns toward Sarah. A thread of a wrinkle appears on her forehead.

"Sarah, I tried to call you the night after Aunt Bossie's funeral. I wanted to tell you about the craziest conversation I had with Miss Willoughby."

"Oh?" Sarah, taking a generous bite of her lemon pie, smiles at Mary Martha.

"About you. Miss Willoughby is worried about you. The day of my aunt's funeral Miss Willoughby came over afterwards. She said she asked you about your mother at the funeral, and you told her your mother was not doing very well." Mary Martha's forehead is now deeply furrowed. "When I told her your mother had been dead two years, she was shocked! She said you did not seem to realize your mother was dead."

Sarah throws back her head and bursts into gales of laughter.

Mary Martha lifts her pointed chin. "Was this your idea of a joke?" she asks.

"Oh, God," Sarah says, still laughing. "I'm such a fool. I don't know why I told Miss Willoughby that. Oh, Mary Martha," and now Sarah is gasping for breath, hand over her abdomen, laughing, "she asked about my mother, about how she was, and she was so utterly grief-stricken about your aunt, and she looked so frail that I thought if I told her Mother was dead, had been dead for some time, Miss Willoughby might just drop dead herself, right there on the church steps. So I said," and here Sarah has to get up and walk around the table, clutching her stomach, bent double with laughter, before she can finish her sentence. "I said, 'Miss Willoughby, Mother's not doing too well right now.'"

And now they are all laughing, and with Isabel's giggling and Gaynor's rollicking laughter and Sarah's throaty chuckle, and, finally, Mary Martha's staccato bursts, like hiccups, there is a chorus of laughter. They laugh until they are sprawled in their chairs, heads thrown back and gasping for breath.

But after Sarah has returned her share of casserole dishes and cake plates to Aunt Bossie's friends, she finds herself remembering the past. The Spring of 1946. The War had ended. Soldiers were coming home. And there had been the four of them. Friends all their lives. They were young, hardly more than children. And how they had loved the Park! Furiously racing their bikes out there. Drinking the ice cold water and splashing it on their faces, their arms and legs. And sharing their momentous secrets: Isabel's confession that Jackson had touched her breasts. And that she liked it! Mary Martha's worry that her parents might be Communists. (And this had set them off.) Cycling along the narrow roads winding through the park, roads that only they ever used. How glorious it had been to be sixteen! How intoxicating!

And then Rosemary had been murdered. And it had all changed. Everything. A sense of unease, of fear, became a part of their lives. At the oddest times, vivid images of the night Rosemary was murdered would appear, as real as if they had happened yesterday—Mary Martha, flushed with excitement, strangely disconcerted, and she, Sarah, with her news about not going off to school—images to be examined and picked over during a sleepless night. Memories would come as sharp as a knife, memories that always ended with the question: *Who murdered Rosemary? And why?* Always unanswered these questions would swirl through her mind to cloud the memory of what it had felt like long ago and once upon a time to be completely happy.

Sarah's Troubles

When Sarah, holding a cup of coffee, opens her bedroom door and steps out into the fresh morning air—the scented air as heady as wine—she decides that even at her age, *especially* at her age, life is mighty intoxicating. Wearing a long cotton gown, she stands on her small terrace looking over the meadows. How calm it is, how still, the birds not yet chirping and trilling among the fluttering leaves. Even before the light came on this morning, she knew summer had come. She could feel it. Smell it. In the summer, clouds gather. Showers come. The sky clears. Gardens flourish. Her antique roses go crazy in the warm East Texas summers. She touches a Queen Elizabeth rose in full bloom and bends to catch its scent. Beyond the low garden wall, she sees the tall pines etched against the faint blush that is, at this moment, beginning to flood the eastern sky.

The mingled scent of roses and the moist, black earth suddenly conjures up, unbidden, memories of Eddie—the angular shape of his face, his chameleon eyes, green or hazel depending on the light, his persuasive voice. For those first years of marriage, she had been Eddie's wife, adored and valued. Especially *valued*, she tells herself wryly, since she was the one with the money.

She has no idea where Eddie might be now. Nor is she even sure Eddie is alive. For that matter Eddie may not even be her husband. But if he had divorced her, she would surely have known it.

Eddie was never a businessman. Ha! Eddie had been a total failure in business! Fully awake now and energized by anger, she hurries into her bedroom, pulls on shabby gray pants and a faded blue T-shirt. Then outside, trowel in hand, she examines the garden with an expert's eye. The rose beds need turning for aeration and water absorption.

Falling to her knees, she furiously trowels, focusing on Eddie's failures. "The Failures of Eddie." A good title for the book she is planning to write about Eddie, a book *using his real name*. She works steadily, turning the fertile, humid earth while counting up Eddie's failed schemes. First, Eddie's tree farm. But after he bought the land *and* the trees, he discovered the trees were too old, too big, too expensive to move from Arkansas to the banks of the Red River in Texas. Then came the catfish restaurant. "It will be posh. Elegant," Eddie said. "Darling, come to bed and let me tell you all about it. It will be the finest restaurant in Cold Springs," he said, kissing her ear, her neck, her mouth. "Hm . . . m, . . . m," he said. "You're getting skinny," he murmured. "And it will be expensive," he said, slipping her gown off and kissing her skinny hipbone. Sarah had never heard of an expensive catfish restaurant and said so. "That's the beauty of it, darling," Eddie said. "Nobody's heard of it."

Next he bought an abandoned church saying that it could easily be remodeled as a restaurant. "Wait until you see those pews, hand-hewn, and the hand-made roofing shingles, but these not in the best shape," Eddie admitted, "and the stained glass windows, and only a few of them broken," he confided, shrugging off the broken windows and the not-in-the-best-of-shape shingles. On their anniversary dinner at the French Room at the Adolphus in Dallas, he said, "Look around, Sarah. Our restaurant will be as fine as this," and he lifted his glass to her.

When he discovered it would cost thousands of dollars to move the church, he invested in a catfish processing plant in Brazil. Then there was the cut flower farm, but it rained so hard the imported bulbs rotted in the ground. One after another of Eddie's schemes failed until her money was gone. And Eddie with it.

At times, she misses Eddie. But if she said this over the bridge table, they would think she was crazy. But without a husband, she would never have had children, at least not these children. She cannot imagine life without Eve and John. She has them. And she has *some* money. When her house burned, she discovered she could buy this cottage (that she adores), and have two hundred thousand dollars left over. She promptly invested it at nine percent. With the interest and her part-time job, she manages just fine. Straightening up, she looks at her watch. She can garden all morning. Tomorrow, their bridge game might get a little wild if someone mentions Jackson again. But with Mary Martha so pure, his name might not even come up.

Satisfied that she has accomplished so much, she stands stiffly and rolls her shoulders. Her back is beginning to ache. Still holding the trowel, she walks over and straddles the garden wall. Sitting here, she might possibly see one of her children. Occasionally, she is rewarded by a glimpse of one or another of them as they speed past the house—John, on his Harley, without a helmet, his long hair flying, his piercings glistening, or Eve in her ten-year-old Mustang, left hand out the window, holding a cigarette high, like a flag.

Sarah knows Eve is too thin. The circles around her eyes have grown darker and larger this past year. However, Eve has been underweight since she was fourteen. During the two years her children most recently lived with her, Eve often expressed a strong desire to wear a size "2" or, at the very most, a size "4." Last Christmas, Eve tearfully refused to try on a size "6" dress, a Christmas present from her mother.

"I'm not that fat!" she cried, tossing the dress into Sarah's lap.

Eve, at 5' 9" tall and weighing 105 pounds, is way too thin. Anorexia? Skinny role models? Thank goodness it's not drugs. Sarah doesn't know where she gets these ideas. But she prays that Eve will gain weight and go back to school. It's not that Eve doesn't use her talents. She has karma and tells fortunes by phone.

When she was twenty years old, Eve had moved out of her mother's house, but she had not done so until the house burned down. When that happened, Isabel had insisted that both Eve and her mother come to her house. "For a few days, for a few months, as long as you need," she said. When Sarah hesitated, Isabel offered more persuasions: "You know I have plenty of room," and "Sometimes I get terribly lonesome," and, finally, "I'm uneasy staying here alone." This last convinced Sarah, but not her daughter.

Late that night Eve had whispered to her mother that she could not stay with Isabel. "It would be awful, like having two mothers," she said. The next day Eve borrowed five hundred dollars from her mother and moved into a one-room apartment.

John, in spite of the ring in his tongue and another below his left eyebrow, in spite of his round blue eyes (Eddie's eyes), that never waver when he fibs to her, John is basically decent, although she had told him he had to move out just before her house had burned down.

Now John is fairly independent. He has two jobs, one as a bartender at the Hut and the other as a waiter at the new country club.

Sarah firmly believes that evicting John has helped him grow up. That afternoon she had come home from her Tuesday bridge and, as soon as she opened the front door, she had smelled something, a funny odor. Acrid. Well, in an old house *that* is enough to set off an alarm. After checking the downstairs, she hurried up the stairs and trotted down the hall, opening every door and sticking her head into every room. When she came to John's room she flung open the door, and there they were: John, lying on his bed without a stitch on, propped up on pillows and with a girl (Who was she? Sarah had never seen her before), also nude, lying across John's stomach. The girl could have been any age, any age at all between fourteen and twenty-four. Sarah couldn't even guess how old she was. As John slid out from under her and reached for his jeans, her straight brown hair fell over breasts hardly bigger than mosquito bites. Shrugging her shoulders, the girl seemed almost bored, only mildly surprised, as if events over which she had no control had overtaken her. She also looked young. Young! Sarah's heart sank. The girl slowly shifted her body so that she lay on her stomach across John's bed. Lacing her fingers together, she propped her chin up and looked up at Sarah. Her mouth had become a sullen pout. *What can you do about this*? her raised eyebrows asked. She made no move to cover herself with sheet or shirt.

Breathe, Sarah told herself. Breathe. Breathe. Then, "John, this is not appropriate behavior," she said.

"Hey, Mom, I didn't hear you knock," he said, slipping into jeans, smiling crookedly at her.

"She didn't," said the girl, clearly insulted by Sarah's behavior.

"Chill out, Mom," John said. "It's just marijuana."

"Get up. Put your clothes on," Sarah told the girl, "and leave this house. John, you go with her."

And with that last, harsh command, Sarah wheeled and left the room, but not before she had seen the expression on the girl's face change from insult to hostility. That very day John had moved out. Their old relationship was severed. But she remains hopeful that a better relationship between two adults is beginning. She has not called him; nor is she waiting for an apology. At times it is better to let things simmer into reason.

Now Sarah's straddled position on the garden wall is beginning to chafe. She stands and gently taps the trowel on the wall, knocking the damp soil from it. She hears the calling of geese and sees that a flock of eastern bluebirds have settled in the holly. Watching the birds, Sarah feels a deep surge of pleasure, followed by the certainty that her children are growing up. Two weeks ago John had stopped by for a cup of coffee and given her a hug when he left. Eve borrowed her vacuum cleaner and returned it in good condition. Slender threads of hope, yet, threads of tensile strength.

Sarah is glad her house burned. The fire had been financially rewarding, although she certainly had nothing to do with it. The police couldn't find the cause. "Maybe a short in the old wiring," they decided. But they had asked about Eddie, asked if he had been in town lately and when she had last seen him.

Sarah loves her new house. Here there are no empty rooms, rooms to be dusted and aired and swept free of spider webs when company comes. She loves her garden, so small that she can watch over every plant. Before she sold her old place, she transplanted the antique roses, the Campanile jonquils and the honeysuckle (this from her grandmother's Tennessee farm), to her new garden.

Later that day, she nibbles on a piece of chicken and leftover apple cobbler. Then she waters the begonias in the window box.

Last night, a neighbor, Emily Hawley, had called to tell her she has seen Mary Martha with a strange man in her car. "Could it have been Jackson Morris?" Emily had asked. "Everybody says that Jackson came home, stayed a couple of weeks and left again," Emily had told her. But neither Emily nor anyone Emily knew had actually seen Jackson.

Finally, after mumbling incoherently about rumors and rumors of rumors, Sarah had told Emily she did not believe it for a minute. But the question took her breath away. When Rosemary had been murdered, Sarah had known that Jackson could be . . . *guilty*, else why would he have run away?

Sarah had gone to bed asking herself that question and had awakened up thinking about it this morning.

Pulling her nightgown off over her head, Sarah wonders if Jackson could have been in Mary Martha's car. Mary Martha was the only one who had talked to the police. Jackson might have known that. If he has come home, he would be the last person in the world to get into Mary Martha's car.

Uneasily, she steps into the shower, soaps her body and turns the shower to cold, sending a shiver down her spine. Since she saw *Psycho,* she has felt a little uneasy taking a shower. But, now, all at once, just the thought that Jackson may have returned is enough to send her stumbling out of the shower, dripping wet and blindly grabbing a towel while her heart beats a thousand times a minute. She snatches a cotton blouse and denim skirt from hangers. She *makes* herself, *forces* herself to calm down. *Silly! Absolutely crazy.* She wishes she had never seen *Psycho* or Janet Leigh in the shower, about to be murdered. Her heart slows. If Jackson has really come home, she will take baths instead of showers.

Calmer now, she stands and, glancing into the mirror, sees her drooping breasts, her rounded stomach. She steps into panties, fastens her bra and, leaning forward, shakes her breasts into the bra. "More gardening. Less food," she tells herself.

Sarah loves playing at Betsy's house, where Gaynor, as soon as she arrived, had immediately become a member of Betsy's household, surprising the whole town. Now that Gaynor has moved to the country to raise, of all things, sheep! Sarah doesn't see her as often. But when it's Gaynor's time to be the host, they play at Betsy's house which smells less *au naturel.*

Betsy lives at the Country Club estates. But driving by you'd never guess the wealth of the people who live there. While the bottom lines of their portfolios are sound through at least three or more future generations, their houses are small in the way an expensive jewel is small. And perfect.

I misjudged Gaynor, Sarah tells herself. *Gaynor never cared about Betsy's money. And Jackson. I may have misjudged Jackson as well. He may not be guilty, but unless the real murderer is found, I will always wonder if he murdered Rosemary.*

Hastily, Sarah applies makeup—powder on her nose and lipstick, both without a mirror. She pulls her skirt over her head and buttons her blouse. Grabbing a handbag and picking up the car keys, she steps outside. A breeze stirs, making a susurrus through the pines. Noticing a small patch of dandelions in the fern bed, she steps off the porch and pulls them out, wondering at the mysterious look of the ferns, their feathery fronds overlapping as if hiding a treasure.

I'll bet Jackson, wherever he is, is still good looking. And thinking this, she tightens her stomach, runs her hands over her plump hips. Noticing the dusty trail this has left on her skirt, she brushes the dirt off her hands and looks at her watch. "Damn it," she says. "I'm going to be late."

Sarah hurries to her car, lowers her car window and puts on her driving gloves, so satisfying these gloves, supple and smelling like fresh-turned earth. In less than fifteen minutes she turns into Betsy's drive.

Daffodils

Sarah is late for bridge, but Sarah is often late. Betsy has opened the door to Isabel and Mary Martha who arrive at the same time.

"Come in, girls," she says. And how reassuring to Isabel, how comforting to have Betsy thinking of them as *girls*. "Gaynor's in the kitchen," Betsy continues. "She'll be bringing in the elevenses. I think she's right, you know. The morning should be simple, and I do love her high teas. It makes the afternoon nicer."

Betsy smiles, and the smile deepens the wrinkles around her mouth and at the corners of her eyes. But the dazed vacancy she had worn on her face after her son's death is gone. Her gray hair has been cut short, but not as short as Gaynor's, and "touched-up" so that it is now ash-blond. Today she is wearing black silk pants and a voluminous white silk shirt that billows out like a small parachute when she walks. Her voice is deeply hoarse, but of course it would be. For years she has tried to limit her smoking to one package of cigarettes a day. On this morning, Betsy has the air of a woman who is absolutely sure about her life.

"Betsy, you look absolutely wonderful," Isabel says.

"Thank you, Isabel. And Mary Martha, I'm glad you decided to come today. I'm sure you'll miss your dear Aunt Bossie. I remember when she went to Spain. In those days, hardly anybody traveled there! Now, here's Gaynor," she says, smiling brightly at Gaynor, bringing a tray of cookies and cups and saucers.

A ray of sunlight, coming from a high window, strikes Gaynor's red hair and the sparkling diamonds in her ears, the earrings her only jewelry except for a small carved silver ring she wears on her right hand. The white tailored shirt, the somewhat frayed riding pants and knee-high mucking boots

Gaynor is wearing make her look as if she's just stepped off
a horse. Isabel envies Gaynor her lack of interest in clothes.
And, too, there's this to envy: Gaynor looks like an aristocrat,
or like Isabel's idea of one, no matter what she's wearing.

"Good morning, Mary Martha. I see you're even a little
early today. No stops at the country market?" Gaynor asks,
grinning wickedly.

"I did stop there," Mary Martha says, "and I brought some
flowers for you. For you and Betsy."

Mary Martha has been standing with her hands behind
her, holding the yellow flowers behind her flowered chiffon
dress, and now she thrusts the bouquet into Gaynor's hands.

"They're lovely. In Ireland we call them daffodils," Gaynor
says, burying her face in the flowers. "Betsy, aren't they
lovely?"

When she lifts her face, astonishingly, her eyes are brimming with tears. "Please, won't you excuse me?" she asks, hurrying from the room.

Turning to Betsy, "What happened?" Mary Martha asks,
her calm gray eyes focused on Betsy. "Was it the flowers? Did
they upset her?"

"It may have been the flowers," Betsy says. "Gaynor told me
that when she and Timothy were on their honeymoon, Timothy brought a picnic lunch and she brought a poem. Imagine.
Bringing a poem to a picnic. It was about daffodils. She says
daffodils grow wild over there, and they were in full bloom,
whole fields of them."

Betsy is a tiny woman, but she stands so marvelously
straight that she appears stalwart. Motioning them to sit
down, she sits in a wingback chair (and in it she seems her
usual tiny self), and crosses her legs. "It's strange," she muses.
"But when Gaynor began to tell me about their life together,
those few weeks they had together, her stories were a marvel-
ous gift for me. Oh, for instance, telling me about their picnic

made it seem, somehow, as if Timmy had lived longer than he did live. Everything she told me about those last days, stories I hadn't heard until Gaynor came, made his death a little easier. She made me know that Timothy lived long enough to fall in love and to marry the woman he loved. They had a little time together. Knowing all that helped." Then, "I'd better see about the cock-a-leekie," she says. Smiling over her shoulder, wrinkling her brow, she adds, "Gaynor says we'll like it."

The two sit silently, different in every way, or so Betsy tells herself as she busily arranges a tray in the kitchen. Isabel, wearing black pants and a black summer sweater, looks perfectly put together, while Mary Martha is wispily modest in her quaint, old-fashioned, pastel ruffled dress. This is not the first time Betsy has marveled at the deep bonds of friendship between all four of the very different women.

Turning to Mary Martha, "What *is* cock-a-leekie?" Isabel asks.

Mary Martha shakes her head. "Maybe a chicken casserole."

"Do you think we'll like it?" Isabel giggles.

Mary Martha puts her finger to her lip.

A clock ticks loudly. When it chimes the quarter hour, Mary Martha looks at Isabel. "The flowers were a mistake."

"No. No. That was a long time ago. It's all right."

"Well, it's not like me," Mary Martha says. "I'm getting to be impulsive," she adds.

"Nothing's wrong with that!" says Isabel staunchly.

Gazing wide-eyed into Isabel's face, Mary Martha smiles. *But you don't know how impulsive I've become,* she thinks. Remembering the astonished look on Albert's face when she had told him she was going to build a new house, small but as nice as Betsy's, her smile widens. When Albert had recovered, he was pleased. "This is great," he said. "I've advised you to do something like this for years. Good. Excellent."

As soon as she signs the papers on the property she is buying, she will tell her friends the news. Over bridge. But now Betsy hurries in, her white silk shirt billowing out behind her as if it is trying to slow her down. "Gaynor's coming right in. She's freshening up a little. And she loves your flowers, Mary Martha. Those flowers, especially."

Suddenly, Betsy's shoulders fall, her chin quivers, she tightens her mouth. Sighing, she straightens. Seeing Betsy overcome with sadness, *Sorrow rides a swift horse,* Isabel tells herself, remembering a story George once told her.

And now the clock is chiming again and the doorbell is ringing and Gaynor is answering the door. "Sarah, I see you've been gardening," Gaynor chuckles.

"For heaven's sakes!" Sarah says, "Look at my skirt," and now the two of them are laughing. "I couldn't resist it. The herb garden was full of weeds."

"Come in! We're just having our elevenses. Come in!" says Gaynor, grinning.

Standing inside the door, Sarah grasps a handful of her skirt in each hand and rubs the dried muddy spots together. Then, coming into the room, "Oh, what a day," Sarah exclaims. "Have you ever seen a prettier day?" Standing, hands on her hips, smiling into their faces, she says, "I'm glad to see you all. I've missed you. Guess what happened to me!" she says. Picking up a cookie, she grins at them. "I almost picked up a hitchhiker. He was wearing a fedora. Remember when our fathers wore fedoras? He had a guitar in one hand and a book in the other. I almost stopped to ask where he was going. He looked so quaint. Really interesting. Now, there's this song. I can't get out of my mind. I can't remember the words but. . . ." Frowning, she began to hum. "La, da, da, da, da, da, da." She breaks into a smile. "Oh, it's . . . *And there he was this young boy, stranger to my eyes/ Strumming my pain with his fingers, killing me softly.* That's it! 'Killing Me Softly.' He made me think of that song! He was walking down the Summerhill Road, and when I saw him, I almost stopped." At a gasp from Mary Martha, the short intake of breath, she looks at her. "Mary Martha, of course I didn't stop. I said I almost stopped."

"Well, this is the strangest thing. I saw him the last time we played bridge," Isabel says. "And I had the strongest feeling I knew him from somewhere."

Mary Martha turns toward the tray and picks up another cookie. When she walks toward a chair, the cup and saucer she holds rattles. *Maybe we were in school with him. But who is he? Has he been watching me?* she wonders. She takes a deep breath. *I'm being silly,* she tells herself firmly. She looks at the cheerful faces of her friends as they cut for partner. *They'll think I'm crazy if I tell them Jackson's been watching me. Jane Austen is right. I need a change.*

But now Mary Martha sits straight in her chair and takes a sip of coffee from her now silent cup and saucer. When the four of them are around the table (Sarah, unable to resist a quick peek at Betsy's garden through the windows, is the last to sit down), Mary Martha deals.

"Jane Austen says a change of place is what's needed," Mary Martha smiles.

"Oh?" Busily arranging her cards, Sarah glances at Mary Martha. Ready to hear more about what Jane Austen says, she folds her cards, lays them on the table.

"Let's play this hand," Mary Martha says. Adroitly arranging her hand, she sighs her usual long, shuddering sigh. "One no-trump," she says.

Isabel passes, and "Three no-trumps," Sarah chuckles. Her freckles dance across her face.

Sarah could never play poker, Mary Martha thinks. *Her face reveals every card she holds in her hand.*

"What's all this about a change of place?" Gaynor asks.

Mary Martha, intent on the game, shakes her head, frowns slightly. *"Not now, Gaynor!"* the gestures say firmly. Isabel leads and Sarah lays her cards down. Mary Martha studies Sarah's hand, her own hand. She begins to play the hand, scooping up the tricks, one-by-one, until nine are in a neat row in front of her. Then she says, "The rest are yours."

"That was perfect," Sarah says. "Two finesses. Now what about Jane Austen?"

"Let's finish the rubber," Mary Martha says.

Now the sigh comes from Sarah, who is, after all, not a fanatic about bridge. After two rubbers (Mary Martha has high score), they trail into Betsy's kitchen where Gaynor is serving their plates. Then they gather around the small table ("So cozy for tea," says Gaynor) in Betsy's sitting room.

"Now, Mary Martha, what's all this about Miss Austen?" asks Sarah, determined still to hear about Jane Austen.

"The Janeites are reading Miss Austen's letters, and in a letter to Cassandra she writes . . ."

"Who's Cassandra?"

"Sarah, Cassandra is Jane's sister. In a letter Jane says that a change of place is helpful. That's all."

"Well, it is!" Isabel says, taking a bite of cock-a-leekie. "Delicious," she pronounces.

"Gaynor, tell them where we're going," Betsy says. "Tell them."

"Home," Gaynor said. "All this time I've been going home, and Betsy has never come with me. But she's coming now. First, we're going to Cork. We'll rent a car there and drive to Sneem. She'll meet my mom and dad and all my cousins. My brothers might be there, too."

"After that, we're going to drive round the Ring of Kerry. We'll go to Yeats's Tower and we'll drive on up to Dromoland Castle. Can you believe it?" says Betsy.

"Betsy, now you tell about Yeats," Gaynor says.

Betsy sets her cup and saucer down. As she leans forward, a smile flickers on her mouth and settles there. She wiggles her hips forward on the loveseat so that she is able to sit perfectly straight. "Before any of you were born, I was in college, down at Austin. There was this teacher who loved Yeats, and I loved this teacher. So I wrote a paper on Yeats's 'Tower Poems,' and I've always wanted to go there. And now I'm going."

"Ireland still has its share of the troubles, but we'll be fine," Gaynor says.

"I'd love to go to Ireland," Sarah says.

Betsy smiles. Gaynor chuckles.

"Find your passport," Gaynor says and, saying it, the weathered pink cottage is before her eyes, the bracing touch of the wind off the sea on her face. She sees her father's face, hears the merriment in his voice. Image follows image: the sweep of the land down to the sea, the gorse and the rape, the colors of the sage, the miles and miles of barley.

"You don't mean that!" Sarah says.

"I do. We do!" Gaynor opens her arms. "I'm going home!" she says. "And you'll all be going with me!"

Frowning, Mary Martha takes a sip of her sherry. "I don't have a passport," she says.

"Nor I," says Sarah.

"Well, I'll just get one!" Mary Martha says sturdily. "A change of place *is* what's needed!"

Her friends, amused, surprised, gaze at her. "Me too," Sarah says. "We'll all go."

Mary Martha is especially pretty today, Isabel thinks. *With her hair curling around her face, she looks younger than any of us. Even Gaynor.*

As the sun begins to set, they stand outside, laughing, chattering. What a glorious day! How good to be alive and saying their usual goodbyes: "Mary Martha, you do need to get a . . ."

"I know. A light." She hiccups. Giggles. "I'm getting a pass-port. I don't need a light. I'm as safe as a rabbit in a burrow out there."

And, "Betsy, can't you talk to Gaynor. Somebody's going to come in on her and cut her throat one of these dark nights. Gaynor, you need to put those diamonds in the bank."

And Betsy, lighting a cigarette, inhaling deeply, smilingly exhales. "I can't say that to Gaynor. I'm taking mine out of the bank!"

This last sets them off again, the sounds of their laughter blending with the hoot of an owl, invisibly perched in the top of one of Betsy's pines and the sound of a small red prop plane flying overhead. On the drive home, it occurs to Isabel that they'll have other days like this. Of course they will. But this one has been especially nice!

PART 3: THE '60S

The Cold Springs Revolutions

The '60s

Years later the women would talk about the sixties in Dick-
ensian terms. The worst of times. One horror after another.
President Kennedy assassinated. Oh how the country loved
him! His bright mind. His humor. The lyrical speeches. The
elegance of Jackie. And just as the country was beginning to
hope again, Martin Luther King, murdered! And two months
later Bobby, the president's brother, lay dying in the kitchen
of a hotel in California. Before the country could recover
from these murders, heinous, unforgivable, there was Kent
State and an image seared into the nation's consciousness of
the young girl kneeling, her hand raised over a fallen classmate shot by an untrained young soldier with the National
Guard because the student was protesting the Vietnam War.
After that, protests to the Vietnam War spiraled out of control. Increasing numbers of soldiers too young, far too young
for the horrors of war, were dying in the steamy jungles of
Vietnam.

In the midst of the horrors, the young people, with their
peaceful resolutions, gave voice, gave hope to the country.
Thank goodness for the flower children and the Peace Corps,
for all those who believed they could make a difference. And
for the gentle lyrics and music of John Lennon's "Imagine"
and Bob Dylan's "Blowin' in the Wind." And thank goodness
for all those who believed the people were better than their
government, and for the Vietnam veterans who came home,
went to college on the G.I. Bill and raised the academic standards of the colleges.

And, thank God for Civil Rights that led to Women's
Rights, the latter giving women freedom to choose where to
work and even when to have a baby. *Peter, Peter pumpkin
eater/ had a wife and couldn't keep her/ put her in a pumpkin*

shell/ and there he kept her very well! some chanted, marching for their rights.

In the middle of the national tragedies, there were the small tragedies, the local ones, heralded by a few lines in the Cold Springs newspaper. There was Gaynor's sad, some would say unwelcome, arrival in 1962 on Betsy's doorstep. And Isabel's husband dead of a heart attack in '66, and Sarah's great old house burning, to the ground! Only Mary Martha escaped the untimely losses her friends suffered.

Despite the national and local tragedies, peaceful revolutions began to spread across the land from as far away as a small Irish farm just outside Sneem in the County of Kerry to the home of a grieving woman in Cold Springs, Texas.

Betsy's House

Betsy Rogers had built her house as a diversion after the death of her husband, the building of it overseen every step of the way by her son Timothy. The house, a small Georgian, befits old money. It has only two bedrooms (Betsy's with its own sitting room), but it is elegant with its small, public rooms, including a library and a small wine cellar. The wide chestnut moldings hand-crafted. The deeply carved panels in the guest room and the library imported from England. Brightly covered rugs, designed by Calder, scattered over the stone floors. The guestroom, now called Gaynor's room, is papered with antique French wallpaper, hand painted with Mironesque birds and trees.

Pictures of Timothy Rogers—an infant in a bassinet, then a baby in Betsy's arms wearing his christening gown and, at two, sitting on a tricycle—stand on tables in Betsy's sitting room. In the hall are still more pictures. Here he's holding a baseball bat over his shoulder, and here he's kneeling, his mouth open with laughter at Lacey, his golden lab, with her paws on his shoulders. And in the kitchen, on the south wall, a picture of five-year-old Timmy sitting on the floor, playing with Ginger's kittens. "See the tenderness in his face," Betsy says, when someone stands gazing at it. In the dining room walls, Timothy fishes and camps and dives in photographs. On the table in Betsy's sitting room stands a silver-framed picture of Timothy, grinning sheepishly, and wearing his first tuxedo. Here's Timothy receiving a diploma from the University of Texas at Austin and another of Timothy receiving a law degree from Southern Methodist University in Dallas. And, finally, a picture of the man Gaynor loved: Timothy Rogers with the Peace Corps in Ghana, his face half-hidden by the peace sign he was making.

Timothy Rogers was all Betsy ever wanted or needed in the way of children. She adored Timothy, had no room in her heart for anyone else, not even for memories of her dead husband. When Timothy's plane crashed—mechanical problem? pilot error? rebel fire?—in Ghana, Betsy took to her bed. She went to bed early and got up late. She took long morning and afternoon naps. Her friends tried to rally her with invitations to travel, to join an "Up from grief" group at the church, to attend cheerful events such as weddings and christenings. They brought trays to her bedside and talked about trivia. Betsy thanked them, saw them out and went back to bed. Her friends decided to wait it out. "Time heals all wounds," they said, through slightly disapproving, painted lips.

Seven months after Timothy was killed, Betsy's doorbell rang, and Betsy answered it only because she was in the foyer and not more than a step or two away from the door, having gone there to place a vase of flowers (unwanted, unappreciated flowers), she had just received on the foyer table. When she looked through the round circle of glass in the heavy mahogany door and saw a woman's pale face, rimmed by a halo of bright red hair, even on this dreary day *bright* red, and wearing diamond earrings (Betsy's mother's earrings), she considered not opening the door. Betsy had accepted the idea that Timmy would not be coming home. She knew *that.* She had buried his remains. *Remains.* A strange and terrible word for all that was meant. That same week President Kennedy had written Betsy a letter, and she *knew* Timothy would not be coming home. But here was this woman. Alone. And Timothy dead. Still, *she* had come. Timmy was dead and here she was. Big as life. Now the woman pressed her face close to the circle of glass in the entrance hall door and, smiling widely, raised her hand and pointed to the family earrings she wore. But it was not the diamonds that caused Betsy to put her hand on the doorknob; it was the desperate expression in her dark eyes (eyes that belied the wide smile), that caused Betsy to step forward and swing the door open.

In a rich Irish brogue, "Mrs. Rogers, I was married to your son, your Timothy," the woman said.

While Betsy absorbed these words, she simultaneously registered, with some dismay, the woman, hardly more than skin and bones, and wearing a wrinkled beige cotton dress, a dress that almost covered her knees (knees white as cotton), and her bare legs, also white and spotted with freckles and (more dismay), the scuffed and worn, brown high-heeled shoes on the woman's feet. Processing all this, Betsy stood frozen. Then she leaned forward and stingily offering her cheek.

She's pitiful, Betsy told herself. *And she saw him last. She saw my Timothy last.*

"I'm Gaynor," the woman said. "Gaynor Trevor-Rogers."

Then Betsy, in mismatched gown and robe, found herself heartily embraced and embraced again, all the while hearing Gaynor's throaty Irish voice: "There now. *There.* What a rough time you've had and without Timothy to help you through it. Well, I'm here, Betsy Rogers. I've come to help," Gaynor told her, and Betsy allowed herself to be led inside and tucked back into bed, with a cold cloth on her head.

That first afternoon Gaynor found the kitchen and made chamomile tea, and by the time she served the tea, Betsy was sitting up, sitting up! although still holding the cold cloth to her head, while Gaynor plumped up her pillows, "Lean forward now," and replaced them, "There. Is that better?" And upon hearing Gaynor's voice that sounded like a teakettle bubbling, "Oh, how he loved his mum. That he did. He said it to me many a time," finally, *finally*, Betsy allowed herself to wake up long enough to cry for the first time since Timothy's funeral, a good long cry. And that on Gaynor's shoulder.

Later that night, Gaynor told Betsy about the pub where she met Timothy and about the current between them, a current so strong that when their eyes first met, they could not look at each other again, until she, Gaynor, was out the door of the pub and riding her bicycle toward home while Timothy jogged beside her in a darkness lit only by a sliver of the moon. And even then they didn't look at each other, not until they reached Gaynor's pink cottage, and only then did he tell her he wanted to see her again. Gaynor told about meeting Timothy the very next day in that same pub called "The Other Bird and Baby," describing the pub's smoke-stained wood, "fine wood all round," and the cheerful electric fire in the room. The next day (and now Timothy was on a bicycle, too), they rode all over Sneem and out into the countryside where "Your President Eisenhower had a grand estate," Gaynor said to Betsy.

While Betsy listened to the words that fell like a lullaby from the woman's lips, she watched Gaynor's eyes dart greedily around the room. *I don't care why she's come,* Betsy told herself. *She, this woman, is the closest I can ever be to Timothy again. Here is his bride, Timmy's bride, sitting on my bed, and I will keep her with me if I can.*

The next evening, over Irish stew followed by bread pudding—comfort food—that Gaynor had prepared for dinner, it was a lightning flash of intuition that made Betsy say: "I want you to stay in this house with me a little while, in this house that Timothy built. Will you stay with me? Here?" she asked Gaynor.

And Gaynor, hesitating just enough to see the anxiety settle on Betsy's face, foolishly replied, "Of course I will. I'll stay."

And so Gaynor had outrageously, noisily arrived in Cold Springs and "swept Betsy off her feet," said Mary Martha. "Back into life," said Isabel. With her red hair, boyishly cut, and flashing diamonds, she looks "a little odd," Sarah said,

and *come to help indeed,* she thought, but said it aloud to
no one. "Flash and trash!" said Isabel gleefully to anybody
who would listen, and immediately decided she, too, needed
a new hairstyle, something equally outlandish. But, surprisingly, it was Mary Martha's judgment that gained acceptance
for Gaynor into their Tuesday bridge games. After Gaynor
had filled in one week, Mary Martha said, "I like Gaynor.
She's real."

Soon, Gaynor was driving Betsy to the doctor's, to her
Highland Park Book Club, to her Methodist Sunday School
class. Then, the two ventured farther afield. "Let's have a bit
of cheer," Gaynor said, and they were off to the Hot Springs
races, to the Chandler gardens in Weatherford, to Dallas to
shop at Neiman's. There Gaynor found just the right sales
woman to help them, and she sat, watching Betsy try on
clothes, and imperially flicking away one dress after another.
"No, dear. That's the wrong color," and "Too old for Mrs. Rogers," and "Mrs. Rogers needs something soft. Something elegant." And when Betsy, having found the dress that suited
them all, started to hand the woman her charge card, Gaynor
stepped forward. "No, Mum, the dress is a present. It's my
present to you."

Nobody had ever paid such careful attention to Betsy's
moods, to her wishes. Lifting her hand, signaling quiet, gesturing toward Betsy, "What is it, Mum?" Gaynor would ask.
"What did you want to say?" Betsy had only to mention that
she hadn't had oysters in a long while and Gaynor would be
at the grocers, begging, bribing the young dark-haired gro-
cer with her throaty voice and wide smile, "Couldn't you
order them? Couldn't you fly them in?" If Betsy felt "a little
tired," Gaynor would have her in bed, perhaps in a new gown
Gaynor had chosen, and bringing homemade potato soup on
a tray to her bedside.

At the Christmas tea at the Club (and this just three months after Gaynor's arrival), Betsy could be heard, exclaiming delightedly: "She calls me 'Mum'. Can you believe it! *Mum*! Isn't that the sweetest thing!"

The Woman from Ireland

Gaynor was twenty-five when she met Timothy and twenty-five when she married him and twenty-five when she became his widow. When they were married and on their honeymoon, she said, "I was in love with another man when we met."

When she said it, Timothy, satiated with love, was stretched out on their picnic blanket, almost dozing in the warmth of the mild Irish sun. He propped himself up on his elbows and grinned at her. "Girl, you jest," he said. He put a hand on the back of her neck, and lying back down, he pulled her over on top of him.

"With an American," she added.

Timothy took a deep breath. She felt his chest expand. "And what is his name? Your American's name?"

She rolled off his body and lay on her back, watching the sunlight dappling the gorse that grew tall around them. Skylarks, dipping and rising against the blue sky, flew low over their blanket. They had made love twice, she, the initiator the second time, unbuttoning each button of his sweater, folding it neatly and placing it at the edge of the blanket, then unbuttoning his shirt, folding it and carefully placing it on his sweater. She pulled her sweater over her head and folded it. Bemused, he watched her face, rapt as if already engaged in the act of love. Then, "Ay!" he exclaimed exultantly and unfastened her bra, tossed it aside and pulled her down beside him.

Afterwards, she turned on her side, put her face close to his and rubbed his nose with hers. "You said, 'Ay.'"

"Ay," he laughed. "I did now. Yes! Yes! What better word for all this," he said running his hand down the length of her body. "Now what about this man, this American, you're in love with?"

"His name is Kennedy," she said. "John Fitzgerald Kennedy."

Timothy chuckled. "He's why I joined the Peace Corps."

"It's grand what your country is doing."

He sat up and, breaking off a stem of the grass, he put it in his mouth. "I've been in Africa for a little over six months, not enough time to be much help. I'm not sure I've changed a thing, but it damn sure changed me."

When, after that first meeting, Timothy had left her in her doorway, Gaynor believed it meant nothing, his promise to come the next morning. He is lonely, she told herself. He has been ill. And she had only to look in a mirror to see she was too big, even by Irish standards, and not a looker. Only through her hair, flaming red and falling below her shoulders in waves and curls, could she lay claim to a kind of beauty. There was not a reason in the world why Timothy Rogers— university educated, schooled to be a lawyer, serving a term in the Peace Corps—should have fallen in love with her, but he had. And she with him! After that first look, in the smoke-filled, ale drinking pub, as she walked through this room and into the smaller room where the women sat, she did not so much as glance his way again. Not even when the singing began and when by their cheering and clapping they urged him to sing and he did, a song about Texas and a yellow rose, even then, she did not look into the room where the men were gathered. She did not need to. Because she loved him, she had seen how thin he was, and, even in that light, how yellow his skin was and how dark were the circles around his eyes. When she got on her bicycle that first night to ride home, he had jogged alongside in a silence broken only by the bleating of lambs, the wind's low murmur and, now and then, the motor of a passing car. When they reached her house, he said, "I'll be here a month. I want to see you tomorrow and the next day and the day after that as well."

"Yes," she said. Then, "You're not well."

"I've been in the hospital. They sent me to the tropical dis-ease center in London where they found a parasite and found the medicine to kill it. I'm fine. I'm gaining weight and feeling better everyday. I'll be in Ireland four weeks, then back to the hospital again and, after that, a final trip to Ghana. I'm out of the Peace Corps. Going back is a formality, and then I'll be coming back here. To be with you," he added, taking her breath away.

That next morning, she took no time with her bath, with her hair, with her clothes. "Timothy Rogers, I'm no Maureen O'Hara. When you come you'll see that you've made a mis-take. If you come," she added, tossing her hairbrush aside.

When Timothy arrived, her father left the lambing, only calling to Henry, the hired boy, to fetch him if a ewe seemed in trouble. All through the morning Timothy and her dad sat in the small parlor, warmed by a peat-fed fire in the small stove, while Timothy talked and her da listened. Timothy told about his father, dead these six years, and his mother who had not wanted him to have anything to do with a cause that took him so far from home. He talked about the presi-dent's call for sacrifice and about the poverty in Africa, the people so poor that they made all of Ireland seem rich.

When she opened the parlor door, neither of the men looked up. She stood a minute before bringing in the tea and saw her father as Timothy must see him, his thick thatch of hair, his round and ruddy face, stubby with the short gray beard, the cleft chin and dimpled cheeks, the callused hands he lifted now and then to shoo away the flies. She saw his round blue eyes, taking in every word and listening to Tim-othy as to a bard, eyes that even at his age held a look of wonder.

"She's all we have now," her father said, beckoning her into the room with a wave of his hand. "We've lost two sons to England. Good lads, both of them."

Timothy, not knowing how to answer, only nodded solemnly.

"She's better with the lambing than her brothers, as good as any vet at knowing when a ewe needs help and when to leave her alone."

Timothy stayed with Gaynor and her family all that day, pegging sheets to the line alongside her mother, protesting, "It's naw work for a man," and Timothy reassuringly, "It's a welcome change from the work I've been doing in Africa." After a farmer's meal of cheese and bread and ale, Timothy helped her da fork the hay into the loft. Then they mucked out a lambing pen and laid down clean straw bedding.

That evening she walked with him to Gleesk pier. They strolled in the gathering darkness, as Gaynor pointed out the harebells and bee plants, the chiming bells. Now and then she broke off a flower so Timothy could catch its scent. Occasionally, a very old man on a rickety bicycle rode slowly past them. At the pier they crossed a bridge over a narrow stream and followed a path of rough stones that led to an old wooden barn-like building. They went into a rectangular room and took seats among old men who sat in straight-back chairs around three sides of the room, the fourth given over to the bar stretching the width of the room.

No sooner had they sat down than a waiter hurried to them. "Would the lady be moving into the next room?" he asked Timothy, as if she were not there. "It has a table where the lady can see and hear from that room as well as in here."

Seeing the surprise on Timothy's face, Gaynor said, "That's how it is here. Tomorrow we'll be the talk of the town."

When they were seated at a small table in the adjoining room, empty except for the two of them, first one and then another of the old men began to sing. "Paddy, would you lay one on for us?" a man would call out. When a spattering of clapping sounded, Paddy or Michael or Hennessey would stand and sing. Their ballads told of children gone to England, or even sadder, across the ocean, and coming back only to put a stone on a mother's grave.

On the way home, "The songs they sang. They were all sad," Timothy said.

"They are. But you must see them at an Irish jig, teasing and telling tall stories. And their jokes. Oh, there's nothing like an Irishman for jokes."

When they reached Gaynor's house, she knew by the lamplight from the windows her father waited. After she brought mulled wine for the three of them, "I wouldn't worry about her in your country," her da said, as though Timothy had already proposed. "Even alone, I wouldn't worry. Not with your fine president." He leaned forward eagerly, his blue eyes dancing in his ruddy face. "Tell me! Do you think your president will be coming to Ireland next year? Oh, what a welcome we'd give him."

Timothy nodded. "He'll come. He loves the Irish."

And hearing this, her father rose, the two men shook hands and Gaynor poured another round.

Early the next morning, Timothy was there again, at her door. Before he lifted the knocker, the door swung open. "She's in the barn," her mother said. "She'll not be coming in until the lambkin's on the ground and safe." As he turned to leave, "Wait," she said. "Will you be taking this tray out to her. Strong tea with cream and sugar is what she'll be needing. I'll get another cup. You'll be having some tea yourself."

When he entered the barn, the smells that assailed his nose were an amniotic mixture of antiseptics, hay, blood and manure. And there was another: the lambs' wool smelling like newly turned soil that had lain fallow for years.

Gaynor was sitting on her heels, her hands palm upward in her lap. So intent was she on the birth, she was unaware of his presence. He stood watching her. She's different from any woman I've ever known, he thought. He tried to imagine her playing bridge or shopping in Cold Springs, and failed. For that matter he could not imagine Gaynor taking part in any of the activities of the women of Cold Springs. But we could live anywhere, anywhere in the world. We could live right here in Ireland, he told himself.

After a minute, she turned the animal around and examined its bottom. Afterwards, the ewe pawed the ground and circled before lying down again.

"Gaynor," he said.

She turned and smiled at him. Then she rose and came toward him. A length of blue cloth that bound Gaynor's hair framed her face. She wore a blue shirt and loose-fitting black pants. He saw that beneath the shirt her breasts were unbound, and he felt a strong arousal.

"The lambkin's almost here," she said. "Do you want to help?" she asked and gestured toward a shelf attached to the barn. The shelf held scissors, iodine, shoulder-length plastic gloves, towels, a heat lamp, syringes—all this and more, a myriad of items that would be needed for the birth.

"You bet. You tell me what you need."

She grinned and returned to her kneeling position. "Here we are. Here it comes," she crooned. "Oh, it's a wee thing, a girl. Hand me a towel," she said. She took it from his hand and wiped the mucus from the tiny creature's mouth and nose. Watching it intently, she said, "It's not breathing. We'll be needing a long straw," and taking it from his hand she tickled the baby's nose with the straw. "Come now. Breathe. You can breathe," she whispered, tickling it again.

The silence was complete, and then there came a faint sound—the lamb's first breath, and when Timothy heard this, he felt an extraordinary sense of relief. Now Gaynor placed the lamb under the ewe's nose, and the animal quickly, frantically, began to lick the baby. "We'll let her get to know her lamb. This will help her expel the afterbirth, and I can remove it. Then we'll finish up," she said. She stood and took his hand in hers. "Let's have that cup of tea, and while we drink it we can tell if she's going to be a good mother."

They added sugar and cream and, turning to watch, they leaned against the wall of the barn and drank the tea. "She's doing well," Gaynor said. "She's bonding with her lamb. Ah! Here it is."

When he saw the glutinous, purple mass in the straw, he frowned.

"The afterbirth," Gaynor said, swooping it up with newspapers and taking it from the pen.

Throughout the delivery he had felt a sense of wonder. Again, he tried to imagine her engaged in the ordinary activities of the Cold Springs women, and he could not.

As they watched, the ewe continued licking her baby. Gaynor said, "Washing the lamb will help her find her baby in a flock of lambs." Handing her cup to Timothy, she returned to the cubicle. "Let's finish up. Hand me the scissors!"

She took them and quickly clipped the umbilical cord. "Now we'll disinfect it. Will you hand me that bowl of iodine on the shelf."

She dipped the umbilical cord into iodine, that odor so strong that the tears came again. "She's a natural mother," Gaynor said. "This is her first baby, and she's doing well. Will you hold her now, and I'll see about her milk. Ah, the plugs are still there," she said.

"Are there plugs?" he asked incredulously.

She chuckled. "Yes."

When she had stripped each teat, she said, "I'll be dragging this baby to the pen you prepared yesterday."

"I'll carry her," he offered.

Again she broke into laughter. Holding the lamb's little hind legs in her hands, she gently dragged it to the lambing pen. "The ewe will follow the trail of smells in the bedding. More bonding."

When the ewe and her lamb were installed, she asked him to bring a bucket of warm water from the kitchen. He set it down beside her. She poured a dollop of molasses into it and swirled it around with her hand. "Now a nice tab of hay. And we're done!"

As she watched the lamb, hungrily nudging the ewe's bag, she put her hands on her hips and tilted her head, frowning slightly. When the lamb fastened onto a teat, she smiled widely.

"You're happy doing all this, aren't you," he said.

"Ay," she said. "The lambing is my favorite time of the year."

When Timothy asked for her hand the next day, her father said, "Son, you're a good lad. I know you'll take care of her," and he pulled out a handkerchief and wiped away the tears streaming down his face.

When they asked if it were possible, Father O'Leary, knowing the mother and the father well and Gaynor, too, shortened the banns. Then, "O Lord, I hope the pope doesn't hear of it!" he said over a whiskey to celebrate.

Two weeks later they were married, she, at twenty-five a spinster, and he at twenty-five, a sought-after Texas bachelor.

On their honeymoon, they drove round the Ring of Kerry, staying in small hotels and inns. Somehow Timothy found the finest hotels and the restaurants which offered the most exquisite menus. Most of the places he chose were filled with American tourists. They dined at small tables in small dining rooms, and their appetites for food were as voracious as for each other. They ordered exotic foods from the menu. One morning he ordered black pudding for breakfast, and she had cheese grits. Each night they fell into bed, made love, slept and waking, made love again.

They told their histories to each other, and every word seemed laden with significance; no detail was too small to tell. She said, "When I was a little girl, I broke a cream pitcher hand painted with baby chickens. My grandmother told me not to cry, and she mended it. It's my favorite thing."

He said, "My father called me Sonny Boy, from the time I was born, I guess. I came home with a bloody nose one day, and he said, 'Sonny Boy, it's a mistake to fight your way through the world.' He didn't ask why I had fought. He just said that."

Over and over again, they relived their first meeting. "I saw your face before you came into the pub. I thought your eyes were black, but they're not. They're navy blue." Then, "I wanted to touch your hair. I almost reached out to touch it," Timothy said.

They had ridden bicycles and stopped to rest by a freshet splashing on rocks at the foot of the mountain. "I knew you had been ill," she said. "I saw that in your face when you smiled at me."

"I didn't smile at you."

"You did."

She giggled wildly and tickled his ribs. He hugged her tightly, binding her arms to her sides. "I give up," she said.

When he released her, she kicked off her shoes and ran up the hill, as nimble as a goat. Laughing, hands on her hips, she watched him laboriously climb to stand by her side.

One night she found a book of Irish poems in the library at the Killarney Hotel where they were staying. She took it upstairs and, in her black silk gown, a present from Timothy, and, with her great mop of red hair reflecting the lamplight, she sat cross-legged on the bed and read poetry to him. He could not take his eyes away. She read *Among Schoolchildren* "by our great Irish poet," she said breathlessly and told him about Yeats and about his love for Maud Gonne. When she came to the lines and read: "And thereupon my heart is driven wild \ She stands before me as a living child," she stopped the reading. "Just think, Mr. Yeats loved her all his life, all his life, even after marrying another woman. Imagine when he first saw her, Maud Gonne, almost six feet tall and wearing her big hat with black feathers and the cages of birds she traveled with. Imagine how beautiful she was!"

"Why didn't they marry?"

"He proposed three times, three times! And three times she refused him."

"How could she when he loved her that much. To write a poem!"

"She loved another. A revolutionary."

He took the book from her hand. "My heart is driven wild," he whispered and took her in his arms.

When they reached the Lake Country of England, he said it reminded him of East Texas, and he told her about Cold Springs with its greenness and lakes and springs and flowering trees. He told her about the house he had helped his mother build. He said that in Cold Springs everybody knew everything about each other.

"Everything? Everything?"

"Almost everything?" His face fell into an expression of solemnity.

"What? What are you thinking about so seriously?"

He hesitated. "Tell me," she said.

"It's just that a long time ago, we had these horrible murders in Cold Springs. A young couple was killed, in the Park, I think. Nobody had ever locked their doors before then, but after that they did. The men bought guns and nailed window screens shut. I was just a kid, but I remember how scared everybody was. I don't think the town has ever recovered."

"Who was it?"

"Nobody knows. To this day nobody knows."

"How awful. I'm not sure I will like Cold Springs."

"That's all in the past. It's over. And we won't stay if you don't like it there. But I want mother to know you. And I want you to see the house. The paneling is old and carved beautifully. And there are wonderful rugs on the stone floors. Bright colors. My mother has a wonderful sense of color. She loves color and clothes and me. And in that order." He smiled and held out his hand to her.

"Will she love me?"

"She'll adore you," he said, walking with her toward the stairs.

"I've heard there's more freedom there. For women. More even than here, in England."

"Aren't you free in Ireland?"

"No. Remember the pub. The men in one room and the women in another. And a baby every year after marriage. More than they can feed or love. I don't want that."

He took her hand and kissed it. "With us, it won't be that way. We will have time to be together, just the two of us. Come on. Let's take that walk."

"Wait a minute." She puts her hand on his arm. "I want you to know that the village thinks I'm wild. Even before I met you they thought that. One day I rode my bicycle to Waterville and had a glass of ale in a pub called 'Dingle Bay.' There was no separate room for women, and I sat with the men and listened to the songs until they asked me to leave. By the next day, the story was all over County Kerry."

"It doesn't matter what they say in County Kerry or in Cold Springs either. Come. Let's walk down around the lake to Wordsworth's house? The innkeeper says it has wonderful gardens."

It was at Michael's Inn in the Lake Country they parted, Timothy saying he'd come back for her, back to Sneem, although the journey would take five days each way. That last week, they hiked from Michael's Inn one day, walking through stands of ash and elder and up into the hills where they made love beside a fallen sheepfold. Afterwards, she dozed and when she woke up, he was gone. She felt a minute's unease, but then he came, carrying a great bunch of white and lavender heather, holding it across his arms, and when she buried her face in it, she thought the heather itself carried the wild scent of their honeymoon.

When he left her there, their room was filled with the heather—in a glass pitcher on the deal dresser and a vase of it by her bed and in a bowl by the bathroom sink. Loving the look of it and the smell of it, Gaynor stayed two days longer than she had thought to stay, and each day she climbed to the sheepfold and sat.

❊

When freshets spring up and converge into crystal brooks tumbling down the mountainsides, and everywhere the green is surgent with spring, and the land, even the fallow land, shoots up pale green tendrils, to hear of death is cruel. When a thin, dark boy on a bicycle came with the telegram that said Timothy's plane had crashed just after takeoff from Ghana, Gaynor went into the kitchen and picked up a knife and hacked off her long, red hair. Keening, she walked out of the house. She walked all that day, and the next and the next, walking away from the anguish of knowing. When Postal Delivery came with the box from Cold Springs, Texas, just three days after the telegram, the box addressed to Timothy Hayes Rogers and with a note from his mother: "Timmy, your heart has always been ardent. Is she, this Irish bride, simply another project like the Peace Corps? But, in any case, here are your grandmother's earrings. Do with them what you wish. They're yours," Gaynor read the letter and put the letter and the box holding the diamond earrings into the bottom drawer of her dresser. She was glad Timothy had not read the note, and she hardened her heart toward his mother.

After Gaynor read the telegram, she had walked, carrying only the grief. Now she walked shrouded in grief and anger. At dawn's first light, she would come down the narrow stairs to drink a cup of the strong black tea and eat thickly sliced, buttered bread in a kitchen not yet warmed by the stove. She walked away from the village, away from society, sometimes walking into the low hills and sometimes walking between the seashore and Lough Currane. Bitterly lamenting her loss, she walked until she was overcome by exhaustion. Then she rested and walked home again. She walked until those in the scattered cottages in the countryside grieved with her, greeting her tenderly and offering food and drink, all of which she turned away. She grew thin with the walking so that, seeing her from afar in her black clothes and with the spiked red hair and the dark, deep-set eyes, she seemed an apparition. In a single day, she walked eighteen miles, walking from Sneem to Waterville and home again. The next day, even before dawn's first light, she was down again, drinking the hot tea and eating the homemade bread, but never tasting a bite of it.

Seeing her leave each morning, her mother was filled with despair. "Jamie, we have to talk to her. She's killing herself. People are saying that already she's a ghost before her own death."

"Let her be, Maggie. The heart has to heal."

"A dying heart can't heal. If you won't talk to her, I will!" But her mother waited.

When a letter came from Texas, Gaynor knew the handwriting and refused to open it.

After twenty-four hours, her father said, "This grief you carry is natural. The hate is not. She was his mother. Open the letter."

Hearing the tenderness in her father's voice, the hard kernel inside her heart softened, and she read the letter. *"How can I go on? How can you? Please come to Texas. I want to know the woman he loved,"* his mother had written. Now the walks grew shorter, and she was able to sleep. And along with her grief and her anger, she felt the stirrings of curiosity.

A month later, she picked out clothes for her journey to Texas, rolled them up, and put them into two green duffle bags. Some of the money from Timothy's insurance was in small, silk envelopes and pinned inside her bra, twenty-five one-hundred dollar bills on one side and twenty-five on the other side for balance.

The three of them walked to the bus stop, her da carrying the duffle bags and her ma holding her hand as if she were a child. As they walked Gaynor made note of the thrushes swooping over their heads and the barley high and golden in the fields. She listened to the bleating of the lambs and the dog barking because he had been penned so he could not follow. She saw the hills, faraway and green against the sky.

When they reached the bus stop, her da set the bags down. "You're sure, Gaynor? You don't have to leave us. Girl, you know that," he said.

"Jamie, don't you be closing her mind to Cold Springs," her ma told him. "You're the one urged her to go."

Hearing the argument, Gaynor threw back her head and laughed, and the sun caught the redness of her hair and, seeing it glistening and full of light, her ma ran her hand over it tenderly, as if touching a wound.

"Will you let it grow long again?"

"Maybe," she said.

When they saw the bus below, lumbering along the curves of Lough Currane, they fell silent. It came toward them slowly. When it stopped and its door swung open, there came a flurry of admonitions. "Gaynor, write us," and "Oh, I will! I will!" and "Da, get two boys to help with the lambing," and, from her mother, "Don't lose your ticket. It's safe inside, with your money," and "Watch out for . . ."

The doors of the bus closed before her ma could finish the warning.

She would not allow herself to look back. Sitting behind the driver, she lowered her head so that the tears fell into her open hands.

In Killarney she stepped into a taxi and asked to be taken to the train station. There she waited two hours for the train to come. During the long journey, she lay awake at night and thought of Timothy, determined to remember every word he had said and the sound of his voice saying it. She thought of how lithe he was and light footed and remembered his stride was long. In the darkness she closed her eyes and saw him casting into the water, and when the lure landed in the willows where he said a fish would be, she saw him flashing a quick grin over his shoulder at her. She remembered his labored climb up the mountain to stand by her side. She saw him laughing at her mother's remonstrance as they pegged the clothes and the look of pride on his face as he helped her father fork the clean hay into the lambing pens.

During the days, she planned what she would say to his mother. On the train to Dublin, she saw herself walking to the door. "He loved me. He did. And I him, " she would tell his mother. Then she would turn away proudly and leave. On the plane, she looked down on the shimmering gray ocean as they took off and thought she would place the earrings in his mother's hand and say, "I knew him better. I loved him more. He was mine."

But when she rang the doorbell and saw Timothy's blue eyes, and these set in Betsy's wrinkled face and filled with sorrow, she could only enfold Betsy into her arms.

※

In Cold Springs she was a misfit. Here the women wore powder over powder. They brushed their eyelids with blue or brown or gray colors. Their lips were bright pink or red or orange. Gaynor wore not a smidgen of makeup. Here the women dressed like the British Royals. Everything matching. Blue suit. Blue shoes. Blue bag, even. Around Betsy's house, Gaynor wore pants and her mucking boots and when she went out, a simple cotton dress and sandals.

When the Cold Springs women talked about bridge and clothes and parties, their voices were serious, their expressions intense. But when they talked about ex-husbands or problem children, they made the stories funny. Was this a Texas trait? Gaynor wondered. She longed to tell them about the sheep and the barley crops and, most of all, about Ireland's "troubles," but she was rendered mute by her own seriousness. She could not find the light-hearted manner of speech they used while speaking of serious, often tragic, subjects.

She was glad she had come. She would always remember the rooms where Timothy had slept and eaten and worked. But, soon, she would be going home. Her father needed her there before the spring's lambing.

Only Betsy seemed to see her as Timothy had seen her. At the country club or at church, "Here's Timothy's bride," Betsy would say warmly. And Mrs. Rose or Mrs. Tilson would take her hand and say how much she was helping with Betsy's recovery. At first, the women stared at her and leaned to whisper in a friend's ear. She wrote her ma and da: "*The town is hot. The people are cold. Betsy begs me to stay, and I will for a while. But I long to see the barley all golden and smell the wind coming off the sea. I'll be coming soon.*

But she did not go home. In some indefinable way, she felt she had not yet finished her journey.

Gaynor and Sarah

It's hot in August and there's talk of frying eggs on the sidewalk. When Betsy told me this, "And then do they eat them?" I asked her. My question tickled Betsy. She has a smoker's laugh, deep and throaty, but surprisingly pleasant, coming from such a small woman. Now Betsy is quick to laugh. When I first came, it was a month before I saw her smile. I'd much rather see Betsy laugh than watch someone fry an egg on the sidewalk. Yuk. I'll remember to say this to her. Anyway, it's that hot today. I miss you. How was Cork? The usual higgledy peggly, I expect. I can imagine the two of you, holding hands and walking along the seashore. A second honeymoon. I like to think of it.

Gaynor put the letter in the envelope and drove in Betsy's old Cadillac to the post office. She stamped the letter, blessed it with a kiss, put it into the box and walked back to the car.

Backing away from the curb, she saw the small, white house in the middle of a stand of great magnolias. Seen that way it looked fresh and clean, nestled among the dappled shade of the dark green leaves and with its dark green shutters against the white of the building. A sign, *Library,* was posted on a stick along the sidewalk. Back she went again, into the same parking place and walked across the street to the library.

Stepping inside, she had to catch her breath. A feeling that she had been swept to County Kerry, wafted there by the smells of horse gear and lambs' feed, was that strong. Taking into her body the smell, like that of the farm in Ireland, she walked across the room to a window that looked out on a golden field. Ay, here it was! The smell of the barley! Coming from the field!

She found a chair by the window, sat in it and studied the room, where she sat—the Adam's style moldings, the worn floors and the casement windows (the windows wide open despite the heat). And here she was, finally, in a library! Not since she had finished St. Mary's College in Cork had she had the grand privilege of walking into a library and choosing a book to take home. She rose and walked among the shelves, savoring the titles. *Thomas Jefferson: An Intimate History; Closing the Ring; Edith Wharton, A Biography; A Tale of Two Cities; Lady Chatterley's Lover; A Primer of Book Collecting.* How to choose? What to choose. She pulled a leather bound edition of *A Tale of Two Cities* from the shelf and ran her fingers across the gold embossed title. Leather. Here was the smell of horse gear.

"What a beautiful book," a woman said, looking over her shoulder.

The woman was a sturdy, pretty woman with freckles scattered across her cheeks, straight blond hair that fell almost to her shoulders and with the prettiest blue eyes, uncannily pretty. Her blue-eyed gaze was so surprisingly direct it took Gaynor's breath for a minute. Below the silky blue dress the woman wore, both her white sandals and her legs were splattered with mud. When she smiled, as she was smiling now, her face, with the wide smile and cozy freckles, took on the merriest expression Gaynor had seen in Cold Springs.

"Are you checking out that book?"

"I don't have a library card, but I'll be asking for one today," Gaynor said. "If I could I'd spend the rest of the day here with the smell of barley and horse gear."

"Barley? Horse gear?"

"The leather books smell like the horses' gear on my da's farm in Ireland. And the field out there, whatever it is, has the smell of lambs' feed."

The woman put her hands on her hips. "Now I know who you are," she said. "You're Timothy Rogers' Irish bride. Widow!" she corrected herself. "I'm Sarah. Sarah Carter."

"Gaynor," she said and held out her hand.

"Yes, of course. Gaynor. I'm checking out a couple of murder mysteries. I'll check out your book on my card. That is, if you don't mind waiting a bit. I can't leave just yet."

Gaynor nodded. "Of course," she said. Then "Ah," as if she understood.

"Oh, no, you don't understand. I don't understand it myself. But Eddie just left me. Again. He's probably out there in the parking lot. Would you step outside and see if he's still there? He's short, about my height, and as thin as a wire. He's driving an old Buick." She put her hands on her hips and leaned forward. She raised her eyebrows. "If he's still out there, maybe you and I could run over him," she whispered.

"I will. I mean I will look outside. I don't think I want to run over anyone today."

She stepped outside and studied the parking lot. *I wouldn't know a Buick from a tinker's cart,* she thought. But this woman, this Sarah Carter, is the most entertaining person I've met in Cold Springs.

Returning, she whispered conspiratorially. "The coast is clear." Then she said, and her voice was solemn. "Tell me. Is the man a danger to you."

"Oh, my. No. A goldfish could scare Eddie. I just don't want to ever see him again."

Saying it, tears filled her eyes, brimmed over, ran down her cheeks. She brushed them away. "I wish I had a gun. No. It's better that I don't."

"I am sorry," Gaynor said, turning as if to leave.

"No, don't leave. I'll check out your book on my card. I hardly ever use it." She ran her fingers along a shelf of books as if they were piano keys and smiled. "It's nice in here, isn't it? Now as soon as you fill out an application for your card, we can walk out together."

In the parking lot, Gaynor tucked her book under her arm and held out her hand. "Thank you, Sarah Carter," she said.

"Wait! I have a fine idea. It's almost one o'clock. Why don't you follow me to my house. I'll make sandwiches, and we'll have lunch in the garden. How's that?"

"I'd like that. But I must call Betsy first to see if she needs her car."

"From my house. As soon as we get there."

Sarah's house was old and creaky and spacious. "I like it. Almost everything in Cold Springs is new, new when compared to the cottages in Sneem."

"Sneem?"

"A little Irish town, near the farm where I grew up."

"My house is falling apart, but we manage. Here's the phone."

Betsy answered before the first ring had finished. Gaynor said, "Betsy, I'm having lunch with a friend unless you need the car just now." And then "Her name? It's Sarah Carter," she said, winking at Sarah. "You know her? Wait. What do you want me to ask? About whom? She's right here. I'll hand the phone to her."

Taking the phone, Sarah listened. Frowning, she shook her head. "No. Not one thing. There's always been gossip about Jackson Morris. No," she said finally. And replacing the receiver, she said, "It's a small town. There's always talk."

Gaynor chuckled. "The same as in Sneem."

Twenty minutes later, Gaynor found herself walking slowly through Sarah's garden as she told the provenance of favorite plants. This antique rose, the Queen Elizabeth, from Brenham in central Texas, the honeysuckle from her grandmother's Tennessee farm, the butterfly bushes, a present from her friend. Sarah spoke slowly, her voice delicately brushing over the "r's" and dropping the -ing's. In this way, her speech was not unlike the Irish, and for Gaynor so far from home, the sound of it was pleasing.

After sandwiches in Sarah's old kitchen, they sat in a creaking swing on Sarah's porch. And Sarah, starting the swing and stopping it to turn and look at Gaynor as she made some point (although at times, Gaynor wasn't sure what the point was), talked lightly about her husband, who had left her several times, making it sound like a comedy. "I was doing fine," Sarah said, "until Eddie came back this time. I hadn't heard from him in months, but here he was, walking into the house like he's never left me. Left us. The children and me." She lifted the hem of her blue dress to wipe away the tears that again filled her eyes. "The children," she said. "I don't care a thing about him. But they do. He came back yesterday. I thought to stay. We went out to dinner, and he said he loved me, but he slept in the guest room. I peeped in this morning, and he was still there, sleeping. He only came for money. Over martinis last night (I should never drink them), he said, 'Baby, I got this stock tip. We can't lose. It's a sure thing. We need ten thousand. In six months it will be worth fifty thousand.'"

She shook her head. "'Forget it!' I told him. But this morning he followed me to the library. 'You're harassing me,' I said. 'I'm calling the police. You're wanted for child support.'" She grinned. "He ran, literally ran out of the library," she said, setting the swing into motion again. Although Sarah's voice was mildly rueful, her smile was genuine. "Eddie couldn't spit to please me now!" she said, laughing. "Let's go inside. There's a pitcher of mint tea and some sugar cookies."

In Sarah's living room they settled into shabby chairs. Sarah kicked off her shoes, squeezed lemon and stirred sugar into her iced tea glass and curled up in her chair. Gaynor's tea was hot and with milk and sugar.

Listening to Sarah, smiling encouragingly, "Tell me about your children," Gaynor said.

Holding her glass up to the light, frowning at it, "Sometimes I think my children will break my heart. They are totally unrealistic. Eve says she is going to New York as soon as she can drive a car. She disdains school. She ignores homework. The teachers are in despair. She failed the first grade. Twice. She's a vegetarian and she collects cats. Finds them. Brings them home."

Eve's irresponsible behavior (her mother's judgment), sounded more like an Irish strange' ling than an immature child to Gaynor. "How old is Eve?"

"She's twelve."

Gaynor could not restrain her laughter.

Sarah smiled. "She's a hippie, a twelve-year-old hippie. I'm at my wits' end! Can you give up on a twelve-year-old? And John, my fourteen-year-old, swears he's going to run away and live with his father, if he can find his father."

Then Sarah sighed, the sound of it profound. Heart-rending. Looking into her face, Gaynor saw that her sapphire blue eyes were beseeching and hopeless.

"I'm sorry," Gaynor said. "I have no children, but I know that lambs grow into quite responsible sheep."

And now Sarah laughed. "Well, here I am, babbling away about my problems and you, oh Gaynor, you just lost. . . ."

"Everything."

"How long has it been?"

"Two hundred and twenty-seven days," said Gaynor, reaching for her handbag and standing. "You see, I can't, I'll never be able to. . . . It's too. . . I have to go."

"Oh, stay. What is it? Can't I help?"

"No," Gaynor said, her voice suddenly formal. "I must go. I enjoyed the lunch and your stories. Thank you. I'll call. Soon."

As she drove through the Park on the way to Betsy's house, Gaynor thought about Sarah. How lightly Sarah talked about betrayal. How amusing her stories were when she spoke about her strange children. What's the matter with me? she wondered. She had sat listening to Sarah, sat in her rambling old house, enjoying the warmth of her voice and the humor of her stories. But when Sarah had said, "How long has it been?" fear had come on so suddenly that her heart contracted. For if the wound were opened, if it were scratched open by a confessional talk of his death, who would staunch the bleeding. Seized by panic, she had fled. Not even to Betsy could she talk about that. To Betsy she spoke about his life, about the days they had together. Never could she speak of the boy who had come on the bicycle or about the message about Timothy he brought that day.

When Gaynor drove away from her house, she believed she would never see Sarah again. But the next week Sarah had called. "Do you play bridge?"

"No. But I can learn," she had said staunchly.

Sarah's Revolution

Sarah emptied the pan under the kitchen sink and replaced it. Eddie was gone for good. So was her money. And her house was falling down. The foundation needed repairs. One could drop a marble on the floor of any room of the house, and it would roll. The roof leaked. There were leaks everywhere. A pipe under the kitchen sink dripped. Water sometimes stood around one of the commodes upstairs. The faucets dripped. Cold air streamed through the window frames. The house needed paint, inside and out. And the rain had gone on for days. Not a strong hardy downpour that came and left a blue sky. Rather, there had been clouds and cold and drizzle. With weather like this, there was nothing to do but stay inside and get something accomplished.

Pulling open a kitchen drawer, Sarah scrambled around among old grocery receipts, pens without ink, erasers that smudged, broken Crayolas, shoelaces and old keys until she found a small tablet and a pen that worked. She walked through the dining room and, crossing the wide entrance hall, she stepped down into the living room. She sat in a chair by the window to make a list of needed repairs and the cost of each. The house was insured for two hundred thousand dollars. She doubted that it was worth that much. But the property was valuable.

Only John's and Eve's attachment to the house had kept her from putting it on the market. Even as she contemplated the possibility, she could hear their protests: "Mom, what are you thinking of? Where would we live? We grew up here. We love this house." This from Eve, and from John, the calm voice of practicality, *his* idea of practicality: "Mom, the house is paid for. I'm thinking about working on the house next summer. I could paint it. I'd start with my room. I'm thinking purple, almost black. And I wouldn't charge much."

Sarah groans. "Oh, dear Lord, deliver me," she prayed.

Tapping the pencil against her teeth, she looked at the first item. Foundation, $50,000. She was pretty sure that number was in the ball park. That's exactly what Isabel's foundation had cost. But she didn't have fifty thousand dollars. She barely had five thousand.

As she was writing the word *roof*, the second repair most needed, the living room suddenly brightened. The blues and yellows in the sofas and the colors in the rug became riotous. The forecast of storms and high winds had been wrong. Storms. What did the weatherman know? She opened the front door and stepped out into sunshine. She looked up at the sky, at the dizzy blue of it, the lazy clouds in it. She saw that the Alexandria rose was filled with hot pink blooms, one or two opened wide. She sighed. Only her garden seemed to flourish. Not the house. Not her children. But her garden was magnificent!

She looked down at the list she carried, the awful list with its dire projections. She tore it in two. Feeling the warmth of the sun, her spirits rose. She went upstairs and picked up the phone in her bedroom. What she needed was a game of tennis. She called Isabel.

"Sarah, are you crazy? Look out your window!"

"I heard the forecast. The front's moving slowly. It won't be here until noon. And the sun just broke through. It's a perfect morning."

Isabel laughed. "Sarah, today's Friday. My trainer's coming. Remember? And with all this flab, I need a workout."

"Well, la-de-da! I've seen your good-looking trainer. Everybody's talking."

Isabel sighed. "Do you think I care?"

But she did care. And Sarah knew she did. "That was mean," she said. "I could cut out my tongue when I say something like that. Nobody's talking. Forgive me."

Isabel's laugh was wicked. "Maybe they should be," she said and hung up.

The truth was that nobody gossiped about Isabel and her trainer, or about Isabel and her financial adviser. Nobody gossiped about Isabel. Period.

From time to time, some man, usually a newcomer, would make a stab at marrying Isabel, or at least sleeping with her. And, apparently, she would enjoy the rush of dinners and flowers and football games (this last horribly boring to Isabel), and then, just as suddenly, it would end. Isabel was not a liberated woman. The sexual revolution was not for her! Isabel was Cold Springs' Elizabeth Taylor. If she ever decided to get involved with another man, her friends felt sure they would know it. There would be a new ring on her finger.

Whatever works, Sarah told herself. She had welcomed the sexual revolution with open arms. She had not seen Eddie for months, until recently. For all she knew, she might never see him again. She was happy about her relationship with Hite. He was easy to be with and eager to enjoy a "frisky romp," as he called it, from time to time. She was fond of Hite, but love? Marriage? Neither she nor Hite was interested in marriage.

Hite might be good for a game this morning. Sarah called him. "How about a quick game this morning?"

He chuckled. "Your place or mine?"

She laughed. "Of tennis, Hite."

"Honey, have you seen the weather report?"

"Hite, I said *quick*!"

"O.K. See you at 10:30. I've got a luncheon appointment."

Thirty minutes later, she was at the club. They played a set, doubles, against Maureen and Richard Ames before the front roared in, sending them scurrying to their cars.

By the time Sarah reached the city limits she had to creep along in order to see the road. The flashes of lightning and bursts of thunder were coming faster. She flipped on the radio.

"Take cover," a voice commanded. "Where ever you are, take cover in the closest building. A tornado has touched down in Cold Springs. It is moving along Main Street at thirty miles an hour. If you are in the vicinity and in a car, take cover immediately. Find shelter in a building."

Sarah had no idea where she was. She drifted to a stop and peered through the windshield. A flash of lightning lit up the street. There was the post office! And, although she couldn't see it, the library was directly opposite. She eased the car toward the library's parking lot, bounced over a curb and turned off the motor. When another burst of lightning came, she ran to the library and pulled the door open. The wind slammed the door shut behind her.

Miss English, Sarah's fourth-grade teacher, stood straight and tall behind the desk. She looked over her glasses, studying Sarah. Raising her eyebrows, "Yes?" she said, like she was talking to a stranger.

"Take cover," Sarah whispered.

"I beg your pardon."

Sarah leaned forward. "We have to take cover," she whispered again.

Miss English looked at the small pool of water gathering at Sarah's feet. "Did you say, 'Take cover'?"Miss English looked to her right and then to her left. "Miss Oates," she said, "could you help me with this lady?"

"Please." Sarah whispered desperately, hopelessly. "Just take cover."

Now another woman, apparently Miss Oates, joined Miss English behind the desk. Miss English turned to her. "She says we have to take cover." Her voice was cool. Detached.

"Oh?"

"I'm taking cover," Sarah announced and, dropping to the floor, she crawled under a table. She stuck her head out. "You need to take cover," she said. "Please!"

But now the thunder seemed to have vanished and the lightning along with it. Miss English fluttered her right hand to the base of her neck and placed her left hand under the right elbow. She frowned. The two women leaned forward in tandem, examining Sarah.

All at once, the absurdity of the situation—herself under the table, the courtesy of the women toward an apparently mad women, registered, sending Sarah into an onslaught of mirth. Crawling from under the table, she laughed. Pulling herself to her feet, she laughed. Trying to explain her behavior, she laughed.

"I was in my car," she said, "and I turned on my radio and the announcer was saying 'take cover,' and I couldn't see past the windshield and there was the announcer with his 'take covers' and the sirens. Yes! There were sirens, and this man telling me a tornado had touched down on Main Street and there was this flash of lightning so that I saw that I was on Main Street and the man was warning me that I had to take cover immediately and there were flashes of lightning and the only thing I could see was the library and. . . ." Leaning against the reception desk, laughing still, she had to stop for breath, and now Miss English had her hand over her mouth, giggling like a teenager, and Miss Oates threw her head back and laughed, a hearty laugh that bounced through the library.

"And even if the library was about to get blown away," Sarah said, "I felt like I had to whisper just like when I was in your fourth grade class and you brought us to the library for a class outing, and we all. . . ." She caught her breath. "Miss English, I didn't know you worked here."

"Why, Sarah Claiborne! I should have known you. You haven't changed a bit. Those sparkling blue eyes and those freckles. Such a cuddly little girl! I remember when I asked you to change the goldfish water and you absent-mindedly let the fish go down the drain. I laughed all the way home about that."

"I remember."

"Now Sarah, this is Miss Oates, our manager. And I work here now fulltime," she said proudly.

Miss Oates was small and wore red. "We need a light-hearted touch in the library," she said and held out her hand.

"Now Sarah, you come on back to my office," Miss English said. "Wearing that short tennis outfit you must be chilled to the bone. I've got a towel back there and a hot cup of tea. And we'll talk. I want to catch up with you. Pauline, I'll take my lunch break now."

"Fine. I have some homemade cookies in my office. Perhaps Miss Claiborne would like that with her tea."

As soon as the office door was closed, Miss English charged into Sarah's life. "Here's a towel. Tea will be ready in a minute. Now. I've been working here, as a volunteer, for a year. Why haven't I seen you in the library? Have you forgotten how to read, Sarah Claiborne?"

"No ma'am. But my life is ruined. Eddie's left me. For good this time. And he spent my inheritance, just about all of it. My children refuse to grow up. And my house is falling apart. Just the new roof would cost thousands of dollars. The repairs my house needs get longer every day."

"What a mess! Sarah, *you* need to grow up. Then, perhaps, your children will be able to. What does your house need the most?"

"A foundation. A new roof. The old one leaks. Money. I need thousands of dollars."

"Sell it!

"Sell the house? It's our home. The only home my children have ever known. Eve and John would have a fit!"

"Let them. Sell it! The property is valuable. Now Sarah, you don't have a job. Why not!"

"I wanted to stay home. I wanted to be a good mother, but I'm not. And I trusted Eddie. I thought he had good sense. He hasn't. Miss English, are you a psychologist?"

"Better. I'm wise. How old are you, Sarah. I'm old enough that I can ask you that."

"Thirty-three."

"That young! One's life cannot be ruined when one is only thirty-three. Sarah, this is a new age for women. Why, nowadays, a woman can do anything. You need a job. A part-time job, maybe, to get you started. I'll go talk to Miss Oates. It won't be much of a job. No benefits. But you can buy groceries and you'll have the beginning of a resume. Now you wait right there. Miss Oates might give you a try."

"But I'm not sure . . ."

"I'm sure. I'm quite sure. Drink your tea," Miss English said. She turned to leave, turned around and sat behind her desk once more. "Sarah," she said, taking a pencil from behind her ear. "I do remember that you and Mary Martha Mercer and Isabel Jessup, why you were Rosemary Winslow's closest friends."

"Yes, we were," Sarah said.

"That young boy, Jackson, who left town so abruptly after Rosemary's death. There are those who still believe. . . After all these years, they still think he may have been guilty." Frowning, she shook her head. "Well, look at me, gossiping. Excuse me."

"I have no idea where Jackson is," Sarah said. "I try not to think about it."

"And why should you!" And with that Miss English left to see Miss Oates.

When Sarah left the library an hour later, Miss Oates had offered and she had accepted a part-time job in the library.

When she got home, she parked the car in front and stared at the house. As she sat there, Miss English's voice resonated— sensible and sure—a voice that brooked no nonsense. "*Sell it!*" Miss English had said. And "*Let them!*" Let Eve and John have a fit. Before she unlocked the front door, she had decided she would put the house on the market. But she had waited. She waited until John was out of high school and then she waited until Eve finished, and by then John was in college. She put off selling it. After all, her husband had come back. Twice. Maybe, someday. . . . Finally, she put the house on the market. But before it could be sold, the house burned. To the ground.

Gaynor's Revolution

When Bobby, the president's brother was assassinated, Gaynor knew she would be going home. She *had* to go. The United States had changed. She needed the solace of home.

On a perfect summer morning, "I have to go home," she told Betsy. "My mother and father need me."

Betsy's kitchen was full of sunshine. The light shone through embroidered curtains to make snowflake patterns on the floor. Betsy shifted her gaze from Gaynor's face to the picture of a five-year-old Timothy playing with a litter of kittens.

"I am going to have a knee replacement in November."

"I didn't know you had scheduled it."

"In a month," Betsy repeated. In the warm sun, her blue eyes gazed serenely at the little boy and his kittens.

"Of course, I'll come back for that. I'll be here for the surgery."

"To stay?"

"I'm not sure. But I'll be with you all through your rehabilitation."

And as simply as that, without rules or boundaries, a gentle skirmish between the two women had begun.

Three days before the surgery, Gaynor returned from Sneem, full of lambing and barley tales, excited about the prospect of her parents' promised visit and made happy by the joy on Betsy's face when she opened the door.

Gaynor stayed with Betsy in the hospital the night before her surgery. After Betsy, dazed and sleepy, and so small, so vulnerable, had been rolled away, the next morning Gaynor went into the waiting room and there they were—Mary Martha, Sarah and Isabel.

"Oh, how I've missed you. I've been so lonesome without you," she said, moving from one warm embrace to the next.

"Thank you for coming. Oh, it's good to be home, to be with the three of you again."

"Your sisters," Sarah said, beaming.

"I've brought you presents. From the tinkers."

"Tinkers?"

"Travelers. Gypsies. The presents are Celtic. Here! Open them!"

The presents were wrapped in silver paper. "They're all alike," Gaynor said.

Exclaiming over the presents—three silver rings that quickly adorned the hands of the women—"They're like yours," Mary Martha said. "The one you always wear."

"And the old Celtic belief is that if you turn the ring three times round your finger, you will call up the wind, the wind that shakes the barley. I don't believe it. Not really. I wear mine as a talisman."

"What kind of wind shakes the barley?" Isabel asked and immediately began to turn her ring.

"A wind that brings the sailor home. And it brings the 'troubles.' A strong wind. Don't," Gaynor said. "Don't do that!"

"Do you believe it? You can't believe it!" Isabel said.

"No, not really. But who knows. Just don't turn it now. Please. Not with Betsy's surgery just beginning."

Isabel put her arm around Gaynor. "I won't. Come over here. Let's sit here, and you'll be telling us all about your parents and your wee lambs."

Laughing at Isabel's attempt at the Irish dialect, Gaynor said, "I'm thinking my da and ma will be visiting me next summer. They've heard so many good things about my life here in Cold Springs, they'll be coming for a visit."

"Good," Sarah said, "And now tell us all about your trip."

They talked together until Dr. Mitchell Young came to say the surgery had gone well and that Betsy would be on the golf course by Spring. Before the week was out, Betsy's rehabilitation was begun, and the two settled again into their old relationship.

It was during the third month of Betsy's rehabilitation that the skirmish between the women began again. Gaynor, in a bitterly cold rain, had driven to the drugstore to pick up a prescription for Betsy.

Waiting for the prescription to be filled, *hurriedly* refilled she hoped, she sat absentmindedly turning her ring. Afterwards, she *clearly* remembered that! she had turned her ring, and she had stopped immediately when she noticed it. Hurrying back to the car, she swung open its door just as a strong gust of wind and rain blew both the car door and the medicine out of her hands. She ran to catch the tumbling package, and when she returned, she saw that a dog had jumped into the front seat of her car.

"Well, hello!" she said. "What's your name? Where do you live?" she said as the dog, wagging its tail, submitted to Gaynor's search for its tags.

"No tags? Now who in the world are you?"

The dog lay down, put its nose between its paws and closed its eyes.

"Well now, aren't you the one, making yourself at home in my car."

Clearly a mutt, the dog was the size of a very large cat. Its coat was silver with black markings around its eyes and on its feet. Beneath the thick hair, the rib cage was bony. She rubbed its head. The tail wagged slowly. "Excuse me," she said and turned it over. A male. She looked at its teeth. "You're rather old," she told the dog. "About eight, I'd guess."

Hurrying, she returned to the store, found the manager and left her phone number with him. "He's a lovely wee thing," she told him. "Quite a nice little dog."

Hurrying down the aisles, she picked up a bag of dog food and a blue collar. Back in the car, "We need a dog," she told it. "And Mum needs a present."

In the utility room, she toweled him off, fed him and left him to dry. In the kitchen, she opened the prescription bottle, poured a glass of water and hurried to Betsy's bedside.

"A dog?" Betsy said.

Seconds passed. Fifteen? Twenty-five? Betsy's mouth grew thin, a frown appeared, her eyes narrowed. When she could no longer hold herself back, "Oh, Gaynor," she cried. "I don't want a dog. In this house! We can't keep a dog here!"

"Of course not," Gaynor said. "What was I thinking?"

Betsy's face slowly returned to its usual contented expression. Smilingly, she squeezed Gaynor's hand. "You do understand," she said.

"Of course," Gaynor said.

Gaynor did understand. She understood fully. She understood that this was not her house. Feeling as young as Timothy was in Betsy's photograph, Gaynor said, "There's an animal hospital in the shopping center. I'll take the dog there. They might know who his owner is."

By the time she reached the new veterinarian's animal hospital, Gaynor knew she had to have a place of her own. She could imagine Betsy's reaction to the news of her parents' approaching visit. "Why Gaynor," she would say. "Your parents coming? Over here? But Gaynor, we don't have another guest room!" And this said with a frown and a stern mouth. In Betsy's house, Irish pallets on the living room floor would not be possible.

It's time to grow up, Gaynor told herself. *I need a place of my own. And that beautiful little jewel of a house was never my home. How could I have thought that it was?*

With Barley under her arm (the name, so completely Irish, had jumped into her head), she opened the door of the veterinarian's office. A bell tinkled. A tall young man, wiping his hands on a paper towel came in. He held out an almost dry hand and shook hers.

"Bill Holly," he said.

He was far too young to be out of school. Was he out of school? "Are you the veterinarian?"

"Barely," he said. "I got my degree in January."

He looked at the dog and at her. He canted his head to the right and smiled. "How can I help you?"

"Barley is lost. He needs a home."

Glancing out the window, he said, "It's beginning to sleet. Come on back. Bring your lost dog, and I'll make a call or two. Maybe I can find Barley a home."

"I need to get back. Betsy's waiting."

"Who's Betsy?"

"My mother-in-law. Sort of. My husband, Timothy, is, *was* in the Peace Corps." Not saying he was dead, still she sighed.

"Look, we'll have a quick cup of coffee. Or hot chocolate."

"I'd love the hot chocolate."

And over the steaming chocolate, she told him about coming to Cold Springs and about Betsy, told him how much she loved Betsy, told him about Ireland—the lambing and the sheepdogs and the vast sweep of their land down to the sea. She told him about her brothers and their families, home from England and helping now, and she told him about the crowded house in Ireland. She still did not say to him, *my husband is dead.* Instead, she said, "I never discuss my problems in Cold Springs. I can't make them funny, even though I know some are. After all, a lost dog! It's silly. But to me it is a problem. And while I waited for Betsy's prescription, I turned my ring."

"Ring?"

"It's a superstition. Silly. But the wind did come. And it was the wind that brought Barley. "

Holding the dog, she sat in a straight-back chair, resting her right ankle on her left knee. *Like a boy,* Bill Holly thought.

"I don't walk under ladders," he said kindly.

Her face was pale. He could not tell whether her blue eyes glittered with anger or with tears as she spoke. He listened intently, immensely enjoying the lilt of her throaty voice, the cadence of her sentences. Nodding, smiling, frowning, his eyes did not leave her face except to respond to the doorbell or the ring of the telephone.

"My parents will be coming for a visit next summer," she said. "And I want a place of my own. But first, I need a job."

Bill Holly rose, placed his cup on an exam table and walked to the window. A hard rain, mixed with the pebbled sounds of hail hitting the windows, fell so that they were isolated, alone together in a room filled with empty cages and closed off from the cold outside world of wind and sleet and snow.

"Excuse me. Sorry," he said, turning to answer the telephone's ring.

Stand up straight, lad, and *Eat a stout breakfast,* she wanted to say to him, for his slightly stooped carriage and the lankiness of his thin frame reminded her of St. John, her youngest brother.

He replaced the receiver, crossed his arms, and apparently studying his shoes, he said, "Would you like a job here? I need someone. Another person. I can't pay much to start, but it might develop into a real job." Now, looking directly at her, he added, "And I can see you like animals." His face was suffused with his blushing. "That's the main thing about this job. It needs someone who likes animals." A smile touched his lips. "Your dog, Barley, could bunk here. With me."

"I'll take it."

"You will? You will! Well, it's done then. Now, about the money. . . ."

At the telephone's interruption, she held up a forefinger for silence, and picked up the receiver. "Good morning," she said. "Dr. Holly's office. And I'll be helping you now. This is Gaynor speaking to you."

Smiling widely, she took pad and pencil from his hand and wrote.

When she walked into Betsy's house, her anger was gone. She took a light supper to her bedside and, before Betsy picked up her soup spoon, Gaynor said, "I have a job."

Betsy put the spoon down and pulled her bed jacket close. "A job?"

Betsy always looked soft. Her bed jacket soft. Soft cashmere. The color was blue. A soft blue. But Betsy was not soft.

"It's a part-time job with a new veterinarian in town. He's just a kid. But I told him all about you and Timothy. And I told him about Ireland. You'll like him, Betsy."

Betsy smiled widely. She sat up straight in bed, reached for a cigarette and lit it. "Gaynor, I'm absolutely delighted. Every woman needs a little independence. Good for you. Now with this job, I'll have no more talk of your leaving me."

Gaynor laughed. "I'll never really leave you. Now taste that soup. It's potato and seasoned the way my ma seasons hers," she said. "Wait a second! I'll fetch a tray and join you. And I'll reheat your soup. Betsy, it's gone cold."

And if it occurred to either of the women that on that day Gaynor stopped calling Betsy "Mum," this was never mentioned.

PART 4: 1980

The Murder

A Person of Interest

Here he is, a fifty-one-year-old man, driving toward Cold Springs, a town he left over thirty years ago. He will not arrive there before darkness falls. Even before he reaches Greenville, the sun has set behind him, leaving the eastern sky tinged with pinks and oranges and blues, delicate colors lightly reflecting the blazing colors of the western sky. Exhausted by the ten-hour flight from London, he had considered and rejected his earlier idea of stopping in Greenville or Mount Vernon, and by the time he reaches Mount Pleasant, he is too close to home to stop. In an attempt to soften Anne Marie's death by recovering this place he has always loved, he has chosen to drive along the old highway 80, a two-lane route that leads him through the middle of small towns. He passes over and under deserted railroad tracks and alongside harvested fields and grazing cattle. The landscape is reassuring, not so much changed, only now and then a new house set back from the highway, the house so enormous that it dwarfs the newly planted trees alongside the drive leading to the house.

Always he has felt this pull toward home, intermittent and sharp, like a fish hitting his lure and spitting it out before he can get his thumb on the reel. Since Anne Marie's death, his longing for home has grown, but equating it with grief, he has dismissed it. Until now.

In the early years of their relationship, simply curious he asked, "Would you marry me and come to Texas?"

As he spoke, the two were sitting on a small balcony in Rome. Remembering the haunting guitar music wafting up from the Spanish Steps, he wonders now if the music evoked his question. Anne Marie, a small, slender woman, had stood, and walked to the balcony's wrought iron railing. Turning to face him, she leaned against the railing, resting her elbows on it. Frowning, she shook her head. "I would not leave my family," she said and added, "or my country."

After that conversation, when they talked about marriage it was always in the context of children. Anne Marie wanted children, but not his children.

"My children will be Italian, and they will be Catholic," she had always said to him.

She never asked if he would be willing to change his religion and take on dual citizenship for her. And he never said, "I love you. Marry me. Our children and I will be Catholic and Italian, and you will be greatly loved." He never said anything *like* that to her.

Their relationship had been deeply satisfying to him and, he believed, to Anne Marie. When he arrived at the airport in Florence, she was always there, irrepressibly joyous, falling into his arms, whispering Italian words of love. When he was in town, they joined her family for their Sunday gatherings amid old Tuscany vineyards. Although her immediate family was small, they were an integral part of her extended family—cousins, uncles, aunts, grandparents, and nieces and nephews. Watching the children, who called him *Tio*, play around the tables that had been set out in the ancient olive grove, tables laden with food, and listening to the passionate and affectionate conversations among the adults, he would say to himself and to her: "This is family enough for us."

When Anne Marie died in a train crash on a bright October day, she was thirty-seven years old, ten years younger than he. Her death had plunged him into the blackest despair. He grieved because he had not loved her enough and because she was too young to die. He grieved because they had not had enough time to sort things out. He grieved because he had not let her go. Had he allowed her, *urged* her to leave him, she might have married an adoring Italian man whose children she would have wanted. She would not have been on a train to Florence to meet him. This is what he told himself.

For years her family continued to invite him to their Sunday picnics. But slowly, imperceptibly, they grew apart. Anne Marie had kept her family close, sending birthday presents, passing along family gossip and jumping into the middle of family crises. Now his warm and loving intermediary was gone.

Three years later, on the anniversary of her death, her mother said to him, "She should have had children. Italian women need children," and, turning away, she cried into her handkerchief. And although Jackson was not fluent in Italian, he heard the bitterness in her voice.

❅

After Anne Marie's death, his urge to return to Cold Springs grew. The way the sun, coming through trees in Caracas, might hit the ground with flickering light; the keening of the coastal winds of Wales; a clothesline hung with laundry on a balcony in Italy—a thousand things reminded him of home.

He never knew when it would happen. Anything could start it up. Once, it happened when he walked into the lobby of a hotel in Madrid and caught a whiff of something, unidentifiable, pungent, hugely familiar. Instantly, he was there, in the high school gym with the band, the cheerleaders, the roar of the crowd, and the weight of the basketball on his finger tips, his feet planted on the line, knees relaxed, his eye on the basket, then, lifting the ball—once, twice and finally, pushing it up into the air. It was all there, whole and intact as if it had happened yesterday. After dinner that night he went to bed and slept, but in the middle of the night he got up and walked until daylight.

In April, he was sitting at a sidewalk café in London when he saw a woman walking down the other side of the street.

Her walk—the languor of it in the easy sway of her hips—was as familiar to him as his own face in the mirror. It had to be Isabel. He threw some money on the table and followed her. Here she was. Unmistakably Isabel, an older Isabel. But when she turned her head to hail a cab, he saw that the woman was not Isabel. He had simply conjured her up. Bemused, he thought about her, knowing she was almost certainly in Cold Springs, Texas, where she had always been.

Now he began to think seriously about going home. Not to see Isabel. Not to open old wounds. He had no reasons he could put on the table to return. His parents were dead. His friends would have either moved away or would have changed beyond recognition. All that remained for him was the place—a pretty town with its shady, graveled roads and ice cold springs and blue lakes; and the clean smell of the pines and the scent of wild plum blossoms in spring. And the river. He longed to be on the river again.

He had been a suspect in the murders. Almost every boy in high school had been a suspect. If he had never left, never run away. . . . Until he left the country, a friend had written, always about the latest news about the murders. Occasionally, an arrest would be made. Or some man in prison would confess. But it had all come to nothing. As far as he knew the crime remained unsolved.

But all that was in the past. He would take his time settling in. Then he would look up some old friends. For the first time since Anne Marie's death, he began to look forward to the future.

The decision made, he sold his interests in the Venezuelan oil service company, but it took a month for his lawyers and his associates' lawyers to satisfy all parties, including both governments. The day after the papers were signed, he packed his bags, checked out of the hotel and caught the next plane to Dallas.

❈

It is three o'clock in the morning when he checks into the Holiday Inn in Cold Springs. He sleeps late. It's after ten o'clock before he showers, shaves and dresses. Then he strolls around the hotel grounds but, fenced in by concrete parking lots and the interstate, he shortens his walk and buys a paper in the lobby, the last one in the machine. He enters the small restaurant, chooses a seat and orders coffee and a ham and eggs breakfast from a blond waitress exuding friendliness.

"Honey, you want those eggs fried or scrambled?" she asks, taking a pencil from behind her ear and scratching her shoulder with it.

He has forgotten how affectionate the Southern banter sounds. Grinning, he says, "Soft-scrambled. Can you do that?"

Walking off, she looks back over her shoulder and winks. "I'll tell the cook," she says.

He reads the front page. President Carter is in Venice with the leaders of the first world countries. They are in agreement on the need for energy independence. The Olympics are to be in Moscow. The Shah of Iran is dead. He wonders how many days the American hostages seized by Iranian students have been held. The news that had seemed urgent to him in Europe now seems a long way off. He walks over to the jukebox, a nice old-fashioned touch, slides in a couple of quarters and plays John Lennon's "Imagine." Then he settles down to enjoy his breakfast.

This morning he had begun to realize how much everything has changed—fast food places along I-30; huge houses replacing the weathered, unpainted farmhouses; more cattle in every pasture; small towns spread miles beyond their city limits—everything has changed. Or almost everything. The sky is still big. The trees green. The heart of the town—the post office, Main Street, the library and the churches—remain unchanged. And the river drifts around the town as it always has.

After breakfast he begins his search, and for eight days he drives through the countryside looking for land. Then he finds it. The Tanner farm is for sale. This farm, bounded on the north by Red River, on the east by a four-acre lake and on the south by a narrow creek flowing into the river, is magnificent. The pecan trees—natives and grafted Stewarts and paper shells—are mature and, once they are fertilized and trimmed, will easily bear 30,000 to 40,000 pounds of pecans a year. The pastures are bountiful. The soybeans green. Jackson has hunted on the place and fished from its banks, and he knows every acre of it. He cannot believe his luck.

The next week, he hunkers down with a real estate agent, going back and forth with the Dallas owner about the price, although it is not far off the mark. The owner lowers his price by 50,000 dollars when Jackson offers cash.

The next day he drives to Genoa to find Oscar Peterson, the only person he had kept up with all these years. He stops at a filling station in Genoa and fills up. The man behind the cash register does not seem interested in whether Jackson pays or not, but he nods when he steps inside. Counting out the dollars into a hand missing an index finger, he says, "I'm looking for a man I used to know. Oscar Peterson. Do you know him?"

The man nods. "I might."

Jackson grins. Was the man's answer motivated by caution or curiosity? He would satisfy the curiosity. "When I was a boy, Mr. Peterson ran a farm on the river about fourteen miles outside Cold Springs. I just bought that place."

The man leans forward. "Strictly confidential. Oscar has a place a half-a-mile down the road, the first turn on the left," he says. He glances around the store and, as if not quite satisfied that the two are alone, he leans even closer. "You'll know it. He's got some mighty fine horses out there."

Ten minutes later, Jackson pulls into a long drive beside a small white frame house. A huge red barn stands behind it. He honks twice, gets out of his car and leans against the fender. When he sees a gray-headed man, slightly stooped, striding toward him from the barn, he walks to meet him.

Ignoring Jackson's outstretched hand, Oscar grabs him in an enthusiastic bear hug. "Son," Oscar says, beaming, "where in the world did you come from? I'm mighty glad to see you. Doggone it. It's been way too long. Now tell me. How in the hell are you?"

"I've come a long way to get here. A lot has happened since I left your place that morning. If you have all day, then I've got a proposition for you."

The men, grinning at each other, stroll toward the front porch, the gray-headed man with an arm thrown over Jackson's shoulders. They sit in chairs, side by side on Oscar's porch—the one, kindly, weathered, bent and the other as eager to please as a boy. Shoulders almost touching, they look straight ahead.

"I never knew a boy who loved the Bottoms the way you did."

"I guess that's the main reason I came home."

"It's not about that woman? Miss Jessup, she was? Did you know that Mr. Arnold, her husband, died more'n ten years ago. As far as I know, she lives alone."

"No. I didn't know that. I've wondered about her. But she's not the reason I came home." He reaches over, slaps Oscar's knee. "I've not forgotten how good you were to me the times I couldn't go home. That last time."

"Anybody would have helped a kid like you." Oscar pulls a knife from his pocket, opens it, picks up a piece of wood. "And if there ever comes a time you need me again, you know where to find me."

"I think the dust has settled from all that. But thanks, I will. I'll holler."

Oscar tilts his chair against the wall of the house and begins to whittle. Jackson smiles. Better than words, whittling is Oscar's way of saying that he has all the time in the world. Satisfied, Jackson stretches out his legs and clasps his hands in his lap.

"The night I came to your place, I was running away because of a promise I'd made. And I didn't want to be questioned again. Or beaten. I was running away from just about everything in Cold Springs."

"Some folks don't need children. They're not cut out for it."

"Things all worked out. With the money you loaned me, I caught the first bus out of town and got a job roughnecking in the oil fields around Houston. Then I got a job with an oil field service company. I worked there almost three years, and then Schlumberger sent me to Venezuela. After a couple of promotions, I advanced to management and a stockholding position. That company sold out to an Italian company that provided services to the Italian oil and gas industry. I spent a lot of time in Rome. God, I loved that city, loved the people. There was a woman . . ." He was silent for a good while. Clearing his throat, he said, "When everything fell apart I started to think about coming back."

The two men sit, shoulder-to-shoulder, both looking straight ahead. Oscar has whittled a piece of wood into a small boat. They sit in silence, watching a hawk high overhead, drifting and turning on invisible air currents until, sighting its prey, it dives down into the pasture.

Oscar chuckles. "Dinner time. I'll fix something."

After a late meal of steak and a pan of onions and fries cooked on Oscar's grill, Jackson drives away, satisfied with a contract sealed by a handshake. He, Jackson, will set up an account at the local bank. Oscar will begin cross fencing the pastures immediately, and, later, he'll buy cattle, Angus cattle. All the invoices submitted by the architect and contractors will be submitted to Oscar or to him for an authorized signature.

When he walks through the gates to the lumberyard the next day, the first thing he sees is a hat on the other side of a stack of lumber. The hat, no more than a gray shard, floats, stops, disappears and reappears.

"Olly, we got that high grade stuff coming in from Colorado," a man, from beneath the hat, says. "Put it inside the barn. It's antique, and it's had enough weathering."

The voice is deeper, more gravelly, but unmistakably Olson's. If Jackson had considered it at all, he would have guessed that Mr. Olson would most likely be dead. Must be well over ninety, Jackson marvels. He walks to the end of the lumber row, turns the corner and almost bumps into Olson. The old man has shrunk. He's all veins and sinew, wiry but without muscle.

Jackson offers his hand. "Good morning, Mr. Olson," he says. "I don't know whether you remember me. Jackson Morris. I see you're still going strong."

Blinking, Olson narrows his green eyes, gone cold as ice, and pushes his head forward past a neck as wrinkled as a turtle's. "You're the kid who started that fire in my lumberyard," he says.

Jackson had forgotten. How could he have forgotten that! He takes a deep breath as the memory of the fire, the smell and smoke of it, flashes over him.

"There were seven or eight of us shooting off fireworks," Jackson says finally. "The Roman candle that started it might have been mine. But I paid for the damages."

Astonishingly, Jackson feels his heart shock into a faster beat. He begins to sweat. Flight or fight? Neither is an option. Starting with Olson was hard luck. But with the old man, shrunken and bent, standing in front of him, he wills himself to try again. Maybe money will warm him up.

"I need some fencing material," Jackson says, again offering his hand.

Olson studies the hand. "Kids," he says, dismissively, and takes it in a firm handclasp. "Son, now how much fencing you gonna need?"

Jackson follows him into his small office, smiling now about this, his first encounter with the past. Olson takes a seat in the swivel chair behind his desk and motions Jackson toward the small, straight-backed chair in front. He draws a long yellow legal tablet close and picks up a pencil.

Seeing the yellow tablet and the pencil poised to take down feet and inches and grade, Jackson smiles. "Oscar Peterson, my farm manager, will be here this week to order the fencing," he says. "Do you know Mr. Peterson?"

"Fine man. A good farmer," Olson growls.

"I'd like to set up a line of credit with you before he comes in. Could we work something out?"

"I'd take a check on a local bank."

"My bank's not local yet. But it will be by Monday. Mr. Peterson will be an authorized signer on the checks."

"Appreciate your business," Olson says.

Without replying, Jackson walks out of the lumberyard. When he opens the car door, he looks back over his shoulder and sees that Olson has followed. Jackson lifts his hand, waves and drives off before Olson can decide whether to return the gesture or not.

His final stop is at Orr's Ford dealership. Now he is even more determined to let the town come to him. Oscar's offer of help signaled that the town is not yet ready to forget the boy who was arrested for starting a fire in a lumberyard, the high school kid who ran away just days before graduation. At Orr's, Jackson half expects to see someone there he knows, but the man who handles the sell is a stranger. He buys a pickup and leases a house trailer.

The next Monday, he drives out to Wendle Brothers Cattle Barn. He takes a seat three rows up and keeps his eye on the cattle, chuckling now and then at the embellishments of the auctioneer's descriptions of the cows and bulls. Oscar buys nine Angus cows, two with calves on them, and a registered, blue ribbon Angus bull. It will be a start.

During the week it takes to get a power line to the house trailer and a propane tank installed, he sleeps at the Holiday Inn, dividing his time between the farm and possible contractors in the area. At night he sketches one idea after another in an attempt to imagine what his house will be like until, exhausted, he falls into bed and sleeps.

When he moves onto the farm, he begins a schedule that almost never varies. Sitting on the trailer steps each morning, he drinks a cup of coffee and has a piece of toast. Then, driven by an urge to know every undulation of the land and every tree, bird, and beast on it, he walks over the farm.

By March the farm is his. His cattle graze in fenced pastures. He knows the trees—the pecans, the sycamores, the willows, the oaks and the bois d'arc. He knows their shapes and sizes. He has studied the curves of the creek as it flows from the lake into the river. When evening falls, he walks up a slight rise that offers the finest view of the sunset: a commingling of colors in sky and water. As he watches the slow enveloping of the day by the night, he feels a sense of ease.

He sets up a meeting with an investment banker in Dallas. Determined to keep a low profile, "No, I'll drive to Dallas," he tells the banker. After a meeting with Henry Drier who knows about money management and investing but nothing about a farm's enticements, he decides to take a different route home, driving due north and then east to Cold Springs. Outside Sherman, he glances at a house under construction, looks at it again and caught by the unexpectedness of form and line and color, he pulls off the highway and stops. Something about the lines of the house and the way it gradually reveals itself (is the roof thatched?) give it a natural beauty.

He stops, backs up and turns into the narrow dirt road that leads to the house. When he closes the car door, he sees a man high on a ladder against the house. "Good afternoon," he calls.

The man hastily climbs down and, ignoring the last two rungs, jumps to the ground. He holds out his hand. "Billy Suggs," he says.

The handshake is firm; the hand roughly calloused. Although Billy's yellow shirt is wet clear through with sweat, his expression is cheerful.

"My name's Jackson. Jackson Morris. I'd like to meet the man who's building this house," Jackson said. "It's different, but, somehow, it fits East Texas."

"Bet you never seen a thatched roof before," Billy says. "We get a lot of lookers."

He puts a small hammer back into the tool belt around his waist, takes his cap off, shakes it and replaces it. "Well, you're in luck. The owner's not here, but the architect, he's around here somewhere. Name's Victor. Victor Siddons. Come on. We'll find him."

Twenty minutes later, Victor has the directions to Jackson's farm tucked into his shirt pocket, and Jackson's grin is as wide as Billy's. Maybe, just maybe, he has found the right man to design his house.

When Jackson steps out of the trailer the next morning, he sees Victor's Ford some distance away and a newspaper on the trailer steps. But no sign of Victor. Bemused, shaking his head, he goes back inside, pours a cup of coffee and sits outside to wait.

Before he finishes his coffee, Victor emerges from the willows along the river and climbs through a barbed wire fence into a pasture. Three or four cows, curious, slowly follow the slender man who occasionally glances over his shoulder at the cows.

"How long have you been here?" Jackson calls.

"Since daybreak. I thought I'd walk over your place, but walking it takes longer than I thought. Four hundred acres. Wow."

Victor's brown eyes shine behind the brown-rimmed glasses. His smile is wide.

"Thanks for the paper. How about a cup of coffee?" Jackson says, wondering if he hasn't made a mistake. Today Victor looks twice as young as he remembered. More like a college kid. Pouring coffee for Victor, *What the hell*, Jackson tells himself now. The kid was enthusiastic about coming over here and he, Jackson, *had* liked the thatched roof. It wasn't the design he wanted, but it had substance and grace. He is glad Victor has come. The only thing either of them has to lose is a few hours.

All day they walk over the land, stopping for sandwiches at high noon and later, stopping to allow Victor's quick sketches of a meadow, the stream, an imagined roofline or great room. In the middle of the afternoon, they stop to have a drink— Dos Equis for Jackson and iced tea for Victor.

Now and then, Victor asks a question. "So you came back home because of the river and pines and lakes. It is pretty country," he says. "After living in Caracas and Rome and London, you came back here. How does *that* feel?"

"I'm not sure yet. I'm keeping in mind what Wolfe said."

"You can't go home again?"

"Yep," Jackson chuckles. "But come on!" he says, springing to his feet. "I've got something to show you!"

He leads the way up to the highest point on the farm and, together, they watch the sun drop below the trees and the sky fill with colors and the river fill with the same colors.

Walking back toward the trailer, Victor says, "I think you've found the site for your house. A house built on the fringe between the woods and the meadows, a house situated there would offer both shelter and repose. Think of it! A house, your house, coupled with the grandeur of the river!"

"I don't want a grand house."

"No," Victor agrees.

Leaning over the kitchen table that night, Victor talks as he sketches ideas that come to him, one following immediately on the heels of another. "Situated at this angle, a man living here would be sheltered from the north winds," he says. And sketching a screened-in terrace, "In the winter you would sit on the south terrace. The sun would be warm," he says, smiling so that Jackson can almost feel the sun's warmth. When he sketches an attached deck leading to an outdoor fireplace on still another terrace, he says, "Here you would entertain old friends from high school," and Jackson imagines Isabel with her head thrown back, laughing.

Bemused by the sketches and the words Victor chooses, Jackson rests an elbow on the table and cups his chin in the palm of his hand.

"What material would you prefer? Let's talk about that."

"Something strong. Sturdy. Maybe pine?" Jackson says.

"And we might look at cypress. Cypress is local to the area. We might even be able to find some cypress that has been dredged up from swamps. This wood is unbelievably rugged. Cypress resists traumas that ordinary wood would succumb to."

"I like that idea," Jackson says. "We'll look at cypress. And the driveway?" Jackson said. "We don't want to take down any trees. The drive will have to wind around them."

"Yes! The drive to the house will be a journey! Mysterious! The house—set back, assured, simple."

And leaning over the table, Victor sketches the long approach, the long journey to a house, a house—set back, assured and simple. The moon is high in the sky when an agreement is reached, the contract signaled by a high five.

Not until the next morning does Jackson realize how much of himself he has revealed to Victor—his strange yearning to return to Cold Springs and his doubts about the wisdom of coming back. And he further realizes that by means of Victor's sketches and his verbal malarkey, his pastures have become meadows, the porches have become terraces, his driveway a journey. The whole farm, a metamorphosis. Jackson likes it.

By early April, the farm is a hive of activity. Once a week Victor, lyrical and practical, impulsive and wise, arrives, some weeks in a propeller-driven plane he flies over from Dallas. Landing on a runway Jackson keeps mowed for him, he climbs out of the plane, carrying drawings and, sometimes, food and beer. He always brings newspapers—the *Dallas Morning News*, the *Cold Springs Gazette*, the *New York Times*—picked up at the Dallas airport.

Jackson reads that scientists believe the *Titanic* has been found. Nigeria has demanded the return of millions of barrels of oil from the Gulf, Mobil and Royal Dutch oil companies. And Ted Kennedy has left the field to Carter.

Jackson finds himself looking forward to Victor's visits and the news. Realizing he misses the give and take of good conversation, he decides to look up an old friend or two, get reacquainted. But then a strange thing happens. Driving to Louisiana to meet a sub, Jackson has reached the city limits of Cold Springs when a warning light on the dashboard of his pickup appears. The engine begins to heat up so rapidly that he pulls over and stops. When a car approaches, he flags it down and walks toward the car, surprised by the fact that a woman has stopped to help. But when he gets close, the woman accelerates and, tires squealing, speeds away in a hail of dust and gravel.

He stands there, in the middle of the highway, and watches the car until it is out of sight. Strangely, the driver reminded him of a girl he once knew. Mary Martha Mercer. Could it have been Mary Martha? No! he tells himself firmly. The woman who sped away was clearly frightened. Mary Martha would have helped him out.

He walks a mile to the nearest service station. By the time he finds a wrecker to pick up his car and rents another one it is too late to keep his appointment.

Later that evening, he walks along the bank of the river trying to rediscover the peace of that early morning. Maybe coming back was a mistake. Thinking of the woman who had driven away, he remembers Mary Martha as a small girl with a lisp who seemed younger than the others. He decides to call her when he returns from Louisiana.

Three days later he heads home, *home,* satisfied with the decisions he has made. When he reaches the farm, the workers have gone, and he walks through the construction site, relishing the idea of what it will mean to him, a place filled with camaraderie and laughter, a place for passionate conversations and lavish meals, a place like an Italian farm without olive groves. Wolfe had it wrong. You *can* go home again.

When they had first walked over the property, Victor had asked, "What do you plan to name the house?"

"I hadn't thought about a name."

"But what if you were to name it? What if it were to have a secret name?"

Jackson had thought of the fish in the river and of the deer making their way across the land. Had thought of the migrations of birds. "If it had a name, *if,*" he answered, "it would be *Wild Thrush Crossing.*"

"That is the house I will build," Victor had said.

Finding Mary Martha

The news is all over town. Everybody has heard it. Jackson Morris has come back home. Been back six months. A year. A few weeks. Who knows? Folks say Jackson has most likely been holed up somewhere, but this morning he came out of hiding and made three stops in Cold Springs. The first stop was at the First National Bank where he deposited a cashier's check to add money to the account he had set up for a house he was building somewhere in the country.

"I want to be sure the paperwork's in place so that Mr. Peterson can sign all checks on that account," he said.

Albert Aston was all smiles when he heard about the deposit. Fifty thousand dollars was a respectable amount of money. And the cashier's check was written on a London bank. Cold Springs didn't get many deposits from overseas banks.

His next stop was at Orr's Chevrolet where he paid cash for a Ford tractor. Then Jackson, accompanied by Oscar Peterson, appeared at the Wendle Brothers' auction in New Boston and bought another dozen Angus cows, costing a right smart of cash money. According to Buck Buchanan, Jackson is as polite and good humored as if he had never left Cold Springs under a cloud. By nightfall everybody in town was wondering about all that money. Late that Friday afternoon, folks caught themselves looking up at the sky, half expecting to catch sight of that red prop plane they had heard about. But the sky remained clear.

Everybody knows Jackson has come back, but nobody knows what to make of it. They sit back, cross their arms and wait for Jackson to make the next move.

❉

On Tuesday, Willie B. is dusting the chandelier in the living room when Isabel stumbles out of bed, pees and splashes cold water on her face. Still in her bright green nightgown, she heads down the hall toward the kitchen for her first cup of coffee. When she glances into the living room and sees Willie B. standing on a chair, dusting the balloon chandelier with a feather duster, she stops. "Willie B. what in the world are you doing?"

"What you see. That's what I'm doing."

"Good lord. What time is it?"

"Late," Willie B. says, too busy to stop her dusting. "You forgetting it's your bridge day?"

"No, I just slept late. I've got to get a cup of coffee."

Coming back into the room, Isabel sits on a sofa, holding the cup cradled in her hands. She takes a swallow of coffee. Then another. "Willie B., a morning cup of coffee is one of the pure pleasures of life."

"You having your bridge ladies today?"

"Why wouldn't I be having them?"

Willie B. takes hold of the back of the chair and carefully steps down. Holding her feather duster in her right hand she puts both hands on her hips so that the feather duster takes on the air of a saucy dance hall girl's adornment. "He's back."

"Jackson."

"How come you didn't know?"

"I went to Dallas yesterday. Drove home late. Who told you?"

"I saw him. Knew it was him. He saw me and touched the brim of his hat, like he was just saying, 'hello.' Lord, have mercy! A shiver went down my spine."

"Where did you see him? When?"

"About ten minutes ago. I was turning into the drive."

At this news, Isabel is suffused with pleasure. She leans forward and, elbows on her knees, rests her chin on hands folded into fists. She sits smiling down at the figure of an oriental warrior on his horse woven into the rug before her. Jackson had been a warrior of sorts.

Willie B. flashes a quick look toward Isabel. "Whatever way you arrange your business, I don't see it as a reason for a smile."

Isabel shrugs. The phone begins to ring.

At the second ring, "Want me to answer it?"

"Yes. And tell whoever it is that, yes, I'm having bridge today. Tell them to come early. Say I'm in the shower. And whoever calls next, tell them the same thing. And the shower's where I'm going right now."

"Nothing good will come of this," Willie B. says woefully, picking up the receiver on its seventh ring. "She's in the shower right now. Yes, ma'am, we surely are. She says to come early." Raising her voice, she calls out to Isabel, who had stopped to listen but is now hurrying down the hall to her bedroom. "That was Mrs. Carter. I told her what you said. You want me to make some soup? It'll be asparagus. The ladies like asparagus. And some cookies? I'll make some cookies."

Isabel stops and walks halfway back. "Willie B., for all anybody will notice, we can have peanut butter and jelly sandwiches today."

"You got that right," Willie B. says.

Stepping into the shower, the thought comes that she, Isabel, has always known this would happen. Jackson would come home. She feels floatingly light-headed, as if it has already happened, maybe in some other life. Now Jackson has come back, and everything will unfold as it should have unfolded all those years ago. She is powerless to stop it. Whatever happens now was meant to happen thirty-four years ago.

When the doorbell rings, she calls out to Willie B., "Tell Sarah to come on back here."

She slips a silk blouse from its hanger and steps into fawn-colored pants. Lacing and tying her oxford shoes, she tells herself, "Sarah's early and the weather's balmy. We'll take a little walk. Not that I want to see Jackson." She puts on her makeup, brushes her hair and, after a minute, "That's not true," she tells herself. "I'm crazy to see Jackson."

When Isabel comes from her dressing room, Sarah is standing in the middle of the room staring at a trowel she holds in her hand. "I didn't know I had it in my hand," she says. Sarah's hair is pulled back and twisted in a small bun at the base of her neck. Her blue-checked dress is pristine, but her shoes are muddy.

Sarah's evident excitement evokes a chuckle from Isabel. "It's true," Isabel says. "Jackson has come back home."

"Who told *you*? Didn't you go to Dallas?"

"Willie B. She saw him this morning. Who told you?"

"I had my hair done yesterday afternoon."

"Josefina."

"She says people can't decide how to feel about Jackson. She asked me what I thought. I said that as far as I know, it's still a free country."

"It's early. Let's take a walk. The sun's out."

"My shoes. . . ."

"Of all days to wear heels! Well, you look great. What's the occasion? Jackson?"

Shaking her head, Sarah says, "I knew you might think that. But Josefina said she heard the newspaper might be out here asking us about Jackson, asking what we think about Jackson coming home."

"Well, let me go tell Willie B. right now that I don't intend to have reporters coming into this house and asking about Jackson. Considering the newspaper and your shoes, let's skip the walk. Come on! I need another cup of coffee and a piece of toast. How about you?"

"Coffee sounds good."

In the kitchen Willie B. has the asparagus on the stove. Now she's rolling out cookie dough for walnut cookies.

Sarah puts her hands on her hips and grins. "Good morning, Willie B. I hear you saw Jackson," she says.

"Yes ma'am. Sure did."

"Is he still good-looking?"

"Mrs. Carter, he never was good looking to me."

"A car's coming," Sarah says then, hurrying to peer out the window. "It's Gaynor."

"Sarah, let her in. Please. I'll bring coffee to the living room." Moving quickly, Isabel gets out a tray, puts stacked cups and saucers on it and pours cream into a pitcher.

Willie B. frowns at the tray Isabel has prepared. "Only Gaynor takes cream," she says, replacing the large pitcher with a smaller one. "You go on in. I'll make a cup of tea for Gaynor."

"Willie B., she's the only one you call by her first name. Why is that?"

"She asked me to."

"Oh," Isabel says. She looks sharply at Willie B., torn between the news about Jackeon that seems to call for some kind of action and her desire to hurry Willie B. into the modern age where her own feet are firmly planted. She is not sure about where Willie B.'s feet are. After a minute, "Well I'm curious to see Jackson. It's crazy, but I want to see him."

"Everybody wants to see him. Maybe they could round him up, put him in a cage and charge admission."

"That's not funny."

"Jackson coming home is what's not funny. Miss Isabel, now you go on. Let me get this tray fixed."

Sarah and Gaynor sit on the long sofa, their attitude one of expectant waiting. Gaynor wears a black cotton dress, flat woven sandals and a necklace of woven cord from which a small wooden cross hangs. Her bright hair, almost shoulder length, is carelessly held up in back with a tortoise shell comb. After greeting each other, they have not said another word. When Isabel comes into the room, they look up at her like children waiting to be told what to do.

"Well," Isabel says. Standing before them, she runs both hands through her hair pushing it off her neck and away from her face. She looks directly at Sarah. "It's started, hasn't it?"

Sarah, usually solid, complete, certain, leans forward. "I'm not sure. I don't know. Maybe," she says.

"Jackson is back. Everything will unfold," Isabel says. Her face, her voice are the embodiment of serenity.

"Or unravel." Now Sarah's voice is crisp and sure.

Crossing her arms, Gaynor leans back against the sofa. "You Texas women with your secrets. Look here now. Betsy's told me about Jackson and those terrible murders. And you think Jackson may be guilty. If you feel uncomfortable talking in front of me, I'll leave. Right now."

Isabel sits in a big chair, kicks off her shoes and, reaching for her ankle, pulls her right leg up beside her. "Gaynor, you stay right where you are," she says. "When Mary Martha gets here, what time is it, anyway? As soon as she comes, we'll talk all this through." And to Willie B., entering with a tray, "You, too, Willie B.," she says mischievously, as Willie B. puts the tray on the table and turns to leave. "You know something about all this."

"No, ma'am. Not me. What I know I'm keeping to my own self. You won't see me messing around in white folks' affairs."

Shaking her head, Isabel watches Willie B. leave the room. "When Willie B.'s cross about something, she talks like that." Smiling broadly, she adds, "And she messes round in my affairs whenever she takes a notion."

Sarah crosses her legs and picks up a deck of cards and shuffles them. Remembering Mary Martha's plan to get a passport, she impatiently replaces the cards on the bridge table and wanders over to look through the windows at Isabel's pitiful garden, considering that Isabel has a full-time gardener. "Isabel, what in the world are you doing?"

Isabel, carrying a small stepladder, has walked to the end of the living room, and is looking up at her balloon chandelier.

"Sarah," she calls, "come hold this light bulb for me. I want to change a bulb that's gone out."

She unscrews one, hands it to Sarah and replaces that one with a new bulb. "Now where in the world is Mary Martha? What time is it anyway?" she says and, as if in answer, the clock begins to chime.

Sarah looks at her watch, "Eleven," she says confirming the clock.

"I'll call her. The news must have completely unsettled her. She may have had second thoughts about coming."

Watching Isabel climb down from the ladder, Sarah says, "Wonder why she hasn't called."

"She should have," Isabel says over her shoulder, crossly.

"I'd like to meet Jackson," Gaynor says. "Betsy said he did their yard work one summer. Timothy was only a little boy following Jackson around trying to help. I wonder what Timothy was like, what they talked about. Do you think I'll ever see Jackson?"

"If they don't put him in jail first," says Sarah.

When Isabel returns, she has thrown her blue silk scarf around her neck.

"She doesn't answer. We'll have lunch as soon as Willie B. can get it on the table. Then, we'll drive out to Mary Martha's. O.K.?"

"Sure."

"Absolutely!"

Walking to the kitchen, Isabel leaves the dining room door swinging. "Willie B., could we have lunch early? We're going out to see about Mary Martha."

Coming back into the room, Isabel sits up straight, both feet on the floor. "We know that something has been going on with her."

"I'll be asking her today what the something is," Gaynor says, taking the comb from her hair and shaking it down around her shoulders.

"Last week I ran into her when she was almost skipping, yes, skipping! out of the bank. Her cheeks were flushed; she was giggly. I said, 'Mary Martha, what in the world is going on with you?' She put her hand over her mouth. I took her hand away and said, 'Tell me.' She said, 'Isabel, I do have a little news, but it will keep until Tuesday.' I thought she'd tell us her news over bridge today. "

Impatiently, Gaynor leans over to fasten her sandal more tightly. "Mary Martha has been quite happy lately," she says. "It's as if she's had a sea change."

"A sea change sounds good," Sarah says.

But, now, here's Willie B. saying lunch is on the table, and from somewhere, like magic, there's the creamy soup and the tomatoes with thinly sliced provolone cheese and homemade rolls. And, for those few minutes over lunch, time is reversed into normalcy.

"We'll take soup out to her," Sarah says.

"What a good idea." And Isabel is off again to the kitchen to ask Willie B. to get the soup into a container and wrap up the rolls and cookies.

After lunch, and this with just one glass of sherry, they get into Isabel's car and in no time at all they are in Mary Martha's driveway where nothing is right because there is a police car in the driveway, its lights flashing and an officer walking over to Isabel's car.

"And what brings you ladies out here in the middle of the day?" he asks and tips his hat, but without a smile on his face and nothing but danger in his voice.

Isabel, ignoring the officer, leaps out of her car and strides up the walk to Mary Martha's front door. And then she's ringing the doorbell and knocking and calling out, "Mary Martha! Mary Martha! For God's sake answer the door!"

The officer is behind her now. Touching her arm, he turns her away from the door. His voice is gruff: "She won't answer. She can't. Your friend, she's dead. She was strangled to death. They found her body this morning. Alongside the creek, in the woods near her house."

And hearing it, but not absorbing it, Isabel stumbles toward Gaynor and Sarah, and they hold each other and weep.

I See the Moon

By early afternoon of that same day, the news about Mary Martha's murder is all over the town. In times of tragedy the people in Cold Springs have their cars washed. And vacuumed. Cars will be needed to pick up people at the airport and at the bus station. Two years ago Sarah had had to drive to Shreveport to collect Isabel's cousins when her mother died. And cars would be needed to take people to the church. And the funeral procession! For the procession the Super Wash would be called for. Sarah's car and Sarah will be indispensable. On her way home from Isabel's, Sarah pulls into Nathan's service station for the Super Wash.

"Oh, David," she says to the car washer who is wiping it dry, polishing the chrome, and opening the car door for her with a flourish, "one of my best friends has been murdered. I feel like I'm having a bad dream." Her voice trembles. Tears flow. She pulls out a tissue and blows her nose.

Speechless at being so close to crime, David merely nods. After Sarah drives off, David finds his voice and tells everybody—those who come for gas or the car wash or Texas Lotto—about the murder. He tells strangers where Bryce's cafeteria is, and then he tells them about Ms. Mercer. "Her friend was just in here, getting her car washed," adding "The Super Wash."

And at the bank, the news spreads. Albert Aston, usually reticent to the point of ridiculous secrecy, stands in the middle of the bank's lobby, pulling a white handkerchief from his pocket and wiping the tears from his eyes. "I just can't believe this. I haven't been as shocked since Rosemary Winslow was murdered. Now why in the world would anybody hurt Mary Martha?" And then remembering her response when he had asked her if she would like to go out with him, he adds,

"Sometimes, she could be a little too honest. But murdered. I feel like there's been a mistake."

Privately, Albert Aston thinks the whole situation is a mistake. Cold Springs' reaction to Mary Martha's death is a mistake. Front page coverage; headlines over that silly little snit. Still, something good might come of it. Maybe the sheriff will get up enough nerve to charge Jackson. It's about time! Everybody in town thinks Jackson murdered Rosemary. And now that Mary Martha's dead, people will put two and two together. The sheriff will have to arrest Jackson, unless he leaves town first.

Everybody who comes into the bank or drives through the drive-by windows or gets money from an ATM hears the news. "Can you believe it!" they say. "Who would do such a thing? Such a wonderful lady. So gentle she wouldn't hurt a flea."

Sarah puts her car in the garage, rubs a tissue over a smudge on the front fender, goes inside and calls Clovis. The first words Clovis utters make her teeth hurt.

"I knew it," said Clovis. "Living out there in the country. I knew something was going to happen to Aunt Mary Martha. I've worried about all of you, all alone, sleeping alone in a house."

"Clovis, we hardly ever sleep alone," Sarah says, knowing that they do, usually, sleep alone. After a minute of silence, she says, "Hello! Are you there?"

Clovis sighs. "Sarah, I'm thinking. The first thing I need to do is secure the house. I have no idea what my aunt has out there. Could you do that? Would you take care of that for me?"

"Clovis, you must be heartbroken. Mary Martha was one of our best friends. Since kindergarten. You know how gentle she was. It's hard to think she had to die that way."

"It's hard for me, too. After all she was my aunt."

"About the house. I'll do what I can."

Twenty minutes later Clovis calls again. "I talked to the sheriff," she says. "They have already secured the house. The sheriff is going to ask you and Isabel and Gaynor to come out to the house tomorrow to see if anything has been stolen. I'm sure it was a robbery."

"A robbery?" Sarah is incredulous.

"Well?"

Remembering the house and its furnishings, "I just don't think it was a robbery," Sarah says. "And Mary Martha never wore jewelry."

"I have to go," Clovis says, but ten minutes later she calls again. "I've made my reservations. My plane's coming into Cold Springs at 2:10 tomorrow afternoon. Could you pick me up?"

"Of course," Sarah answers.

※

After Isabel drops off Sarah and Gaynor, she walks into the house and cries on Willie B.'s shoulder. "I could have been better to her," she sobs. "I could have been a better friend. I wish I had told her how much she meant to me, but the truth is I always thought she was a little odd."

Unable to continue, Isabel puts her head down on the kitchen table and cries. Willie B. cools down a pot of strong coffee with cubes of ice, pours the coffee into tall glasses filled with more ice, and adds dollops of thick cream and teaspoons of sugar.

Isabel sips her coffee, and, as if there has been no interruption, "I didn't know how much I loved her until she was murdered," she says. "There was a . . . oh, a wonderful sweetness about her."

The sobs begin again, deep shuddering sobs that shake the table. When the telephone rings, Willie B. answers, puts her hand over the receiver and says, "It's Sheriff Dallas. Wants to talk to you."

With her head again on the table, Isabel unfolds an arm, holds out a limp hand and takes the phone.

"Rock?" she says. "I can't believe this." Then, "You want us out there tomorrow? At the house?" And after a minute, "Well, I'll try. But I'm not sure I'm up to it." Impatiently, "Well, I *know* she wasn't my sister. I'm hanging up now." And finally, "Well, you can't arrest me for hanging up on you, Rock. You want to be the laughing stock of Cold Springs?"

After that conversation, Isabel takes to her bed. Willie B. makes some calls and the news becomes a tide that floods the town. It isn't long before folks begin putting two and two together. A best friend, one of four best friends, murdered all those years ago. And now, another one, murdered. And Jackson back in town. Sure does seem like *something*, Cold Springs says.

It is late that afternoon when Willie B. leaves for the day. Isabel pulls herself out of bed, puts on her exercise clothes, gets in her car and drives to Sarah's. She finds Sarah, barefooted and wet with perspiration—her face shiny with it, her silk blouse darkened with it—pulling up lantana. Her blue and white spectators, muddy beyond repair, lie abandoned at the front door.

"It's pretty. Why are you pulling it up?"

"It's taking over."

"You gardened. I went to bed," says Isabel, bending to help Sarah pull the lantana.

"Whatever works," says Sarah.

"Rock called, pretending to be a sheriff."

Sarah bursts into laughter. "God, that feels good. I never thought I'd laugh again."

"He wants us to come out to Mary Martha's house tomorrow morning. With Gaynor. He wants her there, too."

"Fine with me," says Sarah. She straightens, and brushing off her hands, she says, "As soon as I got home I called Clovis."

"And?"

"That woman! She asked me to secure the house. She said she had no idea what Mary Martha has in there."

"What did you say?"

"I told her I'd try. She called back later and said she had called the sheriff, *the sheriff,* and he told her the house had been secured. She asked me to pick her up. She's flying in tomorrow afternoon."

"And you said you would."

"But Isabel, you have to go with me. I can't do this alone."

"Sarah, I'll come. Now will you stop pulling lantana so we can talk. I brought wine. It's in your refrigerator. Are you going to start locking your doors?"

"I don't know. I have been uneasy since I heard Jackson was back." Sarah sits back on her knees and looks up at Isabel. "It is strange, isn't it? Jackson leaving town after Rosemary was murdered and now a few weeks after he's come back, Mary Martha has been . . ." Rubbing the chill bumps that have appeared on her arms, she shivers.

"But the murders aren't connected."

"What makes you think that?"

Isabel shakes her head. "The man who murdered Rosemary is probably dead by now or serving a life sentence in prison."

"Isabel, you don't believe that."

"I don't know what to believe." She frowns down at Sarah, again pulling lantana. "Well!" she says, "it is scary. Who knows? We may be next."

Now Sarah is on her feet again. "You don't mean . . . You can't think we're in danger. You don't really think that, do you?"

"No. I don't. But stop gardening. Please stop."

"Well, O.K. I'll stop, but I've got to jump in the tub. I've stopped taking showers since I saw *Psycho.*"

"Fine. Now how about if I put something together—sandwiches, a salad—while you take a bath."

"I don't know what I have."

"I'll find something."

When Sarah appears in a white cotton gown and robe and with a white towel around her wet hair, Isabel, who is now tossing a salad, pauses. "Sarah, you look like you're about sixteen," she says.

Sarah grimaces. "Fat people don't have wrinkles."

Isabel has opened the wine. The salad is fresh pineapple and pears and peaches. While Sarah pours the wine, Isabel adds a sweet dressing and sprinkles the fruit with blue cheese. Then she spreads chopped avocado and onions on garlic rounds. They take trays outside and sit in Sarah's walled garden, watching the sun set and the twilight come on.

"Not exactly comfort food," Isabel says, gazing at the garlic round she holds in her hand. "We need Gaynor. Remember how she cooked for Betsy. Boiled custard. Corn bread."

"Purple hull peas."

"Meatloaf. The meatloaf saved Betsy."

"Let's call Gaynor. Get her over here."

"No, Sarah, we need to talk."

"You mean we need to get ready for Rock. Isabel, we have to tell what we know."

"But not what we don't know. We don't *know* who murdered Mary Martha." She holds up her glass. "A little more?"

Sarah retrieves the bottle of wine from the house, refills their glasses.

"Mary Martha believed Jackson was guilty. She said she would testify against him." Isabel pushes her chair back and walks toward the low garden wall. She wheels and walks back to Sarah. "She wanted to put his head in a noose. "

"Do you think Jackson knew that?"

"Maybe."

"Well, then."

"No. Not, '*Well then*.' Mary Martha's dead. She can't testify."

"Isabel, that sounds cruel."

"I'm not cruel. You know that I'm not."

"I do know it. Sorry," Sarah says. "Here. Sit down. Let's sit here together and think this through."

"Let's just be clear about what we know," Isabel says plaintively. "I know Jackson had a terrible temper. I saw him jerk Jack Bonner out of the car one night like he weighed twenty pounds instead of two hundred. I thought he was going to kill him, but he was immediately sorry. There were tears in his eyes when he apologized. Jackson was very sensitive. Sarah, I'm not telling the sheriff about Jackson's temper when he was just a boy. He did not kill Mary Martha. I'll tell the sheriff that!"

"And that night? Jackson *was* out at the Park that night. Mary Martha said she saw him early the next morning."

"Did you see him?"

"No. But I think I saw Rosemary's convertible in the Park. Eddie said she was driving. We honked but she didn't stop."

"I drove through the Park on the way to your slumber party. And I didn't shoot anybody. Oh, Sarah. Everybody will think Jackson's guilty. But this is about Mary Martha. Not about Rosemary. Let's allow justice to run its course, whatever justice is."

Sarah gathers up the trays and takes them inside the house. Returning, she looks at Isabel, hunched over in her chair.

"I don't know what I'll tell Rock," Isabel says mournfully. "I guess it depends on what he asks."

"Maybe he's already arrested somebody."

"Not Jackson!" Isabel cries.

Sarah shrugs her shoulders, shakes her head. Then, "Look at that moon. It's almost a full moon," she said. "Remember at camp we used to sing: *I see the moon and the moon sees me/ the moon sees the somebody I'd like to see.* Oh, God! She'll never see another moon," says Sarah and saying that, Sarah begins to cry.

"Sarah, if you're going to cry, I'm going home. I've cried all day."

Walking to the garden gate with Isabel, Sarah, sniffing still, blows her nose. "I'll call Gaynor. We'll meet for breakfast in the morning. Some place on the way out to Mary Martha's."

"There's a new Coffee Cup."

"Perfect. We'll go in my car. It's clean."

Isabel opens her car door. "Wait just a minute!!" Sarah says, taking her friend's hand. "Come over here. Let's sing."

"You're tipsy."

"No," says Sarah. "Just sad."

Perched on the garden wall, "This is for you, Mary Martha," Sarah whispers, and they begin to sing, at first tremulously, *I see the moon and the moon sees me.* But their voices gather strength until, singing, *God bless the moon and God bless me/ And God bless the somebody I'd like to see,* they are in full voice.

Clovis

When the women walk into the Coffee Cup the next morning, Sheriff Dallas has just finished his breakfast. Sarah raises her eyebrows. Isabel frowns.

"What?" Gaynor says. Then, "What would the Texas women be telling each other with their facial smoke signals?"

"That's Rock Dallas in the white Stetson. He's pretending to be a real sheriff," Sarah says. "We've known him all our lives. We went to school with him."

"Rock Dallas?" Gaynor said. "That's not his name. It can't be his name!"

"His first name is Oliver. Oliver Dallas. But in high school, his nickname was *Rock*. It stuck."

Now the sheriff is meandering toward their table, his course indirect. But the goal is clear. He has them in his sight. He stops to speak to Loretta Davis, the blue-eyed, gray-headed manager of the Coffee Cup. Obviously in a hurry, Loretta nods briskly and hurries off to clear the table the sheriff has just left.

Isabel nods toward Loretta. "She was in our class in high school. Her gray hair is pretty, isn't it? I've been thinking about letting my gray show."

"I'll believe that when I see it," Sarah says, sliding into the booth alongside Gaynor.

They watch as a thin, black-headed waitress heads toward their table. The sheriff steps in front of her, and taking the coffee pot from her hands, pours himself more coffee.

"Hey, Maggie," Rock says loudly. "Whoa now. Too much in a hurry to stop and talk to old Rock?" He puts an arm around the waitress's shoulders, returns the coffee pot and whispers into her ear.

"Get out of here, Rock Dallas," she laughs, giving his hip a shove with hers.

"Isabel, look who else is here!" says Sarah. "Oops, here he comes! To the rescue!"

A man, smiling widely, is getting up from a table and walking toward the women. His smooth movements, the expensive suit and tie he wears, his coiffed and shoeblack-dyed hair cause him to look as if he might be a dancing teacher introducing the mambo or the president of the Cold Spring Rotary. Maybe, the governor of Texas. He puts a hand on Isabel's shoulder.

"Hello, Trevor," Isabel says, offering her cheek for a kiss.

"Good morning, Gaynor. Sarah. Good to see you both," he says. His voice is soft, his accent more Tennessee than Texas. "I am deeply sad about Mary Martha. And shocked. You all have been friends a long time."

"Forever," Sarah says, her eyes brimming.

Trevor takes Sarah's hand, then Gaynor's. "She was a sweet woman. And such a lady. I can't believe somebody killed her. Are you all right? Anything I can do? Anything at all?"

"We will be all right. We'll get through it together. They'll find the man who did this," Isabel says huskily, "or woman."

Leave it to Isabel to say something ridiculous, Sarah thinks. *Isabel knows it wasn't a woman.* "Clovis is coming in this afternoon," she says.

Frowning, Trevor nods. Then he says, "The sheriff just told me you've been asked to go through the house with him. As your lawyer, I think I'd better tag along."

"Trevor, we don't need a lawyer to tell us if anything has been taken out of the house. We don't need a lawyer at all."

"All right, Isabel. But don't answer a single question about anything or anybody unless I'm present."

"Are we suspects then?" Gaynor asks. "I may go back to Ireland."

"No. I didn't mean that. But you just don't want to get involved." When there's no answer, Trevor says, "Well, if you change your mind, call me. Isabel, you don't need to be involved at all," he says and walks briskly toward the door just as the sheriff heads toward them. Ordinarily, Isabel might have scooted over so the sheriff could sit with them, but now she remains glued to her seat.

Rock Dallas is tall, over six feet even without the boots he wears. He has the white skin that usually accompanies red hair, but his hair is black. He also has a thin, black moustache, grown so that he might appear in a "You must pay the rent!" skit for a Junior League charity.

The women look upward in order to see Rock's face, but after a quick glance, Isabel lowers her eyes to focus on his silver belt buckle depicting a bucking horse.

"Morning, Isabel. Sarah," he says. His voice is surprisingly robust and pleasant. When he speaks, it is as if he might break into song at any minute.

"Good morning, Rock. You know Gaynor."

He touches the brim of his hat. "I know who she is. Good morning, Gaynor. You all coming on out to Mary Martha's after you finish your breakfast? I'll drive on out there ahead of you. See if there's something we've overlooked. Take your time now, ladies."

Without responding, they watch him walk to his car and drive away.

"There's an elephant in the living room," Gaynor says.

"Well, yes," Sarah agrees.

"But we don't want to send it on a rampage," says Isabel.

"Mary Martha was not herself these last few weeks," Sarah says.

"You're right! That's why we have to be careful about what we say to Rock," Isabel says, cupping her coffee with two hands, bringing the cup to her lips. "He's liable to do something crazy."

"Arrest Jackson?"

"Without any evidence? I don't think even Rock would do that."

"We have to be honest," Sarah said.

Isabel shrugs. It's been too long, too many years have passed for honesty, she tells herself.

Silently, the women stir their coffee, tea for Gaynor, and gaze out the window, watching the wind lift and swirl bits of white paper napkins and torn paper bags around the parking lot. Huge drops of rain begin to splatter against the window. The wind rises, howls around the restaurant.

"Who twirled their ring?" Gaynor demands.

Sarah smiles. Isabel gazes out the window.

"I think I'm going into menopause," Gaynor says. "Nausea. Hot flashes. My mother waited until she was fifty."

Isabel says, "Gaynor, everything happens earlier in Texas. Have you talked to your doctor? I'm on hormones."

"I'll call him," Gaynor says. "And set up an appointment."

"I wish . . . " Isabel begins. And Mary Martha's heart-shaped face is suddenly before her. Wordlessly, she shakes her head. After a minute, "We have to protect her. That's all!" she whispers fiercely. "We have to do everything we can to protect her."

"From what, Isabel?"

"I don't know. From unkindness. From talk. She's been so strange lately. That's all."

They finish their breakfast in silence and, heads down, hurry out to the car. By the time they reach Mary Martha's house, both rain and wind have freshened. They sit in the car and listen to the drumming of rain on the car's roof. They watch tree branches blown into frenzied motion by the wind and rain.

"The house knows she's gone," Gaynor says.

"It does look lonely," says Sarah.

"Well, come on!" Isabel says. "Let's get this over with."

Before Isabel can put her finger on the doorbell, Rock Davis has thrown the door open. His ingratiating voice, "Ladies, come in now. Let's do this room-by-room. See what we can discover about Miss Mercer," assaults their senses.

Isabel puts her hands over her ears.

"We need a priest," Gaynor says.

"Was she Catholic?" Rock asks.

Isabel crosses her arms over her chest. "Let's finish with this as soon as we can, Rock."

Standing in the living room, the women stare at the empty places on the wall, places where her family photographs once hung. The photographs are now stacked on the coffee table. A single picture—a small watercolor of an Irish shamrock—hangs there now. Smiling, the women draw close to the watercolor and lean forward, gazing at it.

Isabel's expression hardens. Sarah places a hand over her heart. "She was getting ready to go with us," Gaynor says.

"What?" Rock demands.

"Nothing, Rock," Isabel says. "It's just a water color."

"What about it?"

"She talked about going to Ireland," Sarah says angrily. "She planned to get a passport. And now. . . , well, shit!"

"Now, now, ladies," Rock says. "Who was she going with?"

"Nobody. Us. All of us."

"Maybe Jackson Morris?"

"Rock, don't be an idiot," Isabel says.

"Now, Isabel. I'm paid to investigate. So! You ladies look around, see if anything else in here has been changed? Anything missing? And don't touch a thing. Not even a spider web."

At this Gaynor's mouth falls open. Sarah and Isabel roll their eyes at each other.

"Nothing!" Rock repeats. "Is that clear?"

When no one answers, he stretches both arms out wide and herds the women through the dining room (pausing just long enough to hear Sarah's impatient "No. Nothing's missing here") and into the kitchen.

In Mary Martha's empty cold kitchen the women stand close to each other. They take in the unopened wine bottle on a silver tray. A wine glass. A beer glass. The white linen napkins. And seeing this evidence of hospitality, their eyes meet, dart away. Sarah steals a glance at Isabel's carefully blank face, masking the thought: *Jackson drank beer.* The women smile obligingly at Rock and head toward the stairs.

Moving toward the table, "Well, damn. Excuse me ladies," Rock says and picks up pieces of a saucer he has stumbled over. "What's this doing on the floor?"

The women shrug their shoulders. Then, "Wait a minute," the sheriff says. He draws a glove onto his right hand and begins to gather up the pieces of the saucer.

"Rock, please," Isabel says.

The sheriff refocuses on the table. "Two glasses! Well I never knew Miss Mercer drank. I wonder who she might have been planning to entertain. Any ideas?" He opens the refrigerator door and takes out a bottle of Dos Equis.

"Rock, we came out here at Clovis's request," Sarah says. "She asked us to see if anything was missing. We're not here to answer questions."

"Sarah, don't get your dander up. I'm just wondering who she might have been expecting."

"Whom."

"What?"

"Rock, we don't know," Sarah says. "She had an occasional glass of wine with friends."

"Did she seem worried lately? Upset about anything? Afraid?"

"Sheriff, Mary Martha was going through menopause," Gaynor says, grinning wickedly as Rock turns brick red.

"We're all menopausal," Isabel says firmly. "And bordering on hysteria. And we're upset. Rock, Mary Martha had no enemies. Now. I'm going upstairs," she says and moves so swiftly that the sheriff hurries to follow her.

Then, "Whoops!" he says, suddenly conscious of the Dos Equis bottle in his hand. He turns back toward the kitchen, replaces the bottle and peels off the glove.

Isabel takes the stairs two at a time. Anybody but Rock, she tells herself. She could have tolerated anybody but Rock. The thought of his questions, salacious if given half the chance, is too much. She opens Mary Martha's bedroom door and, in three long steps, she is standing by Mary Martha's bed. Quickly, she takes a red leather book from underneath papers and bills in the bottom drawer of the bedside table and drops it into her handbag. She will not have it. People reading Mary Martha's diary, people who did not love her, did not know her! She can imagine their ribald laughter at the innocence, the naiveté, the suspicions her diary would reveal. Suspicions. She might as well be honest. If she turned this diary over to the police, they might get out a warrant for Jackson's arrest.

When Rock walks in, Isabel is standing in the middle of the room with her handbag over her shoulder. Her hands are clasped behind her back.

"Well?" Rock says.

"Everything looks perfectly normal," Isabel says.

The sheriff moves around the room. In the bathroom he lifts the top off the tank of the commode and flushes it. Returning to the bedroom, he pulls the mattress back and looks under it. When he sees a picture of the four of them on the bedside table, he pulls on his glove, picks up the picture and examines it.

"Where was this taken? What were you all laughing at?"

"Oh, my God," Isabel says. "We were in Jefferson at a bridge tournament."

Now the sheriff is opening all the drawers, one by one. When he opens the bottom drawer of the bedside table, Isabel hears Sarah's quick intake of breath. She crosses her arms, lifts the fingers of her right hand in a reassuring gesture. *It's all right,* the gesture says.

"The court, her bank, somebody will have to go through all these papers," Rock grumbles. He closes the drawer and walks toward a closet.

"No!" Sarah says. "Don't ask me to look at her clothes. Her shoes. I won't do that. It's too hard."

"We're going," Isabel says. "Now."

"Well, all right, but one more thing. And remember. You're not under oath. I'm just wondering. Did Mary Martha suspect anybody of being guilty of those high school murders? Did she suspect Jackson? For instance?"

"We never talked about it," Sarah says. "If Mary Martha had lived . . . Well we wouldn't be out here listening to your questions, for one thing."

"I'll bet she knew something about that murder. Maybe that's why somebody . . ."

"Let's go. Sarah, we have to meet Clovis's plane."

Ushering them out the door, the sheriff says, "You ladies will have to be more forthcoming when you're testifying under oath. Meantime, I'm planning on seeing all three of you at the funeral. You will need to report anybody who looks suspicious. Any strangers who show up."

"Rock, murderers don't go to their victims' funerals. You've been watching too much television."

An hour later, Isabel and Sarah watch Clovis carefully descend the steps of the plane. Although it has landed seven minutes early, they have had time to drop Gaynor off and arrive at the airport in time.

Clovis, at least six feet tall and every bit as thin as Eve, is in a covey of fifteen or twenty passengers, all of them hurrying toward the double glass doors of the waiting room. They see her at once. Her shoulder-length hair, streaked by sun or chemicals (who can tell?) needs shaping. Her black and white checked suit is strictly "dress for success," as is the expensive briefcase she carries. Surprisingly, her high-heeled sandals seem to be sparkling as she strides toward them. When Isabel realizes that the sparkle comes from the rhinestone straps of her sandals, the surprise of it causes her to smile.

Leaving the other passengers behind, Clovis hurries toward them, a single-minded woman with a mission. When she comes through the doors, she offers each a quick smile and a brief handshake.

"Isabel. Sarah," she says, "Thank you for coming." And, after the briefest hesitation, she turns toward the exit.

"Let's get your luggage. This is the baggage room. It will come in here."

"I have everything I need," Clovis says, nodding toward her overnight bag. "I have to leave in the morning."

Sarah stops walking so suddenly that Isabel bumps into her. "In the morning? Clovis, how can you leave in the morning? There's too much to be done."

Without pausing, Clovis opens the door and steps outside onto the rain swept pavement. The sun has come out. The wind has died away.

"There's not much I can do today. Let's get in your car, where is your car? and I'll go over my list."

"There's the funeral?" This from Sarah. And from Isabel, "What about the service?" The two break into a trot to keep up with Clovis.

When Clovis pauses, they lead the way to Sarah's old Buick. Clovis tosses her overnight bag and handbag into the back seat. "Up here," Isabel says, opening the passenger door. "You'll be more comfortable in the front seat."

As Sarah is backing out of her parking place, Clovis snaps open her briefcase and takes out a note pad. "There's not much I can do today. It's so late."

Isabel leans forward. "Clovis, just a minute! Where are you staying?"

"At the Holiday Inn. Now, number one: the house. You've been out to Mary Martha's house. Is everything in order?"

"Some pictures have been taken down," Sarah says. "But other than that, yes."

"Good. Now the second thing: I have a meeting with . . ."

"Clovis, let's get you registered and into your room." Isabel's voice is kind. Motherly. After all, Clovis is alone in the world. She is probably feeling a little frightened. Patience. Patience is what Clovis needs. "We'll get you settled and then we'll help you with your list. We want to do all we can."

"I didn't sleep well last night," Clovis says, an admission of sorts. And then she adds, "I haven't eaten much lately."

"This must be so hard for you."

"I'm doing all right."

Isabel unfastens her seatbelt and leans forward again. "How about this? While you register, I'll have sandwiches sent up. Coffee. Fresh lemonade. We'll have a snack and go over your list."

"And we might add one or two things to it," Sarah says dryly.

Ten minutes later here they are in a room with two double beds, a view overlooking I-30 and the overpowering scent of peach blossoms that does not quite mask the smell of bug spray. Isabel has kicked off her shoes and propped herself up against the headboard of a bed. Sarah has pulled a chair up close. Clovis stows her bag, sits on the empty bed, pulls her briefcase up beside her and opens it.

A knock on the door and a woman's voice, "Room service," sends Sarah hurrying to open the door. "Here," Sarah says, pushing the lamp and the phone book on a small table aside to make room for the tray the woman carries.

The woman is short and dark, her eyes a liquid brown. After she arranges the tray, she turns toward them. "Nada mas?" she asks.

"No. Gracias," Isabel answers.

The woman walks toward the door and opens it. Then, looking at Isabel, sitting cross-legged on the bed, she says, "Lo siento mucho," and allows the door to close softly behind her.

"What did she say?" Sarah asks.

"She said she was sorry," says Isabel. " Maybe she has heard about Mary Martha. Maybe she saw the grief on our faces."

"Small towns!" Clovis scoffs. "They are just downright peculiar."

Sarah begins to hand the sandwiches and the drinks around, coffee for Isabel and Clovis, a glass of lemonade for herself.

Isabel remains propped against the bed's headboard, leisurely eating and drinking, as all the while her eyes move from the sparkling sandals on Clovis's feet to Clovis's solemn face and back again. *At another time a little frivolity might bubble up.* The thought is satisfying.

Now Clovis stands and deposits most of her sandwich on the tray. She turns toward them and crosses her arms. Sighing deeply, she looks first at Sarah, sitting on the edge of the bed, and then at Isabel, propped comfortably on pillows.

"Who could have done this? You knew her better than anybody, even me, *especially* me. Who would have murdered my aunt? She *was* my aunt you know. Just tell me: Does the sheriff have a suspect. Do you? And I want to know if she suffered. Was she? Was she molested?"

In tandem they shake their heads. "We don't know," Sarah says. "Rock told us the police can't reveal any information now."

"This is very hard for me," Clovis says sternly. Then, astonishingly, she puts both hands over her face and begins to cry.

Isabel hurries to comfort her, but when she puts her arm around her shoulders, Clovis draws back and hurries off into the bathroom.

Isabel looks at Sarah. "Just like Mary Martha," she mouths.

"Exactly," whispers Sarah.

When Clovis reappears her eyes are red, her cheeks are flushed, but her voice is matter-of-fact. "She never loved me. She never cared a thing about me. But I didn't want her to die."

"Of course you didn't." Isabel's voice is firm. "And how can you know how much she loved you? Who can measure love? Clovis, you can't leave tomorrow. There's the funeral service to plan. Her estate to be settled. A will to be probated."

"No, no, no. You don't understand. The body won't be released until next week. There has to be an autopsy. I'll fly back then. The only thing I have to do tomorrow morning is to get letters of testamentary, see my aunt's lawyer and get the probate process started."

Clovis sits in the desk chair and, crossing her legs, swings her right foot up and down. The rhinestones sparkle.

She has good legs, Isabel thinks and says: "Clovis, your sandals are beyond cool."

"I don't know what came over me," Clovis says ruefully.

"I like them."

"I just wonder," Clovis says and stops. Then, "I just wonder . . ."

"What? Tell us," Sarah says. "Wonder what? What do you wonder?"

"I wonder about those murders that happened when you were all in high school. Did they ever find . . . ?"

"No." They answer in unison, Isabel's voice sharper than she meant it to be.

"It's strange," Clovis says. "But if you think of anything . . ."

"We'll tell the sheriff," Isabel says.

Sarah, knowing a lie when she hears it, dares not look at Isabel's face that has become unbelievably serene.

"Clovis, you can't stay here alone, in this dreary room. Why don't you have dinner with us tonight. We'll invite Gaynor. She was one of your aunt's best friends. We'll go out to the club. There are so many things we can tell you about Mary Martha. She was very intelligent. One of the smartest women in town."

"And there's your list," says Sarah. "We haven't even started on the list."

"I'll call you tomorrow, but I can't have dinner with you tonight. I'm having dinner with the sheriff. He's coming early to talk to me." She looks at her watch. "He'll be here any minute."

"Oh, the sheriff. Of course. Well, do give us a call in the morning."

"I will. I'll keep in touch."

In the privacy of the hotel elevator, they look at each other. "Well," Sarah says. "Dinner with the sheriff."

"By tomorrow, we'll be Rock's chief suspects."

Hearing this, Sarah bursts into laughter. Isabel joins in so that when the elevator doors open, and they see that the sheriff has arrived to take Clovis to dinner, and knowing how they must seem—two women, bent double with laughter—to Rock Dallas, this too sets them off.

"You two are just plain crazy," Rock growls. "Or drunk."

The two had lingered over dinner and, afterwards, on Sarah's terrace so that when Isabel walks into her own house the tall clock has begun its chiming. Standing in the darkness, she listens. She knows all three cathedral chimes. The Westminster. The Canterbury. The Whittington. The clock is playing the Westminster, her favorite. Knowing it must be at least nine o'clock, she counts the strikes. Ten. An hour later than she had thought.

Sitting on Sarah's terrace, they had talked about everything, everything but Mary Martha. Isabel had told Sarah about her children in California. "They've both had colds," she said mournfully. Sarah had talked about the three hundred tulip bulbs she had ordered from Holland. "I must have been crazy," she had said. "Will you help me plant them?"

"Maybe," Isabel said wryly. Then, "Look up at the clouds rolling in. The wind must be powerful up that high."

"Maybe Gaynor twisted her ring," Sarah had chuckled.

Then Sarah, relishing the telling, said that John was back in school and that Eve always seemed to know when she, Sarah, was thinking about her. "Is that possible, Isabel? Do you believe it?"

"Gaynor believes all that stuff. And it does seem to happen over and over again."

"Do you think Trevor is attractive?" Sarah asked suddenly.

"Not as attractive as Jackson."

"I wasn't asking that! Not tonight."

Worn out by the anguish of loss and the horror of Mary Martha's death, they had not had the courage to mention her name.

❄

When the sound of the clock dies away, Isabel walks through the great room and down the hall. She turns on a bedroom light, puts the red leather diary into the bottom drawer of her bedside table and closes the drawer.

Far into the night, she sits on the south terrace. In the pale light of the sinking moon, the potted rose at the edge of the terrace is luminous. Drawn by the gossamer light of her white robe, a moth lands on her shoulder. She lifts it off and cradles it in her hands. She takes it out into the grass and opens her hands to release it. Reluctant to go to bed, she sits on the terrace steps, listening to the night sounds.

In '46 they had all been so young, so very young, hardly more than children. It seems to her now that they had not chosen silence. Silence had chosen them, had thrown over them a cloak of confusion and fear. They had been children bound by honor, but to whom? And by love, but in what gradation?

And Jackson. Jackson has come home. Does he know she is thinking of him? Now. At this moment. She will see him soon. Perhaps, tomorrow. She will not seek him out, but their paths will cross. When she sees his face, she will know what happened after he left her room that night. She will know he did not murder Rosemary. When she knows this, she will read the diary.

The Funeral

Victor tosses the newspapers onto Jackson's step and, whistling, strolls toward the construction site. There's not a cloud in the sky. Today will be a scorcher. But the framing is finished, and he's hoping the weather will hold so they can finish the roofing by Friday. The shingles are on site, and they're running a little ahead of their target dates.

Despite the heavier than usual rainfall they have had in May, the work is progressing satisfactorily. Victor enjoys the onsite inspections of Jackson's house because Jackson is that rare client who understands that the purity of house design comes about when design springs organically from the site. While Victor's business relationship with Jackson is pleasant, he recognizes that this client's personal life will remain private. However, he often wonders what enticed Jackson back to a small East Texas town after having lived in some of the great cities of the world.

On Monday, the cypress is to be delivered. Last week he had gone to Jefferson to check on it and had stayed an hour or more admiring the wood—its wonderful variations of color, its scarred imperfections. The wood they've chosen has integrity. Dredged up from the swamps of Cypress Lake, it has a strength and beauty no other Texas wood has. It will endure. It will serve Jackson well.

Standing inside the framing, he looks up at the twenty-four-foot joists in the great room, admiring the two huge roof support beams and the angled windows around the top. When he finishes the inside inspection, he walks around the outside of the house, studying it from every angle. He feels an enormous satisfaction about this project. He believes it will be his finest design, as understated and as interesting as Jackson.

After making some notes for the meeting he and the contractor will have this afternoon, he jogs to the riverbank to watch the sun's changing reflections on the river. The reflections he sees, their ever-changing earth tones, might well be used in the interior of the house. He will mention this idea to Jackson.

When he returns to the trailer, Jackson is sitting on the steps reading the paper, a cup of coffee by his side. Wearing jeans and a plaid shirt, Jackson looks rugged. The Marlboro Man.

Turning a page of the newspaper, "Good morning, Victor," Jackson says. Then, folding the paper for more comfortable reading, he glances at it. "Oh, no. Oh, my God! No!" he whispers. Taking off his reading glasses, he stares blankly at Victor, then holds the paper close to his eyes, frowns, shakes his head, trying to comprehend the import of what he has read. The color drains from his face. His shoulders sag. He drops the paper, cradles his head in his hands and furiously begins to rub it.

"What is it? Jackson, what's the matter?"

"A woman's been murdered. God. I can't believe this. Nine or ten days ago." He looks at the paper again. "Ten days ago. Her body was found in the woods close to her house." Beseechingly, he looks up at Victor. "I knew her in high school. I called her after I went to Shreveport. Oh, my God! What day was it? It must have been on the 18th. Or maybe the 17th. She sounded formal, as if she didn't remember me. I told her I remembered her fondly from high school and said I'd like to drop by for a visit." He picks up the paper and turns more pages. In his trembling hands the paper takes on a trembling life of its own. "See! Here's her obituary," he says, jabbing at the paper with his forefinger. "It's short."

He begins to read: *"Mercer, Mary Martha. Born July 14, 1929 and died May 18, 1980."* He swallows, moistens his lips and begins again. *"She is preceded in death by her parents: William Floyd and Maud Evelyn Mercer. A memorial service will be held for Ms. Mercer today at 2:00 o'clock at St. Alban's Episcopal Church on Pine Street."* As he finishes reading, his voice is almost soundless. Then, "Lord God Almighty, have mercy. Have mercy on us all," he whispers.

Rubbing his neck, he slowly stands and rolls his shoulders. "Victor, this is a blow. I'm sorry. I have to think this through. I'll call you next week."

"Sure. About the house . . . the doors."

"I want the construction to continue. Just carry on with everything. Everybody."

"Sure," Victor says again. Turning, he walks toward his car, stops and turns back toward Jackson. "Is there anything I can do?"

"No. But there are some things . . . I've got to see what I can do."

By the time Victor has climbed into his plane, Jackson is in the shower. Cold. Hot. Cold. He steps into shorts and pulls on a pair of jeans. "Damn! This is Cold Springs," he says. "In Cold Springs you wear a suit to a funeral." Pulling off the jeans, he hopes he can find a suit. He hasn't had one on since he moved into the trailer.

The closet door refuses to slide open. He lifts one door, then the other, trying to get them back on track. They swing in every direction, but they refuse to slide open. Damn. Why in the hell is he living in a trailer? A trailer. And suddenly . . .

he feels the lash of his father's belt on his back, hears the rage in his father's voice, the roar of his father's voice. "That'll teach you to start fires in lumberyards. Had enough? Well, damn it! Too proud are you? Well, we're not trailer trash, Mr. Jackson. You tell that to your rich friends."

Ramming the closet doors, hurling his shoulder at them, the voice he hears is lower now, a slow growl. He rams the closet doors again.

Your mother cries. You hear? Hear? She cries. Why don't you cry?

The voice is a whisper. Icy. Without mercy. Jackson steps back, hurls himself at the doors again as, from the bedroom and from far off, his mother's voice, whispering, imploring: *"Please. Please, Vince. You're killing him. Killing me! Stop it! Vince!"* Dying away to a whimper: *"Oh, my dear Lord, help us. Jesus! Help us! Oh, my soul, Jesus!"*

Jackson hurls his body against the sliding doors again and again until they fall at his feet. Hands on his hips, he stands a minute, looking down at the splintered wood before gathering it up and tossing it into a trash barrel. Then, numbed by anger, exhausted by it, he falls onto the trailer steps.

Now that he has shattered the doors, his anger seems to have drained away. He closes his eyes until his heartbeat slows and then he begins to walk. Is this what Wolfe meant? he wonders. Was it memory that had kept him away? Whatever Wolfe's reason, memory has found *him,* Jackson, an earthquake of memories, shaking him to his very core.

Walking along the riverbank, he allows himself to follow the dim threads that lead him back, back to that last time. He remembers that after the small, mewling cries of his mother had faded away, the beating had continued in silence except for the metonymic sound of leather striking flesh. Biting his lips until they bled, he had refused to cry out. There was only the silence. A sixteen-year-old boy's silence. The boy knew that only by his refusal to whimper or beg or cry could he win. It was the boy's silence that never failed to enrage the father. It was the boy's silence that, finally, might cause him to throw down his belt and storm out of the house.

During the beatings, the boy's only recourse was to remove himself from the room, to float high above it, high enough to look down on the man and the boy engaged in their fierce struggle. If the boy's focus was strong enough, he could float above the house and above the pain. He could drift far out over the clouds to the sea.

But that night the boy's focus had been replaced by a hatred so strong that he had cursed and screamed and, finally, sobbed until the man, breathing hard, had said triumphantly, "Well, now, Jackson Boy, you won't forget this night, now will you."

Leaning against the washing machine, sobbing, the boy had watched Vince carefully run his belt through his belt loops. When he saw the lopsided grin on Vince's face, he knew that Jackson, the boy, had lost the battle.

❈

Reaching the bend of the river, Jackson sits down under an old pecan tree and leans against it. A leaf flutters down from the tree, skittering across his lap. A small, blue-winged snake doctor hovers, lights on his hand for a second and helicopters off. His mother had been small, a small, worried woman who always came after the cruelty, tenderly salving his back as soon as his father had stormed off. That last night he had sworn to himself and his mother he would never take another beating from his father. He would kill him first. Or run away.

Watching the flow of the river, he sees that it is running high. He hears the plop of a fish or maybe a frog downstream and the sound of a small motorboat. Can this be enough, he wonders? This river. This house. This view. He closes his eyes, feeling as if he has run a race and finished it. But to see that word, *murder*, in the paper! That had brought it all back. Everything. The F.B.I. questioning high school seniors and soldiers. Even the soldiers! He remembers Isabel's tears, begging him not to tell anyone he had been with her, making him swear on the Bible not to tell they had gone all the way. How quaint the expression sounds now. But he had been in the Park that night. And someone else was there; someone who had waited silently. Someone who had stepped out from behind a tree and killed Rosemary and that boy she was with. And now, Mary Martha has been murdered. Two murders. Could they be connected? The only obvious connection is that there had been four friends, and one of them was murdered. And now, over thirty years later, another one. Murdered. And only two are still alive. But in logic, "B" does not always follow "A."

Anne Marie had once said to him there is a healing, a kind of catharsis in remembering. He does not believe it. Not now. Glancing at his watch, he realizes he has an hour and a half to dress and drive to the church.

In the recesses of his open closet, he finds a blue suit, still in a dry cleaning bag, and a shirt fresh from the laundry. And he has some ties. Somewhere. From a rickety chest, he pulls out a red one. A gold and green striped one. Settles on a gray. After his pants are on, his shirt tucked in and his tie tied, he remembers he has not shaved. Nor has he had breakfast.

He is hungry now. Starved. He makes himself three pieces of toast, scrambles a couple of eggs and pours a tall glass of orange juice. As a kid, he was always hungry. *As a kid,* he muses. Until this morning, he had almost forgotten that six-teen-year-old self. When his English teacher had read a poem about being acquainted with the night, tears had filled his eyes, and Isabel had reached across the aisle and dropped a tissue into his hands. Walking home that day, he had wondered if Robert Frost had been beaten by his father.

After breakfast, he wraps a towel around his neck and shaves. Then he walks up to his house and sits on a sawhorse in the middle of what will be the great room. Looking toward the south, he sees Black Angus cattle grazing out a yellow pasture even though Oscar has scattered sweet, green hay bales around the pasture. The pond is full of water.

The pleasure he has felt these past weeks slowly returns. Not since the years he and Anne Marie were together has he been so contented. But now, coming home. Well. He had opened a newspaper and remembered everything he had tried to forget. Those flimsy doors! Realizing that he has just had a fight with a couple of doors, "Damn," he says. But he has not come back to Cold Springs to be haunted by the past. He let all that go a long time ago.

Feeling deep regret that he had not been able to talk to Mary Martha, will not ever be able to talk to her, he walks back to the trailer, picks up his jacket and drives into Cold Springs to honor her. She had been a part of his youth. Helpless. Never seeming more than a child. He wonders if she had kept the lisp.

When he arrives at the church, the parking lot is full. He parks across the street at the post office. Closing the car door, he notices the heavy coat of red dust on the black Ford. Vincent and Mildred would have hosed it off before a funeral. Walking toward the church, he stops in the middle of the street, struck by the thought that he would never have come back home had either one of them still been alive.

❄

Clovis had called and dropped the service into their two Episcopal laps and one fallen away Catholic lap. They had agreed to meet, briefly, with the new priest, Father Lacey, who would be officiating because the rector was away on his Martha's Vineyard summer holiday. But Father Tom had called both Isabel and Sarah to commiserate and then had said, quite cheerfully, that the service would be meaningful and appropriate under young Lacey's guidance.

Isabel had immediately called Father Lacey to ask if he would come to her house to plan the service. When he walked into the room and saw the women with their prayer books and hymnals in hand, he realized the service had already been planned. Quite a relief that was! Scheduled to tee off at three that afternoon, he had hoped he would not have to cancel his golf game. And there was this: although he had officiated at four funerals and assisted at a dozen or so more, he had never held the burial of the dead service for a murder victim.

Isabel had opened the door for him. "Father," she said, "thank you for coming here." Turning, she had led him into a large room with ceilings so high that the room seemed about to take flight. A golden, beribboned balloon-shaped chandelier hung over a sofa and chairs at one end of the room. Perfect for the room. Intensifying the light-headedness he had experienced when he walked in. He might try to capture the feeling of the room in a painting. In the manner of Matisse. And with watercolors.

Gaynor Trevor-Rogers and Sarah Carter stood when he entered. Seeing them gathered around the coffee table, the word that came to mind was *formidable.* Taking the hand of each one, murmuring condolences, he briefly wondered if leaving the sanctuary of the church's parlor to plan the service had been a mistake.

They smiled at him. They took his hand. "Please," they murmured. "It's Isabel." And "It's Gaynor," and "Sarah, please. Just Sarah."

Despite the polite welcome, Isabel's expression, in the sullen tightness of her mouth and the slight frown on her forehead, was forbidding. Her dress was black, as were her high heels. And her legs were encased in sheer black. Her lipstick was the brightest red he had ever seen. Sarah Carter, a blowsy, yet very pretty woman, kept her handkerchief at the ready, now and then dabbing at her eyes, eyes that were very beautiful and that now, filled with tears, were sparkling like sapphires. The third, Gaynor Trevor-Rogers was in pants and tailored shirt. He knew who she was. The Rector had told him. Because of Gaynor the church has lost a valuable contributor. Betsy Rogers now divided her pledges between the Catholic and Episcopalian churches.

"This is the worst thing," Isabel began. "We can't accept it. When somebody just dies suddenly, or is sick . . ."

"Or even suicide would be easier," Sarah said, tears streaming down her face.

Isabel began to sob. A long, mournful cry, not unlike an animal in pain, came from Gaynor, who was rising and walking toward the glass doors as if to run away. But then Isabel hurried to take her hand and bring her back to the circle.

This is a house of grief, Father Lacey told himself. And he had not expected the deep wounding. After the weeping became muted, he said fervently, "Oh, let us pray. Dear God, help these dear friends in their hour of need. Bring them to a peace that accepts, that forgives. And bless the soul of Mary Martha, their departed friend."

"Thank you, Father," Isabel said. "Now, please sit down." She put her hand on Sarah's shoulder. "Before we begin, there are cookies in the oven. I'll bring a tray."

"Where's Willie B.?"

"Grocery shopping," Isabel said over her shoulder, leaving the kitchen door swinging behind her.

Gaynor smiled. "Father Lacey, where are you from? By that, I mean where did you grow up?"

"New Jersey."

"Oh," Sarah said and leaned forward with another question, but now Isabel had returned with the cookies, a bottle of sherry and four small glasses on a tray.

Sarah and Gaynor sat side-by-side on the wild-flowered sofa, while Isabel and Father Lacey were in chairs across from them. Sarah lifted her glass and the others raised theirs. "To Mary Martha," she said.

Father Lacey took a sip of the sherry and replaced the glass firmly. With the tips of his fingers he pushed it still farther away. "Shall we begin?" he said. They nodded. "There will be the traditional Burial of the Dead service."

"Of course," Isabel said, lifting her glass again and swallowing.

"Father Lacey, would you like me to take notes?" Sarah asked.

"Yes. But please, it's Chip," the priest said and watched Isabel obediently leave the room to fetch paper and pen from the kitchen and, returning, hand them to Sarah.

Now that he understood their grief, he would be able to carry out the duties of his office with a greater sensitivity. Obviously, these women, in their middle fifties, maybe *early* fifties, have suffered a tremendous loss. A most grievous loss. The loss of a friend through murder is unspeakable. Searching their faces, sad but composed, he wondered if they suspected anyone. But that was not a question for him to raise, even mentally, at this time.

Sarah crossed her arms. "Chip, Mary Martha was innocent. I want you to know that about her. Completely innocent," she said tremulously.

"Innocent? Of what?" Chip asked.

"She could have been a nun," Isabel explained, crossing her slender legs. "And there was such a sweetness about her."

Maybe late forties, Father Charles amended. "I see," he says.

"She was pure. Completely pure," Isabel continued somberly, smiling just enough to cause him to notice a dimple in her right cheek. "Father, I would like to say something about her, a few words of remembrance. Her niece suggested it. Something appropriate, based on a verse from the Bible or Shakespeare. Something relevant. Of course, I'll run it by you," she added, smiling more widely now so that her mouth that had earlier seemed almost sullen was now warmly inviting. Pulling a black silk scarf, splashed with roses that were the exact shade of her lipstick, from behind her back and drawing her slender legs up beside her, she lounged against the soft arm of the big chair. The scarf fluttered to the floor beside her slender legs. A watercolor, titled "Roses on Black Water." He might give it a try. Painting was a hobby for Charles Lacey, a necessary diversion after the often sad duties of his priesthood.

He nodded. "Of course," he said.

During the planning of the service, Gaynor's gaze, although directed at him, revealed nothing. She said, "In some ways, Mary Martha seemed younger than her years. There's a song about children: *"One was a doctor, and one was a queen/ And one was a shepherdess on the green.* I've always loved that hymn. Mary Martha was somehow like a child, wasn't she? Could we have that hymn?"

Sarah and Isabel nodded solemnly, and before he could respond to Gaynor's question, Sarah was writing down the title.

Chip did know something about music. It was time for their priest to ease into the planning, he decided. "One of the most gently consoling of Bach's compositions is 'Jesu, Joy of Man's Desiring.' Considering the circumstances I think that the Bach would be a very beautiful as well as an appropriate choice for the processional."

"Oh, Father, yes. I know it. It's a part of the Catholic sacramental music."

The beauty of Gaynor's voice with its Irish lilt and accent had taken him by surprise. He had noticed her hands, how long they were, and her long legs in her black mucking boots. But that voice. Like a bell. And that bright red hair. *Now here is a woman I'd like to know!* he told himself.

"Of course, we'll leave the prescribed service up to you, Father," Sarah said. "As to the recessional, could we have, 'Ode to Joy?'"

And Isabel, her feet on the floor now, sitting up straight, as if she were already in church, had said, "Of course. Yes! And for Mary Martha, let's please have the communal hymn, 'Sing Me to Heaven.'"

"Perfect," Sarah murmured.

Before he could respond, Sarah had written that down. And with that the service was planned and without a word said about the brutality of Mary Martha's death or about the person who had killed her.

❋

Sarah has arrived early for the funeral, determined to save room for her friends. Accordingly, she has spread herself out by leaving a little room between her left side and the pew's end and by stretching out her right hand, palm down, along the pew and then placing her handbag on the other side of her hand. Two seats, maybe three, she is saving.

The church smells of incense and candles burning and England. Sarah has never been to England, but she once read that Noel Coward said of Gertrude Lawrence that "Gertrude loves the Church of England, with all its responses and candles in sconces." Sarah feels that way. The mingled smells of incense and candles burning are a great comfort to her.

Sarah sighs. The church is filling up, people streaming down both aisles and now she sees that Betsy and Gaynor have found a place all the way across two aisles from her. Isabel is probably already seated. No telling where. She looks down at her clasped hands. A manicure would have helped. Carefully, she extracts the dirt from the fingernails of her left hand. Even a week later, everything still seems like a bad dream. She cannot believe that she is here. In church. For Mary Martha's funeral.

Amid the silence, she feels the heightening of tension that always precedes the procession. No. It's not the processional. There's no swell of the organ. Nor is the congregation rising. It might be Clovis. Only the entrance of the family causes this sudden sway in a congregation. Now people turn their heads, craning. Dimly, she realizes there is a man in a blue suit standing at the end of her pew. Relinquishing the seats she's been saving, she takes up her handbag and slides over. The man sits so close she feels his coat sleeve touching her arm. Now, now! the procession begins, and they stand. She catches a glimpse of Isabel, wearing red, near the front.

Of course she's near the front. She'll be reading whatever it is that she has written. Last night she had called Sarah. "I'm going to wear red," she said. "And I've looked in the Bible and Shakespeare. Nothing seems right. So I've written a eulogy. It's short."

Thank goodness for that! Sarah hopes it is appropriate. The church is full. Murder attracts a crowd. She shrugs. This is no place for cynicism, she reminds herself.

The man leans slightly to the right. His shoulder touches hers. "Hello, Sarah," he whispers.

"Jackson," she gasps.

People turn, frown, look away. And now her head is spinning, spinning. Thoughts tumble through her mind faster than she can sort them out. The last time she had seen Jackson. Dare she look at him? Fragments of the service filter through the jumble of thoughts. *We brought nothing into this world.* Hearing that Jackson had come back is one thing. Sitting by him at Mary Martha's funeral is another. *That I may recover my strength.* A prayer. She prays for strength. *In the morning it is green.* Her garden. Every morning. Even in December. She needs to focus on Father Lacey's words. *Thou turnest man to destruction.* Destruction. *Do* murderers come to the funerals of their victims? Was Isabel wrong about that?

The congregation stands to sing. She opens her hymnal. What page? She looks at the printed pages, but Jackson has found the song. Why would Jackson choose Mary Martha's funeral to make a public appearance? He knew that everybody in town would come. He is holding the hymnal for her. Sarah opens her mouth to sing, but not so much as a whisper emerges.

Now Isabel, at a gesture from Father Lacey, is standing and walking slowly, head bowed, climbing the two steps to stand behind the lectern. Why red? Flaunting the color at a friend's funeral. *Tasteless!* Sarah imagines the word on everyone's lips. She had learned long ago to let Isabel be Isabel. Logic. Persuasion. Pleading. All failed with Isabel. She steals a glance at Jackson. He is brown, very brown as if he's just come from Padre. He smiles at her. She had forgotten how blue his eyes are.

Isabel stands quietly for a moment and then begins: "A long time ago, when a husband or a wife or a child died, the clocks were stopped in that household and the bees were told." Her voice is soft and sure. "Doing these things made it possible to make visible our ineffable feelings of sorrow. But how can we in this age show the suffering that comes with the death of a friend? How can I show what her friendship meant to me? I have chosen to wear this red dress because it is a joyful color and our friendship was a joyful thing. When I realize that Mary Martha Mercer is gone, gone, gone, I long to stop the clocks and tell the bees. And so I wear this color. Although not a sister, Mary Martha was a sister to Sarah and Gaynor and me. We loved her. She loved us. Her love was constant. We will miss her every day of our lives. She was our great and good friend. I know you will miss her, too."

"Beautiful. Just perfect," Sarah murmurs as Isabel returns to her seat.

❋

Jackson has come to honor her memory. An impulse. And when he sees the empty place and the woman moving over, he sits by her side. It takes him a minute or two to realize the woman is Sarah Claiborne, and with the same pretty eyes and the freckles. But not until he whispers her name does she recognize him.

But when Isabel walks to the lectern, Jackson recognizes her immediately. In the sway of her hips, the proud angle of her head, although bowed. Before she begins to speak, her mouth seems stern, her face more angular than he remembered. But when she begins her eulogy, her mouth becomes vulnerable, her face gentle. Although her voice is calm, her tears flow constantly as she speaks. She makes no attempt to hide them.

Everybody in town knows or soon will know he had come to the funeral. What a crazy thing for him to do. A huge mistake. But, it's too late now to do anything but take part in the service. And whether the town likes it or not, he is now a part of Cold Springs.

After the service, he takes Sarah's arm and feels it stiffen.

"Jackson, are you coming to the cemetery?"

"Yes."

"I'll see you there."

"Look, why don't you ride with me?" he asks. And he sees her hesitation, for just a second it is there, before she accepts.

At the cemetery, she leaves his side to stand close to Isabel and a tall redheaded woman. Standing apart from the crowd, he watches the three women place roses on the coffin. Moving up the hill for a better view, he sees a man step from a thick stand of young pines and head farther up the hill. With his backpack, a guitar slung over his shoulder and wearing a poet's hat, he looks more like a European than a Texan. Who is he? What is his connection to any of this? And then he understands. The young man has visited another grave and is simply curious about the newest one.

After the service people begin to drift away. And here is Albert Aston with a large handkerchief in full view, but Al's grief is genuine. His eyes are red, his face is swollen.

He catches Jackson's eye, tilts his head back. *Wait a minute,* the gesture says. Jackson shakes his head and turns to speak to Isabel, but she is hurrying off with Sarah on one side and the tall woman with red hair on the other. Sarah, apparently remembering she had ridden with him, turns briefly and gestures toward Isabel. He nods, walks briskly toward his car, sees a man in a white hat, the sheriff, hurrying toward him, cutting across the cemetery graves.

"Mr. Morris? Jackson?"

"Rock? Rock Dallas?"

"I thought you might show up here."

Show up? Jackson has not smoked in years, but now he longs for a cigarette. He would have enjoyed shaking one out, putting it in his mouth and lighting it. *Show up!* Damned if he'll answer to that.

"Jackson, you know about our murders." A half smile curls Rock's upper lip. "Since you are here, we'd appreciate it if you would come down to the station and talk to us, give us an idea, maybe. For example, are they connected?" Nodding as if an agreement had been reached, Rock's voice is conciliatory.

"No."

"No? Did you say 'no?'"

"I am not coming to the station. If you want me to come to the police station, you'll have to get a warrant."

"We got the F.B.I. Her body may have been taken across state lines."

"Then get a warrant. And I'll have representation."

"A lawyer?"

"A lawyer."

"Jackson, how about if I come out there? I'd like to see your place. I hear you're building a pretty nice house out there? How about that?"

"Rock, you're welcome to come. But don't come wearing your white hat."

Rock lifts his chin and runs his finger round the inside of his shirt collar. "When I come, I'll have a warrant," he says. A finger to his hat, saluting, he stalks off, his face mottled with anger.

Dismayed by his own anger and the disgust he feels, Jackson longs to be home, to walk along the river, to talk to Victor, to see friends. *Friends.* Does that word have any meaning for him in this town? He gets into his car and drives. In his rearview mirror, he sees the sheriff's car behind him. He slows. What is the speed limit? It can't be less than thirty-five. He slows to thirty. To twenty. With one eye on the road, the other on his rear view mirror, he watches as Rock Dallas suddenly makes a U-turn and, with lights and siren going, the Ford disappears from his rear view mirror. Jackson grins. He will tell Isabel about Rock when he sees her.

He had liked Isabel's eulogy about Mary Martha. Moving around from one town to another, from one country to another, he hadn't made friends in the sense Isabel meant. He would like to see her. They would talk. A conversation with a friend from the sweetest part of his past is infinitely appealing.

Walking along the river that evening, he considers the turmoil he has just lived through. An emotional roller coaster. God! What an awful day! But when he had felt the urge to go home, it was this home, this place on the river for which he longed. Walking toward the construction, his stride lengthens. He has come home.

PART 5: 1980

A Jury of Her Friends

Isabel and Jackson

After Gaynor had driven her home, Isabel walked into her house and opened the refrigerator. When had she eaten? She gazes at left-over chicken and a broccoli casserole, two over ripe tomatoes and a wilted head of lettuce. She takes a carton of strawberry yogurt from the freezer, dips out a spoonful, stares at it and throws the carton away. She takes a quick shower, slips into a gown and pours herself a glass of wine. Standing by the wine cabinet, she drinks the wine and splashes more into her glass. Then she opens the drawer in her bedside table and retrieves Mary Martha's diary.

Sitting on the south terrace, Isabel holds the diary in her hands. After the long and sorrowful day, she feels numb, unable to mourn the death of Mary Martha, unable to find her way through a fog of memories.

When she finishes the wine, she will read the diary. Right now she's all to pieces. Leaning back against the recliner, she gazes into the darkness. The moon is waning, but the stars are bright. She takes a deep breath and exhales, slowly counting the brightest stars of the Big Dipper.

She tries to weigh the import of the day. The minute Jackson had walked into St. Alban's, she heard the whispers—*Jackson, Jackson, Jackson.* She imagined his name on every lip. The church had filled quickly. She knew some had come because they thought Jackson might appear. Others had come because of the sensational coverage of Mary Martha's death: *History Repeats Itself!* the *Cold Springs Gazette* had trumpeted.

Now, looking out into blackness, Isabel feels as stunned as she had been when the deputy took her arm to tell her Mary Martha had been murdered. Her grief had not been assuaged by the funeral service. Jackson's presence and the brutality of Mary Martha's murder had robbed the age-old sacrament of consolation. Even when she read aloud the eulogy she had written, she had not been thinking about Mary Martha or about the horror of her death. Instead, she had been searching the faces of the congregation, but she had not found Jackson's face.

At the graveside Sarah had whispered: "He's here. He's right behind us."

Isabel's quick nod acknowledged that she heard, but she refused to turn around. She could not bear the thought of seeing Jackson at Mary Martha's fresh grave. Sitting on her terrace tonight, she cannot bear the thought of it now.

Her eyes are adjusting so that the dense forms of the magnolias around the terrace begin to emerge. Her mind is a sieve of memories, of strange, powerful images that on ordinary days would have had no significance. The mournful sound of a train's whistle when they gathered at the grave. A magnolia leaf that fell like a hand on her shoulder when she stepped forward to place a rose on the coffin. A blue heron that flew overhead, flew higher, spiraling upward until it disappeared from sight. Spirits? Spirits singing Mary Martha on her way to heaven. How good to believe in spirits, as Gaynor does, when one loses a friend.

When Isabel had placed her rose on the coffin, Gaynor followed, ceremoniously kissing the white flower before reverently placing it alongside Isabel's. Gaynor, Irish through and through, knows how to mourn properly, she tells herself now.

As Timothy Rogers' widow, it was years before Gaynor looked at another man. But soon after she moved into her own house (Isabel suspects it was then), Gaynor had begun an affair with Bill Holly, a man young enough to be her son. Everybody in town talked about her and Dr. Holly, everybody except Betsy. If Betsy has guessed, she'll never admit it. And why should she?

The one time they met for bridge at Gaynor's farmhouse had been an utter failure as far as their bridge game. But that's when Isabel began to suspect the affair, although Gaynor's house seems an unlikely place for romance. It's drafty, and it's cold in the winter and hot in the summer. It's not well lighted. And it has a wild, feral smell, one that Isabel finds heady after the first few minutes inside the house. And clearly, Gaynor loves every unpainted board, every slanting floor and every leaky window of her *villanelle*, as she calls it.

Isabel has always enjoyed Gaynor's house. When she steps over the threshold, she feels an exuberance for which she cannot quite account. Gaynor's sheepdogs wander in and out; cats curl up on beds and walk overhead on exposed beams. Birds nest under the eaves in spring; in winter, winds blast through chinks in the siding. Hay has to be stacked in the barn; sheep have to be fed. Whether Gaynor is knocking dried mud off her boots with a poker or thrusting armloads of sage into huge pots or wildflowers into small ones, Gaynor is at home in that rustic, old farmhouse as she never was at Betsy's. It was when they last met at Gaynor's house, ostensibly for bridge, that she realized Gaynor was having an affair. Just three days before last Christmas, one of the coldest and the snowiest on record, they had met there when Betsy had been a special guest for the inauguration of Gaynor's new house. The first hand had just been dealt when Bill Holly stepped inside the house, asking Gaynor to take care of an orphaned pig until the following day. "An emergency," he said. "Several cows down on a ranch a hundred miles west of Cold Springs," he had said. Gaynor was to keep the pig in the house for warmth and feed it from a bottle every two hours.

When Gaynor said of course she would help and pushed her chair away from the table, "No, no," Bill said. "You go on with your game. I'll round everything up!"

Doctor Holly knew where to find things. Tall and thin and grinning, he found blankets. Old and new. Matches. Milk. A baby bottle Gaynor uses for lambs. A small heater. When he was ready to leave, Gaynor walked him to the door, and as naturally as breathing, he lifted his hands, took her by the shoulders and leaned to kiss her. Perhaps he remembered Betsy's presence or perhaps it was when his eyes met Isabel's, but, at any rate, he straightened, dropped his hands and stepped back so quickly that he stumbled.

"Gosh dern," he said, grinning widely and then, "Goodbye, ladies." And he was gone before they could respond.

If anybody else realized what was going on, nobody raised an eyebrow. And minutes later, Gaynor had plopped the tiny pig into Betsy's lap. "Betsy," she said, "will you be feeding this baby while I play this hand?"

From Gaynor's perspective, asking Betsy to feed a newborn pig was no more than asking her what time it was. Isabel knew this. She waited, thinking Betsy would refuse. Charmingly. Politely. The idea of a woman as elegant as Betsy feeding a pig was so wildly incongruous that she was afraid to even glance at Sarah for fear it would set them off. But when Betsy held up her arms to receive the pig and obediently bent to her task, it was Mary Martha who laughed so merrily that they had all burst into gales of laughter.

Then Betsy, smiling sheepishly, said firmly, "One does what one must," and this started the laughter all over again. After that, who could pay attention to the bidding! Gaynor had poured tea and passed freshly baked scones and honey around, and bridge was forgotten while the baby pig was passed from one lap to another. Remembering how tickled Mary Martha had gotten that day, Isabel smiles.

She raises her glass to her lips and, mildly surprised to find it empty, sets it under the chaise to keep from stumbling over it. Yawning, she clasps the diary in her hand, stands and, suddenly dizzy, holds to the back of the chaise to steady herself. Gazing across the terrace to the fields beyond, she feels a mist in the air and lifts her face to the night-scented air. She needs sleep. She's had way too much wine to read the diary tonight.

Turning to go inside, she hears the cry of an owl. *Whoo-whoo-whoo* it calls. She listens. It comes again. *Whoo-whoo-whoo-a-will.*

That's not an owl, she thinks. *That's a whippoorwill's call. Jackson! Jackson is out there!*

She stumbles to the edge of the terrace and, peering into the misty darkness, she sees a form emerge from the shadowy magnolias. Seemingly, it begins to float towards her. She steps down into the wet grass.

"Jackson," she calls softly.

Only Jackson's white shirt is visible as he moves steadily towards her. Then he begins to jog, but still there is only silence.

"Jackson?" she calls again.

Without speaking, he continues on a direct path towards her. When he stops he is no more than four feet away, and he is laughing, just as he had laughed when he climbed through her window the night Rosemary was murdered. Her mind spins away. She is lost in time and space.

"Jackson," she whispers. "Remember?"

As she asks, she is vaguely aware of the weight of memory. What is it she asks? Is it too much? She cannot say what it is, that ineffable thing she wants him to remember.

"Jackson," she urges again. "Remember."

He steps close, close enough to touch her, and still he has not spoken. Then, "Ah, Izzy! Izzy!" he groans.

She puts her hands on his shoulders. "You're wet," she tells him. She takes the collar of his shirt and pulls him close. She puts a hand on his cheek and brushes the wetness from it. Frantically, she reaches for both his hands and holds them tightly against her breast.

"You came to her funeral," she whispers.

"How could I not?" he says. "I'm so sorry. Sorry for her. Sorry for you."

He smiles. She covers his smile with her hand.

"I liked your eulogy, " he chuckles, gathering her into his arms.

"I couldn't find the right words," she murmurs.

"And your red dress."

Now he is laughing at her.

"Let's not talk about it," she whispers.

"We can remember the past. Let's begin with that."

The past. The past is his weapon. He could use it against her. Has he come home to ruthlessly demand an alibi? Of course, she would give him an alibi. "Jackson was with me that night, the night Rosemary was murdered," she would say. She would swear to his innocence.

She puts her hands on his chest and steps away from his embrace. Suddenly sober, she says, "Have you talked to Rock Dallas?"

Jackson chuckles. "I told him to get a warrant. He said when he comes to my place, he'll come with a warrant.

"What will you tell him?"

"The truth."

The truth. He has touched a nerve. "I fucked Isabel the night Rosemary was murdered." Is this what Jackson will say to Rock Dallas? The truth. All these years Isabel has swerved away from the truth.

"Let's talk about the past," she says fiercely. "What about promises? Or let's talk about running. You ran away. Why, Jackson? Why?"

"Isabel, stop! Stop it! Why does anybody run away? I ran away because of you. Because of my folks. What are you talking about? I did not murder Rosemary! You know that. I left because there was nothing for me here! Nothing!"

"Everybody thinks you killed Rosemary! And now there's Mary Martha. Jackson, what kind of man are you?" she cries, hurling her weapons against him.

Defeated by the whiplash of her anger, he turns away and in three long strides he reaches the steps of the terrace. He stands with his hands on his hips, looking at her.

Isabel is immediately sorry for what she has said. She would give anything to take it back. Words said cannot be unsaid. She has known that since childhood, and, childlike, remembered it too late. Caught in the unfinished web of their childhood, she can no longer find a way out. Still she must try. She walks to him and puts a hand on his shoulder. "I'm sorry."

He shakes off her hand. "To hell with it! Forget it!" He strides away into the darkness, away from her and her anger. Then, as if continuing the conversation, he begins to whistle slowly, so slowly that his whistling becomes a dirge. *When whippoorwill's call and evening is nigh*, he whistles.

"Jackson, I'm sorry. Jackson?"

He begins to walk faster. Disappearing into darkness, he continues to whistle: *You'll hurry to my blue heaven.*

Dismayed, she falls onto the recliner. It's been too much. A second murder and Jackson back in Cold Springs. No wonder everybody in town thinks he's guilty. They are sure of it now. But Jackson did not kill Rosemary, and he did not kill Mary Martha. She will not believe it. She has to read that diary. Now. Tonight. She gets into bed, turns on the bedside light and opens the diary.

❋

Irritated with himself and with Isabel, Jackson jogs to his pickup. Why had he thought he had to see Isabel? It was a stupid thing to do. Isabel would always be Isabel! Difficult. Passionate. Compelling! When he reaches the Richmond road, he steps on the accelerator, eager to be home and on the river again. "Damn it," he tells himself. "Whatever we had, if we had ever had anything, it's gone. There is nothing between us now. Coming back to Cold Springs was a hell of a mistake, and this has been a hell of a day."

Refusing to waste any energy thinking about Rock's threats, he lowers the window of the pickup to breathe in the rich, fertile smell of the Bottoms. A kind of incense. At the church, the candles, the formal responses, and the incense—all had reminded him of Italy. He is glad he had gone.

❃

When Isabel had walked to the lectern, his first impression had been that she had aged greatly. But when she began to speak, talking so earnestly about stopping the clocks and telling the bees, she seemed innocently beguiling. Holding her head high, she had seemed wonderful and brave in her red dress. When he had first dated, *dated*, dated was too strong a word, he never had enough money, the right clothes, a car, never enough of anything to date; when he first started hanging out with her, she had told him that her church's ceremony was the same for everyone, prince or beggar. He had liked that.

After the graveside service, he had stepped forward to speak to her, but she was chaperoned away by Sarah Carter and that redheaded woman. When the sheriff's car disappeared, he had stopped at Bryce's on the way home. He picked up a chicken-fried steak, mashed potatoes, gravy and chocolate pie "to-go." He had ordered enough for two.

He had had a feeling that Isabel would come out to his place tonight. He had known she was thinking of him. He knew her too well not to believe this. She had deliberately avoided any contact with him at the cemetery, but when she had stood at the lectern, her eyes went everywhere, searching for him.

As a teenager Isabel had always had a mercurial personality. Anything could set her off. Once, after history class, he told her that Truman wasn't as smart as Roosevelt. She had lashed out at him, called him an elitist, and when he said, "It takes one to know one," she snatched her books from his arms, turned and asked Wayne Schuster to take her home.

After Jackson ate the boxed food from Bryce's, he sat in a rocking chair on the structure that was to become his porch. From here he had a clear view of the entrance to his place. Waiting for Isabel, he listened to the tree frogs, to a calf bawling for its mother and to the call of a heron. He dozed off in the rocking chair.

Waking to total darkness, he walked to the trailer, turned on a light and looked at his watch. It was a little after ten. Fairly late by Cold Springs standards. But he could drive by her house, at least that, "Call on her," as her mother would have expressed it.

He had liked Isabel's mother because she treated him like any other boy who came to see her daughter. Yet, Mrs. Jessup had had the most curious sense of propriety. Once, sitting on Isabel's porch, waiting for her to get off the phone, he heard Isabel tell whomever she was talking to that she had to iron a blouse.

When she hung-up, Mrs. Jessup said, "Isabel, darling, don't say you have to iron a blouse. Say press. You have to press a blouse."

Nuances. Subtleties of the South. He grins, remembering.

The idea of seeing Isabel, of talking to her, had begun to take hold so that he found himself picking up his keys and putting his billfold in his pocket. When he walked to his pickup, it had begun to rain, but he would not let himself go back inside for a jacket. When he reached her house, they would catch-up on the years that had passed since they were together.

Until he had actually seen Isabel, her presence had not seemed necessary. But at the funeral, he realized there was still something about Isabel, about the promise of her that made his heart beat faster. Here she was, a fifty-year-old woman, more exciting and interesting than she had been in high school. The French were right. A woman has no excitement, no interest until she is over fifty.

When she opened her door, he would tell her how glad he was to see her. After they had found their way to friendship, he could say, "Isabel, remember the sweetness of that last night. Remember the innocence of it. All these years, I've not forgotten."

When he had reached her house, it was dark. It was late. If he drove up her driveway, lights would come on; there would be a disturbance. Instead, he drove around the block and parked the pickup on the back of the property. Here was the shortcut they used to take from school to her house. He knew the way now, every crook and crevice of the path.

A light was on in the back of her house. When he walked toward it, he saw the gossamer form of Isabel. He began to whistle and walk towards her. Now they would reclaim their past. Blend it with their present. He quickened his pace and began to jog towards her. When he reached her, he was speechless, hardly aware of her questions, swept away by the pleasure of being close to her again.

She had reached out to him, tenderly touched his face. He had put his arms around her, feeling the springy curl in her hair, the silkiness of her body; not knowing where the gown ended and her flesh began. She allowed her head to rest against his chest. He held it there for a minute, enjoying the sweetness of the gesture.

At that very moment she had pushed his arms away, and everything changed. She had lashed out at him; accusation followed accusation: *Everybody thinks you killed Rosemary*!

Then the final charge that knocked the breath out of him: *What kind of man are you?*

Driving back to his place, he tries to grasp what had caused her sudden, wild plunge into anger. *Remember?* she had asked. Then, *Remember*, she said again. But when he started to remember, she lost all control.

He is flummoxed. He no longer understands Isabel. But when did he ever understand her. There can be no ease in her company, if there ever was. Clearly, she had been drinking. Is this what she has become? A woman, growing older, who drinks herself to sleep at night.

The cards are stacked against him. First, Rosemary's murder and now Mary Martha's. He will talk to the authorities. He's heard the F.B.I has taken on the case because Mary Martha's body might have been moved across the Arkansas/Texas line. He will tell the authorities the truth. The truth. This was what set Isabel off. She is afraid of the truth. But who murdered Mary Martha? He hopes to God they find the man who killed her!

Finally, he goes to bed, and, surprisingly, sleeps all night long, sleeps until the sun is well up in the sky.

The Diary

Isabel listens to the striking of the clock. The quarter hour. The half hour. The quarter hour again. Finally, the clock strikes seven. Good! It's not too early to call. Well, yes, it is, she tells herself. It is too early. But they haven't read the diary. If they had read the diary, they would want her to call! She is certain of it.

She picks up the small red book and cradles it in her arms. She will dress and then call, she decides. Hurriedly she showers, pulls on a pink T-shirt, with *"Paris Rocks"* emblazoned with sequins on the front, and steps into faded jeans. She calls Sarah first.

"Isabel, you woke me up!"

"I know I did. Please. Just throw on something and come over here. I'll put on a pot of coffee and call Gaynor."

"I can't get out of bed."

"Yes you can, Sarah. Last night I read Mary Martha's diary. Please come. I want you and Gaynor to read it. We only thought we knew her." When Sarah doesn't respond, she holds the phone away from her ear, looks at it, then, "Sarah, are you there? Sarah?"

"Isabel, that diary is evidence. You're obstructing justice. Burn it!"

"How can I be obstructing justice? I hadn't any idea her diary would help the investigation. I hadn't a clue. "

"Does it say who the murderer is?"

"I'm not sure. Rock may think it does."

"Oh, shit! I'll come."

Thirty minutes after the phone calls, Isabel sits at the kitchen table. She is pale, her face drawn, her mouth stern. In the morning light, circles like faint bruises are clearly visible under her eyes.

Gaynor has arrived before Sarah, although Sarah lives only minutes away. She also arrives before Isabel, reading the diary again, has put the coffee on. Gaynor has dressed; that is, she is not wearing her usual pants and boots, but rather her yellow cotton dress and sandals. Standing in the kitchen, arms crossed, she studies her friend who sits, head bowed, a hand covering her eyes.

"You're wearing a great T-shirt, love, but you don't exactly look like you're rocking. You look awful."

Isabel sits with her chin propped up by her fist. "I feel worse. I can't believe that Mary Martha is gone. Gone. The way she died. Oh, Lord. Her diary just about broke my heart." Her voice trembles. She clears her throat, swallows. "I couldn't sleep, and I drank too much wine. And Jackson came," she adds heavily.

"Ah, Jackson. Talk of Jackson will wait until Sarah comes. For now, we'll be having a bite of breakfast. Shall we?"

Gaynor's voice is the conciliatory voice of a parent to an ailing child. And without waiting for an answer, which is sensible since none is forthcoming, Gaynor butters bread for toast and pours a glass of orange juice for herself and Isabel. Then she finds a skillet and begins to fry bacon.

"Is Sarah on her way?"

"She should be. I called her before I called you."

Turning away from the stove, one hand holding a fork, the other on her hip, Gaynor says, "I thought you might have thrown it in the river by now."

"I was waiting for the right time."

"To drown it?"

"To read it. And, oh Gaynor, I have the most god-awful headache."

"Where are your aspirin?"

"In the medicine cabinet in my bathroom."

"Here's Sarah. I'll let her in. Watch the bacon."

But Sarah has let herself in. "Isabel," she calls from the entrance, and coming into the kitchen, "you need to lock your doors at night. We're not safe in this town. Something's burning! The bacon!" she says, turning off the burner. "Isabel, you look terrible!"

Isabel groans. "Gaynor's already told me how I look. Sarah, Mary Martha's diary sounds as if someone else wrote it. Certainly, not the Mary Martha we knew. Gaynor, remember when you said we didn't really know Mary Martha? You were right."

Handing Isabel a glass of orange juice and a couple of aspirins, Gaynor says, "I'm making a small breakfast. The diary can wait. Don't you think? Why don't you go out and sit on the terrace? God, it's a glorious day! I'll be bringing a tray."

Obediently, the two trail out of the kitchen and a half hour later, the three of them are sitting around the glass-topped table on the terrace. Gaynor and Sarah, eating toast with orange marmalade and bacon, watch Isabel nibble at a piece of bacon. When they finish, Isabel takes the tray into the house. When she returns, she sits down, holding Mary Martha's red book in her lap. Carefully placing her hands, palms down, on either side of her body, she says, "Jackson came last night."

Sarah leans back in her chair. The blue shirt she wears is a shade darker than her eyes; her short, stocky legs are only faintly darker than the white shorts she wears. Folding her hands across her stomach, she says, "Why am I not surprised."

"And?" Gaynor says. "Is he guilty?"

They watch a mockingbird swoop over the table to perch on a chair at the end of the terrace.

"No." Isabel says. Holding out her hands, opening them palms up, she says, "Jackson would never hurt anybody."

"Reading the diary convinced you?"

"No. Seeing Jackson convinced me."

"He told you he is innocent?"

"No. Yes. We didn't talk much about that. I was exhausted and had had too much wine." Running her fingers through her hair, clasping them behind her neck, she says, "When Jackson stepped out of the darkness, I felt like I was in the middle of a nightmare. This week has been horrible. After Mary Martha's murder, nothing seemed real. I lost my temper and accused Jackson of running away after Rosemary was . . . ah, you know." Sighing deeply she clasps her hands protectively over the diary. "And he did. He did run away. Sarah, you remember. And when I said, 'Jackson, what kind of man *are* you?' he left. He walked away whistling."

"He was always whistling," Sarah says. "He could imitate birdcalls." And in that small memory the past is carried to her—the days before graduation, her happiness over that, her tortuous love for Eddie. Overwhelmed by memory, her shoulders slump with the weight of it. "I'd forgotten how Jackson liked to whistle," Sarah says wistfully. And adds, "Apropos of nothing, but I had forgotten it."

"I'd give anything to take back what I said to him. Every word we said to each other got scrambled." Frowning she says, "Our teenage years were scrambled."

"By the murders," Sarah says.

Hugging her knees to her chest, Isabel rests her head on them. After a minute, she puts her feet on the floor and straightens in her chair. "Here. This is where it begins."

She moistens her lips and begins to read.

Tuesday, April 7

It is three o'clock in the morning, but I am too excited to sleep. Miss Eyre has purred herself to sleep and is curled on the foot of my bed, keeping my feet quite cozy. A word about Miss Eyre. Miss Eyre is part of the new direction my life has taken. I have never wanted an animal and certainly not a cat. I have never been fond of cats. But one day, I came home and there she was, sitting on my coffee table with her tail gracefully curled around her feet. I almost named her Isabel. But, considering her even temperament and Isabel's moods, I believe Miss Eyre suits her better.

Isabel stops reading. "I'm not moody," she says calmly. "And I'm not a bit temperamental." Her mouth twitches into a smile. "Not usually," she concedes.

Sarah tilts her head, studying her old friend. She raises an eyebrow.

Smiling ruefully, Isabel says, "Mary Martha's right. Miss Eyre is more appropriate. This next bit is also about the cat:"

Miss Eyre is a soft, gray tabby with the most extraordinary emerald eyes. She is beautiful. When she saw me that first night, she ran upstairs and disappeared. But late that night, I felt her jump up on my bed. She scratched around, making herself a little nest beside my feet. And then she began to purr! I had never before listened to a cat purring, not in my whole life long. Mother would not tolerate cats, but I have found that purring soothes. It comforts me in much the same way Miss Austen's letters do. I listened for a while. Then I closed my eyes thinking I would get up the next minute and put Miss Eyre out. And the next thing I knew it was morning! And Miss Eyre was not to be seen, but all the same, before I left for bridge at Isabel's, I placed a saucer of cream on the floor.

Isabel's voice is soft. She has read the passage slowly as if each word must be heard and remembered.

Sarah lifts her right hand. "Isabel, this is amazing, truly amazing. I didn't know Mary Martha had a cat. Did you? Did you, Gaynor?"

"I never heard a word about a cat! I certainly never saw a cat."

"But she says her life has taken a turn. We know that's true."

"Could a cat have caused it?" Gaynor's voice is full of laughter.

"Let's move to my bedroom," Isabel whispers. "We need a little privacy."

"And I don't want to go to jail," Sarah says, picking up her coffee cup.

Taking their cups and coffee pot with them, they move to the bedroom and close the door, although they know that Isabel will probably tell Willie B. everything as soon as they leave. Or almost everything.

Isabel and Sarah sit on the bed, propped against many pillows. Her red hair frizzed by the humidity, Gaynor wriggles herself into the chintz-covered chair until it conforms to her invisible specifications, and then she hikes her dress up for still more comfort.

While they wait for her to get comfortable, it occurs to Isabel that Gaynor is a very sensual woman. "O.K." she says. "Here we go," and she begins to read:

P.S. April 8th, the next morning,

Since Jackson has returned, I have become utterly fearless. Angrily fearless. Just yesterday, I picked up a hitchhiker on my way to Isabel's for bridge. I thought he was Sarah's son, John, when I stopped, but it was a happy mistake. The young man, Jake Ramsey, carrying a book and a guitar, was perfectly charming. And this morning, I had a delightful walk along the dry creek bed. I have always been hesitant about following the creek bed into the woods, but today, thinking of Miss Austen and her walks, I found it so enjoyable that I plan to walk there again tomorrow.

"A hitchhiker!" Gaynor giggles.

"It might well have been John," Sarah says. "Eve says he sometimes hitchhikes to Dallas. But I can't believe Mary Martha would pick up a stranger!"

"If she thought it was John, she'd stop. But what's this about Miss Austen?" Gaynor says, clearly amused by the diary.

"She was crazy about Jane Austen. Remember, she was a Janeite. They're all supposed to be intelligent," Sarah says, as if this explained the walk and the cat as well as Mary Martha's new-found courage.

Isabel grins. "Wait! Just wait," she says and turns a page:

Thursday, April 9th

> *When I arrived late for bridge, they had looked up, eyebrows raised, half smiles on their faces. But I did not tell them about Miss Eyre because I may decide not to keep her. And I certainly couldn't tell them about the young hitchhiker, although I would have enjoyed the flurry of excitement my telling them would have caused. Today it is as if a window has suddenly opened and there's a fresh wind blowing through my house. Now I'm looking forward to . . . something. I'm not sure what that something is, but I have embarked on a different path!!*

Smoothing out the ribbon marker in the diary, "Can you believe this?" Isabel asks.

"She was not herself," Sarah says sadly.

Handing the diary to Sarah, "You read," Isabel says, and puts her crossed arms behind her head and, leaning back against the pillows, closes her eyes.

Sarah sits cross-legged on the bed, facing both Isabel and Gaynor. Her voice is deeper and more energetic than Isabel's as she begins:

Saturday, April 11th

> *Jackson always had nerve. I admire him for that. And I have always known when he was near me. It's an extra sensory thing. I'm trying to decide what to do about Jackson. I have never told anyone the whole truth about the night Rosemary was murdered. I have never told the ranger that when I drove to the park to meet Jackson,*

I saw Jackson jump into Rosemary's car. With my own eyes, I saw that! That's the truth. And a few hours later Rosemary was murdered.

I'm going to wait. As Isabel says, "Everything will unfold." I know Jackson has come back for a reason. Thank the Lord I'm no longer afraid of him. In fact, he might be afraid of me.

I am afraid of only one thing now. I'm afraid Miss Eyre might leave as suddenly as she came. Love is a dangerous thing.

Sarah, her eyes glistening, says, "It is. Love is hard."

"It's your children, isn't it?" Gaynor says.

"They're growing up. They'll be fine," Sarah says wistfully. And then, impudently, "I think I'll get a cat. They're easier."

"Wait a minute," says Isabel. "Mary Martha never told us or anybody else she saw Jackson in Rosemary's car just before she was murdered. She always said she saw him the next morning, on foot."

"Isabel, we have to face it! Jackson might be guilty."

"No!" says Isabel. "Sarah, what about this hitchhiker with his book and guitar? He's the same man I saw one morning. You saw him, too."

"Yes, and when I mentioned it, Mary Martha's hand shook so that her teacup rattled." Sarah, clearly bemused by something other than the diary she holds, says, "I can't believe the cat."

"It's strange that you both saw the hitchhiker Mary Martha picked up," says Gaynor. And gently taking the book from Sarah's hands, she adds, "He was at the cemetery. He was standing on the hill, almost out of sight in the trees. Who is he? Could he have been following Mary Martha?"

They shake their heads, frown. "Not to her grave," says Isabel. "But we all saw him. This is too much."

"Absolutely!" Gaynor says. "Let's tell the sheriff about this boy. He could question him, at least."

"No!" says Isabel vehemently. "If we tell the sheriff, we'll have to give him the diary."

"All right. Let's finish the diary," says Gaynor. And still reclining in the chair and with her feet propped up on the bed Gaynor begins:

Tuesday, April 14th

Miss Eyre and I drove out to the Tanner farm and saw with our own eyes the red plane everybody thinks is Jackson's. But it's not. A man, looking remarkably like Woody Allen, only taller and more handsome, got in the plane, taxied to a pasture that had a newly mown strip down its center, and took off, clearing the bank of cypress trees along the river by no more than five feet. I saw no other person, but the property is cross fenced and Jackson has black cattle grazing in the pasture. That night I went to bed early and was able to relax with Miss Eyre purring on the foot of my bed.

I have come to the realization that my friends, imperfect as they are, need my advice. I know I would be a better mother than Isabel, who has allowed her children to grow up too fast and now they're off in California, and although she misses them, she's too proud to say it. She needs to get on the phone and say "Ready or not! Here I come!" And Sarah. Oh, that dear girl! Keeping them in the nest far too long. Children are like birds. They have to be eased out of the nest. It's too bad her house had to burn in order to get her children out. Mothering requires balance. Isabel goes too far one way; Sarah too far the other. Miss Eyre and I are in perfect balance. Purring, Miss Eyre stares gently at me, and when I look at her, I smile. Thus we commune with each other.

When Gaynor reads, her expression is solemn, but suddenly there is the sound of pleasure in her voice, like a bell.

She reads this last, looking from one to the other, and then a trill of laughter escapes and still laughing she falls back in her chair, holding the diary over her face.

Unsmiling, Isabel stares at her. "Gaynor, do you hear what Mary Martha is saying? She's adopted a cat and suddenly she's a psychologist. Can you believe this?"

Sarah frowns. "It's pretty good advice. I have always been too protective with John and Eve. I know I have."

Isabel sits up straight and crosses her arms. "This is just crazy. Here's Mary Martha giving advice about being a good parent because she has adopted a cat."

Gaynor chuckles. Then she picks up a glass, drinks and begins again:

Tuesday night, April 21st

I picked up another hitchhiker, a veteran, this morning. This is why I was late for bridge at my own house. I'll never forget this man. The things he told me about the war were horrible. Then, later, we pulled off the road because he was sick. It was as if he were afraid of himself or what he might do.

My friends would think I have gone mad if I tell them. They might even get in touch with Clovis. After they left my house that day, I sat, holding Miss Eyre in my lap, for a long time. In the middle of the night, the cats were howling again, but Miss Eyre sat calmly listening, as if to say, "That is not my tribe." Then we both relaxed, I on my pillow and she, purring, at my feet.

Wednesday, April 22nd

I got up at six this morning, put a bowl of cream on the floor for Miss Eyre (although she doesn't eat enough to keep a bird alive), and took a glass out of my cabinet. The glass was so dusty my fingerprints were left on it. I filled the sink with warm soapy water, washed and rinsed the glasses and the shelves they sit on. Then I began on the plates and the cabinet. With sudsy water all over the place, my skirt wet, the floor slippery, I took a mop, dipped it into the soapy water and mopped the kitchen floor. Stepping outside, I found honeysuckle in bloom. I snapped off some and put that in a yellow cream pitcher over my kitchen sink. After that Miss Eyre and I went upstairs for a nap.

What's come over me? I hardly know, I cannot say why, but life holds promise for me now. It feels like Christmas is just over the horizon. It might be because of the house I'm planning to build or because of my new companion or Miss Austen's letters, but my world is wider now.

One more thing: One day last week, Isabel called to say we needed to talk. She did not say, "about Jackson." But I knew that was what she meant. Then she said, "We need a record to remind us of everything that happened." I said, "I'm keeping a diary. But I only started a few weeks ago." She laughed and said, "Better hide it. Everybody has secrets." I said, "I don't. I keep mine right by my bed. Anybody could read it." But, all the same, I may decide to burn it.

Wednesday, April 29th

I am in danger and Miss Eyre knows it. She sits in the window hour after hour, at times meowing plaintively and, at other times, crouching, claws bared, she hisses. I stand by her side as if to say, "Whoever you are, out there, watching us, we're not afraid of you."

But I am afraid for her. If anything happens to me, I want Gaynor to take care of Miss Eyre. I can hear her saying, "Of course, love. You know I'm fond of cats. She'll be well looked after." I'll put her in my will. And if anything happens to me, I can die with a quiet heart.

Gaynor lays the diary aside. "Excuse me," she says and is off to the bathroom and splashing cold water on her face. Returning, she says briskly, "There's nothing I'd rather have than a cat named Miss Eyre." Pushing the chair closer to the bed, she says, "I'll drive out this afternoon to see if I can find her. Cats love the place, not the people. Let's see. Where was I? Oh, here we are":

> *Oh, about her name. Since my life has taken such a turn, such a dizzying turn, I've been reading something more in tune with my present mood; that is, I'm now reading Charlotte Bronte's "Jane Eyre." Jane has such courage about living her life, just grabbing the rope, swinging out over the water and letting go, as we used to do at Daingerfield Lake. She longs for a wider view, just as men do. A wider view in my own life is what I have recently found.*

> *But those sisters, Jane and Cassandra! They did walk about! All over England. Now I'm going to take a walk. Anything can happen during a walk.*

Gaynor hands the diary to Isabel. "Here," she says. "My throat has gone dry." The women are alert, holding on to every word, breathlessly waiting for yet another revelation. Isabel takes a sip of water and begins:

> *Saturday, May 2nd*

> *I drove out to Jackson's place. When I reached his fence line, I backed the car into the trees and waited. When Jackson left the trailer, I followed him. Miss Eyre came with me and, at one point, she ran across his path. I thought he would surely see her. But he didn't. He sat by the river and watched the sun go down. He seemed lonely. But I must not allow pity to deter me from action.*

> *Monday, May 4th*

> *I picked up a friend today, the man I met weeks ago. His hair is a little longer now than it was a few weeks ago. "Jake Ramsey, do you remember me?" I asked.*

He said, "Yes ma'am. And if you'll stop, I'd like to get out here."

He seemed so alarmed that I laughed. "You were the first hitchhiker I ever picked up," I said merrily, "but now I'm accustomed to it." Then I said, "So you never made it to Dallas."

"No, ma'am. I got so I like Cold Springs." Then, he was silent. I knew he was deep in thought. He said, "Ma'am?"

"Yes?"

"If I were you, I wouldn't be picking up hitchhikers. You might run across a mean one."

His voice cracked when he said this so that I had to laugh. But then I said, "Mr. Ramsey, there's only one thing I'm afraid of."

"What's that?" he said.

"I'm afraid of losing Miss Eyre," I told him.

"Who's Miss Eyre?"

"My cat. She's up here with me, in my lap, and she's purring quite loudly."

"I can't hear her, but if you'll just let me out right here, I'd appreciate it."

I asked him where he wanted to go and when he said the park, I took him out there.

The day was somewhat more eventful than I had planned so I resumed reading Miss Austen's letters. Her idea that most interested me was this:

"What a different set we are now moving in! But seven years, I suppose, are enough to change every part of one's skin and every feeling of one's mind."

Such wisdom. It was as if Miss Austen were lying on the pillow next to mine although the changes in my skin and feelings have come about much more quickly than seven years. It's amazing how happy I am. Tomorrow's bridge. We're playing at Betsy's. I must control the exuberance I feel. They would not understand what I cannot explain.

Tuesday, May 5th

Jackson called and asked if he could come see me. Sounding like Isabel, he said, "We need to talk." I said, "I'm busy next week," because I wanted time to think carefully. I might invite an officer of the law to be here in case Jackson's dangerous. I said, "Remember where I live?" He said, "I know exactly where you live." Further evidence that he's been watching me. He said he would call in a few days.

I arrived late for bridge, but only a little late, because Miss Eyre decided to come along. When we arrived, she leapt from the car to chase a large yellow butterfly and began to race around Betsy's garden like she was having the time of her life. My friends are polite, far too polite to comment on Miss Eyre's behavior. But Gaynor obliquely alluded to mine. She said, "You look like the cat that swallowed the canary." Until then, I had not been aware the Irish knew the Texas folklore. But it was very funny, considering that Miss Eyre was behaving as if she had indeed swallowed a canary.

When Gaynor's our hostess, we play at Betsy's because at Gaynor's house one is never sure what animal is going to drop down onto one's shoulders or jump up into one's lap. And there's the smell.

Isabel stops reading. "Gaynor?" she says.

"Mary Martha is exactly right," Gaynor giggles. "A raccoon came down the chimney this week. And we had the devil of a time getting him out. Go ahead with the book."

Betsy is not a good bridge player, and the cards came my way. I had taken daffodils to Gaynor. They made her sad because they reminded her of her honeymoon in England.

When I got home, my garage seemed so dark I decided I would get a motion detector light for my garage, although I am quite content without it since Miss Eyre curled in a ball at my feet. Betsy and Gaynor are planning a trip to Ireland and invited us all to come along. So, tomorrow I'm applying for a passport and planning a trip abroad. Abroad! The word sends shivers down my spine. Wait until I tell Albert about our trip to Ireland. He'll flip.

"Ah," says Gaynor. "She was that happy writing this."

"And excited," says Isabel.

Here's the last entry," Isabel says . Sitting up straight, she brushes her hair away from her face and, taking a deep breath, hurrying, hurrying, and stumbling over words, she reads:

Wednesday, May 13th

I dropped in on Albert today, just opened the door to his office and walked in. He was salivating over a magazine, but when I said, "Good morning, Albert," he almost destroyed the magazine, trying to close it up and put it away before I could see what it was. All I saw were the words: LAS VEGAS! written diagonally across the cover.

"Well, Albert!" I said, playfully. "A girlie magazine?"

"Business," he mumbled.

I said, "Albert, I've decided to make an offer on that property at the club."

"Good," he said. "And whether you build a house or not, the property is a good investment. When you're ready, let me know and we can decide which equities would be most prudent for us to sell."

Then I saw that Miss Eyre was on his desk, crouched low, claws bared and hissing.

"My cat has taken a dislike to you," I said.

He said, "Mary Martha, I didn't know you had a cat."

"Well, now you know," I said and I scooped Miss Eyre up into my arms. I left, thinking that Mr. Aston, usually so staid, seemed shaken.

Sarah throws her head back and laughs. Isabel giggles. Gaynor says, "Can't you see that banker watching a hissing cat on his desk. Taking her cat into the bank. I can't believe Mary Martha did that!"

"She imagined the cat," Isabel says dryly.

"What!"

Seeing the surprise on Sarah's face, Isabel grins. "Sarah," she says. "Mary Martha had an imaginary cat."

"Isabel, no! The cat is real!" Gaynor says indignantly. "It is! I'm sure of it!"

"Gaynor, please. Let's not quibble about her imaginary cat."

"Whether the cat is real or not her life sounds wonderful," Sarah says. "Adopting a cat, getting ready to build a house, planning to go to Ireland with us! What would Clovis say about her aunt if she knew all this?"

"But the cat couldn't have been real," says Isabel, unable to let the subject go. "Think about it! She didn't bring a cat to my house or take a cat to Jackson's place."

"An imaginary cat, named *Eyre.* And an imaginary walk with Jane Austen," Sarah says tenderly. "It all sounds wonderful. Gaynor, Mary Martha sounds even more Irish than you,"

"Fey," says Gaynor. "Maybe a little crazy. But the hitchhikers were real, and I think the cat was."

"Who killed her then? Jake Ramsey? She picked him up twice."

"What about the other hitchhiker? Or Clovis? Maybe Jackson," says Sarah. It could have been anybody."

"Not Jackson! Never Jackson!" Isabel declares.

"Isabel, she said Jackson called her, and she was planning to see him."

"Sarah, it wasn't Jackson! She imagined a cat. She could have imagined a telephone call from Jackson. It was some crazy man, somebody we don't even know. That happens all the time."

"The Dos Equis beer. That points to Jackson," Sarah insists.

"Sarah, stop it! It's not Jackson! It's not! When he hopped into Rosemary's convertible, he was on his way to my house. He was with me part of that night."

Sarah's mouth falls open.

Isabel smiles. "Yes," she says. "We did."

"Did what?" Gaynor says.

"We went all the way."

Sarah stares at her. "Well!" she says. And after a minute, she smiles. "Well!" she says again.

Seeing the look of astonishment on Sarah's face, Gaynor breaks into laughter, then Isabel joins in and, now Sarah begins to laugh.

"Oh, we were so innocent," Sarah says, wiping tears from her eyes.

"And sure we knew everything," says Isabel.

And for a minute they are silent, remembering their childhood. Finally, Gaynor says, "You say it's not Jackson. Then will it be one of the hitchhikers?"

"Wait a minute," says Sarah. "What about Clovis? People always suspect an heir. Except for the cat you've inherited, Clovis is the sole heir."

"Sarah, you don't think Clovis! Surely not, Clovis."

"It's possible. She wasn't exactly crazy about her aunt. Isabel, somebody needs to know about the diary. Somebody intelligent. We need to turn it over to the F.B.I." Sarah says firmly.

Surprisingly, Gaynor is shaking her head. She gets up and walks to the window. "Not yet. Let's wait a bit. There's something we don't know."

Staring at Gaynor, Isabel frowns. "Something we don't know? Gaynor, what in heaven's name do you mean?"

"I don't know what it is but there are things we don't know; things we haven't allowed ourselves to know." Her voice is vibrant. "We'll be turning the problem over to our subconscious. Together, we have a kind of tribal knowledge."

"Gaynor, I don't have a subconscious. But I'm not turning the diary over to anybody, not right now," Isabel says. Then, relenting, she says, "Gaynor, forget about tribal knowledge and your subconscious. Try to be practical. I'll hold on to the diary, and if Rock asks me for it, I'll hand it over." A smile touches her lips. "But he may not think to ask me," she adds.

"Because he doesn't know there is a diary?" Smiling, Gaynor slowly stands and, stretching her arms over her head, bends to the right, then the left. "I do have to go."

"Why do you have to go? Don't go."

"I'm going out to Mary Martha's to find my cat," she laughs. "No. I do have an appointment. We can talk more later. Just sleep on it, as you Americans say."

Shaking her head, Sarah says, "I'm leaving too, Isabel. I'll call you."

And in another minute, Isabel's house is empty, except for the sound of the Westminster chimes, chiming the hour.

Tribal Knowledge

The women withdraw. From raw grief. From roller coaster emotions. From discussions that lead nowhere. They withdraw from each other. Clovis's lawyer is on vacation and her real estate agent has not been interested in working up an appraisal. July will soon be over, but now, Cold Springs is somnambulant with leaden skies and threatening clouds fueled by dry lightning and rolling thunder. But the rain doesn't come. By mid-morning the humidity has vanished, and the sun blazes down like a hot iron scorching everything in its path.

Sarah, idly running water over an apparently dead hollyhock bush, has planted herself in her garden, but without purpose. Each week she waters longer and more often, but still the leaves shrivel, turn brittle and fall. In late July, all a gardener can do is wait. Looking up at a sky streaked here and there by thin cirrus clouds, she turns the hydrant off and recoils the hose. Unless it rains, she is bound to lose some of her most fragile plants, especially the ferns. And with the temperature over a hundred, even a hard rain may come too late.

Promising herself, as she does each year, that next August will find her someplace other than Texas, she dresses and drives to the library. Reluctant to go home, she works until she finishes the twenty hours a week she has been allotted by the library.

The next morning she showers and begins to perspire before she has finished drying off. She turns the thermostat to seventy. Wrapped in a yellow towel, she calls Hite, thinking that a punishing game of tennis might be just the ticket. After a set in this heat, the thought of the shade offered by the trees around the tennis court is tempting. But Hite's office tells her that he is in Chicago until tomorrow.

When Fall comes, the days will be cooler. But the mild depression she always feels in autumn will be worse this year. *I am projecting,* she tells herself. *By Fall I will have gotten over missing Mary Martha so much. This year I might enjoy September.* Determined to find her way out of the doldrums, she goes to Bryce's and has chicken-fried steak with potatoes and gravy for lunch. Then she buys a lemon meringue pie. When John stops by to repair a lamp, the two of them, rather more cozily than she would have imagined, sit down and eat half the pie.

Afterwards, John gathers the plates and takes them to the sink. He has grown up. Glowing with pride, she watches him load the dishwasher.

"Mom, I know you miss her," he says, putting saucers and forks where the cups usually go.

"I do, John," she says. Her heart melts. John has always been empathetic.

"Would you like for me to move back in? For a month or two? I would do that."

Children are like birds. You have to push them out of the nest. Mary Martha's precise, vertical handwriting is before her eyes.

"Oh, John, I think not. It's something I need to get over alone." She watches John throw his leg over the seat of his Harley, bounce up and down several times, throttle up and take off. The handwriting appears again: *Balance is what's needed.*

She sits in the garden that evening, considering Gaynor's spirit wisdom. Better even than wisdom. Or spiritualism. Or philosophy. Or, maybe, it's psychology! *Turn everything over to your subconscious. Relax. Eat all you want of lemon pie?* She smiles at the idea. This is not what Gaynor meant? Nevertheless, comfort food has its place, she tells herself when she wakes up the next morning, feeling rested and quite capable of managing her life.

Walking through her garden, she sees the ferns are beginning to wilt. She waters them and, using newspapers, fashions a shade covering for them. "There!" she tells them. "You'll be fine."

She pulls a garden chair into the shade of a magnolia and sits down, determined to think. Think hard. Gaynor had said, "Together we know more than we know we know." It sounds vague, arguable, shifting. But when Gaynor explains it, the idea resonates like a conservative-Republican-sound-as-a-dollar platform. The suspects are: one of the hitchhikers? Possibly. Clovis? Somewhat likely. Jackson? Jackson knew Mary Martha. Knew where she lived. Jackson could have murdered their sweet Mary Martha. But Isabel believes with all her heart that Jackson is innocent. And despite wearing red to funerals and going on and on about stopping clocks and telling the bees ("Whatever for," she had asked Isabel after the funeral. "What could the bees do about Death?"), Isabel does have common sense. Therefore, when Jackson and the hitchhikers are ruled out, that leaves Clovis. Clovis was not devoted to her aunt. She, Sarah, would go even further and say that Clovis disliked her aunt. But would she murder her? Possibly. No, *very* possibly. All at once another suspect pops into her head. *Albert Aston.* Albert knew Mary Martha and knew where she lived. And, *and,* further evidence: Mary Martha's imaginary cat, hissing, with her back raised like a Halloween cat. She chuckles at the absurdity of that idea. Albert is dull, too dull to be a murderer. That leaves Clovis. Clovis did not like her aunt. Clovis needed money. Who doesn't? And ninety-nine times out of a hundred, a murder is committed by a member of one's family. Using her subconscious and her common sense, the logical conclusion is that tall, skinny Clovis murdered her aunt for her money.

That afternoon Clovis, ha! Clovis! calls to say she is coming to Cold Spring next week. "So old-fashioned. My lawyer," Clovis grumbles. "Nobody reads wills nowadays. They mail them or something. Sarah, could you meet me next week? I'll fly in on Friday, and I'll take you to lunch. You and Isabel, too, if she wants to come."

Clovis. Clovis. If you only knew, I'm on to you. Sarah's voice is deliberately steely, formally steely: "Clovis, we'll be there. Next week. On Friday."

She puts the receiver down firmly. At breakfast the next morning, she considers questions that would draw Clovis out. Trip her up. This is her chance to study Clovis. If Clovis killed her aunt, a hostile expression, a refusal to meet hers, Sarah's eyes, a gesture—something! is bound to give her away. The night of the murder, Clovis could have driven into town after dark, stalked her aunt, killed her aunt!

She calls Gaynor. "My subconscious is working. I'm meeting Clovis next week and planning to use all my senses. Meet me at Bryce's tomorrow? We'll have lunch and talk. Two heads, et cetera."

"Oh, Sarah. The *thought* of food is too much. I've picked up a virus. Nothing stays on my stomach."

"Could I bring something out? A soda and crackers. That always worked with John and Eve."

"Thanks. I've got sodas and crackers out here. I'll be fine. I'll call you tomorrow."

"Well, darn it!" Sarah says and calls Isabel.

"Sarah, my trainer's here. He's at the door. I'll call you later."

"Wait! Don't hang up, Isabel. I'm meeting Clovis next week. And I think Gaynor's on to something about tribal knowledge."

"What? Oh Sarah, I don't believe in all that stuff. But, sure, I'll go with you."

"Good. There is something to be said for . . ."

"Sarah, I have to hang up. Jeff's about to leave."

Tribal knowledge. What good is it if you can't get the tribe together! After lunch, and somewhat consoled by chocolate pie, Sarah stops at a bookstore on the way home to pick up a mystery. Curling up in a chair, she reads it in one sitting.

❋

When Isabel's trainer leaves, she showers, thinking of that last starlit or, more accurately, star-crossed meeting with Jackson. Since reading the diary, she locks her doors at night, not because she suspects Jackson. Certainly not! But when she's unable to sleep, she wonders if it *is* something she knows that she doesn't know she knows that is keeping her awake. But in the bright morning light, she realizes she is far too practical to have a subconscious. But if she does have one, it's in a coma. But there is a murderer out there, somewhere.

On Monday, she bends and stretches for ten minutes and heads to the kitchen to find that Willie B. has put up the ironing board and sprinkled down a bundle of clothes.

She pours herself a cup of coffee. "Good morning, Willie B.," she says.

Willie B. is too busy to answer. She spits on a finger and taps the iron. Satisfied by the sizzle that ensues, she plops the iron down and begins. Steam rises. Her right hand holds the iron; her left hand, robot like, repositions the cloth she irons. Plop! Hiss. Plop! Willie B. pounds the ironing board.

Coffee cup in hand, Isabel watches her shake out the cloth and again reposition it on the board. "Willie B., are you mad?"

Sizzle. Steam. Plop! The iron is clearly furious.

"Willie B.," she says again. "What are you ironing? That's a sheet! Willie B., you don't need to iron my sheets."

"I ironed your mama's. I'm ironing yours, Miss Isabel."

"Well, don't! And don't call me *Miss!* This is 1980. Don't you know about the Civil Rights?"

"Civil Rights is more'n about who calls who what."

"Willie B., what might your problems be? Do you need to borrow a little money? Is that it?"

"I need a raise."

With her eyes glued to Willie B.'s face, Isabel slowly pulls out a chair and sits at the kitchen table. "Willie B., my expenses are high," she says. "And there's just me living here."

"Isabel, so are mine," Willie B. says, and in one great storm of activity, she whisks the ironing board out of sight, turns the water on full force over the sink, and with a great clatter of cutlery and china, she begins to rinse off last night's dishes.

Isabel stares at her back. "Well," she says. Then, "Well," she says again and stands. With her hands on her hips, she frowns at Willie B's back. "I'll consider it and let you know tomorrow."

Wiping her hands on her apron, Willie B. whirls to face her. "Tomorrow. That's Friday. If I don't get a raise tomorrow, I won't be here next week."

"You're going on strike?"

"I'm resigning."

Speechless, defeated, but wide awake now, Isabel leaves the field of battle, puts on a blue linen dress and drives away from the house *and* Willie B. Without breakfast.

Mad at Willie B., mad at herself, she drives east on I-30. She could visit Mary Martha's grave. Would it make her feel better? Or if she went out to Mary Martha's house, *that* might help. She feels bad about everything this morning. She hadn't known that losing a friend would be so hard. Maybe driving out to Mary Martha's house would be the best thing to do. With Clovis arriving Friday, she could tell her that she, Isabel, had checked on the house.

She's hungry now. And resentful. Willie B. could have been polite, asking. She wheels into the Coffee Cup's parking lot too late for breakfast, too early for lunch. Satisfied that the two eighteen wheelers and the single pickup parked in the parking lot have been parked there by nobody she knows, she goes inside. And there he is. Jackson. In the third booth on the right. She stands watching him. Head lowered, he's sketching something on a paper napkin.

Feeling her gaze, he looks up and his eyes meet hers. He stands, slowly, gesturing toward the empty seat across from his. Wearing a yellow shirt and tan slacks, he, a gray-headed, middle-aged man, looks older than he had on the night he came to her terrace.

"Good morning, Isabel."

"Good morning," she says, taking the seat he has offered. "I'm hungry," she says. "And Willie B. wants a raise."

"And?"

"I'm giving her one. I should have thought of it." She sits back in the booth. "Here I am, like I'm sixteen again, blurting out everything on my mind."

His mouth curls into a smile. "Old habits." He stirs his coffee, takes a sip and replaces the cup.

She leans forward. "I'm sorry about what I said to you that night. I wish I could take it all back. Everything."

Shrugging off her apology, he adds cream to his coffee.

"Jackson, I do have one question. You don't have to tell me if . . ."

"Let's hear it." He crumbles up the paper napkin and tosses it down on the table.

"I'm wondering why you came back?"

"Poor timing," he says, looking up at their waiter, a young Hispanic man, his pencil poised to take their orders. "Isabel?"

"I'd like a poached egg, bacon and fruit juice. Two pieces of toast, buttered. And coffee."

"Double that order. Thanks."

The sleeves of Jackson's shirt are rolled to his elbows, the collar unfastened. Crossing his arms, he leans back.

"Why did I come back?" he says, slowly repeating her question. "It doesn't make sense, does it?"

He says nothing more, and now their breakfast has arrived. He picks up a fork and takes a bite of the poached egg. They eat silently, the silence between them like that of a couple, long married, or, at least this is how it seems to her.

With his fingers, he picks up a last piece of bacon.

"I remember the night you came through my window holding white flowers in your hand."

"A magnolia blossom. Tucked inside my shirt. I needed both hands to climb the tree." A half smile appears. "And, afterwards, my shirt, my pants, shoes—hurled out the window, falling down over my head. I've never been as scared in my life."

"Scared?"

"Of Willie B." Shaking his head, he grins. "She saw me that night."

"Well, my goodness," she giggles. "That's why she never liked you." Suddenly serious again, she reaches to take his hand. "She never said a word, and you're here now. Jackson, why did you come back?"

"When I've thought of home it's *always* been Cold Springs. The smell of the Bottoms in the fall. Like apples. And the blazing red of the big cypresses and forest oaks." Leaning forward, his face is alive. "And the wild plants—the esperanza and yellow stars, the Carolina lilies—like sunshine in the dark woods. The heart-breaking cry of a rabbit trapped. I remembered the early morning songs of the birds, thrilling beyond any opera. And how winter felt when it came and the wonder of an ice storm. It's all here," he said, tapping his forehead. "It's been here all the time."

He speaks earnestly, gesturing, his expression intent, and now it is as if Isabel is seeing him for the first time. A stranger. And in this light, she wonders what kind of life he had lived that would make the words he spoke sound like poetry.

"About Mary Martha." Her voice is soft.

"What about Mary Martha?"

"I know this. I know you didn't kill her."

"Mary Martha's death. That's one thing I hadn't counted on. You were right. Everybody in town is wondering about me. The sheriff will come one of these days with an arrest warrant. Nothing will come of it. But the talk won't go away. Suspicion will hang over my head until I die, unless they find the murderer."

"They never found Rosemary's murderer."

He picks up a piece of toast, looks at it. Replaces it. He reaches across the table to take her hand. "There's this then," he says ruefully. "*You* know I didn't kill anybody."

"Will you leave?"

"No. Not again." Uncurling her hand, he traces her life line with his finger. "What are your plans?" And when there's no answer, "Isabel?" he says again.

"No more Tuesday bridge games. That's for sure." She lowers her head and hesitantly, almost shyly, says, "I've been thinking about my children." She clears her throat. "They're in California and doing quite well. Mary Martha thought I should just invite myself out there. For a visit. I'm thinking about it."

He walks with her to her car, opens the door, and when she's seated, closes it. "If you're out driving, stop by and see my place on the river."

In the furrow across his forehead and the lines around his mouth and his eyes, she sees the years they might have had together. "I will," she says.

Coming into her kitchen later that afternoon, Isabel says, "Something smells good."

"It's rolls and chicken soup. Gaynor's not feeling well. You might want to take her supper out."

"I do. I will. And Willie B., I am giving you a raise. It will be in your next paycheck."

Willie B. nods and turns back to stamping out rolls with a drinking glass.

"I'll put on some jeans and take the soup to Gaynor," Isabel says, over her shoulder. Walking toward her bedroom, she hears Willie B. singing. She has no idea what song she sings, but it's sad. Even with the raise.

Hurriedly, she steps out of her dress, steps into jeans and pulls her pink *Paris Rocks* sequined T-shirt on over her head. She looks at herself in the mirror. Tightens her stomach. She might wear this T-shirt on the plane to California. What would China and George say? Would they look at her admiringly. "Mom! Cool!" they might say. She would love to hear them say that.

When she stops by Gaynor's to deliver the soup and rolls, she finds the house empty. She puts the food in the refrigerator, writes a note and drives out to Jackson's place.

The sun is low in the sky when she arrives, and the workmen, one-by-one, have begun to drive their pickups off the property. Jackson will be at the construction site. Her pink T-shirt is wet with perspiration, the *Paris Rocks* sequins sparkling, by the time she parks her car and walks to the site. When she enters the structure, she sees that the house is gloriously open. The roof is on and the floors laid, though still unfinished. Walls, two or three of them, are up, and, yet, it is wonderfully impossible to tell where one room stops and another begins. Large openings for windows and doors are framed, but the glass has not been set. All through the house there is the fragrant, bitter smell of resin that new houses have.

I hope it's never finished is her first thought. She stands in a large opening for a door and watches the slow setting of the sun accompanied by the fussy twittering of sparrows settling and the evening chirpings of warblers and nuthatches and thrushes.

She sees a cot and blankets, folded and tucked away in a corner. *Does Jackson sleep there?* she wonders and all at once is overcome by weariness. She unfolds the cot and a blanket, lies down and closes her eyes. When she wakes, Jackson is there, looking down at her.

"Hello, Izzy," he says. Though his face is in shadow, she hears the smile in his voice.

She gets up and walks toward him. They stand close, breaths mingling.

Touching her hair, he says, "I remember your hair, the spring in it." He takes her hand. "Come," he says. "I want to show you something."

He pulls the blanket from the cot and leads her to a place where they can see the water flowing toward the long, curving bend of the river. When Jackson spreads the blanket on a bed of pine needles, she remembers the youthful curve of his shoulders, the slight indentation at the base of his neck, his broad hands holding a basketball.

"Sit down," he says. She sits down, leaning against a tree. He sits cross-legged by her side.

From far below, she hears the faint sounds of the river lapping against its bank, and she believes she can smell the river.

He looks toward the curve of the river and, after a minute, turns so he can see her face. "I'd like to know what your life has been? Have you been happy?"

After minutes have passed, two? three? she says, "Most of the time I've been happy." She sighs. "I was engaged to a boy. I thought I loved him. A soldier going off to fight for freedom. Democracy. The flag. When he was killed, I cried for days. Then I began to forget him. Sometimes a whole day would pass, and I wouldn't remember to be sad. Everyone—his family, my family, the teachers, the whole town—had a different timetable for me. *Oh, child, you'll recover. You're young. Six months. Or it may take years. Someday, you'll be able to go on with your life. You may never get over it.* That was hard! I didn't want to wait forever to get on with my life. Six months after he was killed, I married George."

Her candor surprised him. After a minute, she spoke again. "When I married George (And where were you when I married him?), I wanted children, a house and a husband. In that order. But after I married George, I fell in love with him. With his goodness. His fine mind. Head over heels in love. I miss him."

She listens to the night sounds—the call of an owl, the chirping tree frogs, the lapping river. He covers her hand with his.

"Were you ever married? Jackson, do you have children? Have *you* had a good life?"

"No. No children. I've never been married. I lived in South America and Europe. Financially, I've had a good life, but . . . in Italy there was a woman. Anne Marie. She died five years ago in a train accident."

"You miss her."

"Yes."

"You loved her."

"Not enough. I thought we would go on forever, without marriage, without children. She wanted her children to have a Catholic father, an Italian father. I could have converted and taken dual citizenship, but I thought we had years and years ahead of us."

Searching his face, she said, "You talk about this house, this place, the way a woman talks about a baby or a lover."

Her honesty compels his. He says, "I do love this place. It's what I have now. There's one thing more." He stops, begins again. "When I thought of Cold Springs, you were always a part of it," he says slowly. "I had to find you. I wanted to see you again."

The rush into intimacy is coming too fast. She has to retreat, to step away from the urgency in his voice. Abruptly,

"Could we swim?" she asks. "I'm sweating. My mother used to say, 'Don't say *sweat*. Say *perspire*.'"

He laughs. "We'd have to dive from the cliff, about twenty feet down to the river. Isabel, I can't make any plans, beyond building this house, until they find the man who killed Mary Martha. It wouldn't be fair," he adds as matter-of-factly as if he were still talking about a swim.

She takes a deep breath. "And I've lived alone too long to live with anyone now." And saying this to him she feels wretched.

"How about a shower bath?" he says lightly.

"I don't have a swimsuit."

He takes her hand, leads her to the poured concrete that will one day become a terrace. He switches off a single light bulb, swinging from the ceiling and undresses. While he steps outside, picks up a hose and opens the faucet, she undresses in the darkness. Standing on the unfinished terrace, she watches his dark form, holding the hose, move toward her. Starting at her feet, he runs the hose over them, than runs it over her legs, her thighs. Now one hand follows the hose, rubbing her shoulders, her breasts as she steadies herself, resting her hands on his shoulders.

When he finishes, he hands the hose to her and, laughing, she lifts it high over his head and drenches him. They stand on the terrace, drying each other off with their hands. "This is crazy," she says, running both hands over his shoulders. "I'm not sure I ever want to marry again, but I'm glad you've come home."

His response is a pleased chuckle.

Now she draws him close, pressing her breasts against his chest, running her hand over his back. When she feels his bare hipbones, "It's not too soon for this," she says and covers his mouth with hers.

This is why we're here, she tells herself during their love-making and this is what she thinks when the storm of it has passed and they lie on the blanket he has again spread, sleekly perspiring in each other's arms. She rests her head on his shoulder; her hand on his chest.

Then she says, "I am going to California right away. I'll call China first, then George to say I'm coming."

"China? You have a daughter named China?"

"After a school friend. A wonderful Quaker woman."

"And George after his father."

"And grandfather. I don't know how long I'll be gone."

"I'm staying right here."

She steps into jeans, pulls her T-shirt on, and, holding on to his arm, slips into her running shoes. "I won't be leaving for a couple of weeks. Clovis is coming next Friday. I've promised to meet her."

Kneeling to tie her shoes, he says, "I want to see you this week. I'm going over to Dallas tomorrow. I'll call you when I get back."

As they walk through a pasture to her car, she stops and looks back over her shoulder. "A very large animal is following us."

"She won't hurt you."

She holds out her hand. A black cow, snorting, tossing her head, comes close. She rubs its forehead. "Go to bed," she tells it.

When they reach her car, he says, "I always wanted children."

She takes his hand firmly in hers. "They are quite wonderful," and all at once she is happy. Mary Martha was right. Her children are expecting her. Jackson loves her. And so, for this brief time, joy is reclaimed.

❉

The next week, Gaynor, wearing scruffy pants and a blue denim shirt with its sleeves rolled up, sits perched on the table in Isabel's kitchen. One foot on the floor, the other swinging back and forth, she watches Willie B. making a cup of tea for her.

"Willie B., your soup cured me," she says. "And those rolls. You make the best rolls. Ma's are never quite up to being rolls. They never get the courage to rise."

"Well, it might be she needs some Texas yeast."

Pouring steaming water into a cup, Willie B. says, "Gaynor, swinging that foot like a girl! Nobody except you could wear those old pants and swing those muddy boots and look good doing it. Considering what you all have been through, it's enough to put you in the bed."

"We'll survive, I guess." Gaynor takes the cup and smells. "Mint. Perfect! And what might Isabel be up to this morning?"

"You're lucky you caught her at home. I've hardly seen her myself," she says discreetly. "Now you sit right down and make yourself comfortable. Here's your cream and honey. And don't be hurrying yourself in my kitchen. When she comes down that hall, she will be stirring herself up and us too."

Now Isabel *is* coming down the hall, hurrying, calling, "Gaynor, why didn't you come on back?"

"She walks like that when she's feeling good," Willie B. confides.

"Oh, I see you've got your tea. Good. How about a piece of toast to go with it?"

"No, the tea's enough."

Wearing a white linen dress, finished off with a navy monogram on the pocket, Isabel does look remarkably fresh. "Sarah and I are meeting Clovis's plane," she says. "Clovis is taking us to lunch. You want to come with us?"

"I'm on my way to work. Bill's been delivering puppies most of the night. A caesarian. They're labs. Would you like a puppy? They're really very nice little dogs."

"Thank you, Gaynor. No. I'll be flying out to San Francisco to see China and George in a week or two."

"Which will you be staying with? China? More comfortable with a girl, I'm thinking. Or will you be taking turns?"

"Neither. I'll be staying in La Jolla. They'll come to me. I'm crazy about that old hotel out there."

"A pity. Going that far and not staying with your children."

"Do you think so?"

"I do."

"Well, maybe I will stay with them. I'll ask them. That's a good idea!"

At the sound of chimes. Gaynor looks toward the foyer. "The clock?"

"The doorbell," Isabel says, peering out the window, "It's Rock. I'll see what he wants." Coming back into the kitchen, she announces through lips curled with disdain: "The police have a strong suspect. They've been watching 'a person of interest,' as Rock calls Jackson. He wondered if he and I could have a little visit right now."

"I see you sent him packing," Willie B. says, looking out the window.

"Did you tell him you were meeting Clovis?"

"No, I did not, but I have to leave right now. By the time I pick up Sarah her plane will be landing. Oops, where's my bag! Oh, here it is."

The two watch as Isabel strides through the kitchen with her handbag over her shoulder, her keys swinging in her hand. Grinning, she gives them a thumbs up sign and is gone.

Willie B.'s lower lip sinks into a pout. "She's crazy about that Jackson. Always has been."

"And you're crazy about Isabel."

"Spoiled her," Willie B., says gloomily.

When Isabel screeches to a stop in Sarah's driveway, Sarah, chuckling, gets in the car. "Isabel? Isabel. You're bound to get a ticket before we get to the airport."

"No. I'm slowing down. Rock stopped by. Made me late. I'll tell you about it later."

"I have good news. Last night I told John he could not move back home."

"You're pushing him out of the nest? You sound mighty breezy about it."

"An hour later, I called him and said he could move back. For a month. That cheered me up."

Isabel smiles warmly. "You're making progress," she says. Turning off the highway onto State Line, she adds, "I've got some news from the Rocket Ranger."

Sarah's rollicking laughter bounces around the car.

"He came by my house and as good as said they're going to arrest Jackson."

Now, Sarah is quite serious. "Oh, Lord," she says.

"Nothing will come of it. But Rock's got his back up." Now Isabel picks up speed, notices the speedometer's on seventy, and slows. At the airport, she finds a parking place near the passengers' exit. "We'll see what Clovis has to say this morning," she says.

They see Clovis instantly, a head taller than the other passengers. In a bright, green dress and with her rhinestone sandals sparkling, she's hurrying toward them, her eyebrows drawn together by a deep frown. She sees them and waves, imperially, a royal wave of mourning. The Queen at a state funeral.

"She's guilty," Sarah whispers.

"What?" Isabel says, but now Clovis is upon them, and, brightly, to Clovis, she says, "Luggage?"

"No, Isabel. I'm only here until six. Hello, Sarah. My appointment with Mr. Arnold is at two. I do want to take you girls to lunch. How about the new country club? My treat," she says.

"Thank you." Sarah's voice is coldly formal. "I know you've had a world of things to do," she adds, offering a modicum of warmth.

"My life has changed completely. You have no idea."

"*We have some idea*," Isabel thinks.

"I think we have some idea," Sarah says frostily.

Backing out of the parking place, Isabel glances at Clovis, sees that she is fumbling through her handbag, taking out items one by one, until a small stack—lipstick, receipts, parking tickets, deodorant, two more lipsticks, hand lotion, tissues—lies in her lap.

"Your list," Isabel says. "You're looking for your list."

"I left it. Oh, dear. Right by the telephone. I was talking to Sheriff Dallas and left it. I'll have to manage without it."

Arriving at the club, Isabel parks close to the entrance. They follow Clovis inside to be seated in an almost empty, very large dining room. Clovis orders a bottle of wine and studies her menu. "The lobster looks good, doesn't it."

Translating that suggestion into: *Order anything you want*, Isabel orders the lobster; Sarah and Clovis the filets of beef.

Waiting to be served, Sarah sips her wine, sips it quietly, quickly, and reaches to refill her glass as Clovis watches. A slight frown creases Clovis's forehead. "I could order another bottle," she says doubtfully.

"No," Sarah says. "No, this is fine for now. Maybe a glass later. Thank you."

Clovis lifts her hand and summons a waiter. "Another glass for Mrs. Carter," Clovis says. She sighs deeply. "It's strange. I've been really sad about Aunt Mary Martha."

"Do you think it's strange to miss your aunt?" Sarah's voice is steely.

Clovis stares at Sarah. "I guess it's natural," she says weakly.

"Is it? Natural?' Sarah asks, unblinkingly. "The sheriff has a suspect," she adds.

"Well, thank goodness! Who is it?"

"A woman."

"Sarah," Isabel warns.

"A woman," Sarah says defiantly. "A woman who could have slipped into town, murdered her and slipped out. A relative. Maybe."

"Sarah, did the sheriff tell you that? Does he suspect a woman?" Frowning, her eyes narrowed, Clovis stares at Sarah.

Now Sarah's face reveals concern. Sympathy, even.

Clovis nervously fingers her charm bracelet. "I'm her only relative."

"Oh, my dear," Sarah says sorrowfully.

"I'm not a suspect. Am I? Does that ridiculous Rock Dallas suspect me?"

Sarah shakes her head sadly.

Isabel tosses her napkin on the table. "Sarah, I need your help. I've got a pin sticking me. It's down my back. Excuse us, Clovis. We'll be right back."

Before the "Ladies" room door has closed behind them, Isabel hisses, "Sarah, what's the matter with you. Have you gone crazy?"

"You saw her. You saw how nervous she is. How satisfied she is that she's the only heir, she and that cat, to Mary Martha's fortune. Isabel, she killed Mary Martha. She did. I know she did."

"Sarah, no! You're way off base, and Clovis thinks you're crazy. Your subconscious, tribal knowledge. Leave all that to Gaynor. This is not your department. Please! Just calm down. You are not a detective."

When they return, Clovis is standing, hastily untangling her handbag from the chair she's hung it on. "I need to get to the lawyer's office right away. I do need someone to defend me. Sarah is right."

"Clovis, you are not a suspect."

"How do you know? It makes sense. An out-of-town person. Rock is going to arrest me. That's why he's been calling me. Come on! We have to hurry." She no longer looks grim. Or mournful. Her expression is one of utter bewilderment. "What if I run into Rock! I could you know. If I'm a suspect I need to hire someone to defend me. Even if I'm not, not a suspect yet, I have to hire Mr. Arnold anyway. He will charge thousands and thousands of dollars. Probably every penny Aunt Martha left me."

Sarah clears her throat, politely. "Clovis, Mr. Arnold is wills and probate. You need a defense attorney. A criminal lawyer."

"Oh, dear God."

"I'm sorry," Sarah says.

"Clovis, talk to Rock," Isabel says gently. "He'll tell you if he suspects you. I'm sure he does not."

"I'm not talking to anyone until I've seen a lawyer. Do you think I'm crazy?"

"No. I just think . . . Well, I'll drop Sarah off and then we'll go to my house and you can take my car. I won't be going anywhere." Glaring at Sarah, she adds, "Except to bed. With a cold cloth on my head."

Before Isabel has walked through the kitchen and down the hall to her bedroom, the phone has rung three times. "Sarah, I'm not answering. You can talk to yourself. I'm tired. And you are driving me crazy," Isabel tells the phone.

She puts on her gown and dampens a washcloth. Laying it gently on her forehead, she closes her eyes.

Hearing the chime of the clock, she breathes more deeply. When it chimes again, "It's the door," she says, throwing on a robe and hurrying to answer it.

Clovis stands on the porch with her back to the door. She wheels around, her face a mottled red, her eyes flashing. A Fury!

"Clovis?"

"Well, guess what! Mary Martha left her money to her friends."

"What?" Isabel steps back and stands looking at a Clovis who seems to be disintegrating before her eyes.

"Oh, you knew. I'm sure you knew," she snarls.

"No, I did not know. Clovis, come inside. I don't know what you're talking about."

Stepping inside, Clovis bursts into angry loud sobs.

"Clovis, calm down. Please. Tell me what's happened?"

"I don't want to calm down. I'm not going to calm down. What's happened? This is what's happened. Aunt Mary Martha left you and Sarah ten thousand dollars. Each. She left Gaynor more than that because of her cat." And now Clovis is choking with anger. "I didn't even know she had a cat!"

"She didn't. She only imagined she had a cat."

"Do you mean she left twelve hundred dollars to an imaginary cat?"

"Yes. I think she did." Isabel has stepped back.

"I'm about to die," Clovis hisses. "This is too much. A cat. Well, after I give over thirty thousand dollars to her friends and twelve hundred to an imaginary cat, all I'll have left is that run-down, ramshackled old house. Just take me to the airport. I want to go home. And I'm going to contest the will. Never mind the defense lawyer. My aunt was crazy."

They drive, the two of them, to the airport in stony silence. When they are almost there, Isabel says, "Clovis, maybe she *was* sweetly crazy. If you'll stop and think . . ."

"No. Don't talk to me. Don't say a word. Don't! Say! One! Word!"

When they reach the airport, Clovis leaps from the car and dashes into the airport. Without her handbag. "Damn," Isabel says, untangling the handbag from the handle of the car door and hurrying in after her. "Clovis!" she calls. "Here's your handbag!" And holding the handbag high over her head, she stumbles over a black bag, takes three running steps, before grabbing onto the first thing that comes to hand, and finds herself holding on to Albert Aston's right arm.

"Whoa-ho, there girl. Slow down. Where you going in such a hurry? Oh, Mrs. Arnold. Girl, I didn't know it was you."

"I've got to catch Clovis. She left her bag in my car."

Now Clovis has turned and is running toward her. Snatching the bag from Isabel's hand, "You'll be hearing from my lawyers," she says, before sprinting back to the front of the line.

Walking slowly now, Isabel passes Al Aston, standing patiently in line, his bag at his feet. "Sorry, Al," she says.

"I'm on my way to Dallas. Business," he explains, ignoring Isabel's eyes which are riveted to the red luggage tag on his black bag where the words *Las Vegas* in black letters blink up at her. Remembering the "Las Vegas" magazine in Mary Martha's diary, she is barely able to restrain herself from tossing Al a wink.

The Women and Theodore

Sarah has stayed out of the garden all morning, although between coffee and showering and dressing, she has peered through the windows at the falling leaves. But she'll not set foot in her garden today. Today, the women are meeting with the bank president. She intends to disclose her suspicions about Clovis to President White in a reasonable, organized manner. She has three pages of notes in her purse. However, not until she's on her way to the bank does it occur to her that the short, plaid and pleated skirt she is wearing is an absurd dress for a business meeting. How long has it hung in her closet? If John has noticed how unprofessionally she is dressed, he has not commented.

"So, Mom, you're meeting Mr. White at the bank this morning? You and Gaynor?"

"Yes."

"What's the occasion?"

"I'm not sure," she says.

He looks at her, smiling his disbelief.

"John, you're the navigator. Where do you want to be dropped off?"

"Here. Take this exit. It's out the Richmond Road. North about a mile," and then, "O.K. Turn left here. The shop is on the left about a mile down this dirt road."

The road over which she drives is narrow. On either side steep banks fall away to merge with desiccated fields of what had earlier been green with soybeans and clover. Now the road, following a dry creek bed bordered on either side by impenetrable thickets of vines and brambles, is beginning to curve.

"Here," John says. "Turn in here."

The *here* is a huge tin building with motorcycles and parts of motorcycles, in various stages of assembly and disassembly. The odors of gasoline and oil and grease filter into her car. John rolls down his window, takes off his cap and repositions it on his head, backward.

Grinning, he opens the car door. "Thanks, Mom," he says, and a minute later he is leaning into her side of the car. "Mom, in a year, maybe two, I'll own this place or one like it."

His eyes are those of his father's, Eddie's eyes, deceptively free of guile. "Oh, and Johnny," she says sweetly. "Remember. One more week and you're out of my house."

"Sure thing, Mom. No problem."

Sarah watches him walk toward the building, tall, lanky, his blue jeans hugging his hips, a skin-tight, faded-red T-shirt hugging his chest. *You want me to pick you up?* she almost calls out to him, but does not. She backs out of the graveled parking area, turns around and heads back down the dirt road. She looks at her watch. Nine-thirty. She will be at the bank by ten.

❋

A week earlier Sarah had been persuaded that a meeting with the bank's president was necessary. They had met for bridge at Gaynor's house where Gaynor, with a red shawl thrown over her shoulders and with her dark blue eyes shiny as embers, had woven a tapestry of the unconscious and conscious minds together with Shakespeare's spirits and Yeats's dreams and, thus, persuaded Sarah that she, Sarah, could ferret out a murderer. Sarah believes she has done just that. And when Betsy had stepped in with her advice to follow the money, Sarah had said, "I think a meeting with Theodore White is a good idea. Mr. White is a reasonable man," and then defiantly added, "I'm going to tell him I suspect Clovis." Just the mention of Clovis's name had wrung a satisfying torrent of groans and pleas from Isabel "No, Sarah. Don't say a word about Clovis." Now Sarah is even more resolved to lay it all out before Theodore.

Convinced of the logic of Gaynor's persuasion, augmented by Betsy's practicality, she turns off I-30 onto Broad Street and drives toward the Cold Springs National Bank. During the meeting she must forget that John is moving out this week. *And where will he go*? she wonders. She must keep her mind on this business. She has to convince Theodore White that Clovis is most likely a murderer. Thinking of it sends a chill down her spine.

❈

This morning, Isabel has been visited by happiness. It has hung about her, sometimes for as long as several minutes, before slipping away. She first noticed it when she saw the whir-ring red of a hummingbird at the honeysuckle and chuckled.

"Not had your coffee and laughing?" Willie B. said.

"Willie B., see that hummingbird at the honeysuckle! Jack-son said that a hummingbird in the air is like a sea horse in the ocean, at once the frailest and most beautiful of creatures. And I just think that's a wonderful comparison."

"Uh huh," Willie B. said doubtfully. "Well, you have been mighty cheerful here of late. About nothing!"

And then when Sarah had called to say she was not going to rake leaves because she planned to be organized for the meeting with Theodore, Isabel found herself smiling at the solemnity of her promise. Small things. And now, another. She had dressed hurriedly, carelessly for the meeting. Noth-ing would come of it. Why bother! Still, on her way out the door, when she catches sight of the reflection of herself in the French doors—a tall, smiling woman wearing navy blue linen pants and a light silk blouse with a sailor collar—she feels ridiculously happy. A perfect look for a meeting with Theo

White. Smiling at Willie B., she says, "Have a good day," and leaves before Willie B. can say, "Uh huh."

Isabel, like Sarah, had earlier decided that the logical thing is to meet with Theodore White. Her persuasion began days ago when Gaynor called to suggest they resume their Tuesday bridge games at Gaynor's drafty, old house.

"Who would take Mary Martha's place ?" she had asked.

"Isabel, nobody could, but we could ask Betsy to sit in this first time. Betsy's a good bridge player. We can play at my house."

"We could ask Betsy. But she may not . . ."

"Why don't I call Betsy. See if she's up for it. Then I'll call Isabel. Say a week? A week from tomorrow? Could we begin around six? We'll have an early supper and then bridge. Evenings are better for me just now. It's cooler then."

"That works for me," Isabel had said, not at all sure it would work for Sarah, who has never been as crazy about bridge as she, Isabel, has been, nor for Betsy, who has never liked playing in a house full of animals.

Still, however reluctantly, Isabel had found herself at Gaynor's house for bridge on the last Wednesday of August. All day long the skies had been filled with black clouds and claps of rolling thunder, but just as Gaynor was opening the door, greeting her warmly: "Oh, I'm so glad, so glad you're here!" it had begun to rain, and entering the house, she was immediately assailed by the heady smells of sage in great pots on the floor and heather in glass bottles on the table. And when she saw the windows flung wide open despite the rain, evidence of Gaynor's bounteous nature, her spirits spiraled upward.

Then Sarah and Betsy had come forward, Betsy brushing white hairs off her black pants and Sarah laughing at the energy Betsy was pouring into the brushing.

"H-m-m-m, what smells so good?" Isabel said, opening the creaky oven door.

"It's meat pie and whiskey pudding," said Sarah.

"It's delicious," Betsy said. "I've already had a taste." Perched on a kitchen stool, legs crossed, Betsy's right foot had made happy little circles in the air.

"Betsy's brought a fine wine to go with it," said Gaynor.

Jumping up, "I'll pour, shall I?" Betsy said, and to Gaynor, "Where's your glass?"

"I'm having water. This silly virus. I'm not over it yet, not completely."

What is it with Gaynor, Isabel wondered, but when she, prying, had tried to catch her eye, Gaynor had turned away.

They sat down to supper immediately, and Sarah raised her glass. "To Mary Martha," she said.

Gaynor, crossing herself, added, "May God's eternal light shine upon her."

While Sarah served the dessert, Gaynor, with her red shawl around her shoulders, shooed the cats out of the house. When she was again at the table, "Now. Let's use all our senses," she told them. "We need to think carefully about the murderer. Together we know more than. . . ."

"We know we know," Sarah finished. "But I know it's Clovis," she added, eliciting a moan from Isabel.

"We'll start with what we know," Gaynor had said, beginning to sound logical, as she always did sound during talk that circled around her Irish superstitions. "We know Mary Martha had changed."

They nodded their heads, except for Betsy who lit a cigarette.

"Betsy, please, love. Would you be stepping outside for the cigarette?"

"I think it's all nonsense about this smoking," Betsy said as Gaynor leapt to pull her chair out for her and open the door.

"I'll leave the door off the latch," Gaynor said and, as if there had been no interruption, continued, "What else do we know?"

"She had been picking up hitchhikers, but hitchhikers wouldn't have known where she lived," Sarah said. "It is possible that a neighbor, a repair man, maybe a tramp following the creek bed to the river could be guilty."

"Gaynor, Sarah, wait a minute! Let's not go off in a million directions," Isabel said firmly. "Murders are usually committed by someone known to the victim."

"Exactly," said Gaynor. "And that brings us to the cat."

"*That* brings us to the cat!" Sarah exclaimed.

"What cat?" Betsy asked, returning to the table, brushing more hairs off her black pants.

"Mary Martha's cat didn't like Albert Aston," Gaynor said. "Don't forget that!"

The absurdity of Gaynor's comment made them laugh. Then Isabel's "Gaynor, no! Forget that cat!" together with her determined smile damped down their good humor.

"There are spirits," Gaynor said calmly. "I can feel them."

Isabel gazed at her. "Oh, how I wish I could," she said wistfully.

Then Betsy asked, "May I have a little more champagne?"

"Of course," Gaynor said.

"Gaynor, are you feeling up to a little champagne now? Why don't you finish it off?"

"Not just yet."

Three small frowns appeared on Betsy's forehead. "Excuse me," she said. "I'll just step outside for another cigarette with the champagne."

Readjusting her shawl, Gaynor again ushered Betsy out and closed the door behind her. Then she put one hand on her hip and, leaning forward, her bright eyes dancing, she whispered, "I'm pregnant."

Disbelieving, they stared at her!

And then, "You can't mean it!" Sarah exclaimed.

"Are you going to . . . will you keep it?" said Isabel.

"At first I wasn't sure. Now I am. And I don't think I've ever been this happy. I want this baby."

"I haven't rocked a baby in a long time," Sarah said warmly.

Staring at her open hands, "I'm not sure I'm up to mother-hood," Gaynor said. "I'm not going to tell Betsy just yet. I don't know how she'll feel about it."

"I'm beginning to like the idea," Sarah said staunchly, turning to see that Betsy was coming back inside.

"What idea?" said Betsy.

Her eyes still dancing, now with both hands on her hips, Gaynor said, "The idea that I can call spirits from the deep."

Isabel said, "So can I. So can anyone. But when you do call them, will they come?"

"Shakespeare," said Betsy proudly.

And seeing Gaynor, with her blue eyes shining, her hair fiery red and the shawl over her shoulder, at that moment it had seemed to Isabel that anything was possible.

"One should pay attention to all animals," Gaynor said solemnly. "Especially cats. They are intuitive beyond our knowing."

Then, sitting straight in her chair, her feet, in high-heeled pumps, side-by-side, Betsy had said, "Follow the money." And in her deep smoker's voice. "Pay attention to the money," she said again.

Isabel crossed her arms, Gaynor leaned forward, Sarah frowned. "Can it be that simple?" Sarah had asked.

"Yes. Absolutely. Follow the money."

"Betsy, there isn't any money. Or, at least, not much. We thought there was. A lot of money."

"Mary Martha knew there was. She was planning to build a house close to yours at the club. Now, where *is* all that money she was planning to spend?" Isabel sat back in her chair and made a pyramid with her fingers. After a moment, she smiled and said, "We have to go to the bank and talk to Theodore White."

"I'll call Theo," Betsy offered. "Shall I say that the three of you will be in?"

"Yes!" Isabel said breathlessly. For what Isabel cared about now was her own happiness that had somehow become inextricably tangled with Jackson's. "Yes, tell him that," she said.

⁂

As soon as Betsy had walked into Gaynor's house, she had known the evening would be difficult. There was the odor, or rather odors, for one thing, making her sneeze, each sneeze followed by Gaynor's blessing. And when she hung her jacket on a hook just inside the door, she had seen the other jacket, a man's jacket, hanging there. And then, with all the windows wide open, when she had grown a little chilly and so had to put her jacket on again, there it was, still, the other jacket, hanging there as if it had some right that superseded hers. She would not allow herself to think whose it might be. The pipe on the kitchen counter could be overlooked. Betsy had always liked the smell of a pipe, and if she were, for example, in Europe, France maybe, she might buy one, smaller, more feminine than the pipe on Gaynor's counter, and smoke it.

When Isabel had arrived, Betsy had begun to enjoy herself. Isabel sat cozily by Betsy's side at the table, looking into her face as if every word Betsy spoke was the gospel truth. It was during their conversation that Betsy had realized that the sullen expression that was often Isabel's had disappeared. As the evening continued, Isabel frowned and made wry faces and lifted her eyebrows, but the stern look of denial was gone. Sex. Betsy knew it was that. Some women could live forever without that kind of love, but Isabel was not one of those women. She had often thought that Isabel should probably see a counselor. Counselors are good about sex.

As for herself, she could do without it. But then she was older. However, after Timothy's father died there had been that one nice little fling with Theo, between Theo's wives of course, but she was mostly content now. And she took a vicarious pleasure in all kinds of things, just now in enjoying Isabel's happiness. Now that Jackson has come back, she hoped he would be able to clear his name. These women would never admit it, but that is what it amounted to. Until Mary Martha's murderer was found and charged, Jackson's name would be under a cloud.

But right before the whiskey pudding, Betsy's evening had fallen into chaos. Although Gaynor had told her about her upset stomach, "just a little virus," Betsy had not thought a thing about it. And when she noticed the jacket and the pipe, the truth did not dawn on her. Even when Gaynor asked her to smoke outside, even then, she wasn't sure. But when Gaynor refused the champagne a second time, it struck her: *Gaynor is pregnant.* And worse, Bill Holly was probably the father. Oh, surely not. Surely not. Betsy had rather the father be a door-to-door salesman than that clumsy boy young enough to be Gaynor's son. But with this realization, her heart sank. Gaynor was too old to have a child. Having a child at forty-three could be dangerous. For Gaynor. For the child. But the only thing she could do right now was wait to be told. And that, too, would be hard.

A meeting with Theo would come to nothing. She was sure of it. Theo would think she was daft, as Gaynor would say, when she called him. However, she would make the call. But it had been the dire possibilities that the future held for her precious Gaynor that had driven her from the table to smoke a second cigarette so soon after the first. She would be there for Gaynor, certainly. And, perhaps, it was not too early to think about knitting. Modern mothers prize handmade things for their babies. Knitting would keep her hands busy, if not her mind. She would pick up the yarn, yellow, it should be yellow, tomorrow.

※

Gaynor had risen early because she wanted to feed the animals before she left for the meeting. She is accustomed to it now, the queasy feeling she has every morning, but if she avoids the smell of coffee and slowly eats a bowl of oatmeal, she soon recovers. It is the silliest thing, the most wondrous thing—what's happening to her now. Here she is, forty-three years old and expecting a baby. Pulling her long gray skirt over her head, she zips and buttons it easily. Last week, the doctor had said, "Now, girl. You don't need to lose weight. You need to be gaining a little at this point."

She has written her ma and da that she'll be coming home for the birth. Her ma had been thrilled. Her da, too. Both of them calling her up all the way from Ireland, though it cost a pretty penny, and as soon as she said, "Ma, I'm going to have a baby," both crying so hard they couldn't talk and so the money was wasted. Isabel and Sarah had been astonished, as she had known they would be, and during the rest of the evening the two of them grinned so foolishly at her, at Betsy, and at each other that she was sure that Betsy would soon be asking questions. But they would be right by her side, whatever decision she made about marrying Bill.

Bill would be honorable: "Of course, I'll marry you." He would offer that sincerely and have to be persuaded that marriage wouldn't be necessary. Carefully polishing her boots, Gaynor considered Betsy. Betsy might well think having a baby with no public father would be a betrayal of her and of her son.

When she turns down Broadway, Gaynor realizes she will be late for the meeting. She had never met Betsy's bank president, although when she lived with Betsy, she had always known it was Mr. White calling when Betsy's voice ("Oh, Theo!" she would cry), became dulcet, almost girlish. With the morning queasiness behind her, Gaynor was looking forward to the meeting. She needed to be there to see that the meeting proceeded in a business fashion.

❊

Now here they are. Three women seated at an oblong conference table in the Cold Springs National Bank. At each of their places is a glass of ice water, a yellow tablet and a blue pen embossed with *Cold Springs National Bank* in white letters. Sarah draws a smiling face on her tablet and holds it up for Gaynor to see. Isabel turns the smile upside down and holds it up for Sarah to see. Sarah shrugs.

The door opens and Theodore White, wearing a gray, pinstriped suit and a military mustache, steps into the room. He shakes hands with each of the women, adjusts the cuffs of his white shirt and addresses them formally, lingering over Gaynor's hand. "Is it Mrs. Rogers?" he asks.

"Trevor-Rogers, with a hyphen," Gaynor says, adding, "Please, just Gaynor."

"Theo, how good of you to see us," Isabel says.

Pulling out his chair, Theo asks, "Could we get you anything? A cold drink? Coffee?"

A chorus of "We're fine," "No thank you," polite murmurs, comes from the women.

"H-m-m-m-m," he says, centering his yellow pad on the table. Taking a pen from his shirt pocket, he clears his throat. "Mrs. Rogers has informed me that you have some concerns about Miss Mercer's estate. However, uh, as I told Mrs. Rogers, that information is h-m-m-m-m, uh, privileged."

He smiles steadily, carefully dividing his smile between the women.

Isabel folds her hands on the table. "We do know that, Theo. We came to give you some information. Mary Martha left each one of us ten thousand dollars. She left Gaynor a little more because of the cat."

"Well, yes, I did know about your inheritances. Miss Mercer's niece told me about that." Sitting back in his chair, he makes a pyramid with his fingers. A furrow crosses his forehead. "A cat? Did you say there was a cat?"

"Not a real cat," Isabel says firmly. "Miss Mercer had an imaginary cat."

As soon as the words are out of her mouth, Isabel knows she has made a mistake. She should never have mentioned the cat. She would have to get the discussion back on track. She opens her mouth to speak, but before she can say a word, "Miss Eyre did not like Mr. Aston," Gaynor says, doggedly staying on her own loopy track.

"Miss Eyre?"

"The cat."

"H-m-m-m-m. I see you ladies are in a, uh, playful mood this, uh, morning," Theo says. Studying Gaynor, he cants his head and smiles crisply.

"Let's forget about the cat. We thought the estate was larger than it is. Quite a bit larger," Isabel says.

"Miss Eyre is not an imaginary cat," Gaynor says, determined to stay in the Land of Oz.

Theo folds his arms, leans back. "H-m-m-m-m-m, interesting, the cat, I mean. An interesting cat. Apparently."

Well, she's pregnant, Isabel reminds herself, *and determined to remain pregnant. Who can blame her for fuzzy thinking?* "Gaynor, please!" she says, and turning to face Theodore, "Let's get back to the estate. We thought it would be much larger. Mary Martha thought so, too. She was planning to build a new house and go to Ireland."

Theo's eyes dart around the table. He repositions his cuffs. "If Mr. Aston were here, I'd ask him to come in. He has managed the estate for years. But Mr. Aston is in Dallas. I can say no more than that."

"Mr. Aston is in Las Vegas," says Isabel.

Sarah raises her eyebrows. "You don't suppose Clovis and Albert were flying off together."

"What!" Theo says. "Albert flying off with Miss Mercer's niece!"

"Sarah, not now!" says Isabel. "Remember what Betsy said."

"I'd be interested in anything Mrs. Rogers had to say."

"Betsy said, 'Follow the money.' And we told her there wasn't much money to follow. But, Theo, I don't believe Mr. Aston is in Dallas. When I saw Mr. Aston at the airport, his luggage tags said, 'Las Vegas.'"

"I'm quite sure that Mr. Aston is in Dallas. He goes there frequently on business."

"Mary Martha said that when she told Albert about Ireland he would flip," Sarah says.

Theo smiles benevolently. "Mr. Aston flipping! You ladies *are* highly imaginative."

"Another thing, Mr. White. We know the cat was imaginary," Sarah says. "But Mary Martha was careful about money. We are not imagining that."

"She was smart. The best bridge player in town."

"A Janeite," says Gaynor.

"H-m-m-m-m-m, a Janeite." He fingers the knot in his tie. His smile fades. "I had never thought of Miss Mercer as a liberal."

"Theo, being a Janeite has nothing to do with politics. Miss Mercer was a saint."

"Catholic? I thought she was Episcopalian, although her parents were Methodists. Fine, fine!" Lifting his chin, Theo wriggles the tie's knot back and forth, loosening it slightly. "Ladies, I will certainly look into this matter. Now, if you'll excuse me, I do have a meeting. And please, give Mrs. Rogers my regards."

Standing, Theo pulls Gaynor's chair out for her and watches as she—a beautiful woman, a beautiful, confused woman, and doubtless, a wealthy woman—leisurely stands, stretches her shoulders and turns toward the doorway. Thinking of her wealth, after all she is Betsy's daughter-in-law, Theo hurries to take her elbow, and with his other arm sweeps them all toward the elevator.

When the elevator's doors close, Gaynor says, "He doesn't have a meeting. He's calling a bank examiner right now."

"I hope so."

"If he isn't, we'll have to depend on Rock."

"Never!" Isabel says. "Not in a million years."

"We will hear from Theo White," Gaynor promises.

"We've found the killer," Isabel says. "Albert Aston murdered Mary Martha."

"Isabel, I'm not sure. Albert Aston doesn't seem like a murderer," says Sarah.

"Miss Eyre knew he is guilty," Gaynor says. "Just wait! You'll see!"

When the elevator doors open, they step outside and Isabel, chuckling, reaches to give Gaynor a hug. "Can an imaginary cat solve a crime?" she says.

"Ay, just wait 'til we're all in Ireland together. You'll be getting a taste of the spirit world," Gaynor says. And the lilt in her voice is there, and the warmth of it, too, as she adds, "And don't you be forgetting that we'll be playing at Betsy's the first Tuesday in December. And we'll be hearing from Theo before then."

"I just hope we hear ... something!" Sarah calls over her shoulder.

"And soon," Isabel tells herself, turning on the ignition of her car. "I hope to God it's soon."

Convinced that Mr. White, with the frosty smile and the doubt on his face, will be calling one of them right away, Gaynor closes the door of Bill's old Ford and inserts a tape of "Danny Boy and Other Irish Tunes" into the player.

Waiting

Theo will call Betsy. It will be Betsy, or possibly Gaynor, since he had fallen all over himself paying attention to her during the meeting at the bank. As the women wait, the days grow shorter. Colder. A week passes. Then another. And still Theodore White has not called.

As Gaynor waits she finds herself constantly seeking her lover's presence. At the animal hospital, she assists as he examines and treats the animals, and she is by his side during surgery and there when he consoles clients whose animals are quite ill or, at times, about to undergo euthanasia. And in bed at night, she curves her body, spoon like, inside his. Preparing for lactation her breasts grow firm and tender so that when he caresses them, kisses them, she suspects that he knows. How could he not? He must know. A veterinarian treating all animals?

It's a chilly late September and Bill makes a fire in the fireplace and comes, bringing breakfast to her bed. "There's a nip in the air," he says. "Stay in bed awhile."

Reaching for the breakfast tray, she realizes that she, like all animals carrying their young, has been seeking the warmth and protection of her mate. She looks up at him, her face alight with the pleasure of the sudden knowing.

Bill places the tray on her lap. Tilting his head, smiling, he looks down at her.

"You are a bonny young man," she says and touches his chin.

"And you, Gaynor, you are unusually beautiful this morning."

"I am delirious with happiness."

He leans to brush a lock of hair from her face. "Why? Any special reason?"

"Quite special. I'm pregnant."

Taking her in his arms, "Gaynor, are you sure?" he whispers. "I thought. . . I don't know what I thought."

"I thought the same thing."

"Of course, we'll be married," he says.

"Ah, William Holly," she says. "It's too soon to be talking of that. Pregnancy is naw a reason to be marrying."

"Gaynor, be serious."

She breaks into deep throaty laughter. "I am serious."

"You're not thinking of an abortion," he says sternly.

"No. I'm going to have this baby. But I am not going to marry you, not just yet."

"Gaynor, I don't understand you," he says and takes her in his arms again.

"Billy, it's all going to be wonderful. The three of us will be just fine."

❈

In early October, Isabel pulls on jeans and a sweater and drives out to Jackson's place. Painfully aware of the barrier that has found its way into her relationship with Jackson, an emotional and physical barrier as certain as a stone wall, *I must see him,* she tells herself. Too many subjects—her suspicions of Albert Aston, Rosemary's murder, their future together, their separate pasts—are off the table for discussion. At least, they can talk comfortably about his nearly finished house.

She drives to the farm under dreary, overcast skies and over roads rutted by fall rains. Black, spiky trees fill the landscape on either side of the road. Coming up to the pedestrian gate at the house, she marvels that she had thought that this drab, lifeless place was beautiful? The needles of the pine trees are yellowing, as is the grass, and the water standing in the fields has muddied into an opaque blackness.

Jackson's prized black cattle stand motionless in the pasture, sorrowfully watching as she opens the car door and steps into mud as deep as a pig's wallow. "Damn!" she says. Now the wind rises, a cold, West Texas howling moan sloughing through the yellowing pines, a wind that insults her senses. By the time she reaches the house, *his cold, dreary, unfinished house*, she is ankle deep in mud and carrying her mud-covered shoes in her hand.

Jackson comes to the door, seemingly unperturbed at seeing her feet clad only in mud. Without comment, he takes her shoes and sets them on newspapers he spreads on the unfinished floor. Then with paper towels and damp cloths, he begins to clean them.

"Jackson, what about my feet!" she says. "Look at my cold, wet, tired, dirty feet!"

"Izzy, you can take care of your feet," he says kindly, studying a damp cloth he holds in his hand. Discarding the cloth, he picks up a paper towel and begins to rub the heel of a shoe.

"Jackson, I came out here to talk!"

"So talk."

"Jackson, I want to know if you and I have a future together."

Now he begins to scrape the sole of the shoe. Frowning at the shoe, he says, "I'm not sure. I thought I was coming home, but whatever the word *home* means, I haven't found it here." Finishing one shoe, he picks up the other and begins to scrape the sole of it.

"Isabel, will you come to Europe with me?" he asks. His flat, cold voice is that of a surgeon, asking for a scalpel during a hopeless operation.

She hands him a fresh rag. "For a visit?"

"For a lifelong visit and with my ring on your finger."

"Not now. I don't know. To live in Europe, forever? No. No. As soon as we hear from Theodore White, I'm going to see my children. They're expecting me."

"Then it's settled." He glances at her. "You know where the bathroom is if you'd like to wash your feet."

"Thank you."

She carefully, slowly, walks to the bathroom. Then she sits on the commode and thinks angry, petty, childish thoughts. She gathers them up in the apron of her mind, practicing the list of accusations she will confront him with when he comes to see about her. She furiously turns on the faucets in the tub, sits on its side and puts her feet into the warm water. Slowly her anger dissolves. "*Isabel, you're fifty-one-years old. Grow up!*" she tells herself.

After a long while, he taps on the door. "Izzy, may I come in?"

"Yes."

Opening the door, he hands a cup of hot tea in to her. Then he disappears and returns, carrying her clean, polished shoes in one hand. Silently, he lifts each foot from the water and carefully dries it. He slips her feet into her shoes.

Breaking the silence, he says, "I've got a fire going. Come in the kitchen. I'll make dinner for us. How about catfish, roasted potatoes and a salad?"

She sits at the bar, watching him cook, smiling at the grace of his movements, enjoying the hint of a dimple that appears and disappears as he tells her a story about glimpsing a woman on a London street, a woman whom he thought was she, Isabel, tells of this woman, older and more beautiful than she had been in high school, a woman who looked "just as you do now, sitting on a bar stool in my kitchen." He finishes slicing a tomato and carefully puts the knife down. He walks to the bar and leans on his crossed arms so that his face is almost touching hers. "That's when I began to think seriously about coming home. It was on that street in London, seeing a woman who looked like you, who moved like you."

"Maybe I will come with you," she says.

Grinning, he shakes his head. "And maybe you won't. Izzy, this may not work for us. Small towns have old memories.

Even if they find the man who killed Mary Martha, I'll still be under suspicion."

"No, you won't. I'll tell everyone you were with me the night Rosemary was murdered."

"We have this night together," he says firmly. "We can enjoy it."

She nods and rises to light the candles on the small table in front of the fireplace. The smell of basil and garlic and olive oil fills Jackson's kitchen. They sit on the floor and eat and talk about a Rita Hayworth movie, called *Gilda*, a movie she had seen at the Paramount years earlier and which he had seen more recently in Italy, with Italian subtitles. They talk about Sarah's garden. Gaynor's sheep. They make love, and, afterwards, she falls asleep and drives home the next morning. But the wall between them remains.

※

Sarah has been invited to dinner. Before the invitation, each time the phone rang, she expected to hear Theodore White's voice. But now she has stopped worrying about Theodore White's phone call or about Albert Aston's guilt. Even her grief over Mary Martha's death has been mitigated by Eve's invitation that, to Sarah, signals nothing less than Eve's entrance into adulthood.

John is to ferry her out to Eve's house on his motorcycle. At first she had declined his offer. "John, we'll go in my car. I'll come to the garage, and we'll drive out together."

"Oh, come on, Mom! Have you ever even been on a motorcycle?"

"No."

"Well, then. Here's your chance. I'll be home by five. O.K.?"

When she calls Hite, he asks, "Where does Eve live?'

"I don't know. Someplace on the other side of the viaduct. This is my first invitation."

"And you're going on a motorcycle."

"Yes."

"I'll be at the club when you need me."

When. The word is so patronizing that she hangs up without saying goodbye.

Preparation for the evening consists of dressing down. She puts on a T-shirt and heavy socks and jeans. She pulls a woolen cap down over her head. When John comes, he eyes her up and down.

"Mom, it's chilly. Here. You take my jacket. I've got enough stuff on."

Wearing his blue jeans jacket, Sarah climbs up on the motorcycle behind him. "Hold on," he says, and they're off.

Arms wrapped around him, she ducks her head behind his back to escape the wind. When they arrive, she dismounts from the motorcycle into a small yard in front of a smaller house. She has made up her mind not to ask a single question. Not one! About anything. But the first thing she says is: "John, why does Eve have three bathtubs in her front yard?"

John laughs. "One is for herbs, one for cut flowers, and one for vegetables. In November she planted a hundred daffodil bulbs for Spring. She plans to sell all this."

Sarah imagines golden daffodils, piquant herbs and ripened vegetables springing from the enameled tubs. "Don't you think Eve's a lot like me, the gardening, I mean?" she asks, her voice warm with satisfaction.

"Mom, John, hello!" Eve, with fluttering shawls and scarves and swinging beads, comes running down a broken sidewalk to give her a warm embrace. "Mom, you came on John's motorcycle! Cool," she says. And then, her arm still around her mother's waist, "Watch it!" she says. "The sidewalk's uneven here. Come in. Come right in."

Stepping over the threshold, Sarah sees that the house is essentially one room, and that room is filled with the smell of incense and many, many burning candles. Wondering if the candles are not a vain attempt to hide the scarcity of furnishings, "Eve, this is lovely," Sarah says.

"Thanks, Mom. Now you just sit right here, in this chair," *the only chair,* Sarah notes, "and Mom, I've got great news for you! John, shall I tell her now?"

"If you don't, she'll find it out soon enough."

Oh, Lord, either she's pregnant or she's adopted a Chinese baby. "Eve, I can hear this standing up," she says. "Tell me now."

"I'm a vegetarian."

Relaxing into the chair, grinning widely, she says, "Eve, you don't know, you can't even imagine, how delighted I am to hear you say that."

"Mom?" Eve says doubtfully.

And now they're both looking at her, John frowning, Eve with a thin smile on her lips.

"Well! It's perfectly wonderful, your being a vegetarian. Wonderful! I'm just very pleased!"

"Maybe it's just a fad. I may not always be a vegetarian. I may become a vegan, and that's really hard."

"Either would be nice," Sarah says gamely.

"Now, for dinner. Everything's ready except for stir-frying the vegetables. Come in the kitchen while I finish up."

Three steps and Sarah is in the kitchen, watching her daughter sauté asparagus, lettuce, mushrooms and spinach in a blend of olive oil and garlic and lemon. Eve's cheeks are flushed. Her thick hair, ordinarily masses of curls, hangs in a braid down her back tonight.

"Eve, you look especially pretty tonight, doesn't she, John?"

"Thank you, Mom. Now. I have some real news for you. I could hardly wait for you to get here."

Real news. Sarah cringes; she steels herself. She has always disliked hearing *real* news from her children.

"Mom, I've going to join Greenpeace. They're trying to save the whales, and I am going to help them."

Another subject would be safer. Any subject. Sarah sips water from the glass John has handed her and swallows carefully. "Save the whales," she echoes, watching Eve happily sprinkle herbs over each serving and add a piece of hot, buttered bread to each plate. "Eve, the bread smells deliciously yeasty."

"I made it. Mom, have *you* thought about saving the whales? I know you love animals."

"No. But I do remember Haight-Ashbury and the flower children. Joan Baez and Bob Dylan. All that," she says, standing so John can draw Eve's one chair close to a wooden crate covered with a brightly colored shawl.

She watches Eve and John put their plates on the crate and settle cross-legged on the floor beside it to eat.

"Mom, Greenpeace is important. Save the whales. Save the planet," Eve says sternly.

"Your dinner is delicious," Sarah says, tearing off a piece of the bread. "The vegetables. All so fresh. Sweetie, it is all so good."

Eve sighs, a hopeless, long sigh. "You don't think whales are important. I know you don't," she says, frowning down at her plate, and then, accusingly, to John, "I told you she wouldn't care about the whales."

Sarah sips more water. She has always been a little afraid of her children, afraid of losing them, afraid of their anger. She summons up the image of Mary Martha's vertical, precise handwriting—*Balance. Balance is what's needed.* It is before her eyes, a rope to hold on to.

"Of course, I want to save the whales. I saw them once. Majestic, beautiful animals. And I'm very proud of you. Saving the whales. It's a fine thing to want to do."

"I'll need money to fly over there."

"I hope you can find a way to earn it," Sarah says. "Now what is that wonderful music on your stereo?"

"A recording of the whales' songs," Eve says dully.

"Their songs are accompanied by harps and silver flutes and tambours," John adds.

"And by the sound of the earth's resonance," Eve says, "but I know *you* can't hear it."

Sarah tilts her head, listening. After a minute, she says, "No, I don't hear it."

Eve remains quiet, staving off any possibility of pleasure for the rest of the evening with monosyllabic answers and great yawns and long sighs though she does allow a stiff hug and is able to muster up a cool *goodnight* when they leave.

When they reach Sarah's house, John says, "Mom, I'm sorry."

Dismounting stiffly from the motorcycle, Sarah says, "John, don't be. Eve is growing up. You both are. And remember, next week."

"I'm out of your house," he says grinning.

"Oh! And John, one more thing! Can you hear it?"

"Hear what?"

"The earth's resonance."

"No," he says with a reassuring pat on her shoulder. "And neither can Eve."

"Good!" Sarah says.

Getting ready for bed, Sarah reminds herself: "My children have always been strange. And, actually, Eve is a lot like I was at that age. Saving whales is bound to be a lot easier for Eve than saving Eddie was for me," she muses, settling herself on her feather pillow.

※

Gaynor is dreaming. In her dream, the bell in the tower of Saint Margaret's in Sneem is ringing. It is her wedding day, and Timothy, thin and gaunt, but with the sweetest smile on his face, is waiting for her at the altar. Then, suddenly, she's in a house she's never before seen and walking into his arms. Now the ringing in her dream becomes the insistent ring of a telephone, *her* telephone, and only half awake, she stumbles to the kitchen and picks up the receiver.

"I was having the nicest dream," she says grumpily.

"Mrs. Trevor-Rogers, Rock Davis calling? Sheriff Dallas? I have some news for you girls, if . . . Are you sitting down Mrs. Trevor-Rogers?"

"No. I am standing."

"Well, this news will wake you up. Maybe you'd better sit down. "

"What is it, Sheriff? Is this about Miss Mercer? We know Albert Aston murdered her."

"You don't know the half of it."

"Has he been arrested?"

"Yes ma'am. He sure has. Late last night. And they got it all on tape."

"Have you called Mrs. Arnold and Mrs. Carter?"

"I thought I'd ask you to do that."

"I shall. Thank you, Sheriff Dallas."

"Wait just a minute now. Hold your horses. There's one more thing. They're holding Aston in Las Vegas, but we're holding some evidence down here. We'd like you ladies to come down to see what you can make of it."

"Thank you, Sheriff. We'll be down."

"One-at-a-time."

"Goodbye, Mr. Dallas."

Replacing the phone, Gaynor sees that her hand is trembling. Sitting in a kitchen chair, she studies her hand. She looks at her watch. Eight-thirty. Finally. Confirmation of Albert Aston's guilt has come. She cannot, will not, allow her mind to follow the dangerous and dark places of a mind like

Albert Aston's, a mind that would drive a man to stalk Mary Martha as she walked along a lonely creek bed and murder her. She hopes that Mary Martha was on an imaginary walk with Jane Austen when she died, prays that death had come so suddenly that Mary Martha had felt no pain and that in her last moment of consciousness she was looking at some beautiful thing like the wings of a yellow butterfly opening on a green sprig of wild parsley. Holding to that thought, she takes her rosary in her hands and kneels. *"Hail Mary, full of grace, the Lord is with thee,"* she prays. Then, she steps into her pants, pulls on her boots, slips into a heavy blue sweater and drives to Isabel's house.

Willie B. answers the door. "Gaynor. Bless my bones. Here you are blossoming out all over the place. She told me already. If you need me for some heavy cleaning down the road, you just call." Hands on her hips, Willie B. focuses narrowed eyes on Gaynor's stomach. "You want to know?"

"I do."

"It's gonna be a girl."

"Thank you, Willie B. Now I'll be choosing her name. It's that important to a girl. What would you be thinking of Margaret Elizabeth?"

"Calling her after your mama?"

"And Timothy's ma."

"A girl could stand behind a name like that. But now you go right on back. She's not feeling so good this morning. Don't know why."

Walking down the hall, Gaynor sees the sun shining on the chandelier and on the faded rugs and on a bouquet of red zinnias in a crystal vase on the library table. Welcoming the beauty and familiarity of the room, she calls out, "Isabel, it's Gaynor. I'll be coming in. May I?"

Isabel, frowning, comes from her bathroom. Wearing panties and a bra and with a towel round her head, she asks, "Gaynor, are you all right?"

"I'm fine. The Rocket Ranger telephoned this morning with news."

"Oh? Well just a minute, Gaynor. I'll be right back." She returns immediately, with her green robe swirling, her hair dripping wet and a hair brush in hand. "Now, tell me."

"They've arrested Albert Aston in Las Vegas. He confessed to Mary Martha's murder. And, Isabel, he killed Rosemary. And that boy she was with."

Isabel sinks into her chintz-covered chair. "So it *was* Albert," she says slowly. "We knew it. That morning at the bank, we put it all together." She moves to the bed now and, pulling her robe close, she asks, "Is it cold in here to you?"

"You have chill bumps. It's the shock. You and Sarah were Rosemary's best friends.

Gesturing toward the empty chair, Isabel says, "Gaynor. Sit down. Even if we were sure it was Albert Aston, it's still astonishing. Shocking. In high school, he was always . . . ," she begins, but unable to finish her thought, her voice falters.

"Always what?"

"I don't know. Always by himself, I guess." Studying the brush in her hand, Isabel says, "I'll get dressed. Let me do that and we'll drive over to Sarah's and tell her." She pushes herself out of her chair, walks towards her dressing room and turns around. "Will you call Sarah?"

"Ah, Isabel, you're crying," Gaynor says. "I've already called her, and she'll be waiting for us."

❈

When Rock ushers them into his office, the women see Rock's desk with a big leather chair behind it and three smaller chairs in front of it.

"Gaynor, here. Sit in the middle," Isabel says, pulling a chair away from Rock's desk.

Rock Dallas, seated now, watches them arrange themselves in a semicircle in front of his desk.

"This won't take long, will it Rock?"

"Isabel, no more time than it needs." He opens the door, turns back, his hand still on the doorknob. "A Texas Ranger is on his way in from the airport. As a courtesy, we've asked him to join us. His name is Gonzales," Rock says, closing the door behind him. And then, opening the door again, he sticks his head in. "He has been on this case since '46," Rock adds, before again closing the door.

Listening to the sound of Rock's boots on the stairs, Gaynor asks, "Did he say 1946?"

"I think so."

"And would he not be speaking of all those years ago, and the four of you no more than children?"

Before they can respond, the sheriff has returned with the Ranger—a slight, wiry man wearing the alert expression one sees on the faces of small animals.

The Ranger takes each woman's hand in his, and, at a gesture from the sheriff, sits down in the sheriff's chair. Quickly, the sheriff pulls up a chair by the Ranger's side and sits down. The Ranger crosses his arms on the desk and leans forward toward the women. "I worked a murder case here in 1946," he says slowly. "It spilled over into '47 and '48. And there's not been a day since then that I haven't thought about those youngsters. Murdered. God almighty, I wanted to find the man who killed those kids." Gazing at the window high over their heads, he rubs his hand across the deep wrinkles on his forehead. Shaking his head, he clears his throat, and then, "Well, it just seems to me that every town has its great and small mysteries." And now it's as if the Ranger is talking to himself, thinking, wondering as he continues: "A man in a small town fifteen miles from here shoots himself on his honeymoon."

"Clifford Smiley," Isabel says.

Now looking into their faces, the Ranger nods. "Now why would a man do that? Or how is it that a girl gets off a train in Denton and disappears from the face of the earth?"

"Virginia Carpenter," whispers Sarah.

"Or take this case: a woman goes out with a man for twelve years, and, finally, marries him. Two days later she comes home and files for a divorce. The man goes missing."

"Jacqueline Butler," Sarah says.

Naming the characters in his stories, Isabel and Sarah are caught up in the story telling, nodding, agreeing with the Ranger.

The Ranger glances sideways at Rock, lifts his eyebrows. "Jump in here anytime, Sheriff."

Shaking his head, "It's your show," Rock says, pushing his chair back, crossing his legs.

The Ranger folds his hands on the desk. "I thought we had that kind of a mystery here," he says evenly. "How is it that a sixteen-year-old girl is strangled, her friend bludgeoned to death with a tire tool and her murderer is never found. And now, thirty-four years later a woman who had been one of the Winslow girl's best friends is also murdered. Well, these cases are closed now or will be soon. Albert Aston has confessed to the murders."

"Why?" exclaims Sarah.

"Is he crazy?" Isabel asks.

Shaking his head, the Ranger says, "The sheriff in Las Vegas said that when Aston started talking his lawyer couldn't shut him up."

"But why? Did he have a motive? "

"The Hollins boy was changing a tire. A flashlight was found on the ground and the bloodied wrench. Your friend was probably holding the flashlight so the Hollins boy could change the tire. We think the Hollins boy saw Aston and went after him with the wrench or his bare hands. We don't have all the details yet. Albert said the Hollins boy tried to kill him, and he picked up the wrench and killed him. He said he had to kill Rosemary because she recognized him."

"This will all come out in court," Isabel says.

"Every bit of it will."

The air in the room feels heavy to Gaynor. She stands and moves her chair a little farther from the desk, takes a deep breath and sits down again.

"One last thing," Rock says. "Ranger Gonzales and I have discussed it. *Modus operandi.* What that means is . . . usually, the murderer kills using the same weapon and for the same reason. This case is rare because, although the same man committed the murders, he killed with whatever was at hand. Different weapons—a wrench, his hands—were used. But we now believe and Aston confirms it, that Miss Mercer's murder was premeditated. That right, Gonzales?"

"Yep, I expect that's so. Except for Miss Mercer's murder, Aston is what you might call an impulse murderer. You see, he hadn't planned to murder the young couple. But he confessed he followed Miss Mercer down the creek bed. It was premeditated and vicious. Aston said, 'I couldn't depend on her any longer. She was planning on spending all her money. She would have put me in prison.' "

"Money he had lost in Las Vegas," Isabel says.

"Mr. Gonzales, aren't you the one who questioned Mary Martha?" asks Sarah.

"I am. When I questioned her all those years ago, she was as scared as a rabbit in a trap." He looks at his folded hands and then says, "Let's look at the evidence, Rock."

Ceremoniously, Rock places a Cold Springs High School annual, a small ring, and a small metal object on the desk.

Sarah leans to look at the items on the desk. "It's Mary Martha's ring. Her birthstone. July. A ruby. It was a graduation present from her folks. She wore it on her little finger."

"Where did you find it?"

"Isabel, we'll be asking the questions," Rock says.

"Sheriff, these ladies were Miss Mercer's friends," Ranger Gonzales says kindly. "I think we can tell them where we found the ring. It was in Aston's desk drawer in his office at the bank."

He picks up the annual and opens it to a place marked by a protruding envelope. "Will you look at this picture, sort it out for me?"

"It's the four of us, taken on class day at Daingerfield," says Sarah. "That's Rosemary on the left."

"Her swim suit was brown. It matched her eyes."

"What's the big yellow 'x'? Look! Rosemary has been crossed out. So has Mary Martha," says Gaynor.

"I'm not sure what it means. He knew you were friends," the Ranger says, and pointing to the metal object on the desk, "And what about this?" he asks.

Sarah and Isabel shake their heads. Gaynor picks it up. "I know what this is. It's Saint Christopher, the patron saint of travelers."

"Mary Martha wasn't a Catholic," says Sarah.

"She was planning a trip," says Isabel. "We were going to Ireland."

"It was Mary Martha's," says Gaynor. "It was one of the charms on her charm bracelet."

Isabel moistens her lips and leans forward. "Mr. Gonzales, I'd like to speak with you," she says. Her eyes fill with unshed tears. She places a hand on her throat. "Privately," she whispers.

Sarah cringes. She knows that look. God knows what Isabel is getting ready to tell the Ranger, and all that's missing is her red dress. If she gives him the diary, and she might; she likes him, she trusts him, and the Ranger is a man of the law. He would have to take some action. He might charge the three of them with withholding evidence.

"Ladies. Rock. If you will excuse us," the Ranger says. "The reception area will be comfortable. If you'll wait out there, please."

In a few minutes, the Ranger opens the door and nods. "Come in!" the nod says. When they are seated again, he says, "Isabel and I have had a private conversation, and I have assured her that it will remain private. These murders have been solved. No other person in Cold Springs is under suspicion. And Miss Mercer's private life will remain private. I know the sheriff agrees."

The Women

Two days before Thanksgiving, Sarah and Isabel reach Betsy's house at the same time, and Gaynor, wearing her bright shawl, hurries them into Betsy's sitting room. They stand in front of the fireplace warming their hands against the first hard freeze of the year.

"It might be snowing by Thursday," Sarah says, rubbing her hands together. "And everything can return to normal."

"Normal?" Betsy says, coming into the room with a tray of cups and saucers.

"Well, look at you, Betsy Rogers, in your gorgeous blue!" Isabel exclaims. "What a wonderful color!"

"Thank you, Isabel. But as for normal, I'm not sure anymore what normal is. But we're having chamomile tea today. After the hard time you girls have had, you need a little pampering."

Sarah and Isabel sit side-by-side on the loveseat. Sarah is wearing khaki pants, clean khakis, and muddy running shoes. Isabel wears a black silk suit with her black, rose-covered scarf thrown round her neck. Her heels are high. Her black hair falls to her shoulders. The length of her hair makes her look older, or so Sarah thinks.

"Sarah, would you pour?" Betsy says.

"Sure," Sarah says and, beginning with Betsy, she pours tea into thin china teacups. "Betsy, I've been thinking about the meeting we had with Theodore White. He was bumfuzzled before it was half way over."

"Bumfuzzled, how."

"Isabel mentioned the cat's inheritance. And then to clear that up, she told . . . ," and now Sarah is giggling and Isabel is smiling, "she told Theo the cat was imaginary."

"And then I said Miss Eyre did not like Albert," Gaynor says merrily, and Theo said, 'Who's Miss Eyre?' And then, I said, oh my Lord, I actually said, 'Her very real cat,' and Betsy, if you could have seen the look on Theo's face!"

"Betsy, pay no attention to Isabel," says Gaynor. "Miss Eyre is a real cat. I know she is. But, oh, thinking back, it was quite a funny conversation."

"Betsy, the only thing Theodore White understood was your advice to follow the money," says Sarah.

"As a matter of fact, Theo called the day after your meeting and thanked me," Betsy says, wiping tears of laughter from her eyes, and then, sipping the tea, frowning, she says, "Too bland," and then she grins. "He also said the three of you were quite formidable around that conference table."

"Betsy, would you ever in a million years have thought that Albert Aston was a murderer? I thought Clovis murdered Mary Martha."

"No, Sarah. I never thought about Mr. Aston. And the idea that Clovis was guilty never entered my mind. I was afraid it was Jackson. Thank God it wasn't."

"And all the saints in heaven!" Gaynor says fervently.

"I thought we might never know who it was," Isabel says, "And that would have been horrible. For Jackson most of all."

Untying her silk scarf, Isabel folds it into a sash and ties it round her waist. Giving the scarf a reassuring pat, she smiles at it. Having quietly captured their full attention with the scarf, she chuckles and says, "I'm going to marry Jackson. I've always loved him. Even when I was madly in love with George, there was always a place in my heart for Jackson."

The women gaze at Isabel, taking in the idea of an Isabel who loved two men at the same time. Isabel shrugs her shoulders, puts a hand over her mouth and giggles. "It's true," she said. "I've always loved him. I called him last night and told him." Smiling demurely now, she adds, "He's not quite sure about marriage."

"Not sure?" Sarah gasps.

"He's not sure, but I am." And grinning, she adds, "I'm sure enough for both of us."

"Oh, Isabel, Isabel, of course, he will marry you," Betsy says staunchly. "He just doesn't know it yet. Now, we'll have a little sherry, shall we?"

When Gaynor accepts a glass, Isabel's shakes her head in a barely perceptible gesture of disapproval. When Gaynor sees that, she defiantly lifts her chin. Sarah frowns and clears her throat. Gaynor shrugs, sips the sherry and smiles. And then Betsy, astonishingly, collects the sherry glasses hardly anybody has touched.

After a minute, "Life will never be the same again," Isabel says.

"No," Betsy says. "Everything changes. But I have made peace with change," she says huskily.

The women are silent. *Change.* The word hangs in the air. Sarah knows her house will soon be empty again. John's boxes and garbage bags are piled in the entrance, waiting for her to come take him and his things to the garage where he'll be living, "for awhile, Mom," he had told her. "I'm moving out and moving up. You'll see!" Remembering the enthusiasm in his voice, she feels a surge of energy. At times, an empty house is nice, she tells herself, She might even go to school and become a Master Gardener.

Isabel thinks of Jackson, waiting for her at his place on the river. When he sees her, his face lights up. She thinks of her children, looking forward to her arrival in California. Her visit will be a start. Her life with Jackson is a beginning. The town will get to know him.

Gaynor smiles broadly. This time next year her baby will be almost six months old, sitting up and smiling when she (Willie B. is most likely right about its being a girl), sees her mother's face. She looks at Betsy, stalwart in her straight chair, her feet side-by-side, her ash blond hair brushed up and away from her face, her suit the color of hyacinths. Suddenly anxious, she asks, "Betsy, what can I do to help with supper?"

"If you'll get the chairs round the table, I'll serve the plates. It's shepherd's pie. Your recipe," and saying this, Betsy vanishes into the kitchen.

"Gaynor, Gaynor," Sarah reprimands, taking a chair from her hands. "You get the drinks. We'll get the chairs."

Gaynor shrugs, and says, "Tea? Coffee? Champagne all round?"

"I hope it's not champagne all around," Sarah whispers to Isabel as the door into the kitchen swings shut behind Gaynor.

And now Gaynor is returning with champagne glasses, the champagne and a bottle of ginger ale. "You're like a bunch of mother hens," she hisses. "I'm perfectly healthy and I'm going to tell Betsy tonight," she says softly.

They nod. "Good," says Isabel and "Perfect!" says Sarah.

When they are again around the table, Sarah says, "The meat pie is delicious. Gaynor, why is it called shepherd's pie?"

"It's pub food. Pub food is always plain and good in Ireland. You'll see when we get there. And we are going to Ireland. We are still going, aren't we?" Gaynor says.

"Of course, we are," Betsy says.

"I have some news," Sarah says wryly. "Clovis called this morning. She said it would take a long time to receive her inheritance, but her funds are insured, and the estate is what she had thought it would be, well over a million dollars. She is putting the house and its contents on the market next week. She says she doesn't want a single thing in the house."

"And she wants us to meet her plane."

"No. She wants us to go out to the house and choose something, a keepsake. 'One thing,' she said. 'You can each pick one thing.' And she said that if we see something else we want, we're to buy it from the estate."

"Why am I not surprised," Isabel says wryly.

"And we're to pick up a key at the real estate office."

"Late tomorrow afternoon would be good for me. After work. Let's go then," Gaynor says and stands as if to leave the room, but then she turns to face them all. She takes a deep breath. "This is hard," she says, taking the shawl from her shoulders. "I don't know why, but it is." When she takes a step toward the three women, they see her flushed face, her trembling lips.

"Betsy, I'm going to have a baby," she says. "And I know, I do know, how Cold Springs is. People will talk. Your friends will. They will talk about me. About a baby and no father."

Sitting straight in her chair, Betsy's face has turned to stone. Frowning, she shakes her head. When she stands, it seems at first as if she might be standing to comfort Gaynor, but no, she's hurrying from the room. Gaynor shrugs her shoulders, turns and walks to the window. She stands there gazing out at Betsy's azalea bushes; her tightly clenched hands hang by her side.

But then Betsy is hurrying in, hurrying to Gaynor. Taking her by the shoulders, Betsy turns her around. "I have a present for you," she says triumphantly, kissing her on one cheek and then on the other, "Sit down. Open it!" she says.

Searching Betsy's face, Gaynor sits on the love seat and unwraps the yellow blanket, shakes it out, holds it up. "You knew," she breathes.

Isabel breaks into laughter. "Oh, Betsy," she giggles, "that's why you swept up our sherry glasses before anyone had taken a sip."

Betsy's eyes twinkle. Smiling, she puts her hands on her hips. "I've already started on the cap and booties," she says proudly. "And do you think I care what Cold Springs says? Well, I don't. Now when am I to be a grandmother?"

"In April."

"Such a lovely time to have a baby," Betsy beams.

"Perfect!" says Sarah.

"And what does Dr. Holly say?" Isabel asks.

"He wants to marry me."

"And what do you say?"

"I'm not sure about the marriage bit. But I am sure about this baby. Bill seems happy about it," Gaynor says, holding the yellow blanket to her breasts as if there were already a baby in it.

"What you're doing, this baby, it's thrilling," exclaims Isabel.

"And brave," says Sarah.

"Let's play a rubber of bridge," Gaynor says, folding the blanket, nestling it again in the tissue paper. "And tomorrow we'll go out to Mary Martha's."

"For closure," says Sarah.

"Closure," Isabel says. "Is there such a thing? Let's cut for deal," and then, "Gaynor, we're partners. Your deal."

"What's wrong with closure?"

"Closure is a phony word. It's psycho babble. There's no such thing!"

Deftly arranging her cards, Sarah says, "We'll go to say goodbye. How's that?"

"Better. Partner, I bid four clubs. Betsy, do you play club convention?"

"I invented the bid," Betsy says. Swinging their chairs around, they settle around the table as Gaynor deals the cards.

Miss Eyre

The women stop by the agent's office for the key. When they reach Mary Martha's house, they see the overgrown and dying grass and the leaf-littered walkway leading to the forlorn, deserted house.

Gaynor says, "The house knows she's gone."

"Oh, Gaynor," Isabel sighs. She puts the key in the lock, pulls the door tightly shut as she has seen Mary Martha do, and turns the key. The door squeaks open. They tiptoe inside, see the dusty photographs still stacked on the table and gaze at the watercolor of the four-leaf clover on the wall.

Isabel takes it down. "Gaynor?"

Gaynor shakes her head and replaces it.

Upstairs, Sarah picks up the picture of the four of them. "I'll have copies made."

Isabel picks up a worn, leather-bound book. "I'd like this. I'll read every letter, and then I'll read every novel." Walking downstairs, she adds, "I might become a Janeite."

They close the door quietly, lock it and walk toward the car. "Wait a minute! The wood violets!" Sarah cries.

The key is turned again, the door reopened, newspapers found and hosed until they are dripping. In the utility room, Gaynor finds a trowel. Scrambling down into the creek bed, "I can transplant them. They'll multiply," Sarah says, "and in a year or two, I'll divide them."

Isabel watches Sarah dig around the delicate, green plants, lift them gently and place them on the wet newspapers.

Gaynor has wandered off along the creek. Glancing over her shoulder, she sees that Sarah has climbed out of the creek bed and begun to fold the wet newspapers into a cone for the plants. Turning, Gaynor begins to walk back toward the women. "Kitty, kitty, kitty," she calls. She walks slowly, calling, "C'mere, kitty. Here kitty. Kitty, kitty, kitty," peering into the creek bed. Coming closer, she laughs. "I can call spirits from the deep."

"Oh, Gaynor, there's no cat out here. Let's go," Sarah says.

"Kitty, kitty, kitty," Gaynor calls again, her voice as sweet and pure as water. "Kitty, kitty, kitty," she coaxes, peering down into the creek bed until, swept along by the tenderness in her voice, her friends, almost believing, stare into the emptiness of the dry creek bed.

"We need to go," says Isabel.

"Wait!" Gaynor whispers.

And a gray cat appears, steps slowly from a bed of maidenhair fern, steps softly, comes stepping, stepping and purring, comes purring, winding itself in and out round the legs of the women until Gaynor sweeps it into her arms. "Ha!" she exclaims. "Sometimes they come. Sometimes they do come!" And in the irrefragable light of evening, the women draw close to gaze at the cat purring in Gaynor's arms.